THE
IDIOM
AND THE
ODDITY

Intentionality must be posited for a critical reading of text, life. Still, particular choices of persons, places, times, situations will always be a blend of the simmering cosmic cholent pot of history and happenings; a potpourri of known and unknown impressions, imaginings and memories. Could have, should have, might have bubbling into words and sounds spilling over onto the page.

The Idiom and the Oddity

Published by A.B. Ruth Associates

© 2017 • All rights reserved

ISBN: 978-965-92626-0-1 (print)
ISBN: 978-965-92626-1-8 (ebook)

Foreword

So there I was walking in the cool of late October on the Coney Island beach, and I noticed a canister washing up on the sand. I picked it up, opened it and I found this manuscript. Of course I read it. Sort of roman a clef – yes and no, more of a clef-hanger, a coming of outrage kind of thing. Kind of a sermon on the mound, wandering with a wondering Jew.

So here it is.
It was signed: "An unnamed Marrano centerfielder."

and dedicated to:
M. Beilis, A. Dreyfus and L. Frank.

Preface I

In 1949 the jurors (amongst them t.s. eliot, E. E. Cummings, W. H. Auden and Allen Tate) of the Bollingen Prize (subsidized by the Library of Congress) awarded the prize to Ezra Pound.

"Pound is a fascist and a traitor."

"He may be but this has nothing to do with his poetry."

"...To permit other considerations than that of poetic achievement to sway the decision would destroy the significance of the award and would in principle deny the validity of that objective perception of value on which civilized society must rest." Juror press release.

Whereas

"Shoeless" Joe Jackson with the third highest lifetime batting average of any major leaguer .356, was not admitted to the Hall of Fame for allegedly fixing the World Series.

Preface II

Mr. Twain once introduced a book by declaring it had no 'weather.' He was convinced that too much time is spent by writers on describing weather and slows up the narrative.

For those people who like weather he appended a few pages of the best excerpted weather that he could find that they might insert anywhere they like.

This work is without any explicit sexual description. The modern reader would seem not to need any help in this regard.

BOOK ONE
The Idiom

*"Whoever wants to know the heart
and mind of America had better learn
baseball, the rules and realities of the game."*

Jacques Barzun 1954

Hearses come on time. Since the horn stopped working, the Beth Asher *shofar* (ram's horn) hung by a string to the dashboard. Now and then Meshugana Morris was impressed into duty to beep and bellow. But that was only on occasion. Making my groggy way to the window the hoarse rasp of the shofar-hearse-honk was confirmed. Marty and Bam had arrived and were waiting alongside the glistening grey black topped hearse, both still in bathing suits. Marty had on his Marrano team black and yellow polo shirt and black baseball cap with the big badge-like yellow letter "M." Quickly those sho-far sounds were drowned by the thunderous roar of a plane circling overhead heading to Idlewild. Mom said the plane roars were louder and more unpleasant than the elevated train back in Brooklyn. Dad said the train-din was grating, nastier and harsher. Like the *chazzan* (cantor) and Reb Shimshon Cohen at Beth Asher in Brownsville we had learned to wait till those crashing glacial noise bursts passed over. Waving, Marty and Bam called out reminding me they were hungry.

Shortly after our purchase of that overhauled, resurrected, vehicle, already in our initial runs, Marty had noted a suddenly emerging promptness. Notwithstanding its new incarnation—serving us today primarily for off-duty tooling and cruising about—it still held true, this uncanny, punctuality. Even has-been hearses mysteriously come on time.

Once, when stopped for driving a commercial vehicle on the Belt Parkway that was my plea to the policeman: We were today a civilian carrier, a retired hearse, long mustered out of active service—the livery plates were vestigial, a mere re-hearse. Hadn't Bam, Marty, Tony and I, soul-searchingly discursively discussed and analyzed the "*sugya*" (subject discussion) with commentaries, and decided that even with our occa-sional loaning of the hearse to Pastor Earl Thomas for a freelance funeral in his black Baptist community in Laurelton, and our subsequent receiving of an honorarium, nevertheless that should not in principle impair our essentially amateur status. We were yet eligible for the Olympics, as our primary mileage was of non-profitable roaming and cruising. So what, if here and there, it was sprinkled with an occasional Hessian jaunt. That was a negligible percentage of our overall driving.

Another time, we took the opposite defense, as a policeman was pulling up Marty quickly jumped to the back, lay down, rolled his eyes back and pulling a beach blanket over his face, prepared to hold his breath. Sneakers and Marrano cap still on, he stretched out, dead to all the world.

All through the years growing up together, Marty had been the best dead man not just on our block, but for blocks around. Over untold shootouts. Cowboys and Indians, Cops and Robbers, G.I.s versus Germans or Japs—throughout those encounters Marty was a dead man without compare. For what seemed to be hours he could lie motionless without a hint of breathing. Later, when I met Izzy at the *yeshivah* and we put him to the test, he proved to be in a league with Marty. But Izzy had on-the-job training, extensive clinical practice to work the kinks out of his method. As a beleaguered intern at Cook County Hospital, in the summer, seeking out a cool quiet respite from his sleep-starved rounds, he once landed at the morgue and stretched out on an empty cot. Concluding it to be the quietest, coolest place in the area, he began dropping by regularly and stretching out on an available table for his mid-rounds rest. Izzy learned to blend in with his lifeless neighbors.

Marty was first-class at being dead without any apprenticeship at a morgue. Playing dead came naturally, he said. It ran in his family. According to Rubenstein family lore, more than once, great-grandfathers, great-uncles, and other relations, had escaped various Cossacks, Polaks and Russians, Ukrainians—even in Kishinev—by playing dead. There was a tradition of sorts in the family.

The Irish cop that stopped us that time pulled the sandy blanket from off Marty's face: "Tsk tsk." Crossed himself. "So young, so young." Sending us on our way, he extended a fatherly caution to stay off the Parkway. Noting the cap and sneakers: "Imagine, he musta been in the middle of a game, tsk tsk. What inning was it?"

"Second."

"My, my, not even an official game."

Though Marty held the neighborhood trophy for being dead, Bam was according to most opinions the best die-er. He fell from stoops, hanging fire escape ladders, from windows, from on top of parked cars, all with stunning and desperate abandon, twisting and turning, contorting and convulsing with assorted, accumulated wounds inflicted by countless shots, arrows, bayonets, and blades.

Today, of all days, I thought Marty and Bam would be late. Earlier this morning, driving to the schoolyard the motor had stalled a few times. Pastor Thomas had complained last week about the stalling, and as usual about the baseball equipment and women's articles in the back of the hearse. "It is a genuine actual undignity fellahs and you fellahs know I run a genuine bona fide dignified operation." At 8 a.m. this morning as we were chalking in on the concrete alongside the first baseline for our Auld Lang Syne Sunday morning softball game in the schoolyard, Marty was busy on the street, his torso half hidden, hanging over the engine under the yawning open-hooded hearse, tinkering with the carburetor. Like that metallic alligator was about to swallow him.

Returnees, recidivists, guys coming back, coming home, to where they—and we'd—played as boys: To the PS 189 schoolyard. Guys had moved on, to Flatbush, Canarsie, Manhattan, New Jersey, Long Island, Westchester, yet still atavistically returning to this Brownsville yard to play with these same guys Saturday and Sunday mornings. Ye Olde Yard with Ye Olde Guys. Guys in their twenties and thirties, and a few forty-year-olds. For years I watched before I could play. Each year a few guys stopped playing. Some of the retirees returned to "kibitz" (running commentary) and watch. Most stopped showing. Either way that made room for youngster-draftees.

Most players had no social contact outside of these games. From the first twenty names chalked onto the list each Saturday or Sunday morning, two seasoned, self-appointed — yet by common consent — pitchers were chosen to choose. They then would do the ceremonial holding the bat by the bottom knob and spinning each around his head, the pitcher who outlasted, chose first. Now, in retrospect that ritual remindful of pre-Yom Kippur *kapparos*, (atonement ritual) but then I wasn't all that into, in fact in at all, to *kapparos* though a bit aware of Yom Kippur. Pitchers could then alternatingly choose their teams one by one. Much prestige hung on getting picked early. We played with a short center, like *davening*, (praying) we also needed ten men in the field. Winners stayed on for the second game. Latecomers to the chalk list and refugees from the losing team comprised their opponents. During the second game today, Marty had pronounced the hearse once again roadworthy. Reverseless, hornless, but cruise-capable.

Once upon a time it was understood that one had to give one's all for the Marranos. Even that cavalcade of sad sack clowns who posed as teachers in the after-public-school afternoon Talmud Torah classes in the basement of Stalin's *Shul* — so named after a dispute over whether to recite a *misheberach* (blessing) for the Russians during World War II. The already elderly rabbi, Reb Shimshon, with his loyal *baalei batim* (lay leadership) sometimes referred to as Joe Weiss and his seven dwarfs — went for the recitation explaining that as evil as Stalin was, now Russia was our ally, and the priority at hand was to best Hitler. A group of passionate dissenters bolted and formed their own anti-Stalinist synagogue the "Veisse *Shul*", (the White *Shul*) a few blocks away, off Linden Boulevard and Rockaway Avenue. Classes in the basement at Stalin's *Shul* were a study in how not to teach and inspire. Nevertheless, despite those ne're-do-well, incompetent, mock-opera teachers one could not drain the outrage awakened from so many of those historic happenings. Those "teachers" serving as they did as undercover agents of secularity, even they could not trivialize the core–cutting poignancy of so much of our people's hurts and heroism — like the story of the Marranos. Anger, hate, compassion and loyalty were reflexive. And so when it came time to name our softball team, most of us in our second year of junior high school, discussions offered "Broncos,"

"Apaches," "Eagles," I pushed "Marranos." Standing there in Howie's sporting goods shop on Sutter and Howard Avenue one time, I could already laugh at having once been convinced that the street had been named after Howie. Amidst the spell of all those magical scents, and sights—soft crafted, tightly bound Rawlings and Wilsons new leather gloves, spanking white virginal clinchers, smooth grained blond, brown, and black, bats with the regal imprint of Louisville Slugger, that coat of arms, that seal of endorsement — "*hechsher*" (to determine kosher) — then and there when Bam and Marty and I ordered the yellow embossed black shirts, and fifty-plus-year-old, paunchy, gravel-voiced Howie so unknowingly, irritatingly, aloof to the plush beauties of his merchandise, like a eunuch in a harem, Howie looking up over his glasses, "You guys sure that's what you want? 'Marranos'?"

And after we reassured him, "Well it's your money and your shirts but if you ask me..."

"We are not asking you Howie."

Tony, reviewing, commiserating, how he was regularly taken for Jewish — dark-haired, aquiline nosed, and how regularly I was taken for not Jewish — blond hair and straight nosed — Tony asked, "Does a *goy* score points in the celestial scoreboard in the sky for suffering anti-Semitism?" Tony traced the origin of his frequently mistaken identity to those years when he played as undercover goy on the Marranos. Often he would say to me, "Given our givens, you are the consummate Marrano and I the inverse Marrano." When we in turn called his attention to his natural endowments of nose and coloring and suggested that perhaps the wristbands in the nursery at the maternity ward had been switched, Tony pointed out "One day we would see." He and his neighborhood would not go black. Whereas since Jewish and Irish neighborhoods all eventually turned black it must be, that blacks are Irish and Jews just, turned inside out! Maybe the Phillies sold Chuck Klein even after he won the Triple Crown in 1933, 'cause they thought he was Jewish.

If the playing hard and giving one's all for the Marranos was understandable, yet, one might have thought that choose-up schoolyard games would not be played that hard. After all, today's team was chance, an ephemeral formulation, a quirky fleeting serendipitous whim of circumstance and fate. But. There was the yard as Tabernacle. As temple. And the game as rite. The spiritual aesthetic of stretching oneself stoically to perform, with pitching, hitting, fielding as *mitzvahs*. (Torah ordained good deeds) Pitchers, though more self-appointed than chosen, were endorsed and they were possessive expecting team loyalty. Standing there off the first base line, after the spinning of the bat ritual, choosing from the chalked-in lists, it was a mystical moment, utter epiphany; this is the team for whom you should play this week. While there were only four or five potential pitchers in the orbit and they each had their favorite players, still, different weeks saw different pitchers and new teams. Absence, lateness, occasional newcomers and whim, conspired to precipitate changing configurations. Yet a measure of homage was in order, to that very revolving Randomness. Our act of faith in the act of fate that put this shortstop and this second baseman together this week. So what if last week I played against Coffee, Biggie and Zip and this week with them. Now the muses, (Providential Guidance – "*Hashgacha*" Winters and the guys at the *yeshivah* would say) had made this the lineup this week. Often during the traditional pre-game in-field peppering and double-play practice I would think that no matter how much you tinker-about-it's-forever-chance, yet in today's incarnation these were my team-mates. Are China, Japan, Germany, Russia so different? Wait a minute, give me the scorecard. Who chalked in today? Last week's enemies, today's allies? Is the difference between hours and years quantitative or qualitative? Which is a closer reflection of our condition, the uniformed team game, or the ad-hoc chalked-in choose-up team? So it was, with these choose-up games, they were played with dedication, genuine hunger to win. Perhaps in one corner of my soul there was also a certain pleasure of sorts in that I did not have to disappear as me, enveloped by the team. No nullification of identity. I was playing today with this team, and in fact I would give my all with playing as *mitzvah*. Next week there would be a new grouping, and that would still be me, my *mitzvah*. Yet, when the Dodgers sold Pete Reiser after he had cracked his skull on their walls trying to intercept extra base-blasts, that sale was an ignominious act. Ultimately rationalized for the greater good of the team and its mission, it did not work. It hurt. Maybe the Coleridgean aesthetic was at work with the game as poetry: The best possible players in the best possible order. Perhaps tragic rather than pathetic; the necessary that yet pained?

Despite this morning's stallings, Marty, and Bam were in fact on time. Once upon a time I did not wear a watch. Dad had railed, cajoled but to no avail. As such debates often go, we pretty much had our steady scripts with some ad-libbing here and there.

"A *mentsch* wears a watch."

"I imagine you would agree that the converse is not necessarily true."

"Come on, get off it — the bare minimum of day-to-day functioning with responsibility that's all I ask."

"Like I told you, Dad, I eat when I am hungry and sleep when I am tired, for other times I do somehow manage."

"Those *ladygeyer* (colloquial slurring of ladik goers — empty amblers) bohemian friends, all that hanging around the Village."

Refusing to wear a watch was for Dad my application of Greenwich Mean Time.

Bam, Marty, Tony and I, did often hit the Village. After a while Marty stopped coming, declaring that everyone there, the guys, the girls, the couples walking in the streets were all looking for something that wasn't and won't be there. Coffee shops and bars were not destinations, rather stop-overs between roaming, rambling, milling as ends not means. To see and be seen. As we studied others, so we were studied. A human zoo where the cages had been opened and spectators and animals had mingled and gotten all mixed and confused, andit was no longer clear which were the viewers and which were the viewed. An on-going play with no objective correlative, all flurry of staged action and inaction and its theatrical business never succeeding in portraying any intent.

Tony came regularly to the Village and said of the coffee house poet's recitations "They wrote and read shopping lists and laundry lists, mentioners, not writers." Some years later Rav Winters was to tell me of a *rebbi* (teacher) of his who, when guys before they had thought out what they wanted to say asked questions in *shiur* (class) the *rebbi* would cut them off with, "Bunches of words you give me, I should choose from them. Better you should choose first, and then give me the chosen words!" Groucho-like Marty concluded that he did not want to see those people that had come to see him. And if they really wanted to see him they could come to Brooklyn. Besides which the beers and girls were pretty much the same all over, and in Coney Island you can get rides and hot corn.

Sometimes we went to Union Square Park, across from Klein's 14th Street, (our bargain basement Hyde Park) to hear, watch the speakers under the statue, under the horse's tail. Melvin looked, spoke, moved and gestured like a de-frocked cantor. He rhapsodized about American democracy to the standing, shifting crowd. A black guy pushed forward and interrupted Melvin, "Hey man this here ain't no equality here. Over there in Russia that there's real equality...," in a boozy somewhat slurring manner.

"What are you talking about?" Melvin continuing, "At least as you and we all here can see, you can talk, speak your mind. There, they lock you up for talking." A big guy from the back with his hands in his coat pockets. "I been over dere, I know what is over dere, it vas hell under de Czar, and it's now two times hell by Stalin. Ask Miss Emma Goldman. The only vones vhat's tinking is dere all de time a holiday is de ones vhats not dere! You standing here and you talking from something dat you not even knowing!"

"Don't you go gettin' psychological with me man," stressing the psycho. "I know them there tricks! I damn well know equality when I sees it. And here's where it ain't, so don't go getting psychological with me, you hear me man!"

"Ye ever hear about the Ironed Curtain mister man?" The little old fellow with the curly grey hair adjusting his pants. "You know vhat is dat?"

"Man I told ye don't go gettin psychological with me and let me tell you man, Mississippi dat dere's my Iron Curtain!"

One hot August night sitting in a coffee shop on West 4th sipping bitter espresso and munching on some stale tasteless crackers that managed to be soggy as well, listening to Wendy with her irritatingly whining voice explain that she knew a guy who had read "War and Peace" in five languages in order to really understand what it meant, and me telling her that reading it twice in the original was more likely to achieve an understanding of what the author meant. All the while, through her wide-eyed hyperbolic protestations, she continued carefully sweeping silverware off the table into her purse. Midway through her peroration Malcolm Cohen appeared. Dressed in a too tight black turtle neck that traced his obesity, the too small black leather vest, khaki Bermuda shorts, removing his pith helmet revealing his long disheveled tumbling locks that reached to his neck, Malcolm waddled over to our table. Graceless Malcolm had been the worst ball player on the block, the neighborhood, the borough, the state, and according to many, in the history of the world. Reluctantly, chosen into games when we were short of a *minyan* (ten males to pray) to make the team even then guys argued they would sooner go it with nine rather than with Mal but schoolyard-stickler *halachasists* insisted on a full *minyan*, like for *davening*, claiming that otherwise the game would not be recorded for posterity in the Cosmic Scoreboard in the sky. Sharing a rotating catcher with the offensive team was never considered at the outset of a game; only under emergency conditions, - if someone got hurt or left in the middle of a game with no bench — only then was the shared rotating- catcher the option.—"*Bidi'eved*" (post facto) as my recently discovered *halachasists* (proponents of Talmudic law) would say. Despite Malcolm's ineptness, or, according to some, because of it, his butcher-cum-real estate investor father and his broad-shouldered mother always had Malcolm decked out with the newest, slickest gloves, sneakers and miscellaneous paraphernalia of the game. Halloween night of 1949 at a cub scout masquerade contest party at PS 189 Malcolm won first prize dressed in black face and Dodgers uniform number 42; Jackie Robinson. Marty said it was like squeezing a zeppelin into a flying tiger! Bam spoke for many when he complained that it was genuine *chutzpah*, downright immoral for a world-class *klutz* to portray any sports great let alone the nimble lithe Jackie.

After years, now watching the overgrown Mal there in that basement coffee shop in the village stroking his carefully-kempt-unkempt long locks, I pictured his mother leaning on the window-sill from her third floor apartment monitoring the children's play downstairs in the street screaming out from time to time in her thick powerful contralto for one child or another to either do something or not do something pertaining to Mal. Occasionally she would sit in her fold-up chair in front of the tenement. I was sure I noticed "director" emblazoned on the banner on the back of her seat. Now, restudying Mal I thought of Tennyson's appearance at the Oxford Theatre to receive an honorary degree, he with his locks wonderfully, studiedly disheveled, and someone from the audience calling, "Did your mother call you early dear?"

Today Mal had his trusty copy of "Howl." He carried it with him all the time. Wendy Smith reminded me of Popeye's Olive Oyl. A stick-slim girl with the palest of complexions. She always carried "The Fountainhead."

"There is a conspiracy of the reactionary academic establishment to keep Rand out of literature courses." Wendy- Olive Oyl with deep seriousness. "That's cos she was really a socialist though a lot of people don't know it and the establishment are all ultra-conservative."

"A socialist? Our own home-grown reactionary Ann Rosenbaum? A socialist?" Me, with wonder.

"Sure! Everyone knows all those Russian Jews were socialists! Anyone knows that!" Wendy–Olive Oyl dropping another knife and fork from the table into her purse.

"How do you like that? Little old Ann, all those years posing for Buster Brown shoe ads and deep down she is an undercover socialist." Marty.

"Lifts and Rands notwithstanding, think of all those sales and the movie to boot, Rand was pretty well heeled for an antisocial socialist!" Me.

Watch-watchers versus ladygeyers. Like the car games at the penny arcade going out of lane signals, bells sirens, warning noise for an irate Dad. Invariably during such confrontations I watched Dad's left temple. He was a redhead, not a bright orange-red, like Sroly the Chassidic butcher, but rather an ochre-rust-red. Still, red enough to fit into the family lore which had it that redheads were severely short-tempered. Red Moish in the schoolyard who consistently slammed fists, gloves, balls and bats on the concrete, fences and people as well; and Harvey the Red from Legion Street who got a dishonorable discharge for hitting an officer were cases in point that I knew. In and around the family kith and kin and non-kith and non-kin were cited to substantiate the thesis. With Dad, as he angered, the pulse in his left temple began to throb, first a bit and then furiously. That was my "whether vein" determining "whether" to push my point forward or to quit. As exception that proves the rule, bright orange, red-headed Sroly — a bit of a mutant —

anger and energy had evolved into song and dance.

At the window checking my watch, I confirmed Marty and Bam's once again on-time hearse arrival. Irony of ironies! Now that I did don a timepiece it afforded Dad no *nachas* (spiritual satisfaction) — wearing it as I now did, to determine when it was time for *Minchah* (afternoon prayer) or how long it had been since I ate meat. However new and experimental for me, but in Dad's studied opinion time honored *halachic* habits were remote, outdated, outmoded, outvoted. Dad's own time piece had a special alarm for the anachronistic which in his lexicon, and according to his hermeneutic principles appeared alongside (hence related) to the anarchistic: adversaries each, to the even keel, straight and narrow, middle of the road, norm of norms.

From the beginning, Dad was destined not to reap *nachas* from my timekeeping. Somewhere, deeply buried in my dresser, a few of my erstwhile watches that had timed my early, dubious, short-lived career as timekeeper. One watch, purchased for my tenth birthday, had read "waterproof." Dad repeatedly cautioned that he would not rely on the claim. And so that Saturday rushing into the Rockaway waters, those choppy grey surging waves — somewhere there were blue oceans but here they were grey — with me clinging to his back, Dad swam further out, beyond the other swimmers, not too far, but far enough to feel beyond, then pivoting, and turning back with the gathering surge of the heightening wave, we laughed and gasped as the growing wall of sea rushed at us, over us, as if through us, pushing, pulling us shoreward, splashing and sliding we hit the shallows, shells, stones and sand of the beach. Lo and behold I was watchless. Then Dad, standing upright, arms akimbo, his-ochre rust hair wetted down slick and brighter now in the August sun. "I told you not to wear it." And I replied, "But you did not say not to wear it because I might lose it, you said 'cause it wasn't waterproof." He stared, thought and laughed as he grabbed me and threw me into the air, both of us then falling to the cooling cushion of shorefront sea. We rolled and lay and rolled and lay in the swishing swirl of sea water and we laughed even when he said it again. "I told you not to wear it." Over the years he was to mention it again. And again. It was evidence of what happens when fathers are not heeded. At first he would quote the price of the lost watch and Mom often corrected him citing that it had cost less. And so it was then in years to come, on later visits to that ocean, that I considered putting a notice on the beach or an ad in one of those journals for budding young poets, read only by their mothers, sisters, girlfriends, competitors; advising one and all that this sea could no longer accurately be reckoned as timeless.

Then there was that lazy Sunday afternoon when Cousin Gregory and I began taking apart our bar mitzvah watches. His, that new model silent watch to find out what made it not tick. And mine to determine why it was running slowly. On being reassembled, a week later at "Murray Goldman's New and Old Gold Jewelry Shop and Watch Repair" on Pitkin Avenue, (Dad had gone to school with Murray, Mom distrusted him), Greg's previously silent watch began to tick and run slowly and mine now ran silently and fast. Rather quickly Greg despaired of putting the pieces together - *yiush, shelo midas*? (abandoning hope without knowing) Though I tried encouraging him to keep at it, "We have all the parts. Let's keep trying, by infinity its got to work." For a long time I kept checking both watches to see if it was infinity yet. Eventually, I traded my watch away for a female mutt, Heidi, part Spitz, part German shepherd. Dad objected to having a dog in our Brooklyn apartment, but Mom said we were scheduled to move in a few months to Lawrence, Long Island, so we might as well keep the dog. I was 16 at the move and shortly afterwards my kid brother Teddy, ten at the time, was romping with Heidi and a next door neighbor Great Dane, Rex, and Teddy reported that Gregg's once-silent-now-ticking watch had fallen, and Rex had swallowed it. Some kids in the neighborhood said that Rex ticked afterwards. Others said he didn't. Even those that said he ticked said it was only sometimes. Most agreed that he ran more slowly.

Then for years I was watchless until Pat McQuade registering her displeasure with my inveterate tardiness (and pleasure with me), purchased a watch for me as a gift for my twentieth birthday. My suggesting that Pat and Dad now had common cause set off the "whether vein." "Don't put me in a category with some *shiksah*." (gentile woman)

"She's not some *shiksah*, she has a name."

"*Shiksahs* have no names."

And I responded with "Hath not a *goy* eyes? Hath not a *goy* hands, organs, dimensions, senses, affections, passions? Fed with the same food, hurt with the same weapons, subject to the same diseases, healed by the same means, warmed and cooled by the same winter and summer as a Jew is? If you prick them do they not bleed? If you tickle them do they not laugh? If you poison them do they not die? And if you wrong them shall they not revenge? If they are like you in the rest they will resemble you in that."

Dad had his racing theory of race. "It's all of it, all of history like one long race. One extended marathon from the beginning until today — and they are running against you, all those *goyim*, but because there are so many more of them—they're also the referees, not just the competitors; contestants and rule makers as well. So when you start running fast, then they try to trip you up, and there is no one to talk to 'cause they're also the referees. So you just have to learn to run even better and even faster, and then they start knocking you down even harder and you have to learn to get up again and to run from a kneeling position like feigning giving up and then from that bowed position on the ground, like straight from the floor with a jump and to weave and to zigzag and to master those moves. And because they are the refs, and everything is theirs, they keep getting away with it, the knocking you down and then cheating you out of your just wins. And the faster you learn to run, and the better you get at it, your legs get smarter, you learn to run with more brains and you don't give up, and you get even smarter and faster, gutsier and savvier and deep down they hate you even more. But you have no choice. And all you want is to live like a *mentsch*, the bare minimum that any human being needs and wants and they don't *fargin* (wholeheartedly grant) —they begrudge you that. And to marry out, is to give those bastards a win, a victory they do not deserve. It's not coming to them, and you go and hand it to them like that on a silver platter."

One Sunday morning in the kitchen over coffee, toast, and the comics I asked, "So what if you find a place, a time, a new track and they allow you your lane to run your race?"

"No such thing, it never happened yet."

"Well what if..."

"I said it never happened."

"So just theoretically I am asking what if it would?"

"Just like it never was it never will be... I have lived a little longer than you and I have learned to see through those phony setups the bluff the blah, blah, bluff of tolerance. Why do you think a father tells his son what he does? It's for you not me." As frequently happened in such confrontations, Mom and Teddy walked in and hung around, first as spectators, and then as referees to help quell any sudden storming of players on the field. Teddy his signature smile less than dimpled but a touch of cheek impression. He and mom speaking silently with their eyes and reaching-to-be-hopeful smiles.

"So, like what about your father, Dad, what did he want from you, for you. Surely to keep kosher and wear *tefillin* (phylacteries) and do those other things that made him proud to be different, and which he was convinced were so important — more than important — crucial for Jews. But if we eat, drink, sing, dress and dance just like those *goyim*, so where's the difference?"

"That's the point for G-d's sake, for them there is always a difference. They will never let you forget the difference, it's a fact of life that difference! And besides which my father was really different, he was European, and brought those customs to America and a lot of them just didn't and don't fit here. There is no *mitzvah* to stoke the coals of their prejudices."

"'Don't fit' says who? Those goy referees? Your father and a lot of people that I have met thought and think they do fit, even here."

"That's again the point, he didn't realize that his habits weren't for here, for this place and this time, and I made up my mind that I did not ever want my son to have that problem — I remember standing in his dry goods store on Utica Avenue like it was yesterday, and those two Irish girls that kept coming in and out and asking each time about some sweaters and skirts and every time they tried to get him to say 'Ah hundrit pertzent vool' and they would crack up and get crazy giggling and run out and then come back again for more… and when I asked him why he didn't just throw them out he says, 'De veil dey buying from me stockings and gloves and scarves so dey laugh, so vot.' But you also know, how Stephen, while he was alive and visiting us, even though we ate non-kosher outside the house, for him we kept kosher in the house."

"Aha! So maybe I ought to have a raven-haired Rebecca at home, and a blond, blue-eyed Rowena outside the house!"

From across the kitchen he heaved a box of Rice Krispies at me. I ducked, and a ceramic coffee pot on the counter and a vase crashed to the tile floor of the kitchen and smashed and splattered. "Robert!" Mom screaming to Dad swallowing hard holding the next scream down with her hand on her mouth.

"And here I thought they just snapped, crackled and popped!… You could've at least passed the milk," as I stood up and exited the room. I had neglected to note the 'whether vein.'"

The poles of our magnets were lined up wrongly our ironies repelled. He never got to savor my dropping of Pat. Truth was, that I never formally decided or declared that dropping. And maybe she did some dropping. But mostly it was Topsy like—it was not born, it just grew into being.

In order to posit, that one-true-blue-so-help-me-God-til-death-do-us-part-love, doesn't it presuppose that Absolute Producer-Director Himself "so help me God." And while men might need that romantic hypothesis to accept monogamy, hadn't Will James during that opium stupor written —"Higgamus hoggamus women are monog-amous/Hoggamus higgamus men are bigamus." and women needed it to apologize for biology — still it — that one true-blue thesis wasn't always all that convincing. While driving from our house in Lawrence, north to those dates in Suffolk County with Pat in Babylon, Long Island, how many streets with how many houses with how many women had I passed en-route? Right at this very moment, wasn't there someone at that end of the world threading his way towards Lawrence, even as I weaved my way towards Babylon, he like me, to pick up his love of loves. Maybe we could compare photos, maps, notes, routes, numbers and pull a switch. Or we could advertise: Looking to trade: One low mileage well-kept *shiksah* driven mainly on weekends, for trade, seeking similar chassis model closer to home. Save time and mileage. Or I could stop at the next traffic light and park. Try a few doors. Just inquiring. Is the lady or the tiger in? And then what? There is always someone else around the block and/or around the corner. Who is to say this then is my girl of girls? Then maybe, the only escape from rampant maybe-ism was to posit that Absolute *Shadchan* (matchmaker) in the sky who has Providentially set me up to take that course at that hour with that instructor and place me in that seat alongside that *shiksah* who looked like Daisy Mae — which was after all, one Jewish boy's conception of The American Girl. However if I did posit that Omniscient, Ubiquitous *Shaddchan* of *Shadchans*, wasn't it He that had fixed me up with my people as well. My people and its cumulative baggage. And lookee — there were *tzitzis* (ritual fringes) and *tefillin* hanging from the bag. Like the story that Winters told of the little Russian Jew in that third class train-car returning from the Rebbe's *tish* (festive holiday table), glancing out of the window as the steppes unfolded, sparsely speckled with occasional peasant dwellings, he, all the while humming to himself the melody he had heard at the *tish* of the Rebbe. The anti-Semitic Russian conductor rushing into the car, his eyes and face filled with hate screaming "*Zhid! Chamadanchik!*" "Jew! The suitcase!" The Jew oblivious to the scream-ing of the conductor continues his entranced rendition of the *niggun* (melody), from the *tish*. A few minutes later the conductor rushes back in and again screams "*Zhid! Chama-danchik!*" Over the next fifteen minutes a third and a fourth time. Then the conductor lifting the suitcase flings it out the window and the train rushes on.

Here, the little Jew finally turns from the window towards the conductor and continuing his sing-song rendition of the niggun, he now adds a lyric — "It wasn't my suitcase!" How many Western Jews forfeited their Jewish baggage to anti-Semitic con-ductors though neither they nor the conductors bothered to investigate the contents of that baggage? How many of those first generation arrivals had themselves tossed over-board suitcases with tefillin, *tzitzis* and *sheitels*. And so their sons had never learned to identify those suitcases nor their contents. Jewish baggage? Baggage of Jews?

As the great Dane of existentialism was fond of saying, wasn't it, "Either, Or." Nor was there any perpetual emotion machine, never, ever. All and every great love in history merely summer romances, schoolyard chalk-in dalliances. Yet to be played with utmost allegiance, loyalty and aplomb. The law of the game. But without some Deus ex Machina, the randomness sapped the orderly flow of heat to energy, and instead there was an atrophying, paralyzing entropy — a molecularly quintessential uncertainty — ever to remain uncertain whether there is or isn't something even more uncertain. Who knows where I will be at any given moment? Or should be. But I do know approximately where I will ultimately be, i.e. not be. Or, or. And while I was or-ing about, I lost hold of the oars, and as they sank into the deep I drifted further and further out to sea. To see, and check other ports of call. By the time I tired somewhat of my harbor hopping, Daisy Mae was gone. Re-entered into the Sadie Hawkins Day Meet. And even if she sent signals that she expected me to join her to re-run that race I was by then already dizzy from running Dad's marathon. Like Charlie Chaplin, I had turned a corner and surprisingly received that red flag of a baton, unwittingly off and running up front, unknowingly leading a parade, a demonstration, a marathon, Dad's marathon. And lo and behold I was up front but was I leading or escaping the crescendo of that burgeoning pack of Patriarchs, Prophets, and Pharisees. By now I wasn't sure, whether, where, and when to stop. Were those fellows behind me also running the marathon fellow travelers, chased by my pursuers as well, or were they chasing me? Now I was in that passing lane, on that track, following close after those Super-Jews who had streaked through the pages of history with all their cumulative, accelerated, excellence. So maybe you did have to be faster in the classroom, in the market place, in the town hall, even in the schoolyard. Faster than a speeding bullet, leaping tall buildings at a single bound more powerful than a locomotive... After all that was two Jewish boys' — Schuster & Segal's — "American" (Jewish) conception, Superman. Then, like that film episode where a startled Thomas Mitchell, (and if he wasn't Jewish then Goldwyn-Mayer and the Warner Brothers et al were) seized with fright, his face contorting with pain, reporting that while he was walking the docks that very day, his soul, "Just upped and left." Poof!! It was gone! And as he talked, the fire of his madness cooled just a little but continued to crouch in the corners of his pained eyes. So, in mirror image it was with me: It had come to pass, that one day looking into the mirror, of a moment, suddenly, there was a Jew looking back at me! Perhaps, a free-floating unemployed dybbuk had latched on for the ride. Or some musty, dusty, chained Marrano soul from the dungeon of my unconscious, at first furtively, then openly appearing, escaping suffocation. Once underground now surfacing, this *tallis*-clad circumcised be-*yarmulke*-ed uninvited Marrano soul had come up for air making me his home. However experimental, my present novitiate *yeshivah bachur* (unmarried student) status was for me, which, at best was partial —constantly partial — and I was decidedly partial to its remaining partial. Yet for Dad *yeshivah* life was just another version of diversion, an inverted Bohemianism, much like Kafka's father's response. Dad found it "flagrant, flaunting, missing the point, the mark, the boat."

And as cousin Franz put it,

I found little means of escape from you in Judaism. Here some escape would, in principle, have been thinkable, but more than that, it would have been thinkable that we might both have found each other in Judaism or even that we might have begun from there in harmony. But what sort of Judaism was it I got from you? In the course of the years I have taken roughly three different attitudes to it.

As a child I reproached myself, in accord with you, for not going to the synagogue enough, for not fasting, and so on. I thought that in this way I was doing a wrong not to myself but to you, and I was penetrated by a sense of guilt, which was, of course, always already at hand.

Later, as a young man, I could not understand how, with the insignificant scrap of Judaism you yourself possessed, you could reproach me for not (if for no more than the sake of piety, as you put it) making an effort to cling to a similar insignificant scrap. It was indeed really, so far as I could see, a mere scrap, a joke, not even a joke. On four days in the year you went to the synagogue, where you were, to say the least, closer to the indifferent than to those who took it seriously, [you] patiently went through the prayers by way of formality, [you] sometimes amazed me by being able to show me in the prayer book the passage that was being said in the moment, and for the rest, so long as I was in the synagogue (and this was the main thing) I was allowed to hang about wherever I liked. And so I yawned and dozed through the many hours (I don't think I was ever again so bored, except later at dancing lessons) and I did my best to enjoy the few little bits of variety there was, as, for instance, when the Ark of the Covenant was opened, which always reminded me of the shooting galleries where a cupboard door would open in the same way whenever one got a bull's eye, only with the difference that something interesting always came out and here it was always just the same old dolls with no heads. Incidentally, it was also very frightening for me there, not only, as goes without saying, because all of the people one came into close contact with, but also because you mentioned, by the way, that I too might be called up to read the Torah. That was something I went in dread of for years. But otherwise I was not fundamentally disturbed in my state of boredom, unless it was by the bar mitzvah, but that meant no more than some ridiculous learning by heart, in other words, led to nothing but something like a ridiculous passing of an examination, and then, as far as you were concerned, by little, not very significant incidents, as when you were called up to read the Torah and came well out of the affair, which to my way of feeling was purely social, or when you stayed on in the synagogue for the prayers for the dead, and I was sent away, which for a long time, obviously because of being sent away and lacking, as I did, any deeper interest, aroused in me the more or less unconscious feeling that what was about to take place was something indecent. – That was how it was in the synagogue..."

Dad was similarly betrayed. "You're either dancing with *shiksahs* or with rabbis!

There is no happy medium with you." Each time he uttered "happy medium" I pictured a grinning, turbaned conjurer, smoothing his crystal ball and tuning in to my newly arrived *dybbuk*. Maybe there was a Jewess in the Ford in my future. Henry might have been upset to know that.

Dad was, and wasn't, like Kafka's father. Like Kafka's father, Dad did not want me to be more traditional or less. He'd already carefully marked the terrain, and struck his stake—our stake. That's where the lines were drawn and how we were to be. Mom and Dad each identified with me. With all his being, Dad wanted me to be like him; with all her soul Mom wanted me to be. As long as I played the game on his grid, according to Robert's Rules of Order, according to his criteria, honoring those rules of his turf, then any success of mine was an extension of himself. Stephen Bloom son of Robert Bloom. Unlike Kafka's father, Dad hoped and actually worked for me to outdistance him, but on his track, in his meet, for his trophies.

Wasn't my new-old Schwinn still in the garage? How he insisted on buying that new Schwinn even then, in ante-bellum Brooklyn before the evacuation. Predating his big hit with his piece of that real estate deal in the Manhattan office building—though Mom and I had said that cousin Gregory's old Monarch bike, which Uncle Sid had given us, was good enough—Dad had refused the hand-me-down bicycle. It had to be the new Schwinn, cost was not a factor.

Holding the handlebars together Dad running with me astride that spanking new blue and white, slick Schwinn, he puffing as he ran. Though he was in pretty good shape from the blackball handball games he played Saturdays, first in Betsy Head and then in Lincoln Terrace Park, but by then he was less regular, and tiring after an hour of chasing with me up and down around the schoolyard. Me falling, and tumbling, and mounting the bike again. And again. Suddenly, that mystically ordained moment when seemingly doing what you were doing all along, at that predetermined moment, it worked. I coasted and raced, now circling the bases. That magical moment of willing motion into being, from my mind to my legs to the bike; Dad beamed. He'd been vindicated. I circled the bases from home plate cutting the corners of the bases as I rode out my scoring.

It was a year now since I moved back to Brooklyn, to join the likes of Rabbi Winters and Reb Shimshon, the last of the Mohicans holding out on the Brownsville Reservation. That move, prompted to facilitate my learning some *Mishnah* (first recording of oral commentary – beginning of 3rd century) and *Gemara* (elucidation and analysis of Mishnah – 500 C.E.) with Winters in the evenings and to be closer to my afternoon English teaching job, which employment Winters had found for me in a *yeshivah* in Crown Heights, one L station and subway stop away from my Brownsville – East Flatbush divide room. And to be within easier commute to Brooklyn College evening classes in deeper Flatbush about forty minutes on the El and Subway. For Dad it was the most unkindest cut of all, "Only a *goy* moves out of his house before he is married, Jews get married from their homes."

Sundays I did visit the new family homestead, my weekend place in the suburbs. Now, as I rested in my latterly/erstwhile bedroom, with its tastefully appointed impeccably matched autumnal colors, olive green and rust wallpaper, the colonial highboy chest, the big photo of Jackie Robinson stealing home plate, the team photo of the Marranos after we beat the Union Street "Eagles." Down in the kitchen Mom was preparing victuals for what she viewed as my extended Brooklyn picnic on the green glens of Brownsville – East Flatbush nature reserve. Meanwhile my regular Sunday pilgrimages from Brooklyn to the Lawrence homestead and the leaving of my main belongings in Lawrence were supportive of her thesis. For Dad, my returning to the Brownsville war zone was an affront. Why? For what? Traffic was going the other way. So was the race. His Jewish-American marathon. I was running in the wrong direction! It was veritably anti-Jewish, not just non-Jewish, to go that route. This was not how he had dreamed and planned it. Not what he worked for. Yet, was it *goy*-like to move out of one's house in order to learn Mishnah and Gemara regularly and to facilitate a quotidian keeping of kosher; was that being more or less Jewish? Maybe that landing of an unlanded generation of "greeners" while they worked feverishly they were yet drone-like haploids, they could not produce sons, only grandsons. May-bee. To bee or not to bee…..Brooklyn.

Often exiting Ebbets Field, the crowding of homebound fans climbing up Bedford Avenue towards the subway on Eastern Parkway seemed Pamplona-like, maybe the bulls would be set loose. City-folk seemed to always have some level of anxiety. Ever prepared to dodge and run. Sometimes I suspected that in an earlier epoch free-roaming bulls, bisons and mastodons had pounded this turf and in some watershed act of Providence had been frozen, squared and cornered, atrophied as buildings, shorter, taller, wider, narrower: One day when the reckoning would come, to be set loose again. Maybe that was the ever-present root palpable tension of the urban tribe. Dodging and dodgers. When? Who knows? Escaping the boredom, the pervasive clouding of ennui, exiting our games.

Was The Brith of Sisyphus a possibility? Attempting to award to that endless circular emptiness; emblematically carving focus and purpose into the very body of the seemingly relentless redundancy.

Waking up one day and finding that people who had seemed to be just extras, milling around at the edge of the movie set of one's life, that they, had of a moment, come forward and graduated into lead roles. While it sparkled with discovery, yet it rubbed with a touch of awkward embarrassment as well. Where were they–I–until now? True, Reb Shimshon always had an ambivalent role. On the one hand, that tall gaunt, Yiddish-speaking, grey-bearded, black-hatted, black-frocked rabbinic figure was removed by light years from my planet. Grandpa Bloom's stories of Reb Shimshon's feats in the *shtetl*, of those battles with *goyim* and *maskilim* (proponents of enlightenment), (however de rigueur) nevertheless physically and conceptually had earned Reb Shimshon a vague, if heroic aura–spirit, indomitable defiant in the face of harsh circumstances. Yet, he was for us, me, uncomfortably, hopelessly old-worldly, otherworldly. Confrontations and collisions with *baalei batim* of Beth Asher (Stalin's *Shul*) did lend him a noble, rebel-like charm, an intriguingly dogged-underdog dimension. Righteous loner stopping, demounting to daven *Minchah* before sunset, then remounting riding off towards that descending orange pink, incandescence on the horizon. Alone. Even when accompanied, alone. With or without Sancho, at times a Litvishe (Lithuanian) Lone Ranger, other times a *heimishe* (home-like) Don Quixote: Citizen and resident of the chimerical and fantastical estates of his own mind. His dwindling posse of septuagenarian dwarfs notwithstanding. However charming yet removed—of a different time and a different world. Those heroic escapades were not first hand. And Yiddish just wasn't the language of my heroes. Then for sure. Now, still not quite. Yet, Reb Shimshon's very causes and lists of issues had tipped him more toward Kosher Don Quixote than urban Lone Ranger. Literarily, that enhanced the charm, but practically that distanced him further from my world. So it seemed, then. However sadly, ironically the intensity of Grandpa Bloom's support reinforced my doubts. If I sympathized with Grandpa Bloom and with Reb Shimshon it was from a distance. I rooted for Grandpa Bloom and Reb Shimshon, but not quite as passionately as I rooted for the Dodgers. Age, language–first heard rhymes, first felt rhythms, pulsed, churned, conspired and dictated that Grandpa Bloom's, Reb Shimshon's points of contact with my life would be limited. Neither the lyrics nor the melodies of their anthems were mine. They did not know from Gil Hodges and Vic Raschi and I did not yet know from Rashi-Rashi, Rambam and Ramban, but there were moments along the way that, perhaps, because of that distance, there was a larger than life persona, looming, hovering over Reb Shimshon's escapades, mysterious tragic-fantastic, comic, by turns, together, by turns.

Arriving alone in America in 1936 with the plan of bringing his family over after he had made some money, Reb Shimshon landed a job as a *shochet* (ritual slaughterer) in a Hoboken slaughterhouse, which position was shorter lived than the beef. Finding the *halachic* standards woefully inadequate, Reb Shimshon soon quit. He bounced around between a few part-time *hashgachah* (kosher supervision) jobs at some small catering halls and restaurants. Some had similar *halachic* problems, others were just poorly managed or under booked. With emerging ghetto-gentrification moving from the East Side to Williamsburg and Brownsville, and edging from Brownsville West into East Flatbush, Grandpa Bloom, the Rosenberg brothers, Zaks, Katz, and some other old-timers and dwarfs organized the purchase of the triangular lot on Saratoga near Linden Boulevard, across from the schoolyard and planned the Beth Asher *Shul*. Meantime that storefront parish was at best a part-time *parnassah* (livelihood). A *landsman* (countryman), Grandpa Bloom, pushed the appointment of Reb Shimshon as rabbi and when other candidates, who were less *talmidei chachamim* (Talmudic scholars) were brought forward, Grandpa offered to pay the first year's part-time salary. That clinched the deal. Only the basement was up in August 1937 when they moved in for the High Holy Days. Plans were for completing an imposing building for Beth Asher but "they started off on the left foot." The first point of contention was Reb Shimshon's insistence that they design the synagogue with the ark in the east, as per accepted tradition for congregations anywhere west of Jerusalem, to pray towards Jerusalem. Because of the triangular shape of the lot, the architect had designed plans, and already constructed the basement level, with the ark positioned in the west. Standing tall in that temporary pulpit in the basement, Reb Shimshon, for weeks quoted responsa, chapter and verse, explaining, emphasizing the significance of placing the ark against the east wall of the *shul*. Then, one night after *Maariv* (evening prayer), Reb Shimshon, Grandpa Bloom, Rosenberg, Zaks and a few dwarfs moved the temporary ark and the pulpit around to the east wall of that basement sanctuary. Though opposition to the face-east coalition was large, once Reb Shimshon and his loyalists had moved the ark to the base of the triangle in the east there was a reluctance to confront him, them. If the pro-west coalition was relatively and mumblingly reticent, they communicated that they were marking time.

More and more frightening news leaked from Europe, and even the sparse mail stopped. At first more slowly, then completely. Reb Shimshon made three false starts, two in the winters of '39 and '40 to return to Europe. Only in the fall of '41 did he succeed in getting into Hungary in search of his family. He wasn't to return until the end of '45. During that long absence the *shul* was completed according to the architect's original plans with the elaborate carved wood ark in the west: *Der Shul mit die fahrkerter aron*—the *shul* with the opposite facing ark. Reb Shimshon lost that battle. Over the years Grandpa Bloom had regaled us with stories he had gleaned of Reb Shimshon's adventures in those pre-war years and then hearsay reports from the occasional refugee about what might have been or not have been Reb Shimshon from the thick of the war-front, bits and pieces. Once he returned, Reb Shimshon refused to talk about those years but here from someone at the nursing home, and there from someone at a different nursing home, and people that drifted through the Brownsville scene, shards and splinters, some shrapnel of stories. Reb Shimshon had tried a number of times to get over to Budapest where the Rebbetzin had moved in with her sister. Although of Lithuanian stock himself, Reb Shimshon grew up in Belgrade where his father held a rabbinic position in the small Serbian Ashkenazic community. As a young man, his father had sent him back to Lithuania, that center of Talmudic scholarship, to study. During a visit back to Belgrade the shidduch (match) was proposed with the daughter of a Hungarian merchant, and the couple were married and settled for a while in Pressburg. With five young children at home, late in 1936-7 Reb Shimshon set out alone for the States. Then when it became evident that it was taking longer than planned to put the savings together to bring the family, and with more horrible stories drifting back he made those attempts in '39 and '40 to return and was each time spurned. Once getting as far as London, and once re-routed to Denmark, both times, after waiting it out for a month, he returned to Brooklyn with the resolve to try again. Meanwhile by questionable unclear word of mouth from fleeing refugees it seemed that the Rebbetzin and children were hiding out in Budapest, working on escape.

In October of '41 Reb Shimshon took off again, and this time he succeeded in getting into Hungary. But he never found the Rebbetzin and the children. Some wet-behind-the-wings-rooky-angel on what was probably his inaugural flight, managed to collect and pluck the Rebbetzin, Benny and Miriam Cohen out of the maelstrom. Five children, Itzik, Channi, Perele, Yossel and Yankele were deported. Never to be seen or heard from again. Like Roosevelt and Churchill, maybe rooky-angels had quotas or at that time all angels, for saving Jews. Miraculously, the Rebbetzin, Benny and Miriam were transported to Switzerland from there to London and after a few months to New York. For the following four years, Reb Shimshon roamed the inferno searching for clues, evading the streaking flames and beasts of destruction, unable to find any trace of his family, all that time, unaware that the Rebbetzin, Benny and Miriam had made it to Brooklyn. The Rebbetzin and children and the Beth Asher people were equally unaware of Reb Shimshon's whereabouts, unsure of his very existence. During his absence from Beth Asher a number of rabbis on trial came and went. An uneasy coalition was formed between those who wanted no rabbi at all, and those who wanted to wait it out for Reb Shimshon. Mr. Zaks said he could do all his shopping for years by taking test model cars from neighborhood agencies for trial runs around the block. He encouraged ongoing auditioning.

While Reb Shimshon was away the Weiss did play. Eddie Weiss, his cousins Morris and Isaac and the Roses and their group of *baalei batim* began almost immediately whittling away at the *mechitzah* (divider). First the one in the basement, and then the one in the newly built sanctuary above. Though the just completed Beth Asher sanctuary had a balcony for women, some of the older women had difficulty climbing the steps and petitioned to cordon off a section downstairs for them to be able to daven. A *halachic mechitzah* was erected downstairs to divide off about sixty seats at the back. Over-all room capacity was about three hundred. Only on High Holidays did that main sanctuary fill, when all kinds of neighborhood and out of neighborhood ringers appeared. On a regular Shabbos, there were about forty men and fifteen women.

Talmudic psychology had it that the threshold for male sexual arousal was low, imminent, casual. Female sexuality was slower to respond and relationship oriented. Viewing the female was potentially distracting for the male. The way Rabbi Winters and the *bachurim* at the *yeshivah* spoke of it, *halachic* modesty was kind of the difference between new money and old money. New money was an adolescent romp. Spendthrift, garish, demonstrative, ostentatious. Some lived their entire lives as nouveau–riche adolescents. *Halachic* norms define human sexuality as old money. It's been in the family for generations. There was due recognition for it. But, those long-time wealthy have less need to prove and demonstrate their wealth. It's there. A given. They respect and appreciate it. But they are unhurried. Like F. Scott Fitzgerald said, "The rich, they are different from you and me" even if Hemingway disagreed. Whereas I could have seen my once-resident *shiksah*—Pat McQuade—going for the *mechitzah* idea. She'd have liked a kind of portable *mechitzah* on wheels to contain my peripheral vision as we promenaded through the avenues and boulevards, the parks and beaches of the city. In Barbusse's novel the anti-hero of a hero wonders at his own response to a new stimulation so immediately after, on the heels of, an indulgence. Wilson cites that as credentials for, "outsiderhood"; mere physical pleasure being less than fulfilling. Someone should tell Barbusse and Wilson, that "insiders" suffer that too. Some more consciously, others less consciously. The Talmudists would have smiled knowingly, "No man dies with having fulfilled half his appetites." Wilson underestimated, over-rationalized and romanticized the essential id. Predestined to plague the omnivore's chronic appetite, rooted in the necessary and continuing discrepancy between expectation and delivery, it came with the territory. Perhaps that very disillusionment and disappointment helped propel the cycle forward. Endlessly. Hopelessly. Endlessly. Barbusse's fellow had more masquerading as else. Not much else was available at the market place.

Spiritual vacuum, ennui? The rabbis say that perforce demonizes the unfocused act of pleasure. Abstinence? Unreasonable. Harnessing? Productive. To deny channels for expressing root needs was unrealistic, counterproductive; whereas undirected indulgence was condemned to that endless spinning redundancy, the bottomless abyss of disappearing satisfactions. They, the Talmudists talked of three criteria for the focused act—time, place, people. Optimal merging of the variables produced a productive, meaningful act, less than that was neutral or destructive. To eat the day before Yom Kippur was a *mitzvah*, to fast on Yom Kippur was a *mitzvah*. On Purim one fasted the day before and feted the day of Purim. Neither eating nor fasting was inherently holy or unholy. Context, shaped by *halachic* criteria, defined positive or negative. *Halachah*: from the root form *halach*, to go, the manner in which a man went through the business of his life or should go through the business of his life. The very same actions could be uplifting, when focused through *halachic* criteria. Of course all this meant that one had to accept the givens of the *halachah* as being primary and essential molds for shaping ideal behavior. Given their givens they had a game plan those Torah Jews. But maybe you had to be in a giving mood to grant those givens— to sympathize with that case for *davening* as a time for undivided attention it followed that you needed a divider.

And so, as was with the fabric of so many American *mechitzahs*, they were not shrink-proof, so it was with Beth Asher during Reb Shimshon's absence. Though less and less women, and no younger women, came to the synagogue, fewer of those that did come were prepared to climb the steps to the balcony. The improvised *mechitzah* down-stairs shrank during Reb Shimshon's absence. Returning on a Wednesday in August of '45 he spent Thursday night through the night with a few of his dwarfs and other remaining loyalists rebuilding the *mechitzah* to its *halachic* height. The only can of paint was white and Reb Shimshon and his people painted that *mechitzah* white and decorated it with some flowers. I was eleven at the time and remember Grandpa Bloom went along to help. It isn't everyday a man gets a chance to whitewash a *mechitzah*.

"But dis is America. Is ah free country and here if I vont to sit mit mine veib (wife) ahm entitle."

"Ahm [1] not knowink Veiss that you are knowink so good de geography, so dis is America, *azai gor...*" Reb Shimshon, continuing "So how come Veiss before ahm goink for 4 years over der to dat *gehinnom* over dere, your *veib* vas tellink me and crynk that you are never home even ven you are not vorkink you playink cards and drinkink mit you cronies. So *punkt* den ven its de time to *daven*, punkt den dats ven you vant to sit mit your veib? Another time you can't find? I'm telling you vy, 'cause you vantink to givink your *veib* time from the *Ribono Shel Olam*'s (Master of the Universe) time, not from you own time, dat's vy. But you no havink any real *sechel* (wisdom), is all de time alvays the *Ribono Shel Olam*'s time and soon iz cominck dat time ven you knowink dat, Veiss, but yesterday and today you not knowink dat yet." Weiss with the Roses and Katz nodding in agreement.

During those four years while Reb Shimshon was wandering through the

---

1 For the benefit of those who do not speak Yinglish, please see the translation in the Appendix, page 205.

devastation of that continent gone berserk, the Rebbetzin, Miriam and Benny made it to Brownsville. Reb Shimshon had a small two-room basement apartment on Thatford. Horowitz now gave the Rebbetzin, Miriam and Benny a larger apartment in his tenement on Bristol Street, Kaulkstein got her a job in Cohen's Bakery on Riverdale Avenue near Sarotoga where he was a silent partner. Cohen said Kaulkstein wasn't so silent.

At their Brooklyn arrival Benny was 12 and Miriam 15. When people addressed Reb Shimshon's wife as "Rebbetzin" she looked pained and tearfully rejected the title saying that she wouldn't be "Rebbetzin" until Reb Shimshon returned. Walking the streets from her apartment to Cohen's bakery and back again in her white uniform–Cohen required the sales people to wear white–Zaks said "The whole world – the bakers dey wearing white and the salespeople dey are wearing anyting what dey want. By Cohen its *Moshe Kappoyeh* (opposite). The salespeople dey wearing white and de bakers dey are dressing like "plumbbers" and "carpentners." Trudging through the streets the white figure of the Rebbetzin appeared ghostlike. Grandpa Bloom said the Rebbetzin had been a beautiful woman. From her home to the bakery was a distance of only a few blocks yet each time I saw her she seemed lost like she was about to take the wrong turn and somehow at the last moment she went right. So it was before Benny's bar mitzvah debacle which was one really bad day at Beth Asher. From that day on it was more rapidly downhill.

Benny and Miriam hit the pavements and schools of Brooklyn with running starts. With Benny more the schoolyard than the school. At twelve he just started throwing, fielding and hitting as if he had always done it, and done it a lot better than anyone else. The exploits of that dark-haired lithesome figure, with the Yiddish accent were quickly passed by word of mouth throughout the neighborhood. Already at twelve years old a budding star. Perhaps because of that accent he hardly spoke, Benny. But he played. And played with a graceful excellence that was stunning. In softball, and stickball, his pegs and fastballs zipped and hopped, in blazing streaks. Soon came the Parade Grounds and hardball games again starring even when playing against sixteen and seventeen year olds. Meanwhile, black-eyed fiery Miriam picked up occasional singing and dancing engagements at Yiddish speaking parties in the neighborhood around Brooklyn and even Manhattan. In Reb Shimon's absence she supplemented the meager income of the family with spot performances in the Yiddish theater as well. While the Rebbetzin disapproved, and some *baalei batim* tried to dissuade Miriam, she went about her business independently.

As Benny's bar mitzvah neared, arrangements were made by the *baalei batim* and the *gabbaim* (sextons) for Benny's *aliyah* (calling to recite blessing at Torah reading) to the Torah to be followed by a festive *kiddush* (traditional small morning repast for occasions, sometimes not so small). Although it wasn't expressed, it was thought by all— who knows whether or not Reb Shimshon is even alive? Yet the bar mitzvah day must be marked at its proper Jewish calendar date. "A bar mitzvah is a bar mitzvah." Grandpa Bloom and Zaks went with the Rebbetzin and Benny to Ripley's on Eastern Parkway and Utica to get Benny his de-rigueur double-breasted navy blue suit. New shirt, new tie and new shoes were purchased on Pitkin Avenue. Even then, a seven year old like myself had heard that Benny was destined for greatness to pitch for some major league team when the time came. Probably just because of Reb Shimshon's absence and the Rebbetzin's situation, the *baalei batim* had taken to preparing a more lavish *kiddush* than might have been the norm.

The morning of the bar mitzvah arrived. Throughout the Shabbos prayers, distracting aromas of simmering *cholent* and *kugel* (traditional Shabbos dishes) wafted up from the kitchen in the basement to the main sanctuary a floor above. Mr. Rubinoff who fancied himself a world-class *chazzan* (cantor) led the *Shacharis* prayers. Barrel-chested Rubinoff had the problem of always wanting to lead the prayers but feeling the need to reserve his performances for occasions that were special, such as holidays and *simchahs* (joyous moments of *mitzvah* to celebrate) — significant times worthy of his grand talents. Much to the chagrin of most of the muttering congregants, his style was to drag out the *Shacharis* prayer longer, filling the air and time with trills and flights of *chazzanus* (cantorial rendition). Longer and longer. Delays and stalling notwithstanding the time came to remove the Torah scroll from the ark for the Shabbos reading... and no Benny. Continuing the reading and adding the maximum amount of permissible *aliyahs*, still no Benny. *Maftir* (concluding *Aliyah* reserved for bar mitzvah) was reached – Benny's turn to bat and still no Benny. The *baalei batim* huddled, stalled and huddled and reluctantly the service was continued. Rubinfeld got *maftir*. Benny was a no-show. Instead, that Shabbos morning thirteen-year-old Benny pitched a no hitter for the Flatbush Knights against the Park Slope Cowboys in a hardball game at the Parade Grounds, where all the other team members on both sides were sixteen-year-olds and older.

According to the women that were at Stalin's *Shul* that Shabbos, the Rebbetzin sat transfixed, affixed to her seat up in the balcony long after all the congregants had left for the *kiddush* in the basement. Hovering high overhead the vaulted ceiling of Beth Asher, its naive murals of the zodiac, she sat staring down to the unpeopled pews and *bimah* (synagogue table dedicated for Torah reading), empty sanctuary for hours without moving. Some *baalei batim* left for home, others proceeded with the *kiddush* – pity to waste all that good food and *schnapps*. But the Rebbetzin would not come down to join. Nor to leave her seat in the balcony. Sixteen-year-old Miriam tended to her frozen mother, but the Rebbetzin was unresponsive. So it was that the Rebbetzin was to become Beth Asher's Miss Havisham. She took to showing up every Shabbos in that same black and white polka dot dress with the rounded white collar sitting through the *davening* and long after all had gone, staring down for hours toward the *bimah* scrutinizing that vacated space. For years she had waited for her husband, Reb Shimshon. Now she was also waiting for her *Chassan HaBar Mitzvah* (groom-like state of bar mitzvah) boy to show. And for years neither showed. She virtually stopped speaking.

During the week, now trudging more slowly, traipsing to and from Cohen's bakery her steps were even heavier. Like she was towing an invisible shopping cart laden with terribly heavy goods she would stop as if to rest, then strain and tug and pull that invisible cart on. No longer able to deal with customers. Cohen removed her to inside the baking area, and then let her go. Even then, Cohen along with other *baalei batim*, Kaulkstein, Horowitz, Rosenberg and Grandpa Bloom continued to financially support the family. Miriam refused their support and took on more evening performances, eventually, landing steady work as a waitress at Uncle Sid's Mermaid's Tale. Benny also drifted towards Coney Island, where he hung around the midway. He quickly mastered hustling along the Coney Island carny strip, pitching milk bottles, popping baskets and rifle shots at the gallery. Stalking, setting up his prey, betting, initially feigning incompetence, climaxing with accuracy and winning. A reticent hustler but a hustler nonetheless. Then a waiter, and then on to managing the Mermaid's Tale, the fish and chips bar and restaurant just off Mermaid Avenue where Uncle Sid still owned a piece of the action and had endorsed Benny's appointment. After all Benny had been a schoolyard hero, a generation after Sid but a schoolyard hero. After Benny's notorious no-show, one Thursday morning Zaks, Grandpa Bloom and a few other *baalei batim* caught Benny and brought him to Beth Asher for a quickie Marrano-like weekday basement *bar mitzvah aliyah*. Someone was dispatched to bring the Rebbetzin but she refused to come. Miss Havisham-like she was to continue her Shabbos vigil.

Early on Sammy and Gabriel promoted the Mermaid's Tale as a meeting place for many Yiddish theatre types and émigré bohemians residing in Brighton Beach, Coney Island, Flatbush, Brownsville and even East New York. Miriam and Benny's presence encouraged those customers. Deep into the wee hours of the morning, spring and summer, ex-performers and never-wasses came to reminisce, argue, fantasize, drink and eat at the Mermaid's Tale. Miriam had found her way to the Workman's Circle building on Ralph Avenue becoming a group leader often during the evenings delivering firebrand lectures around the city mostly on Sacco and Vanzetti. Brownsville's own Rosa Luxemburg, Emma Goldman. Black-eyed Miriam dressed like a socialist, a worker woman, yet performed like an actress. Between campaigns for Norman Thomas, just before

Reb Shimshon's return from the European hell, Miriam married a fellow socialist, Solly Zemeroff, a writer for the Daily Forward. By the time Reb Shimshon surfaced in '45, Miriam and Solly and Benny had long jettisoned whatever traditional cargo they had brought along from the old country. Miriam and her husband moved first to Manhattan and then to Jackson Heights. Old Torah traditions had been replaced, upstaged by the newer testament of socialist credos and dogmas. If more modern, yet for these socialists already a tradition, a code of customs with set times for ritually fixed liturgical recitations. When challenged how he, arch capitalist that he was, tolerated Miriam's hot-brand radical speeches at the Mermaid's Tale, Uncle Sid replied, "Socialists are good for business." Since Sid and Sammy held firmly, a restaurant should always be full, requests for credit were frequently honored. Sammy inaugurated a policy of giving discounts to people branded with the blue numbers from a concentration camp. One Romanian Jew was twice caught having penned simulated blue numbers onto his arm to gain the discount.

Even while Benny's formal residence was still the Rebbetzin's domicile, he was rarely there. And then he moved out at about his 17th birthday just before Reb Shimshon returned. Yet Benny continued to contribute to the Rebbetzin's household upkeep – some said regularly, others said irregularly. Until her marriage Miriam tended the Rebbetzin's home. It was said that even though she did not keep kosher any longer personally, she respected the Rebbetzin's criteria for *kashrus* in that home. After her move from Brooklyn, Miriam continued coming once a week. Friday nights Mrs. Rosenzweig from Thatford Street or the Schwartz family from Bristol Street would walk up to the Rebbetzin's third floor apartment and find her sitting alone at the candle lit holiday-like, white cloth covered table, set for four guests. At times it was set for nine. Repeated invitations from Beth Asher families to the Rebbetzin to join them for Shabbos and holiday meals were spurned. It was increasingly hard to get her to speak. If at all she spoke it was about her childhood, her parents, the early days in Budapest, about the disappeared Itzik, Channi, Yankele, Perele, Yossel and Reb Shimshon.

Upon his return in '45, Reb Shimshon took over the household and care of the Rebbetzin. Benny, between pitching for Tilden High School and working at the Mermaid's Tale, was rarely around. Though baseball remained his first love, he went to LIU on a basketball scholarship. After about two years, dropping out of school he worked full time at the Mermaid's Tale as manager. For a few seasons Benny continued showing up now and then for Saturday, Sunday softball games at the PS 189 schoolyard. Shortly after signing a contract with the Giants, he broke his leg sliding into third in a schoolyard softball game. Benny never made it to spring training that year. Delay after delay, and one thing did not lead to another, Benny never did make it to the Polo Grounds.

Two pictures with Benny hung in my Lawrence room; one at a Saturday morning schoolyard contest, Marty had snapped the shot as Benny greeted me at the plate after
I homered. Benny was our pitcher that day and wore the mantle of home run greeter. The
second shot was of Pat and myself with Benny on a date at the Mermaid's Tale. Dad had
demanded that I remove that picture. Mom said she would prefer that it be removed, but
that I had a right to my privacy. When I moved back to Brooklyn, Teddy cited Dad's in-
trusion into my privacy as the cause. When he walked me to the car he smiled that Teddy
smile as we parted. The picture was removed by Dad shortly after I left.

Now looking from the bedroom window of our Lawrence abode– my
short-weekend (Sunday) cottage in the suburbs–I espied the glistening hood of the black
topped hearse jutting out beyond the neatly cropped bushes of Dr. Weissman's mansion
on the corner. Marty and Bam were honoring Dad's injunction not to park the hearse
in front of the house. Two vehicles banned from parking there: The hearse and Sroly's
piebald rusted dented delivery van. Post-beach Marty and Bam again confirmed that they
were hungry. It was "The Nine Days" and I had not gone to the beach with them. Real
yeshivah bachurim would not go mixed-swimming any time during the year. *Halachic*
norms for Jewish modesty were predicated on the male vulnerability for casual, visual,
stimulation. Responsible halachic behavior required anticipating consequences, setting
up the scenario to increase the probability of the *halachic* goal being achieved. Those
inclinations, propensities to be mandated exclusively for focused application within the
halachic ideal. Marriage, family, community; team and buddy loyalty, enhancing relation-
ships, productivity. Pat would have found that poetic, romantic.

During The Nine Days there is a prohibition against any swimming. From the
First of Av through and climaxing with the Ninth of Av was a period of intense mourning
for the destruction of the two Temples on that very same day. But even extra innings –
end. Last play, last out, game finished. When the inventory of bullpen, bench clemency
has been exhausted it's over and even those extra innings constitute a game completed
as if it had been nine innings, the ninth of Av...but, yet, – "wait till next year." Peculiarly enough while Rosh Hashanah begins the month of Tishrei, yet the counting of the
months of the Jewish calendar starts with the month of Nissan. When necessary a month
will be added so the lunar calendar can catch up with the solar calculation – Pesach must
be spring time – baseball season.

In keeping with the Jewish credo holidays were not merely commemorated but
rather existentially re-lived, revisiting that place in time, one behaved in rhythm with
the motif of that calendric zone within which one re-found Jewish history, the Jewish
people, one's self, in that actual temporal-space. Dancing in step to the beat of the hour

we were now approaching "Lamentations"! Like some intellectual-cum-theological strat-egy for survival. Jewish judo! Turning the opponents thrust to our advantage. Thank you Pharaoh, Nebuchadnezzar, Haman, Hitler, Stalin, for reminding us that we are Jews. Heinous and dastardly as your crimes have been through history, we owe you bastards a begrudging debt. Your hateful, hostile crimes have regretfully served us. Jew-Jitsu! Tishah B'Av – that day from time immemorial, set aside for retribution when we spiritually bottom out. Pre-calamity and post-calamity is all the difference. Life is to be cherished. We are enjoined to protect and better the gift of our lives every step of the way. Only three transgressions require self-sacrifice: Idolatry, adultery and murder. In concentric circles we are dedicated to building ourselves, our families, our communities, our people, the world. But post calamity searching for Providential Guidance even when not finding His signature we own up to His authorship. Sighingly to re-read the ancient prophetic tomes that anticipated and anguished about those happened-now- happening events. And if His penmanship often seemed so illegible, perhaps the problem was my lack of training, skill and sensitivity in deciphering that Cosmic script. If it so often came on as incoherent scribble, batches and patches of suffering and chaos, then that too, ironically enough, that very illegibility had itself been predicted and projected. In the *beis medrash* (study hall) at the *yeshivah* those *bachurim* amateur and expert Aramaic graphologists scrutinizing the layers of text, searching, attempting to divine the Divine, collecting the elliptic clues of the Cosmic scrawl from those ancient scrolls; on the gross level, if not the specific level. Somewhat akin to that uncertainty principle where the larger picture might be predict-able but the particulars ever elusive...Like facing Bob Feller, strike out, likely; yet, if/when connecting belting it for the longball. Didn't the winning Robin Roberts give up more home runs than anyone? Jew-jitsu. Hitting Esau's fastball.

Most hours of most days I now behaved more similarly to the less pious segment of the Orthodox community, so called "modernists" where lines had been drawn and a pick-and-choose syndrome instituted. Unlike Conservative and Reform this group was *halachically* committed to Shabbos, kashrus, post marital family purity, prayer, while yet often comfortably leapfrogging other *halachic* norms. At the left end of the *halachically* observant continuum they yet stood committedly to the right of the non-*halachic* com-munity. Philosophically and theologically, I did identify with the *yeshivah* community on the right - right. A Rabbi Shmuel Yaakov was quoted as defining "*Charedi*" as someone who had internalized as his primary goal to connect to his Creator; unlike someone who discharged the *mitzvahs* as external obligations always looking for loopholes to beat the system, like having a good accountant that can save you taxes. For the *Charedi* the élan vital of one's existence had become connecting to The Source. Anyone can fail, but the one measures himself, his very existence, by the reaching for that excellence, the other as incidental to the essential thrust of his being.

Regarding non-*halachasists*, Rabbi Gordon quoted a Rabbi Wasserman as telling that a synthetic potato had been developed in America. It looked, felt and even tasted like a potato. Yet when planted it could not produce more potatoes. Such was the measure of authenticity – does it produce succeeding generations? It did seem to be "either/or." The *Halachah*. One day? Maybe. Meanwhile I still hit the beaches with Bam and Marty on plain old civilian Sundays. But today was different. The Nine Days had an increasingly tangible heaviness. More today, *erev, erev* Tishah B'Av than yesterday. Tomorrow night was the planned caper. And though we had agreed we would not be talking about it, surely we were all thinking about tomorrow night's planned Tishah B'Av mission with Reb Shimshon. Bam claimed being nervous made him hungrier. Marty said it was not possible to be hungrier than Bam normally was. I wondered whether the rabbis would have enacted a *gezeirah* (edict) not to think about tomorrow night in order not to come to speak about it. And what about thinking about thinking about it? Operation Jeremiah!

Of late, Mom prepared the victuals for my kosher jaunt back to the glens of pastoral Brownville over the barbecue in the back yard. I connected Grandpa Bloom's passing with the removal of the last vestige of the kashrus ritual at our home to that single altar in the garden. Banished, exiled. Actually the banishment took place a year before Grandpa's death when he had already stopped visiting us. Till then we ate like Jews in the confines of our home and like *goyim* in the outside world. Gourmet gastronomic Marranos. One snowy December night during Grandpa Bloom's last winter, after it had been agreed with the doctors not to take him out of the nursing home at all till warmer weather, if then, suddenly one snowy December night he appeared unannounced on our doorstep. Some good Samaritan of a volunteer had given Grandpa a ride without clearing the visit with the doctors or nurses. Dad and Mom, after their initial shock, scrambled about to give him something to eat. Refusing Dad's suggestion to offer some tuna and vegetables, Mom with tears in her eyes declared that Grandpa Bloom must have something "substantial" and warm. There was no choice but to get the barbecue going.

"Barbecue? In a snow storm, ridiculous." Dad.

"Yes! A barbecue! You should have thought of that before we stopped keeping kosher in the kitchen." Mom.

With Grandpa Bloom sitting in the den, patiently waiting in front of the TV, eleven-year-old Teddy and I watched through the sliding glass doors of the kitchen as Mom and Dad donned coats, gloves and scarves, and braving the cold wind plunged into the gusting snow and began struggling to light the barbecue. Not the surreal ballet, the absurd-grace, and soft elegant antics of Charlie Chaplin, not even the mock-farce-operetta of Laurel and Hardy; but rather a more harsh and foolhardy jerkiness, stand-ins for Abbott and Costello at the North Pole. A confused slapstick charade of haplessness and helplessness. Twice I offered to go out and help, and Dad said if he could not do it there was nothing more that I could do. Coughing out bursts of smoky blurbs, stumbling about in the blowing snow. Finally they gave up after a seemingly endless hour or so, escaping the blustering storm and returned to the house. Grandpa Bloom had tuna and tears – Starkist and Mom's. That was two years ago. Grandpa Bloom died a year after that visit.

Tishah B'Av was to be tears without tuna. As one version had it, Napoleon riding around Paris Tishah B'Av night after questioning why Jews sat on the floors and read by candlelight that night, and it having been explained to him he replied "If after 1,700 plus years they still mourn that loss, they will make it back to rebuild." Meantime I had decided to respect this for-me recently discovered tradition not to eat meat during The Nine Days, I would have tuna instead. Mom had been tipped off. She had never heard of The Nine Days and their prohibitions until I told her. Tomorrow night and Tuesday day there would be no eating. Post Tishah B'Av I would be able to eat at night, but meat or wine only after the following midday. All this to be in step with that rhythm, that beat of the pulse of the Jewish people, its historic calendar. Preparing my supplies for the coming week, as usual Mom would put in extras for Marty and Bam and tonight for Izzy as well. He was in town, and would be joining us. We would pick him up on the way to Brooklyn. Izzy, like me would be on a meatless diet. Marty and Bam held they were not limited to fish now or for that matter kosher at all. Nor were we, they thought. And we thought we and they were. At times, at least, I thought that it was so or might be so. Possibility sometimes becoming probability. Oft times just possibility, but actually possible to become probability. "Actual?" "Satisfactual?" – Possibly.

Rabbi Gordon quoted the Spanish Jewish commentary, Abarbanel, who rejecting Ferdinand's offer to stay on, choosing instead to join his brethren expelled from Spain as saying that – "Had the king and queen realized how they had re-confirmed the faith of so many as that decree had fallen on Tishah B'Av – had Ferdinand and Isabel understood that, they might have rescinded the decree." It was also pointed out that many historians viewed World War II as a direct extension of World War I. And World War 1, Russia and Germany had declared war on each other during those Nine Days.

As had become Dad's habit over the last year, since my move back to Brooklyn, on my Sunday visits weather allowing, he adjourned to the yard to read or play catch with Teddy. No greeting. No words were exchanged between us. Like our allotted quota of words had been used up, and no new shipment was in the offing. Perhaps there is a passion quotient that accounts for quantity as well. Once more today, upon my arrival, Dad invited Teddy to the backyard to play catch.

I could hear Mom in the kitchen opening and closing the doors to the refrigerator and cabinets, folding, wrapping sandwiches, and plastic containers of fish and meat from the barbecue, cookies and fruit for the week. Leaning on the hearse parked at the corner, Marty and Bam waved up to my window and I signaled them that I would be out shortly. Those high neatly clipped hedges of Dr. Weissman's property across the way partially blocked my view of his yard. Ironically, since we had moved across the street I had not been behind those hedges. Nine years ago, when I was eleven, and we were still coming out to Lawrence from Brooklyn on the average of two Sundays a month, to visit with Uncle Sid and Aunt Fran, one fateful, infamous Sunday I had been behind those hedges. Uncle Sid was said to have been born with a smile on his face, while he spoke that smile never left. It seemed to say – "You may know what I have in mind, but so what, I will out-last you, out-smile you." More than just having internalized street savvy, he'd succeeded instead in externalizing the core of human personality, the root inner being had for Sid become purely cutaneous. Perhaps this explained his affinity to theatre. Feeling, anger, hate, love were donned and shed, purely external, passing with each scene. And that smile was confirmation that all the hullabaloo was merely a lot of sound and fury not signifying much. Never meriting too much agitation. Even at his funeral, people viewing the bier agreed his countenance had a smile. While he spoke, that smile never left, through whatever stress and duress, the smile was omnipresent.

Tripping into the coat business during his jaunt as a borscht belt saxophonist and *tummler* (a generator of action), that original factory was in fact picked up for a "song." Some of those old-time theater people and garment district people later became regulars at the Mermaid's Tale. Sid was a promoter's promoter, i.e promoting those who thrived on promotion. He initiated and organized Perlmutter's hiring of the Spanish galleon for Reb Shimshon's star-crossed Columbus Day voyage, Reb Shimshon's sole journey as a seafaring *mashgiach* that ended in mutiny and exile.

Dad said that when Sid and he were just fifteen years old, often walking Pitkin Avenue together, Sid would point out the occasional Cadillac, swear and bet that before he was twenty five he would own a new one. He beat his deadline by two years. One of those summers up in the Catskills he joined a small makeshift textile plant. Uncle Sid brought their wares to market in the city. Not long after he teamed up with Sammy and Gabriel the Romanian refugee identical twins who although they only spoke Romanian and Yiddish were doing a pantomime and magic act around the borscht belt. Sammy would appear alone on the stage and after being duly bound, chained and locked in boxes and safes, then Gabriel would emerge unfettered from alongside. Before and after shows, one of the two would be disguised with mustache and dark glasses. Sammy said all other actors get made up for their performances, they, the identical twins, got made up between performances. Within a year Uncle Sid and the twins opened their own small children's wear factory near Monticello. A few years later they moved the operation to Greenpoint section of Brooklyn and started manufacturing women's coats. During the summers, from '53 - '55 I worked there in the shipping department. Sammy and Gabriel were both initially inside men and Uncle Sid did the selling. Along the way Sammy learned enough English to hit the streets and markets. Gabriel went on to study chemistry. But Uncle Sid remained the salesman par excellence.

Chutzpah, while it partakes of insolence and impudence, yet it has something more. *Chutzpah* is a song, a dance, an entertainment. It touches the other's repressed unconscious; that frequently blocked brazenness of the more decorous. As performance, *chutzpah* is riveting and cathartic. Impudence is foolhardy, insolence supercilious, but *chutzpah* has charm. Impudence is expedited with a horse laugh, insolence a sneer, and *chutzpah* a smile. Uncle Sid smiled. Each such performance was discharged "fair and square." *Chutzpah* expects, requires applause and that requirement is a compliment to the audience. We need, and want your recognition. You are our public. You are crucial to our act. Whatever other emotions are engendered by that theatric effrontery–catharsis entertainment and appreciation are there as well. And oft times, worth the price of entry. No less a dignitary than Abie Rellis had been a fan of Sid's brashness, following an incident in the pool room under the El on Livonia Avenue near Saratoga when Sid had laid out one of Abie's boys. Then one day Abie pulled up in a big limo with a number of goons and challenged Sid to do it again. There, on the street in front of the schoolyard without much ado Sid promptly repeated his decking of Abie's boy. Some said that Abie offered him a job, others say he pronounced, "I just wanted to make sure you did it fair and square kid." One version had it that Sid did some odd jobs for Abie over the years. How odd? No one discussed. Uncle Sid was one of the mourners that day not far from the scene of Rellis' last plunge. The parachute jump, Ferris wheels, roller coaster, were all closed for winter when Abie Rellis took his infamous parachute–less–parachute–jump from the Half Moon Hotel sixth floor window in Coney Island.

Sid's ubiquitous smile atoned for a fair amount of sinning. "That's Sid" was sometimes a condemnation, but more often than not, an explanation and submission to Sid's spell.

What Sid lacked in being avuncular he more than made up in flamboyance. "He made a parade out of stroll." And that flamboyance simultaneously drew and irked those around him. Always the Clark Bar, "the center of attraction." In its audacious energy *chutzpah* rivets even critics.

Fran was my anti-auntie. She was anti-Dean Martin, "He's nothing without Lewis." Anti-Dewey, "He looks like a waiter at Ratners." Anti-Truman, "He's got no class, and if he worked in my haberdashery I woulda fired him too." Anti-conspicuous consumption. "Who are they trying to impress?" Anti-frugality, "If they have it why don't they spend it?" Anti-girls-with-nose jobs, "Who is she kidding, I remember her with the old nose." Anti-girls-without-nose jobs, "With all they spend how much would it have cost already to fix that nose?" Fran and Sid met one summer up in the Catskills when Fran was singing with a summer stock company.

Despite the smile, Dorian Gray-like, Uncle Sid's face told of the effort he had put into indulgence. It had not come easy. Reading the lines, between the lines, in his face told the story. That boyish grin belied the fatiguing effort dedicated to the ethic of enjoyment. But the etched-in lines on that face testified to the effort. Dad was 'on the outs' with Sid and Fran for while after Greg's bar mitzvah - whereat Sammy of the twins had said, "There had been much Bar and little Mitzvah." After having promised to accommodate Grandpa Bloom and have the affair catered kosher, Sid and Fran reneged. Dad was outraged, and did not want to attend. That was bout two, a rematch of the fifteen rounds Mom and Dad had gone with Sid and Fran a year earlier at the Old Age Home. Two years before we moved to Lawrence Sid and Fran upped and moved to Westchester. They said they wanted more "genteel" surroundings. Too many people from Brooklyn, and the Bronx, had come out to the five towns. Dad read 'gentile' for 'genteel.' While they still lived in Lawrence, we drove out once or twice a month on a Saturday or Sunday to visit. Our Brooklyn outing to the Island. They were gracious, if somewhat condescending hosts. Their children—Roberta, six years, and Gregory three years my senior—hardly joined us. A great collector, Gregory occasionally allowed me access to his classic comics, baseball cards, and autographs. That kept me going for hours. Of a mood, Gregory would deign to share his encyclopedic knowledge of baseball players, their batting averages, RBI's, earned run averages etc. His erudition was impressive and atoned partially for Gregory's lack of active participation in sports. At that time we kept kosher only at home and ate the going fare when in Rome. Sid and Fran's place was Rome. But when Dad and Mom discovered that Sid and Fran had been bringing Grandpa Bloom non-kosher food at the Jewish Old Age Home in Rockaway which facility was kosher, Dad and Mom protested. In rebuttal Fran and Sid pointed to our family's culinary peccadilloes.

"So don't make like you are some religious who-knows-what, you know what I mean, you pack away plenty of that stuff yourself. Okay?" Sid winking and smiling.

"That's not the point dammit, who the blazes cares what I eat. Don't you understand that my father never ate non-kosher and you fed it to him not to me, to him for G-d's sake?"

"Come on, who says he never ate non-kosher even with all those labels, some of those rabbis will put their name on anything for a buck, who knows what he really ate. Besides which my cooking is a lot better than the greasy stuff that the 'home' serves." Fran with indignation.

"That's ridiculous, my father never knowingly ate anything non-kosher in his life." Dad.

"That is the point, you know as well as I do that he is out of it most of the time now and he hardly knows what he eats. So what difference does it make, and besides what do you mean MY father, he happens to be my father as well." Fran.

"So act like it dammit, treat him with respect instead of insulting him. I don't care if you could fool him or not, but we both know that if he knew it was non-kosher he wouldn't eat it. Even if you held a gun to his head. Any child can see that what you have done has destroyed his dignity, any little dignity he had left. You have no license to do that to anyone let alone a father."

"Okay, so she has no license, but a learner's permit she's got—you know if you tasted her soufflés you would know it was only a learner's permit." Sid smiling, beaming.

"So what kind of way is that to talk about my cooking? You don't look undernourished for G-d's sake." Fran.

"You know I am just kidding Fran." Sid.

"Yeah I know you should have stayed at the Nevele or at Grossingers...And you tell it to me straight Robert, you don't think G-d gives a hoot what you eat, do you? He has got more important business to attend to. All those outdated customs and rituals, all that European stuff is passé here." Fran.

Dad began whistling Yankee Doodle Dandy. Tante (Aunt) Bella of blessed memory, Grandpa Bloom's sister, called Jews hell-bent on assimilation "Yankee Doodle Dandies."

"Says who?" Mom for the first time.

"Says me." Fran turning to mother and continuing, "I think some rabbis and kosher butchers drummed up the whole deal if you ask me." Fran.

"No one is asking you." Dad.

"This much I'll tell you Fran, if it's up to Jews like us to carry on the tradition it's going to disappear, only those Jews that keep those things will survive, " Mom.

"So who needs Jews to survive? Trying to survive hasn't got us such great reviews." Sid.

More strains of "Yankee Doodle Dandy" from Dad. "Cheese and crackers." Dad. Grandpa Bloom's objection to invoking Jesus Christ had brought into the family lexicon "cheese and crackers" as an alternative expletive.

"You keep missing the point." Dad continuing. "You violated my father's basic dignity. That's what I'm talking about and that's exactly what you did, and that's what counts and that's the thing I will never forgive."

"Here we shlep all the way from Westchester to bring this gourmet food and that's the way you talk." Sid again tossing his head back so that the hair hanging on this forehead would shift a bit, still smiling all the time.

"Who asked you to move or to *shlep*, you're not doing anyone any favors." Dad.

Gregory's bar mitzvah celebrations came to pass on the evening of Sunday December 7th 1947. Like to a modern day ark, rows of twos, of furry and wooly looking creatures began streaming up the ramp to the ship-like concrete structure on the old World's Fair Grounds near LaGuardia airport. Male and female mammals, some exotic, some ordinary, bunching, trotting, scampering aboard. Set after set discarding their mobile metallic shells at the entrance to the ark, lessening the weight that the ship would carry, ascending the ramp. Once inside, then removing their sleek coats of mink, ermine, Persian lamb, cashmere, leather, wool – many La-Vine coat creations. Splendidly coiffed women in spangled, perfumed gowns, bedecked, bedizened with glitter; accompanied by sartorial gents all spit and polish. Ceiling high mirrored walls massively reflecting, amplifying the strolling, parading, the preening, strutting, sashaying. All bordered by lower panels of marble and upper panels of flower embossed white satin trimmed with white on white, braided flowers, set off with cornices and sashes of red and blue. Miscellaneous ambling sybarites stopping to study themselves in the mirrors, more women, more scrutiny, but men as well. Sometimes with all that earnestness slipping into fun-house mirror distortions. Spinning clumps of people randomly grouping, winding, unwinding. Spools of couples and singles raveling, regathering. On the stage a full orchestra alternating between Hit Parade Tunes, Broadway Classics, and dance music. Endless streams of white-gloved formally attired waiters and waitresses carrying, displaying, flaunting, steaming trays of delicacies. Waiters dressed like minstrels, others like clowns, or strolling musicians weaving, roaming the ballroom floor. Acrobats, cartwheeling, and dancing, prancing their way from the kitchen to the tables and back again, balancing their aromatic delicacies and assorted drinks.

Suddenly the lights dimmed, a few mellow honks, if shofarless yet chauffeur driven, a white Cadillac open top convertible gliding onto the scene, Gregory sitting up on high on the folded top in his white cutaway full dress suit, his feet dangling down but not quite reaching the back seat. A scepter in one hand, with his other hand adjusting the gold crown on his head. Coasting through the huge ballroom, around the tables, Gregory bowed regally, from the waist, continually adjusting the slipping crown as the band played "Long Live the King." The crowd loved Gregory. They screamed and applauded. Gregory loved being loved. Another round of mellow honks, the band with "Here Comes the Bride" and another white Cadillac convertible pulling a float with a stage front open like a doll house façade, white picket fence below, two floors open to the interior. In the living room sitting on love seats, waving, nodding, Sid and Fran throwing kisses to their guests. Loud whistling, laughter, applause and foot stomping. Moving majestically, the white Cadillac towing its float, through the wide lanes, quickly followed by further floats. Dozens of clowns and acrobatic waiters and waitresses gracefully leaping from floats with more exotic dishes. Now Sid in tails and top hat and Fran in evening gown doing a Fred Astaire, Ginger Rogers routine. A Gregory-as-a-toddler-look-a-like, taking his first steps, throwing his first pitch. More waiters, more food, and another float to the tune of "Take me out to the ballgame." High up on a pyramid of bats either Joe DiMaggio, or a look-a-like. Gregory and Sid below wearing New York Yankee uniforms. Dad never accepted that it was DiMaggio. A mere look-a-like. Some underemployed borscht-belt dropout doppelganger for hire, for weddings and *bar mitzvahs*.

"But if Sid swears it was Joe DiMaggio why are you so adamant that it wasn't?" Mom to Dad.

"Because Sid swears it was."

"That's not nice."

"Sid's not nice."

Sid was to make an appointment to take Dad to meet DiMaggio, to verify the appearance. Each time the appointment was made, it was cancelled. Later that night of the floats, Sid and Fran appeared as Roy Rogers and Dale Evans, Sid-Roy strumming his guitar and doing "Happy Trails." And the final float, Sid in Jolson blackface singing first to

Fran "The Anniversary Waltz", and then to Gregory, "Sonny Boy." Then like at the Macy's Thanksgiving Day parade, three larger than life balloons of Sid, Fran and Gregory held with ropes by midget clowns on unicycles, racing around the room.

Of a moment it began to "snow" inside the ballroom. Blowers in the ceiling thrusting out clouds, gusts of snow-white confetti all through the room, white flakes coated the orchestra as they played "Jingle Bells", then "White Christmas" amid loud laughter and happy screams. Waiters, like Eskimos driving teams of huskies plowed through the confetti covered floors. The snow became heavier and heavier, the blasting storm from above reaching blizzard proportions. As if the ark had hit a glacier precipitating a massive snow slide. Everything, everyone was inundated by the sticking, piling white flakes of confetti. Floors slippery and wet from spilled drinks. People slipping, tripping and falling. Angry yelling, screaming, from all sides. Some isolated laughter and cackling all but drowned by the hollering and growing rage and hysteria. "Shut the damned fans!" "Idiots, I'll sue. I'll sue Sid, I'll sue the management." "Stop the madness!" Women cried and screamed. A few men and more women lay sprawled on and in the accumulating white blanket. Hurting, afraid, they remained lying where they'd fallen in the burgeoning white. From somewhere inside the kitchen in panic, "It's jammed, we can't get it right!" "It's jammed!" More crying, coughing and raging threats. Holding removed shoes, guests gliding, limping, slogging toward exits. A few guys laughing, drunk or drunk-like, staggering, spilling their drinks, rolling snowballs and pitching them around the hall. The crescendo of crying and hysteria growing louder...Louder!

The storm halted. More than half the guests had escaped. "Sid's Blizzard" as it came to be called in the family and by friends, had ended.

That night Sid had a massive heart attack. Dad was torn between anger at the bar mitzvah and sympathy for a felled favorite anti-hero. Old angers and combatants engender a loyalty and nostalgia all their own. Batman would really miss the Penguin if he didn't turn up next issue.

Mom and Dad visited Sid in the hospital. Not long after, Sid returned home, and we resumed our drives to visit, but now to Westchester and only once every seven or eight weeks. Mom would often say she wasn't going out there again, until Fran and Sid returned a visit with us in Brooklyn. Dad would then make the case that driving up to the Westchester to Sid and Fran with their yard and barbecue was kind of an outing, getting away from the city. So Mom settled for cooking, baking, transportable dishes to bring along. Sid enjoyed an audience and he rarely failed to note Mom's superior culinary skills.

"Leah should give cooking lessons." Sid.

"And who do you think her student should be?" Fran.

"We'll offer scholarships and see." Sid with the ubiquitous smile, set in that lined, tired boy-man face. In the earlier years, first Pesach Seder, Fran and Sid and their children usually came to us. A few times a year Sid would appear alone at our Brooklyn apartment, on his way to or from the Mermaid's Tale and his adjacent atelier. If Fran were a decisor of halachic law then the bachelor studio above the Mermaid's Tale would have been a Torah prohibition, and dropping by us to eat merely a rabbinic one. She was kept equally unaware of each infraction.

"So how come we got three refrigerators, two huge freezers and I mean huge, like these commercial jobs, and if someone comes by and Fran did not know they were coming she's got nothing to give them. And here, with your one *farshtunkener* (lousy) Frigidaire, any time I come you always got something for me? Explain it to me?" Sid with wonder.

"Maybe Fran thinks the way you and your friends drink that you gave up on eating." Dad.

"Not a chance Rob, not a chance." Sid. Punctuating his gulping of chicken and kugel with smiles.

Dad said Sid couldn't even give a compliment without putting someone down along the way. Mom said it was a compliment to us. Dad said, "To you, Leah, but our '*farshtunkener* Frigidaire' was aimed at me." Mom said Dad was over-interpreting.

The coup de grace of Sid's fall from grace was that Sunday visit to Lawrence about a year and a half after Gregory's bar mitzvah. I was about eleven, and we had taken my new Schwinn with us, "So you would not have to borrow Gregory's bike." Dad had insisted. Not long after we arrived, I hopped a curb and losing control, wobbled onto the road into an oncoming car. Within seconds, I was in Dad's arms as he ran towards Sid's car. The elderly driver of the hit car was too shook up to help. Sid's brand new powder blue Caddy was blocking Dad's aged bottle green DeSoto. Dad, running to the Caddy, "Fast Sid, he's bleeding like crazy." Sid hesitated. "No sense in staining up this new up- holstery. I'll move the Caddy and we will take the DeSoto." With the reddening towels wrapped around my head Dad gently placed me down on the back seat of the DeSoto and slammed the door locked. Sid carefully backed the Caddy into the street and Dad screeched out in reverse, leaving Sid behind standing in the driveway waving for us to wait as we sped off to the hospital.

"It will be okay, Stevie, don't worry it will be okay," Dad, trying to assure himself, as much as me. At the emergency room in St. Joseph's hospital in Far Rockaway an Irish nurse with what Mom would have called 'a twinkle' in her eyes pulled Dad aside after the x-rays and told him that there was no internal injury and I merely needed stitches; but, given that there were only interns on duty now, if it were her son she would take him to Dr. Weissman the surgeon with "the magic hands" who had a private clinic in his home in Lawrence and wasn't at the hospital today. After giving us the address, she added that since it was Sunday we had better just go without calling. Back to the Batmobile and off we zoomed to Dr. Weissman's clinic.

The mansion which housed Dr. Weissman's domicile and private clinic was set far back off Central Avenue, hidden from the street by a wall of high neatly cropped bushes. Inside that tall thick green crew cut fence of hedges, the meticulously arranged grid of paths, lined with flowers, and plants, a botanical maze that turned in, on a squared-off lily pond at the center, and then back around the maze. Mumbling, grunting, with short breath, Dad ran carrying me from one stone-lined path to the next. I wanted to walk but he wouldn't let me. Doing the whole thing horizontally, I thought of Laurel and Hardy lost and anxious in Oxford Gardens. Finally, Dad let me down. Standing in front of what seemed to be the great doors of a majestic castle, Dad rang and knocked with the big brass knocker impatiently. A black maid answered the door, and promptly referred us to either St. Joseph's Hospital or Jamaica Hospital, vouchsafing that Dr. Weissman did not have office hours on Sundays. Jamming his foot in the door, Dad pushed us through. We weren't leaving until we saw the doctor, announced Dad. She turned, and her quick footsteps rang and echoed over the marble floors as she disappeared down the hallway. I was dizzy and Dad picked me up again. I looked up to the flashing tiered blades of glass of the great chandelier above magically cascading, sparkling reds, blues and oranges threading through its brilliant white illumination. Emanating from the ceiling about three stories up, the light pouring down over frozen icicles of white light splashed with color. Like sentinels, two larger-than-man sized black vases with pink and green floral patterns sat at either side of the lobby entrance. I was sure that I saw Laurel pop up from one, and heard Hardy grunting and struggling to free himself from the other. That yodel of a scream, "Stan!" Any second Ollie's vase would begin shaking, first slightly and then widely and wildly, and topple, and crumble exposing Oliver.

With his "magic" hands, except for the thumbs, in the pockets of his grey tweed vest, in shirtsleeves with gold cufflinks, a grey-haired Dr. Weissman appeared. Unsmiling, slight of figure, impeccably groomed, stiff and officious, part concert pianist, part Long Island Railroad conductor. What could, would those "magic hands" do? Rabbits? Birds? Coins? Dad placed me down and related the details of the fall and the hospital visit. Without any noticeable facial expression Dr. Weissman repeated the maid's words.

"Sunday the clinic is closed." His lips hardly moved as he spoke. Like an understudy ventriloquist, he had mastered part of the routine, but hadn't learned to throw his voice yet. As the doctor spoke Dad started drifting towards the living room. I had never seen such a high-storied large room in a private home. Nor a room with more furniture—other than Phil Cohen's furniture showroom on Rockaway Avenue near Pitkin. Leaning on an ornately carved mantelpiece Dad began describing how easily it might be dismantled. He bet he could do it with his bare hands in a matter of minutes. Bending down and pointing to where it could be pulled off the wall without the aid of tools, he said "Like if someone was leaving in a real hurry and wanted to take the mantelpiece with him." Dad straightened up and stared at Weissman. Weissman was still. I sensed that whoever broke the silence lost. Tight lipped as earlier, Weissman barely uttered that it just so happened that his nurse was there today. She rarely is there on Sundays. They were going over some bookkeeping. Escorting us through the house to the clinic, he said next time we come we had better use the clinic entrance on the south side of the house.

In under an hour we were done. To me Dad whispered that the doctor's hands were in fact magical. To Dr. Weissman, Dad smiled and said that his own Uncle Sam had been a tailor and he appreciated quality stitching. Weissman offered no reaction other than that he preferred to be paid in cash rather than check.

For a few years Sid and Fran skipped coming to us for *Pesach Seder*. Then in April of '51, our last Seder in Brooklyn, they joined us again. Traditionally Grandpa Bloom had led the family Seder. It had been a strain for him the preceding year. This year though he would come from the nursing home to the Seder he had announced that he had now passed on the stewardship of that ritual Seder. Dad and Mom thought he might change his mind or forget by the time he arrived. In his mid-eighties he was tuning in and out, lucid when in, but forgetful mostly regarding recent matters, and repetitive when out.

Using a text Dad could recite the *Kiddush* (blessing of sanctification) over the wine even if he could not translate the words and stumbled over some of the Hebrew pronunciations, but basically he had the tune. For the rest of the Haggadah he would simply follow the English translation and directions in the illustrated paperbacked Maxwell House Haggadahs that we had. Teddy, as the youngest in the family was invited to recite the Four Questions. Till about a quarter of the way through the *Haggadah* Dad sort of led, the one-eyed man in the land of the blind. From that point the blind leading the blind. Early on, Dad had abandoned his mangling attempts at the Hebrew phrases and also dropped the stiff translations. Shifting to speed-reading, rushing by the text like scenery along the train tracks in the dining car, caught between intermittent gulp-glancing mouthfuls of gefilte fish, matzah and swigs of that too sweet wine. And none of the table discussion revolved around the *Hagaddah* text or the evening's requirement of *mitzvahs* or *Seder* customs. Truman, MacArthur, the Yankees, the Giants, the Dodgers were the *Seder*-table talk.

Though we had stopped keeping kosher, except for a few utensils that were reserved for the barbecue in the yard, yet in the basement Mom still had entire sets of separate utensils for Passover. "Pesach was Pesach." Pots, pans, dishes, silverware, packed in corrugated brown boxes most of which I'd *shnorred* (begged) from LaVine Fashions during my summer employment there. Pesach equipment, kept apart from the all-year-round *chametz* (wheat product prohibited on Pesach) and in our case, all-year-round treif. From time immemorial, Jews had their minimal survival gear packed, and ready for a sudden exodus—another quick getaway from one more host nation turned hostile.

It followed a fortiori that if while Grandpa Bloom had presided over the Seder we had cut the *Hagaddah* short to dig into the gefilte fish and *kneidles* (matzah balls), surely with Dad at the helm it would be an adumbrated Seder. So in April '51 with the baseball season just under way—how little did we know it would end with Branca and Thompson. I was fourteen and Teddy was eight. He recited the four questions by rote, without seeming too concerned about receiving answers but with eight-year-old charm and grace he enjoyed the spotlight, he enjoyed being enjoyed and we all enjoyed his enjoying being enjoyed. That was six years ago. This last Pesach, a few months ago, I was at the Winters' *Seder* table, and the action was furious. Those foods and dishes spread over the table were as listed in the *Haggadah* which now read as gourmet-mitzvah-menu-manual. At the Winters it was contest time as well. With score cards. The air tingled with import. At the Winters' *Seder* table it was like the actual game had begun, the pennant race was on. Each *Mitzvah*, ritual, custom, precisely calibrated and linked to text and discussion, eating and drinking. Yet it all centered around the children. Quiz-show-like question provoking, that script. Resolutions, ranging from classic to innovative. Adults focused on the children, children performing for the adults. Like this connecting of generations helped connect all of us to history, son to father, to grandfather, to great grandfather to… singing, the vigorously engaged exploration of text and taste all merging on the tongues of young and old. Here each morsel of *matzah* and measure of *maror* (bitter herbs), every chomp and gulp set in the music and lyric of that family operetta bursting with song and laughter munching as meaning. The air was festive, dramatic, exciting, earnest yet joyous. While being recorded on High, officially being scored by the only real Official Scorer. It worked as it culminated the schedule of spring training and serious season games with others, with ourselves, stretching, reaching for achievement…whereas six years ago in '51, none of us brought any Torah knowledge or mitzvah commitment to the table. Ours was not even quite a chalked-in schoolyard choose up game either. More like hanging around without enough guys to start a game and taking turns banging the ball around, lazily waiting at our *seder* for something to happen getting more hungry, more bored, more hungry.

Only the fifth question that *Seder* night with Sid and Fran livened up the table. Seventeen-year-old cousin Gregory asked Dad who he thought was right, MacArthur or Truman. Dad supported Truman and Uncle Sid was a MacArthur man. "You Brooklyn Jews all think it's a *mitzvah* to vote Democrat, like Moses was a Democrat or something. Like all that sneaky, undercover, socialism is good for the Jews and the US. So let me tell you, I know those Russians, I fought alongside them in Poland and Germany, and they're just waiting until they're good and ready to take over everything, Europe, and Asia and us, and you need a guy with class and guts to face those bastards down." Sid triumphantly.

"Vestchester, Shmestester," Dad feigning a Yiddish accent. "As one Brooklyn Jew to another you can take the boy out of Brooklyn but you can't take Brooklyn out of the boy. So tell me, what's your plan, let's give it all to the generals to run? Huh? Let's just become another banana republic with periodic revolutions. Let's trust decisions and rights of minorities to military dictators? That's the answer? It's positively asinine!"

"You really believe that some cut-rate haberdasher can run this operation better than a genius like MacArthur? Who beat the Japs in World War II? Who chased them around the Pacific? Who landed at Inchon and turned Korea round? If Truman would have been successful in business he never would have gone into politics!" Sid.

"Yes, so you tell me who dropped the bomb to beat the Japs? Who?" Dad.

"What the hell does Truman know from military operations—MacArthur is a West Point man a proven quantity and that's what leadership is all about!"

Much to Uncle Sid's consternation Gregory sided with Dad. Though I felt an attraction to the dashing hero image of MacArthur, yet something about Truman was decent—a kind of homey reliability. Besides which, if Aunt Fran and Uncle Sid were so down on Truman, there had to be something right about him. Yet, I still wasn't comfortable writing off MacArthur. More recently the guys at the *yeshivah* quoted a rabbi who critiqued Hiroshima at the time. Perhaps the Japanese should have witnessed some desolate island being blown to bits by an atom bomb before it was actually dropped on human population. Perhaps that would have had them capitulate without that enormous loss of life. Others argued that even after Hiroshima there was resistance till Nagasaki. Perhaps the full extent of the devastation had not yet set in.

As *yeshivah* guys would later put it–"at fourteen years old 'I heard' MacArthur, and 'I heard' Truman. But I went Truman."

Dad had to once again come to the defense of the Democrats while sitting *shivah* (traditional week of mourning) for his father last year. Uncle Sid came for a *shivah* call with his partner Sammy and Sammy's twin Gabriel. Sammy, I knew from my summers at the La-Vine Fashions factory. Gabriel I met frequently at the Mermaid's Tale where he hung out with some of his Yiddishist buddies.

"When it's my turn to go they can skip that *Kaddish* stuff and just play 'Happy Trails' or 'Home on the Range,' that will be good enough for me." Uncle Sid smiling.

"You and FDR, that was his favorite song, 'Home on the Range', you should have picked a Republican melody." Dad.

"That *mamzer* (bastard), him and Churchill, the whole bunch they could have saved millions of Jews and they let the Nazi *chayas* (beasts) gas them, shoot them, murder them." Gabriel.

"That's no way to talk about a president of the United States and a great one at that. He was a friend of the Jews." Dad with agitation.

"From what are you talking? Don't you know they kept the quotas down not to let in Jews?! Even when the Nazis were still then ready to send them out in '40 and '41. So that's what made Hitler understand he could get away with what he wants. Regner in Geneva told them already in '39, at the beginning, what was going on and they didn't do nothing. Not them here and not the British, they wanted it quiet, they squashed it. Palestine should not be open, even they sent boats back filled with Jews trying, crying, desperate to escape. The Americans sending back the St. Louis to Europe for those Jews to die and the British 'The Struma.'" Gabriel.

"That's a bloody lie! I won't let you desecrate FDR's memory like that in my home. Do you hear me? He was a great president." Dad.

"You are just like all the naive Americans you all boy scouts. Not even, maybe cubby scouts. One day maybe you actual bother to search around to know the honest true history and then you all seeing: FDR, Churchill, talk, nice talk, diplomatic talk, while men, women and kids is being murdered every day, and they delaying and delaying so should be no immigration. Millions of Jews they could still save but they sending memos and talking and talking." Gabriel.

"What the hell you want him to do in the middle of a war, phone up Hitler and say 'Hey Dolphi, do me a favor and let out some Jews will you?' That's absurd, absolutely absurd!" Dad with exasperation.

"But they could have let Jews in here. But the unions didn't want them. They keeping their quotas. Even when those Nazi madmen were murdering children and were ready to stop and send out some children, just twenty thousand. And how easy they could bomb the tracks going to the gas chambers, the maps they had from the Czech underground and the crematoriums it's for sure they had the maps and they didn't do nothing, too many people without jobs, they were afraid of their jobs in the US so you couldn't bring in more immigrants, especial Jews. No one is caring that those people, men, women, children being killed. Votes, jobs, money, that's what counts," Gabriel his fists and his face tightening.

"Dad, it fits your racing theory of race, and that they always knock us down so we have to run faster and smarter, according to you. According to Gabriel they acted true to form. Now you say Roosevelt was immune?" Me.

"Sure. That's the way it is for each and every individual goy out there. But the country and the president that's different. They need to prove it to the world, for history, to uphold the ideals of this democracy, otherwise everything falls apart. America is special and even if one to one, *goy* to Jew, deep down they can't stomach us, there is that gentleman's agreement, like the Pope's Jews. Americans go for that ceremony. And I am telling you FDR even meant it, really. He was president of all the people." Dad.

"Maybe *takke* (actually) like the Pope's Jews—they kept us around to fill that prophecy of our suffering. They needed us around and close by to make sure that it was happening that way." Sammy continuing.

"They all got blood on their hands, Churchill, Roosevelt, the diplomats, the whole government and the American Jews here what was keeping quiet." Gabriel.

"You're *meshugah*." Dad

"It's true about those unions." Sid picking up. "They will kill for another few jobs - that's the difference, the Republicans, at least even if they don't love the Jews, they know damn well that Jews are good for business. Jews are hustlers, they get the merchandise out, they move it, and that's what makes the world go round. So they say what the hell if they don't like our noses, our pushiness and customs and all that, the bottom line is that it's good for business and that's what counts. So that's the kind of people you can do business with—I don't need no one to love me, don't do me no favors, just tell me what you want to order and that's all I want to know." Uncle Sid with triumphant sagacity.

I checked Sammy to see how he had reacted to Sid's soliloquy. Sammy had a way of half smiling, sipping, not gulping the ludicrous. Not a Sid smile, rather a minimalist, tight-lipped, skeptical partial smile, like it wasn't worth the effort or investment of a fully committed gesture. How many times had I sat by in Sid's office at the plant when one or another of the salesmen had come in to complain about Sid switching styles and colors in filling orders.

"Sid, you're killing me and this business for G-d's sake. You can't do that to customers. How can I go back and talk to the buyer from Penny or Sears after you practically ignore their orders and deliver them all your leftovers? How, just tell me how?" Eddie Shapiro with tears in his voice.

"Get off it Eddie, you're a big boy, tell us the whole story, you just didn't *shmear* (bribe) that buyer enough that's all. Someone else did a better job at it and beat you to it. That's all there is to it, don't give me no sob stories." Sid.

"It's not true Sid, those are big operations, Penny and Sears and they watch the stores like hawks, they know what's moving and what's not moving, you dump goods on them like that Sid, and you just can't get away with it. It's like killing the goose that laid the golden egg I swear it is." Eddie with pain. "They just won't come back again, I won't get another shot."

"To hell with them then. I can't do business with people like that. People that just want what they order! What the hell, a coat's a coat! Let them go to some fly-by-night fink operation that will bend down, bow down and kiss their toes. Me, I run my place the way I like!" Staring at Eddie, Sid, punctuating his peroration with his spooky non-sequitur Richard Widmark smile.

"What do you mean a coat's a coat? So why the heck do we break our backs creating all those styles and colors if a coat's a coat? That's just crazy, positively crazy." Eddie.

"You heard me, a coat's a coat and that's all there is to it! That's the whole story. Only some guys know how to sell coats and some guys don't! That's it, simple as that Eddie!" Sid, still smiling but signaling that the conversation was over.

I watched Eddie as he turned pale. And paler. Gradually he seemed to evaporate. Total etiolation. No more arguments. No more talk. No more Eddie. Like "poof!" he just disappeared from the room, maybe from the earth. Sammy was quiet. He had no problem with switching orders or salesmen. But he was more disciplined, more selective. There were customers, and there were customers. There were salesmen and salesmen. While for Sid, a principle was a principle.

Last summer driving by the Greenpoint plant I dropped in to chat with Sammy.

He indicated he'd heard about my recent *yeshivah* involvement. After exchanging some pleasantries he looked at me and said. "So I hear that you're on G-d's team now! You should know Stevie your G-d is like us here in the *shmattah* business (rag-trade, garment business). All dose Jews over dere in Europe dey putting in orders, boy dey are sending orders and orders. And also He don't deliver according to dose orders! Dey ordering and ordering. But no delivery. Just like us Stevie!" Sammy took out a twenty dollar bill and stuffed it into the *pushka* (charity coin box) at the end of his desk.

"So how come you stuff twenty dollar bills in *pushkas* if that's the way you feel?" Me.

"So I will tell you Stevie, mostly I'm mad on Him, but I'm sometimes thinking, maybe because He's not doing such a good job your G-d, maybe He needs some help."

Often, after pitched battles between Sid and a salesman, Sid gulped down a water glass, or even two, of bourbon and exited to the delivery yard.

Religiously, twice a week two of the black guys from the shipping department— Leroy and Warren—polished Sid's powder blue Caddy parked between the loading and unloading trucks. Sid then came down that wide-open pen of a massive freight elevator, descending to the receiving yard to do his ritual inspection. Circling the Caddy he studied it from every angle. Then coming close, running his hand over the hood, doors and roof, like an Orthodox Jew examining the perfection of an *esrog* (citron) before Sukkos (Festival of Tabernacles). Like a sculptor lovingly tracing the lines of his handiwork. As if he had actually sculpted that sleek, powder blue vehicle.

In the La-Vine Fashions factory they still talked of the big strike that shut down the operation for three weeks in 1950 three years before I began my summer employment there. Sid crossing the picket lines caught some bullets in the tires and a rock that smashed his windshield. He had to be pulled away from the immobilized vehicle as he stood paralyzed, tears in his eyes, yet still smiling in the midst of a deluge of raining rocks.

As accountant and then lawyer as well, for Sid and Sammy, Dad sometimes took a piece of the action of some of their real estate transactions. When Sid and Sammy bought the rooming house on Mermaid Avenue with the restaurant and bar downstairs, Dad had a financial interest in the deal. Reb Shimshon's Benny was drafted by Sid to run The Mermaid's Tale. "Sea food of choice." Non-kosher of course. Upstairs, Sid maintained an even less kosher bachelor suite. His atelier. His court for games away from home. While Dad and Sid had had their business differences as well, that atelier outraged Dad and exacerbated their other problems. After two years Sid bought Dad out of the Mermaid's Tale. Before the split Mom and Dad often took us for supper at the Mermaid's Tale.

Strolling in the salt air through Coney Island midway in the day, the bathers, the corn and the franks all heating, cooking. With dusk, less bathers, more hawkers, barkers, gaming stands, and rides, all coming alive jumping with fun-seeking people. Still, the franks and the corn, tourists and Carnies, flavoring the Coney salt-sea air pungency. The tattooed and the tattooers, the reddened, the tanned, the bleached and the black and brown, the hustlers and the hustled, the dredging and the dredged. Early in his Coney Island career, Benny used to hang out a lot at the Cow's Pail bottle pitching booth. Stalking his prey he proceeded to flip some poor shots, work up some betting, and then as the stakes increased he finally tumbled everything in sight with amazing speed and accuracy. For a number of years Benny managed the Mermaid's Tale. Till Miriam and her husband Solly moved to Queens, Miriam worked there part-time as well. Sammy and Gabriel were fond of bringing their old borscht belt buddies, and other *landsleit* (countrymen) that hadn't gone the borscht belt route, to the Mermaid's Tale as clients. Waiters, chefs, barkeeps were recruited from *landsleit* with preference given to the borscht belt people. Former performers and hangers-on collected. But those acts that had gone over well in the borscht belt, on the same menu with all that excess of food during vacation time in the cool mountain air of the Catskills, those same acts, just didn't work in the stern concrete and bleak stone of the workaday city. Even with the backdrop-backup of the Coney Island midway, the fantasy, the carny mood, those acts just did not take. With time, the clientele at the Mermaid's Tale was mixed, Jewish and non-Jewish. Long after the performances stopped, one singing waiter from Odessa remained. Still, through the years, the Mermaid's Tale remained a hang-out for numbers of ex-Yiddish and a few English speaking theater people. Has-beens, almost and never-wases, musicians, writers and artists, some residents of Coney Island and Brighton Beach but many came from afar. Sid and Sam each had his own circle of hangers-on, many of whom were subsidized. Both had agreed to give free drinks and discounts to clients with blue numbers on their forearms. Gregor Wladkowsky of Krakow tossing his mane of white hair to calculated effect, was for years working on a Yiddish translation of the Iliad and the Odyssey. Mendel Schweber from Minsk claimed to have some backing for a Yiddish opera company. Mendel said he already had Molly Picon signed up for Carmen.

Sid changed the name from the "Mermaid's Saloon" to the "Mermaid's Tale", and commissioned me with the task of coming up with a story that would be the saga of the Mermaid's Tale. And so it came to be: A local legend was born. A Delaware Indian princess, a favored one of the tribe. Laurel-Eye, who had bested all in the swimming races, was then blessed with longevity by the Sachem—the tribal elders. Many of the secrets of the sea were confided to her, including the breeding grounds of the Coney fish, which when later she divulged those whereabouts to Dutch fishermen, she was brought to task by the Sachem.

Upon being found guilty the winsome Laurel-Eye was transformed into a mermaid. The irrevocable blessing of longevity notwithstanding, she was condemned to a limbo existence, unnatural in the sea and unnatural on land. Her revenge then for decades—she surfaced and reclined on rock breakers or at the edge of the sea, appearing, luring ships and swimmers out to their doom. Between dusk and dawn her song could be heard and she could even be sighted. From Gravesend Bay to Coney Island, Brighton Beach, Manhattan Beach, Sheepshead Bay, and Dead Horse Inlet, haunting evocative, provocative refrains. Glimpses of that apparitional image, half-woman, half-fish were sighted; casualties, in those waters, sunken boats and drownings were attributed to Laurel-Eye.

Bam and I were surprised one night to find his second cousin Bertha Stein, who had been saved from the Budapest death march by Raoul Wallenberg, at a table in the Mermaid's Tale. She had been a harpist and her fingers had gone numb yet her love of music had never slackened. Of all people that night she brought Eddie Borenstein who taught Shakespeare at Brooklyn College. Marty and I had taken a course with Eddie. After a while he became a Thursday night regular. Slight of build and squinting through his thick glasses, he argued that it was mistaken to read Shylock as hero. Elizabethan audiences laughed at his "When you prick me do I not bleed" those lines were penned just after poor Dr. Lopez, the Jewish-Spanish doctor to the court, had been framed and convicted of espionage. Duly tortured, killed, and quartered with various pieces of his anatomy hung from the palace towers. Shylock appeared upon the heels of Lopez, figuratively, literally. Jews rejecting as they did the message of Christianity, had always been somewhere on the continuum between despicable and laughable. The Bard hit it just right for his audience.

Sitting at our corner table with red and white checkered table-cloth, we could hear from outside on the midway the canned cackling of that mad hag of a mannequin-cuckoo popping in and out of the opening and closing shutters of her high-up window perch above the haunted house entrance. Louder and louder that crescendoing, that delight-in-fright happy-screaming from the racing, careening cars of the roller coaster, and the spinning, climbing, falling ferris wheel. Anxious, hesitating, deep-breath bursts of laughter, rhythmically softening slowly disappearing, then so quickly again faintly to be heard, gradually loudening, exploding with cymbalistic metallic clankingly tense joy and then once more gradually melting and evaporating.

One of Borenstein's favorite and oft quoted lines. "If cows could talk they would serve pasteurized milk in heaven" had gotten me into some difficulties with him. "But not steak" had gotten me a respectable number of snickers. Whereupon quickly I began to moo. In stages many joined me, amidst the smothered giggling and suppressed laughter more and more mooed along. After that, every time G-d or heaven or hell was mentioned in class, someone would let loose some low key mooing. When we first met that night, after two years of not having seen each other, there was a moment of strained silence and then he proceeded to moo. We had a few beers together with Marty and Bam. Borenstein began showing up weekly at the Mermaid's Tale. One night some months ago Gabriel asked Borenstein if he liked Ezra Pound. Borenstein admitted to enjoying Pound.

"Then you probably like Wagner's music also?"

"Being an anti-Semite doesn't change the quality of literature or music does it?"

"Of course it does. There is blood on every word and in every note. They were written in blood. And that's why those Nazi butchers while they were murdering men, women and children, slashing babies to bits—they played Wagner, 'cause he himself was a vicious anti-Semite. In one camp there was a Jewish slave orchestra with confiscated stolen instruments that had belonged to Jews, these slave musicians performed until the minute they themselves were sent one by one to be killed."

"I still fail to see what that had to do with the actual poetry or notes of music."

"Would you listen to music that was written by the man that murdered your children?" Gabriel.

"I don't have or intend to have any children, but I imagine that would be hard for someone that did. But essentially that would not change the quality of the music even if someone had an emotional problem with it."

"Your wife is Jewish?" Gabriel.

"No."

"Now I know why you didn't have children."

"Why?" Borenstein perking up with curiosity.

"Because I think deep down you also don't trust *goyim*!"

❑   ❑

Though I hadn't spoken much over the years with Reb Shimshon, Rabbi Winters quoted him regularly. Winters said that Reb Shimshon said that Americans were not good haters. That came from not being good lovers. Like the British, Americans merely liked and disliked. King Arthur and Cowboy Cool. If they had either loved mankind or hated evil enough, they could not have consciously stalled and delayed while those millions of Jews, men, women and children were being murdered. Gabriel regularly held forth about FDR and the State Department and immigration quotas. But he especially had it in for the British. Arab oil resources had been a lot more important than Jewish lives. It wasn't just keeping us out of England. It was keeping us out of Palestine. Though that was to have been ours, Biblically, historically, Balfourly, scout's honor. Her Majesty's minister's word. So they "promised!" So what? Those lives were merely Jewish lives.

Ever since Sammy and Gabriel had first argued that case during Grandpa's *shiva*, I had read and talked with more people about allied negligence-cum-complicity during the war. And so it came to pass that, post Struma and St. Louis it became hard for me to think of the Cardinals, of Musial, Schoendinst, Marion and Slaughter, without thinking of that other slaughter—the slaughter to which most of those Jews of the St. Louis and millions like them were sent. Wasn't t.s. eliot from St. Louis? All that carefully constructed iambic venom. Bleistein's swimming his sewers, so despicably cultured. So now however vicariously, added to the twisting and sometimes seething sibilants of my simmering soul, to schoolyards, synagogues, *shuls*, Jewesses, *shiksahs*, seas, Spanish Inquisitions and swastikas were now added St. Louis, Struma and Slaughter.

Marty said all of life was only a game anyway. Just like in any game, some you win, some you lose. Like D'Lisle-Adam, "As for living that was for our servants," contemplating the nuances of the bustling business of it all was the gentleman's role. Much to the chagrin of his teammates Marty would tend to recline in right field in the middle of plays explaining the improbability of a ball coming out to him. His was to consider and describe, not to engage. Exertion was for plebeians. Or just early retirement.

A few nights a week, Bam, Marty and I would sit around, amidst the ship-like décor, at our corner table, at the Mermaid's Tale, watching Reb Shimshon's Benny receiving his guests with a friendly kind of reserve. Now and then Sid would appear, and tumult up a storm. In fact he had apprenticed in the Catskills at a number of hotels as official full-time "*tummler*"— part-time saxophonist. Hired to up the tempo, the traffic, the action of those Catskill scenes. Today as well at the Mermaid's Tale the energy increased with Sid's arrival, decreased with his departure. Benny—more reticent, ruggedly handsome— was our mysterious Marlboro Man, though he smoked Camels. At the pinnacle of his sandlot career Benny had signed with the Giants, and promptly gone on to break his leg sliding into third base on the concrete in a schoolyard softball game. That was in '47 the year Jackie Robinson came up. Somehow after that, things never came together for

Benny. A long recuperation, and a lack of commitment, most guys said. Korea followed by the Mermaid's Tale, and his frequent disappearances. To roam. And roam. For a few weeks or more at a time every few months Benny would disappear and Sid would re-hire him upon his return. One version had it that Benny had a girl in Chicago. Another said 'girls.' A third had it, that it wasn't lust-wander but instead wanderlust. "That's the way he is Benny, when it comes time to go, he just ups and goes." To snatches of Frankie Laine singing "Roaming Man."

One summer night in 1950 Mom and Dad and Teddy and I were at the Mermaid's Tale when Gil Hodges came in with Cal Abrams. Benny received them a bit more cordially than the usual guests. Although the Mermaid's Tale served non-kosher food, Sid had a penchant for gefilte fish and it appeared regularly on the menu. Each time we turned up Uncle Sid made a point of saying the gefilte fish would never compare to Mom's. Cal and Gil were brought portions of gefilte fish—on the house—"Like Mom used to make," winked the waiter to Cal.

Though Jackie Robinson always remained my favorite player - his electric presence, the versatility, hitting for extra bases or bunting to get on, the thrilling dance off the bases, that delicious tension as he threatened to run, so suddenly that pigeon-toed explosion of speed, bursting out as he ran towards second, and especially towards home and the hook slide around and under the tag. All of that on top of the heroic stance of defying prejudices and breaking barriers. The beautiful and the just, that remained. Yet Cal Abrams caught a certain corner of my heart for some months as well. New Jew upstart on the block. Starting and startling, Abrams, though he was a lefty, slapping hits to left field, day after day. Incredibly, those first weeks batting over three fifty. Even when they pulled a right-handed-pull-hitter-shift on him. Still he punched his hits through the shift to left and to center. If he didn't have Jackie's power, speed and pizzazz, still he was ours. And he hit! When queried why a lefty hit to left field, I replied that we Jews read from right to left. In fact baseball runs Jewishly from right to left. We and baseball run counter-clockwise, transcending time. Perhaps scoring meant coming home for each?

Though I was only to learn years later of the principle from Winters, still I kind of intuited it already then, the relationship between the people and the Messiah. Abrams must have been destined to be the Messiah – a Jewish boy on the Dodgers hitting over three fifty! Without a doubt! But, the Messiah's appearance is rooted in the merits of the people, and we just didn't deserve him yet. So Cal began popping up and striking out. My visions of Gladys Gooding playing "Shalom Aleichem" and "Hatikvah" from that right field scoreboard would have to be postponed. Eventually, Cal was sent into exile. Today, seven years later, all the Dodgers were preparing to go into exile. Soon after the Temple would be destroyed. But back then, that night in 1950 when Hodges and Abrams came in to the Mermaid's Tale Cal talked about the day's taunts coming from the St. Louis dugout, "Fill your nose with nickels Jew boy and go home." "How come Hitler missed you?" To Jackie they'd regularly held up black cats and called out "Nigger." Every team had their offenders but the Cardinals were the worst St. Louis-Struma.

Cal told the story of the kid that waited nine consecutive home games, taking Cal's autograph each time. After giving the ninth signature Cal told the boy he was very touched that the lad wanted so many of his autographs but why on earth did he need nine of them? The boy sheepishly replied. "I'll tell you the truth, my friend Louis told me if I give him ten of yours he'll give me one Carl Furillo."

Sitting around with Marty, sometimes Tony, and Pat and Borenstein at the Mermaid's Tale we talked shop.

"Hemingway was a Maglie, he didn't have that naturally great fast ball but he made up for it with smart breaking pitches. With savvy sliders and curves." Sipping my beer.

"And Faulkner, I suppose was a Furillo?" Marty.

"No Faulkner is heavier, more weight and power, but he strikes out a lot too like Snider, and like Snider he hits righties well and deep but he can't hit lefties." Me.

"Fitzgerald was a Dom DiMaggio or Billy Cox–quick, slick, smooth glove darting into the stands to snatch a foul ball. But with a weak stick and Tom Wolfe was a Johnny Mize or Johnny Lindell very selected moments of power interspersing the overall that was fair to middling." Tony picking up.

"So what about Joe, the Yankee clipper? Consistent greatness!" Melville all grace and power!" Borenstein.

"Musial is a Tolstoy. All depth of courtly class. The inimitable stance that coiled, timed, power and dramatic art, whereas Ted Williams is a Dostoyevsky sheer blasting release of awesome power, but less beauty than Melville or Tolstoy whereas Jackie's lesser, edgy, kind of power, informed and complemented by a poetically elegant savviness, a smaller greatness–Hawthorne." Me.

Over the years Reb Shimshon made two state visits to the Mermaid's Tale. I was not there for either but heard tell of each. Guys on the block had always said that Reb Shimshon did not walk into a place or onto a scene in steps or stages, instead he just flapped his cape of a caftan and appeared. Like out of nowhere. That's the way it was, said the adults when he returned to Brownsville and Beth Asher after his four-year sojourn in the European Hell, the Gdanske *sefer* Torah in his arms at the end of '45. Notwithstanding the added intensity that he now embodied, he took to business as usual. Admittedly the *sefer* Torah with blood on the parchment was unusual, yet in a way it fit for where it and he had been.

Like that first time Reb Shimshon appeared at the Mermaid's Tale three years ago, he stood in the doorway they said as if he'd just landed from another planet. He refused to enter the premises and signaled to the maitre d', Isaac Vladimovsky, to call Benny. Miriam had collapsed the day before, May 1st, at a May Day rally in Brownsville and was in Beth El Hospital at the Brownsville East Flatbush divide, not far from Beth Asher. She had asked to see Benny. After conferring for a few moments Benny gave some instructions to the waiters and exited with Reb Shimshon. The unlikely pair. The taller older man with the flowing Rip Van Winkle beard exaggerating his high broad shouldered, yet gaunt frame, alongside the younger athletic Benny, in his floral patterned opened collared shirt – he, ever the tourist on this planet, his graceful stride, a player between games.

Isaac Vladimovsky's elderly brother Berel still lived near Beth Asher and was one of those who had conflicted directly with Reb Shimshon. Berel Vladimovsky was a workman's circle Yiddishist, who championed the redirecting of the emptied Beth Asher synagogue facility for use as a Yiddish Theater Center. That was one of the five great battles that Reb Shimshon had fought over the years. There had been the skirmish over naming the *shul* "Beth Asher" as Mr. Asher Goldstein had given the largest donation to the building and although he had opposed Reb Shimshon on a number of matters and the Rabbi's allies wanted the name removed yet Reb Shimshon refused to go back on the agreement. Reb Shimshon also explained that the verse in the Torah when Jacob blesses the tribe of Asher describes how affluent that tribe will be and later in *Devorim* (Deuteronomy) the verse predicts that in the final phase of history more Jews will go away because of affluence rather than from poverty, and so Beth Asher fits for America.

The earliest of Reb Shimshon's wars was his commitment to design the planned facility of Beth Asher so the ark would appear in the east. Though Reb Shimshon had reorganized the basement *minyan* facing east, nevertheless that battle was lost during World War II with his absence. While he was searching for his family in that Teutonic–conquered hell called Europe, the new *aron kodesh* (holy ark) in the just-finished sanctuary was established against the west wall. Before and during his absence, battle number two was the *mechitzah*. There had been border skirmishes around and about that shrinking *mechitzah* pre and post-war periods. An uneasy truce was established retarding if not preventing *mechitzah* shrinkage. Now with his return he reconstructed that *mechitzah* to its original halachic height, and once more guerilla war broke out, civil and uncivil. Before Reb Shimshon's departure the third conflict was the *misheberach* for the Russians which had resulted in defections and the establishment of the "Veisse *Shul*," and their designation of Beth Asher as "Stalin's *Shul*." Asher Goldstein in fact joined the Veisse *Shul* yet Reb Shimshon persisted in maintaining the name Beth Asher.

Four, the *sefer* Torah with the blood. Wandering somewhere through that flaming nether-world, amidst all those macabre happenings, somewhere between purgatory and oblivion, that inferno of prussic acid and Prussian sadists, Reb Shimshon met a displaced Polish Jew from Gdansk, who had succeeded in rescuing that *sefer* Torah from the central *shul* before it had been destroyed by the Jews themselves who had elected, painfully, to execute the eleventh hour destruction rather than hand over the sanctity of that synagogue to the Nazis and have them gloat with satisfaction by turning another *shul* into a gymnasium, stable, or brothel, as they had done with other Polish synagogues. Miraculously that Polish Jew saving the *sefer* Torah had run the Hades of destruction with the *sefer* Torah in his arms. Blood spots in the parchment borders did not obstruct the words, hence the *sefer* Torah was deemed kosher. Before he died, the Polish Jew gave the *sefer* Torah to Reb Shimshon and had him promise that if Reb Shimshon made it to freedom he would place the *sefer* Torah in a *shul* where it would be used regularly, and the blood stains would never be removed.

Overnight the blood-stained *sefer* Torah became a cause celebre. Together with Grandpa Bloom, Rosenfeld, Rosenbloom and Zaks defended Reb Shimshon against Katz, Kaufman, the Roses and Weiss leading the pack that demanded that either the bloodstains be removed or they use a different *sefer* Torah. Reb Shimshon offered the compromise of using the Gdanske *sefer* Torah only for Mondays and Thursdays and another *sefer* Torah for Shabbos and holidays. That would be sufficient to fulfill his commitment that it be read "regularly." A different *sefer* Torah would then be used on Shabbos and Holidays though the Shabbos *minyan* was more populated than the weekday *minyan*, "No go," answered Manny Rose, his brothers, cousins and cohorts. And so Reb Shimshon used the *sefer* Torah with the blood stains for Shabbos and Yom Tov as well. The opposition and fellow travelling *baalei batim* went on strike, refusing to accept *aliyahs*. Mr. Zaks, the Beth Asher *gabbai* (sexton) for years opined that inasmuch as awarding the limited number of aliyahs was always a problem with so many perceived slights, he would recommend that all synagogues adopt a policy of sprinkling blood in the borders of the parchments and there would then be so many less candidates for *aliyahs*. A case in point, Mr. Edelstein in later years complained bitterly about not getting an *aliyah* at the Sunday morning bussed in *minyan*, even after being explained that the *sefer* Torah was only taken out Monday, Thursday, Shabbos, *Rosh Chodesh* (first of the month) and Holidays. For weeks he boycotted the Sunday *minyan* and then showed up on one Sunday late that happened to be *Rosh Chodesh* as they were putting the *sefer* Torah back. "Aha, I caught you, you do take out the *sefer* Torah when I am not here!"

"Dat's de trouble, de main part from de trouble mit you people. By you in de *sefer* Torah is no blood in him!…If he had in him blood de *sefer* Torah by you, it would be a lot difference a lot of tings. Ah big difference. Iz all de *sefer* Torahs alvays havink in dem blood, ven iz alive but is inside de ledders like by de *mentsch*. Dis vone vat iz givink me *der Gdansker yid*, iz de *sefer* himself beink stabbed mit ah knife so iz bleedink, but by you not believink iz blood in de *sefer* Torah in de first beginnink altogedder,…coz its not alive by you dat Torah…so is by you upsettink you den de blood vot's *fuhn* inside him." Reb Shimshon to his opposition.

Then came the infamous sauna proposal, primarily to turn the existing *minyan* in the main sanctuary into a liberal *minyan*, mixed seating and modified liturgy; whereas to satisfy the original Beth Asher charter requirements, a small Orthodox *minyan* would be maintained in the basement until it literally and figuratively died of old age. Most importantly to add a new men's club and sauna to the Beth Asher faculty.

The existing building would have to come down and a new structure would go up, but the case was made that with more relaxed standards for prayer, encouraging Shabbos travel highlighting the men's club and sauna facility, many of the people that had moved out of the neighborhood would yet commute back for such services and amenities. A *halachic minyan* was dependent on locals, predicated upon Shabbos proximity, given the requirement to walk to *shul*. While emphasizing the sauna yet flavored with a bit of nostalgia a hybrid Reform / Conservative package would find commuting takers. Again Reb Shimshon resisted. Even after permits had been secured for tearing down the Beth Asher building, Reb Shimshon succeeded in resisting.

Today, the final battle—the proposed sale of the building. There weren't many offers. Berel Vladimovsky in his prime had been an organizer–impresario–actor at the Parkway Theatre for Yiddish plays and at one point had been ousted in a backstage scene that was purported to have been sufficiently histrionic to have been on the stage at the Parkway. Later, he got it into his head that the continuing disappearance of congregants from Beth Asher justified, required, having the facility redirected for other uses for the Jewish community. The logical alternative was a Yiddish theater. Though people were less interested in religion they weren't as culturally disaffected. Once again the thesis that out-of-the-neighborhood people could be attracted back but for quality theater performances. Sauna and even Conservative-cum-Reform rituals could be had in the newer neighborhoods and suburbs without travelling. A Yiddish theater belonged in the old neighborhood, here, tinged with an integral nostalgia. Berel still had contact with many of his Yiddish theater troupe many of whom had once performed at the now defunct Parkway, and more recently frequented the Mermaid's Tale. With time Jews from nearby neighborhoods would attend a reconstituted Yiddish theatre at the vacated Beth Asher building. While many called his plan hare–brained Berel Vladimovsky was single-minded. Some said he was living out his greatest stage role which he would never get to perform before the klieg lights.

Uncle Sid had dated Vladimovsky's sister Zelda. She and Reb Shimshon's Miriam had been the local up and coming talent in the Yiddish theater. Pretty early on, though, Miriam went ideological and Zelda was hit and killed by a car on Linden Boulevard. With the years Vladimovsky encouraged Sid's sentimental hindsight of the liaison. Dad said it was utter fabrication. Vladimovsky seeded, not just watered, newborn memories and with an especially green thumb grew them carefully. "Dollar green" said dad. Between re-seedings, waterings, Vladimovsky hit Sid for subsidizing one Yiddish troupe or another that "was keeping Zelda and Miriam's dream alive." As the Beth Asher crunch moment came closer Vladimovsky pressed Uncle Sid to help champion, promote, the transforming of Beth Asher into that new Yiddish theater. After all, the facility was built and developed by Jews for Jews. Religion in any form was on the way out in the new country, yet a moral obligation remained that such resource be harnessed for its cultural and symbolic attachments for the community. With the right packaging the very neighborhood and its personal and historic associations could be factored into the emotional-cultural-nostalgic equation for promoting a Yiddish theatre being re-established in the Beth Asher building. Though a synagogue sauna would not work, a Yiddish Winter Garden could work. Packaging was the key. Uncle Sid was the great packager.

For a number of years Uncle Sid had been interested in making a grand reunion for Brownsville neighborhood émigrés, ex-contemporaries. Bring back old guys and girls with their Caddys, Lincolns, and Chryslers and Packards and occasional Jags to a frank and pastrami fest at the PS 189 schoolyard deep in the old country ghetto of Brownsville.

Each time the idea surfaced with a certain degree of momentum Reb Shimshon campaigned against it. It was not returning home, he said, but rather importing and showcasing an ostentatious display of affluence in a now under-privileged black and Puerto Rican community. That was morally objectionable and practically counterproductive. It would fan the glowing embers of jealousy and anger of the indigenous indigent. Don't celebrate your escape from the ghetto at the doorpost of those that are still there. Uncle Sid countered, "We paid our dues and got to where we did, so let the climb of the 'Jew-Boys' from the cellars to the penthouses and skyscrapers be a model." It was educational and inspirational. Reb Shimshon rebutted, "By dem you not de model."

There was already a latent—and sometimes not so latent—black anti-Semitism that could be felt. Reb Shimshon quoted the story of the man who had a free loan fund and when dispensing the loans he gave each borrower a small pebble. When asked what the significance of that pebble was he explained, "Since ahm doink dem de favor is for sure dey going to trow on me rocks, better should be a small one dan a big one." Jews did too many favors to help the blacks. Around Bed-Stuy, Brownsville, East New York one could hear "Jew" as profanation. For some blacks such usage gave them immediate membership in the larger white world of *goyim*—us against those upstart Jews, an act of entitlement, enfranchisement. One Brownsville minister Dr. Mark Reginald Hood (a Detroit émigré black catholic turned Baptist), regularly boldly, baldly scored Jews. Too many Jews had worked too hard for black civil rights. Surely, a) that was philosophically and practically paternalistic colonialism condescendingly treating the black natives as the Jew boy's burden, like the blacks were too infantile to do it on their own; b) those Jews must have had guilty consciences otherwise they could not have invested so much of their time, money and energy and very lives in the enterprise of helping another, especially blacks. Normal people don't do that. And that meant somewhere along the way, Jews must be guilty.

Here rabbis and historians seemed to agree, obsessed as we are with *Tikun Ha-Olom*, (improving, perfecting the world) invariably irresistibly thrusting our aqualine noses into the moral business of the other. We never were or will be a 'normal' people.

Hood claimed to have been a radio technician and to have worked with C.E. Coughlin before Father Coughlin was quieted. Andy White said Hood was not very popular in the Brownsville black community. His storefront church congregation was not growing. Maybe black Baptist Brownsville parishioners were suspicious of a converted Catholic. Over the years swastikas had been painted a few times on the Beth Asher building and the Hebrew Home for the Aged, the two remaining Jewish facilities in this formerly Jewish neighborhood. Andy and Whalen both attributed the swastikas to Hood's agitation. Mr. Zaks said it had nothing to do with anti-Semitism, rather with Hood wanting to purchase the Beth Asher building (he had sent a number of proposals) simply figuring he would push the price down and the sale forward by making it uncomfortable for Reb Shimshon and the few remaining holdouts.

Reb Shimshon did not want to sell to any church let alone to Hood. A Puerto Rican church group also wanted the building. Hood and the Puerto Ricans threatened Reb Shimshon and each other.

Meanwhile Uncle Sid, encouraged by Vladimovsky, who saw it as a launching of his Beth Asher Yiddish troupe, enthusiastically went ahead with his reunion plans. Reb Shimshon, Miriam heading a committee of her fellow socialists–activists, and a few Beth Asher *baalei batim* formed an awkward coalition to get Sid off his reunion idea. Reb Shimshon's steadfast opposition ruled out Sid's first choice of the use of the Beth Asher facilities for the event. The PS 189 schoolyard was chosen as fair grounds for the gala event. Vladimovsky himself an ex-carpenter supervised the building of a small stage for a few short skits and Sid organized the food—some from the Mermaid's Tale, and some from a delicatessen in Crown Heights. To keep the neighborhood kids and troublemakers busy that evening of the August festivities Sid arranged for free sodas and ice cream at a number of neighborhood candy stores within a radius of five or six blocks from the schoolyard. He also hired a few local black hoods to supervise the proceedings and arranged for parking VIP guests cars inside the schoolyard along the foul lines and outfield. Tables with various goodies were set up across the infield.

The night before the grand reunion, Beth Asher and the Hebrew Home for the Aged were once again decorated with swastikas and this time the schoolyard floor as well. Most were done in chalk but a few with paint. Still, at 8 p.m. on the appointed humid New York August night, Caddys, Lincolns, Chryslers, Packards and a sprinkling of plebian vehicles hopped the curb and glid into parking positions along the foul lines of the PS 189 schoolyard. Most of the older cars had to seek parking along the streets. Dated Chevys, Plymouths and Fords and at least one Hornet and one Studebaker circled the block searching for parking spaces. A seven-piece band blasted out "The Star Spangled Banner," "America the Beautiful," "My Country 'Tis of Thee," "Take Me Out To The Ball Game," "Somewhere Over The Rainbow" and select Hit–Parade tunes. Then, "My Yiddishe Mamma" and a medley of secular Yiddish melodies. Others of Vladimovsky's troupe and Mermaid's Tale émigré hangers-on, either came by El or bus. Schoolyard parking was reserved for about twenty of the carriage trade cars. With about one hundred and twenty people showing, the proceedings began with reading of Solomon Bloomgarten's Yiddish translation of Hiawatha. Vladimovsky beamed. Sid's ubiquitous smile stretched. Miriam and friends boycotted.

Notwithstanding all the free goodies being distributed at different neighborhood locations around the schoolyard nevertheless local spectators began gathering, crowding — first kids, then adults, numbers growing and growing — first outside the schoolyard, hanging on the wire fences and peering in then gradually moving in to participate, and overtake the food tables. Uncle Sid's local black Hessian hoods were bested, inept, or undercover hoods of Hood. While a number of the black adults and children were charmed by Sid's smiles and Vladirmovsky's diplomatic pontifications, with all the black–back–

slapping, and working of the variegated gathering, still the thickening crowd became more and more unmanageable. Nasty exchanges, pushing, scraping, some punching, a few snatched purses, some broken glass, punctured tires, bloodletting. Police.

Despite the grand union debacle Vladimovsky and his cohorts persisted with their Yiddish theatre plan. When challenged that since the change of the neighborhood was the cause of the demise of Parkway Theatre and Beth Asher as well, then why should a little Yiddish theatre group today at the edge of Brownsville in a now black and Puerto Rican community be any different, Vladimovsky repeatedly countered that with proper management the Parkway Theater could have survived even in the present neighborhood. Secondly the location of the Beth Asher building at the nexus of Linden Boulevard, Kings Highway and Pennsylvania Avenue, so close to The Belt Parkway offered direct and easy access to all of Brooklyn and Long Island. Even a Conservative synagogue was unnatural in a non-Jewish neighborhood. A theatre was not. And he already had his core of pre-committed, subscribed attendees — Yiddishists, socialists, and bundists who were devoutly colorblind. Reb Shimshon told them that they may be colorblind, but the blacks in the neighborhood weren't. Since eight years prior when the attempted sauna program had been vigorously resisted by Reb Shimshon, meantime, a lot more players had moved to Flatbush, Long Island and a growing number to the final exits off those parkways at the edges of Long Island and New Jersey wastelands, those final ingathering Jewish neighborhoods that would not change; those Jewish cemeteries bordering the edges of the suburban barrenness. Through all the battles Rosenman, Rosenberg, Grandpa Bloom and Mr. Zacks and the dwindling dwarf pack had been with Reb Shimshon leading the defense in Reb Shimshon's ongoing War of the Roses against Weiss, Katz, Rosenkrantz, Kaufman, the brothers Rose, Berkowitz and Vladimovsky.

Reb Shimshon's saga was replete with drama and tragedy. It was still being played out. The denouement was approaching. Even if my allegiance to Reb Shimshon was less than to the Dodgers in those early years, still, rooting for him as an underdog holding out as he had for tradition and principles—albeit not necessarily my principles—there was a kind of heroic romance of sorts that he inspired. His opponents represented the crass pressures of the bad-guy-*baalei batim*, motivated solely by expedience. Katz, the dapper dresser in his "three–G" suits and broad colored silk ties had a way of saying "Good morning" or "It's going to rain today" as if he had said something original and worthy of quote. After all, it had come from under that grey homburg, the president's homburg. Melvin Katz, the president's son was a classmate of Dad's in law school. Dad said Melvin also always spoke as if he was wearing a homburg. He and Dad had studied under Alvin Thomas who modeled himself as a part Clarence Darrow part William Jennings Bryan. Amateur Shakespeare actor Thomas had Katz and Dad practicing monologues in front of mirrors. Classmates — competitors more than friends, Melvin went on to become an assistant prosecutor in the D.A.'s office and Dad went on into a combined accounting and law firm practice. Katz senior ever referred to Melvin as the next D.A. and eventual governor. Though president Katz posed as neutral, yet he and Melvin were critical of Reb Shimshon. Melvin was more outspoken. I sensed that some of Dad's mixed affinity for Reb Shimshon had to do with Melvin's dislike of Reb Shimshon.

There were two Reb Shimshon stories that caught me somewhere in that uncharted region between heart and head, in that gut of the imagination. For one we had eyewitnesses, for the other we heard tell.

When Reb Shimshon arrived in America in 1936 with the plan of earning some money, and then bringing the family over, his first job was as a *shochet* in a Hoboken slaughterhouse. Finding the halachic standards below his requirements he quickly left. Next, some classes at a local *yeshivah* but knowing no English and there being few takers for Yiddish, it hadn't gone very well. The few Yiddish speaking positions were oversubscribed and under paid. A few more fill-in hashgachah jobs, for off-Main Street off-Broadway catering establishments came up now and then. Again most of the setups couldn't satisfy Reb Shimshon's kashrus standards. Then early in 1937 when Beth Asher was being established Reb Shimshon was installed in the part-time position as rabbi. He continued doing some teaching and tutoring. Horowitz the painter, a congregant, had a cousin, Goldenberg who was opening a new kosher hotel in Belle Harbor. Uncle Sid was contacted (before Sid and Francine had fled Brooklyn for Lawrence and then to Westchester). Sid was, like Dad, basically a no-show member at Beth Asher, but also a member at the Conservative synagogue on Remsen Avenue. Yom Kippur, Dad sat longer at Beth Asher sanctuary than Sid, who made it known that his good behavior for the time he served earned him an early release. Dad also showed for part of Rosh Hashanah.

Sid was our home grown expert on promotion. A scheme was hatched to publicize Goldenberg's new hotel in Belle Harbor in flamboyant Sid-like fashion. An agreement with a movie company was reached for renting a Spanish galleon docked in Sheepshead Bay waiting for a film making. Hired for a pirate film that was to be done around the upper Hudson area, Sid contracted the ship for a gala cruise around Manhattan Island with sixty select paying passengers that would have an on-going buffet smorgasbord of Goldenberg's special delicacies. Scheduled to leave from Fulton Fish Market, sailing north up the East River, around the upper tip of Manhattan Island bringing the passengers back south through the Hudson down the West Side to the lower tip of Manhattan, then east past Red Hook, Coney Island to Belle Harbor where they would be picked up by lifeboats that would bring them to shore at Goldenberg's hotel. Goldenberg would never have opted for having a *mashgiach* on board but the hotel was kosher and the Queens-Rockaways Rabbinical Council required the promotional voyage to be *mashgiach*-manned as well. As Goldenberg's new seafront kosher hotel was to be called Goldenberg's Columbus House, the date for the promotional pilgrimage was set for Sunday October 12th, Columbus Day. When the engaged *mashgiach* took sick an S.O.S. was sent out to find a substitute quickly. After trying one after another of unavailable rabbis in Queens and Brooklyn, Reb Shimshon was contacted through Sid's recommendation. After investigating the track record of the first *mashgiach*, Reb Shimshon rechecked the source of the meat and utensils and the basic standards that had been established by the first *mashgiach*, and found them adequate. Reb Shimshon was given the documentation and inventory of food and the utensils including a generator powered unit for warming dishes. Boarding that square-rigged full-rigged ship, on Columbus Day, the jolly guests, greeted by their Columbus–era–lookalike–uniformed sailors, passengers and crew in the best of spirits. A mild October day, brilliant white sails, gently puffing out, flying jib to spanker, all the crew decked out in their period costumes. Amidst wafting aromas of Goldenberg's gourmet delicacies, all ready to set sail.

The seven piece band played "Cruising Down the River on a Sunday Afternoon" as the passengers ascended the gangplank to the Santa Maria as she had been dubbed for the voyage. Passengers in their Sunday best out for a gala outing at seventy-five dollars a head, top price being paid for what promised to be a special experience. With all the guests assembled on the forecastle deck the accordionist doing the vocal solo accompanied by the band delivering, "Star Spangled Banner." "America the Beautiful" and "My Country 'Tis of Thee." Ending with "*Hatikvah*." Under a clear sky, and in calm waters, that early Sunday morning, they began the cruise uptown, starting from the Fulton Fish Market. Food was plentiful, the band lively, and loud, and the milling passengers moving fore and aft indulging and indulged. All smart and jovial. Lovely weather, joyous music, the Columbus Day pilgrimage, the Goldenberg's Columbus House in Belle Harbor promised to be launched with genuine success. Things carried on that way for a short while. About two hours into the voyage passengers took note of loud voices emanating from below. From down under the decks, a heated argument was taking place. Yiddish, English, Russian—but mostly Yiddish. Sailing through the narrows, west around to the Hudson and heading south now, the conflict exploded from down in the hull underneath, to up on deck. Reb Shimshon had discovered discrepancies in identifying the food inventory and when questioning the waiters in charge it was revealed that substitutions had been made at the last moment from some non-kosher restaurant near the dock. Somewhere between Grant's Tomb and Hell's Kitchen Reb Shimshon announced to the passengers his discovery asking, cautioning, begging, warning the people not to eat from the non-kosher food. Of the sixty passengers more than half were from Goldenberg's select private party and they and the others shouted Reb Shimshon down. They were free adults and could choose to eat what they like. "True," said Reb Shimshon, but a contract had been entered into with Reb Shimshon taking responsibility for the kashrus of the fare served on the voyage. Goldenberg, Reb Shimshon, all parties were bound by that agreement. Again he was shouted down, "When I pay, I eat what I like!" Suddenly Reb Shimshon ran to the buffet table, spread so elegantly with its steaming meats and delicacies, and began to pick up dishes and trays and throw them overboard. Tossing full platters and bowls, one after another, into the Hudson River. Initially too shocked to respond guests stood paralyzed as Reb Shimshon then joined by one of the guests, a red-headed giant of a Russian Jew, running up and back across the deck from tables to the railing of the ship flipping portion after portion of meat and entrees overboard. "He's gone mad!" "Toss him overboard!" "I paid for dis mit mein own money, none from his damned business." "In America iz ah free country." If I wasn't there, still I could close my eyes and picture Reb Shimshon darting fore and aft, long beard and caftan flying in the wind feeding those Hudson River fish, that gourmet repast.

Three people from Goldenberg's party finally subdued Reb Shimshon and held him still. The big brute of a Russian Jew turned and said, "Listen de whole year I am also not eating de kosher. But iz vas here advertising dat iz being kosher and de Rabbi he is taking de responsible, den he is one hundred per cent and I am telling you iz a good idea to leave him to go because me ahm starting to get mad. And anyvone vat is knowing me, is knowing iz not healty ven I'm getting mad. Not healty mostly for yenem, on de udder side from me." Releasing Reb Shimshon, they began to negotiate. Reb Shimshon was prepared to accept being let down on shore before the end of the trip. Once he had announced to others the state of the non-kosher food he was *halachically* no longer responsible. By the time all was agreed, they were in downtown waters, and Reb Shimshon opted to be lowered in a boat and dropped at Bedloes Island. Some reported it was Governors Island. The Russian Jew and his wife jumped ship with Reb Shimshon. For that story we had eyewitnesses.

The other story had come in bits and pieces. While it was hard to picture Reb Shimshon talking about it, yet even if he had not been the source, it seems he tacitly confirmed it. Over the years Grandpa Bloom as confidant had pieced it together. When the liberating Russians had come into Poland they found Reb Shimshon, wounded and recuperating in a makeshift Russian battlefront hospital. At least at one point Reb Shimshon had been taken by the Nazis, and subsequently escaped. Running, hiding from forest to farm and back again he had been caught and wounded more than once, and somehow each time had miraculously escaped. Still in his tattered prison uniform, he lay there in that improvised hospital, semi-conscious for days, just beginning to recuperate as the Russian cavalry reinforcements arrived. Upon release, Reb Shimshon was recruited by that Russian cavalry group—he, the only identifiable Jew in the group, to ride with them on their mission to retrieve thousands of horses that had been set loose during the mayhem. For three months riding bareback through the war torn Polish–Russian countryside rounding up wild-eyed, half crazed, all crazed, starved horses, terrorized, stricken, fleeing, escaping man and his engines of destruction. That countryside in shambles, gouged with craters, fields strewn with the debris of war, remnants of immobilized burnt-out war torn vehicles. Man and horse carcasses and an occasional stiff dog. One day, a few soldiers and Reb Shimshon stopped at a deserted farmhouse and as the soldiers went through the closets they found a moth-eaten cutaway swallow-tailed full dress suit and top hat. A number of soldiers tried them on but they didn't fit. The full dress suit and top hat were awarded to the tall *zhid* by default. And while they were lice-infested Reb Shimshon preferred them to his Nazi prison uniform. Thus he rode galloping with that Russian posse over the devastated countryside with his tails, the horses' tails, flapping in the wind. Sometimes with his new old top hat, sometimes a sporting khaki stocking cap he had taken from a dead Polish soldier. With the beginnings of his re-growing beard, top hat or stocking cap and cutaway tails, riding through the countryside that still echoed the hoof beats the guttural cries and curses of countless hordes of headless, heartless horsemen, Reb Shimshon rode to that last roundup.

Later at the *yeshivah* in Ellenville I was to hear the story of a friend of the *Rosh Yeshivah* who was in a Soviet prison with a former White Russian officer. On a regular basis the officer disappeared to some unknown place in the compound. One day the friend followed the officer and found him wearing his old officer's uniform posing in front of a broken mirror. He then explained that he had hidden the uniform and on a daily basis performed this ritual, "to remind myself who I really am." Who was Reb Shimshon, really? Who was, am I really?

Once when I had pranced with the other boys and girls up and down those peeling, hardening, chipping oil-cloth-covered steps to those mock classes in that unventilated basement, those after–school Talmud Torah classes, Reb Shimshon's spooky presence hovered at the edge of those non-happenings. Imposter, pedagogues, "ah, aw, beh-ing" mechanically, listlessly, at us second generation Marrano children. *Yarmulkes* were for cellars. We boys donned *yarmulkes* on the way down to those dank, poorly lit cubicles in the basement, and we promptly shed those *yarmulkes* as we hit the street, light and air— re–entering the real world of goyim, to appear once again as goyim amongst *goyim*. And while the kids continued to say that the tall, gaunt, long bearded, be–kaftaned figure was one genuinely spooky presence, and that he merely flapped that kaftan to zip from place to place, yet we viewed him—spookiness and all—as a leftover from another world, another time and place; a remnant, a loser, albeit a hauntingly heroically romantic loser. He had won some battles, but lost the war. However arete-dik, tragic but fact. Did not history—the world— abound with such winner/losers—Ossip Mandelstam, Isaac Rosenberg, Pete Reiser, Satchel Paige, Byron, Shelley, Benny Cohen? Guys who with slightly different turns of the cosmic kaleidoscope their abundant talents would have found such stellar expression. Quirks, breaks, sickness, wars, plagues, holocausts. How many were potentially to have penned epic poems compose and discover, disclose their inner songs and remedies for Man? How many children who were to have children? The perennial perning of the global gyre. Admittedly with Reb Shimshon some of his mini triumphs, escapades, did provide a tragic poetic touch to his losses. If he never came across as cranky and crotchety, still he was sad, and somewhat pitiable in his present irrelevance. An old civil war veteran. Which is then sadder, being locked into the frames of those long-gone quasi-quixotic heroic gambits, frozen in glacial nostalgia, or, succumbing to pandemic tinsel consumerism Yankee – Doodle –Dandy—driven, amateurs at the Fred Astaire school of dance, stepping so carefully, so warily, fitting their footsteps on to the prepainted steps of the dance floor. De rigueur rhythmic movements ever and anxiously updating the stylish Zeitgeist, shedding old habits and ideas like worn work shoes and donning today's more fashionable gear. Then all fitting so cozily together onto those prepared steps. Reb Shimshon continued to resist that suffocating encroachment.

A kosher Quixote piercing windbags if not windmills. Even in his occasional scoring inescapably sad. To what avail? Today he patrolled the all but Jewless deserted turf around the haunted Beth Asher castle with his Sancho, Andy White the black handyman. Oft times Winters was not far behind.

There is something disconcerting, to wake up one day and find that people who had been merely extras on the film location of one's life milling, aimlessly about the corners of one's existence, that of a moment, suddenly they had been re–cast, promoted to supporting roles of prominence, nay, even stardom. Today, Reb Shimshon loomed larger than life. Three dimensional. In a starring role. Where was he, I, till now? While there was the exhilaration of discovery yet there was the humbling of having bumbled as well. How come I hadn't noted that stellar-potential? Who was the casting director around here anyway? However deferential I had now become to the stamina and commitment of this Talmudic Lou Gehrig, playing together on the same team, wasn't there the anachronistic mystical *shaatnez*–like (halachic prohibition of joining certain items to be worn) mix of old-timer, new-timer? Today, as participant in Reb Shimshon's caper, on his team, on his court, was I playing in an old-timer's game? The antiquated and the precocious?

Anticipating tonight's operation had me on edge. Marty, Bam and Izzy who had come down from the *yeshivah* in Ellenville for the mission—we all agreed not to talk about Reb Shimshon's Operation Jeremiah. Only what was specifically necessary for planning. Chewing it over "*stam*"(generally) was counter-productive. It made us jumpier. Again I wondered whether the rabbis would have enacted a *gezeirah* (edict) not to think about it. And what about thinking about thinking about it?

Post our family's move to Lawrence six years ago, and pre-driver's license— spring and summer, if I did not sleep over at Marty's place the night before, then I would take public transportation or hitch in to the PS 189 schoolyard for Saturday and Sunday morning softball games. When they got their licenses, Marty and Bam, respectively a year and a year and a half older than me, they usually drove me back to Lawrence. In warm weather on the way there or back we hit the Rockaway beaches.

Now, post my *yeshivah* tour of duty and my return to live in Brooklyn, summer Sundays I went round trip with them—for me a Lawrence visit to the "family" and then beach and back to my inverted garret, my basement apartment on the East Flatbush– Brownsville divide. Bam's folks had moved to Canarsie. Marty, since his father died now lived with his mother deeper in Flatbush. During the two years since I had moved back to Brooklyn, Dad's fury had not abated. When he reiterated his arguments at my leaving, I frequently pointed out that it was only six years since they had moved to Lawrence, and that in fact, I was merely continuing our prior Brooklyn residence. They had in truth left me.

Beth Asher: Yesteryear's congregants had been evacuated, yet even if those erst- while urban Jews had fled to their suburban diasporas maybe G-d had not. Maybe He still hung around His old ghetto haunts. Maybe He was still more at home amidst the clutter of archaic musty, dusty volumes, the unmatched cholent of benches, chairs, stools and tables which needs have randomly sprouted, "*Galusdik*"(exile-like). Who could have planned such décor–in–chaos? If galus as option was Providentially ordained, yet opera- tively it was enacted as Hidden Countenance. Scripted yet inviting, requiring ad-libbing from within those texts.

A new stop, another stop on the exile express, a commuter stop. Might there perhaps be commuted judgments for regular commuters. Beth Asher's walls and ceil- ings, the peeling floors, motley splintering furnishings yellowing crumbling prayer books and Torah books had along the way absorbed moments, selected seconds of fleeting but genuine Jewish joy and Jewish hurt. Those "greeners" had recited *Kaddish* for their par- ents but had not produced a generation that would recite it for themselves. Maybe these immigrant Jews—greeners in the *goldene medinah* (golden country), heaven-bent on a better life for their children, forsaking the *cholent*–pot for the melting pot—deep down they knew that their own children would never recite that *Kaddish* for them. Hence their own recitation of Kaddish was two-tiered, reciting it for their lost parents but also knowing it was for themselves as well. *Kaddish*—that liturgy of linkage connecting generations—was here a declamation, a haunting confessional of unlinking. By definition one could not *halachically* recite *Kaddish* for oneself so these ambivalent refugee recitations were especially, darkly poignant, penetrating, portentously painfully doomed. A surreal harmonizing of antinomies. Two-teared.

Dutifully, yet comfortably and lovingly Reb Shimshon moving through that décor–in–chaos, like that's the way it had to be, here now *galusdik*.

Designer and design Hiding and Hidden. Yet present. Reb Shimshon sensing that clinging Divine Presence as willing hostage to His Cosmic Covenant to accompany His people through galus. Saturating, infusing these tear-soaked walls, furnishings and premises.

However contradictory, however paradoxical and ironic, however shortsighted and wrong-headed yet the plaster and paint, the ceilings and floors were witness to a certain quantity of *mitzvahs*, if oft times lackluster, nevertheless strands, fibers, bits and sparks of energy that coalesced into the very substance of this space, these grainy, pickled pews and briny benches, their odor, their texture. Years upon years of sapping up the bitter-sweet resin of those tears and sweat of the running and climbing of those immigrant Jews, all that scrambling, reaching, stretching for the greener's America, greenbacks chasing after green bucks, to service their born-in-America children. Still oblivious to the new and widening fault lines, that spreading abyss between immigrant and newborn terrain. Some spiritual Richter scale could have picked up the vibrations and reverberations, the echoes foretelling the incipient eruption, the tearing, piercing poignancy of those two tiered *Kaddeshim* that their children could not or would not recite and they, the newcomers, knowingly – unknowingly chanted for their own souls. And just as somewhere out in the dark and stretching cosmos those sounds continued to ebb and echo so also could they still be heard, felt, right here hanging in the air at Beth Asher.

Jews who recited *Shema* (prayer declaring commitment and belief) and *Shemoneh Esrei* (*Amidah* recited three times daily) inside Beth Asher and sang and danced to "Yankee Doodle Dandy" on the pavements of Brooklyn—so do souls have inner sanctums. American Marranos, in the cellars of their souls they first suspected, and later knew that they had failed. Today the emptied edifice of Beth Asher stood as monument to that tragic–cum–epical saga. Maybe the sleek young temples on the Island, new and sprawling smooth wipe–clean surfaces of those architecturally interchangeable, designed – to be benign, modern structures in the suburbs connecting conveniently to area shopping malls interlinking all to massive common parking lots that afforded such ease of access in and out, to glide unscathed, unmarked, untouched. Not the narrow streets and alleys of piled upon dwellings, not the crowding chockablock scampering and bumping of pedestrians and vehicles for a little corner of space. Those suburban roomy lots kept fenders and bumpers, souls and persons undented, untouched.

Yeats had it that Byzantium was not a country for the old; conversely Beth Asher was no synagogue for the young. Ranch house-like designed synagogues were untiered, no place for absorbing tears. Not those idiosyncratic niches and crannies, nor all the sinewy rough surfaces and scratchy places of the soul so carefully paneled over, hermetically, formica-wipe-clean-sealed. No places for crying. Not for laughing too much either. Surely not so loudly. Not like those greeners who mangled language, and lacked decorum, those, that had cried and laughed so freely and had walked and talked like Jews in pageant. Decidedly secular but unequivocally so Jewish even as they sought to escape that designation. As Mr. Sartre was to say, the assimilating Jew must expend an energy to overcome that initial Jewish designation that the gentile has no need to submerge. That mock operetta was no longer funny. Vladimovsky notwithstanding.

So maybe G-d thought otherwise. Reb Shimshon held–felt–thought He did. And if all the other guys on the block had quit and taken off, then Reb Shimshon was not a flat-leaver. He also stayed on; sticking it out with G-d, he wouldn't leave G-d flat, and thus being held in such Cosmic Thrall lent a peculiarly elegiac, yet quirkily sanguine, quality to Reb Shimshon.

His dark penetrating eyes, first he looked at you, then through you and beyond you, but always coming back to look at you. Those eyes also flickered, just enough, especially at the corners, igniting first those eyes, then the smile as he stared at you, beyond you, through you. Or perhaps because he stared through-you, at-you. Perhaps he penetrated more deeply into the precincts and hideouts of that Marrano soul. Maybe Reb Shimshon had tied himself to the mast of the HMS Beth Asher and in that gathering storm of assimilation, as so much Jewish cargo jettisoned - cast out, and so many of the crew already jumped.

"The good ship nodded, teetered crazily,

Planks peeling under the lashing of the sea:

What though the mast now be blown overboard,

The cable broke, the holding anchor lost

And half of our sailors swallowed in the flood

Yet lives our pilot still?"

Or was it misplaced obstinacy bordering on madness, Ahab–like. Was Reb Shimshon – Sir Francis Drake–like, Columbus–like onto something that the others had gotten off or never grasped? Or, or...

It was long told that Reb Shimshon still delivered *drashos* (sermons) in the deserted main sanctuary to the empty pews. Usually late in the afternoon on Shabbos. After *davening* with Winters at the Old Age Home which was the only Shabbos *minyan* within walking distance, and then eating his Shabbos meal at home, Reb Shimshon would in the afternoon head back to Beth Asher to the unlit, vacant, vaulted sanctuary, ascend the steps to the pulpit and begin addressing his bodily-absentee yet ghostly returning congregants, those hovering invisible yet tangible presences with whom he connected. Winters, Zaks and others occasionally whispered about those *drashah* (sermon) performances. Winters maintained that it was normal enough amongst Talmudic scholars to express their ideas and insights verbally even when alone, so to clarify nuances and delicate points which through articulation became clearer. Later at the *yeshivah* I did see rebbes and bachurim in the beis medrash, scholars sitting alone, or pacing to and fro reading, reciting passages of tight, hinting texts of *Gemara* in haunting rhythms out loud to themselves, stretching, straining to elucidate, explaining, as if to another, complicated concepts verbalizing while yet alone; like rehearsing for their *chavrusa* interaction or for *shiurim*. Monologues in preparation for dialogues. In actual discourse with Rabbi Akiva, Abaye and Rava, The Rambam, Rav Yosef Karo, The Vilna Gaon. All those discussions, words once heard, retasted, reingested, recycled. Now. All tangible. Also for Reb Shimshon one could feel that he actually sensed the lingering breathing presence of those long gone, long since disembodied, congregants, and that gave the haunting touch, the apparitional dimension to his drashos. Like he and they were there now, that phantasmagoric quorum, those returning ghosts, who now must come back to Beth Asher to recite that *Kaddish* for themselves—that *Kaddish* that their children could not or would not recite.

Or maybe, Reb Shimshon, and Rav Winters were fending off windmills, protecting the ramparts and drawbridges of the castles and palaces of their own minds. Maps of their own making—some fantastic dream cartography—tracing the route from Alexandria to Rome to Madrid to Minsk to Pinsk, with some stops in Oz and Camelot, but Auschwitz, Hades and Sodom as well. Our Semitic glatt kosher Quixote with his loyal Sancho, both congenial, sincere, devoutly chimerical.

Worse yet, might it not be that I'd chalked in for a voyage on that Pequod of

HMS Beth Asher, and that he of the caftan and limping leg—maybe he wasn't just that rejected *tzaddik*, schooled in the esoteric wisdom and ways of our ancient law, lore and tradition; maybe instead, all that cataloging, collecting and explication of seeming contradictions, that ritual stitching and suturing of Jewish text and Jewish suffering—instead, all those sleight of mind moves were merely dazzlingly ingenious intricate brainy games, that stretched one just enough to cleverly pluck the chords of one's heart as well. Really and actually, no more than some men's—and here one man's — on-going obsession with tracking down, reining in and recording, walling in, all that accumulated plaintive wailing. And was I now a part of that doomed expeditionary wailing crew.

Dad dated the turning point for my enlisting or being impressed into service and services as seafarer on the HMS Beth Asher-cum-Pequod setting out to brave the sea of Talmud, two years ago, from that first Shabbos I spent at the Winters' home. Those years that I commuted for Saturday and Sunday games from Lawrence to the schoolyard, often stopping on Sundays to pick up our meat order at Mendel's butcher shop in Brooklyn. Now that Mendel was semi-retired Sroly made the deliveries. Besides saving Sroly the extra lap from the Old Age Home it also saved Dad the allergic shortness of breath and hives that attacked him with each of Sroly's visits to our new — elegant neighborhood, that piebald dented van, Sroly's flying orange peyos, conjured his antic dancing at heimishe *chasunahs* (community weddings) to raise money for the poor, encouraging celebrating the growth of that ghetto world on this American soil. That Shabbos, that watershed Shabbos came about through just such a Sunday pick up at Sroly's. Mom had no problem with my going for Shabbos nor with my subsequent *yeshivah* odyssey. Dad already had a problem with my opting then for the visit, and now a fortiori for enlisting for the voyage. While Sroly and Winters learned together some evenings as well, Sunday—always a slow time in the shop—remained prime *chavrusa*-time. They were really going at each other when I came in, and Winters turned to me like he was expecting me, and stammering a number of times before he got it out, he asked, "If you nnneed *yiush* (abandoning hope) after the loss of an object—to have taken place before the ffffinder can take legal possession, then what about if we knew for sure that if the loser would be aware that he lost the object, then he would dddespair of finding it, but he happens now not to bbbbe aware yet that he lost said object, should that potential *yiush* be ttttantamount to in fact actually knowing, and giving up hope, (i.e. yiush without knowing?) Bbbbut how can one know more than ppprobability that he would be *meya'esh* (giving up hope)? Furthermore how come it then says..." Winters' face reflected the strumming, and humming of his mind. Grimacing, constricting, stretching, smiling as he savored the words and thoughts first faster, and then a little longer than others, as he stammered for words. One could feel the tremors of the ideas as they crossed his face, childlike, from eyes to mouth, reverberating through his entirety, from his head through his trunk, through his arms, animating his hands and fingers, ideogramatically drawing invisible pictures in the air. If most of Winters' face like Wally Cox was glasses and nose, yet as he fielded Sroly's questions with consummate *sangs foire*, that cool grace was more Billy Cox darting out with the big glove at the last split second snaring the hot grounder or foul ball right out of the third base stands. Winters and Sroly carried on quickly losing me along the way: I / me contemplating whether I was lost, and had I been *meya'esh*. Was I subject or object, and could I retrieve myself, as lost object, or was I up for grabs? Such and other nonesuch considerations. At one point Winters turned to me, and though I had seen the coming attractions when he in the past had invited me for a Shabbos and I had politely smiled and refused, but this time it felt like leaving the heroine on the tracks with the oncoming train and the serial film would wait until next showing for the denouement. There were *kashas* (questions) that had not been resolved. First it seemed harder to go than not to go. Suddenly the adrenaline pushed to go. Then it seemed harder not to go than to go. Meanwhile a "yes" was heard. Someone had said it. It wasn't Sroly and it wasn't Winters. So it must have been me. Like a converse Goldwynism – I had been excluded in. Though for the life of me I could not remember pushing the "yes" button. But clearly they heard it and I heard it and it sure sounded like my voice. So there I was, committed to return from Lawrence to East Flatbush not just for the Saturday and Sunday morning softball game at the schoolyard, but for my first "*Shabbosdike*" Shabbos.(halachically Shabbos) During that week Dad provided me with a number of different scripts of how to back out. Mom said it would be insulting to Rebbetzin Winters and Mom was sure that the Rebbetzin was a great cook and it would be a good experience. I would enjoy it. Dad pined and opined, not only was the venue wrong, "Normal people don't go from Lawrence to Brownsville for weekends and especially to hosts that are stuck somewhere in 18th century Eastern Europe."

Suddenly, it was Friday afternoon and there I was at the Brownsville–East Flatbush Divide, at the upstairs apartment of the Winters' abode, in that row of four family units squeezed between now black and Puerto Rican tenements, arriving as instructed three-quarters of an hour before candle lighting (which official time was eighteen minutes before sunset). Boom, varoom, like I had hit the scene smack into the middle of a helter skelter madcap silent film, except not so silent and featuring a chorus of Lilliputian circus clowns scampering hither and thither, some in pajamas, some all ready decked out like they were going to a party, some in the process of getting decked out. Kids, all shapes and sizes, popping out from under tables, chairs, from behind bureaus, and out of closets. Dozens of them, it seemed, from those in diapers up and on to adolescence. Like somebody was filming a family biography, and there were stand-ins, and a kid for each age and sequence for each year. I must have counted seventy kids in all as they skipped in and around that whirling room. Rebbetzin Winters appeared with an infant in her arms. She dressed like the good cowboy Randolph Scott's wife, high necked, long sleeved dress, with a white apron and kerchief, covering her hair. She smiled, asked me my name and with her free hand put down a cup of coffee. Dvory the fourteen year old was right behind with milk, sugar, and some freshly baked cake. The Rebbetzin said Dvory had baked the cake herself. Dvory said Tzippy and Itzik had helped her. Nine-year old Itzik said that ten-year old Tzippy had just cracked open the eggs and mixed the batter; though Tzippy also later put on the icing he reluctantly added. The dining room table was set for Shabbos, and I was guided to a small table-desk in an alcove off the large dining room. Ceiling-to-floor bookshelves surrounded that area. As suddenly as she had appeared, the Rebbetzin disappeared back into the kitchen. If I thought of those illustrations of the old woman who lived in a shoe, who had so many children she didn't know what to do, with kids popping up between the laces, hanging on to the eyelets, sliding down the ankle, and the high rounded toe, yet Rebbetzin Winters did not have the harried look. Busy yes, harried no. Her work force was organized. Dvory, the fourteen-year-old baker, was take-charge foreman as well, managing operations, liaising between headquarters in the kitch-en and field workers. Orders flew up and back. Some of the furnishings of the tri-purpose living room/dining room/study, were arranged by waves of assorted elves and fairies. Just-bathed cherubs now tumbled out from the back rooms and the bathroom off the long hallway. Winters brought up the rear guard. He glad-handed me and proceeded to turn on lamps and lights and then some off, scooping up pens and coins from his desk and dumping them into drawers. Coming closer to candle lighting time the pace increased to that of a film on fast forward. Then, like someone hit a gong, and like an hydraulic brake had been pulled, the entire leaping carousel of kinetic action halted. The Rebbetzin and Rabbi Winters' mother, the gathered girls were all decked out to go somewhere, except the somewhere was right here, to this table, to greet the Shabbos queen who was arriving. Here. Now. With their lighting, the women ushered in a tangibly incipient calm, a mys-tically whispering feminine–cum–spiritual softness wafted in. Like their grandmothers and mothers, these women's ceremonial lighting surrounded by all those spick and span shining children, here now again effecting that distaffly quilted tranquility, descending suffusing the room. Gathered together at the white-clothed dining room table festively set for about fourteen or so places, the candles lit, the Rebbetzin, her mother-in-law each covering her eyes and whispering prayers. At home Mom usually lit the candles without the prayer. But we never learned where that special lever was, we never got to pull that hidden hydraulic brake. With us there was less action before, and continuing action af-terwards; i.e. business as usual. No incipient tranquility wafting in, suffusing, permeating.

This kind of Shabbos required a special menu and special conduct, in rhythm with the setting and its sense of drama and purpose. Winters suggested that I unload my *muktzeh* (items one refrains from using on Shabbat), the props of the weekday stage—money, pens etc. into a drawer of his desk for safe keeping until after Shabbos. A kind of regal flame, the Shabbos candles, an honor guard of orange spearheads atop their white wax poles, the Shabbos queen had arrived.

Winters and five boys—four were Winters and one was a class-mate visiting for Shabbos—and two Winters girls and two guest friends all donned their fine Shabbos coats and hats for the twenty minute walk to the Old Age Home to daven. Pouring down the steps, Yankie and Moishe jumping two steps at a time, two of the other boys rat-tat-tatting, machine gunning their legs down the metal–tipped linoleum covered wood steps.

On the way a few of the older black men standing at the corner or at the front of their buildings said "*Gut Shabbos*," one more elderly gent tipping his hat as he said it. The only outsiders attending the in–house *minyan* at the Old Age Home were Reb Shimshon, the Winters family, and me. The rest were residents, patients. For a while now they were under house arrest, confined to the premises. Once upon a time they could walk the streets around the home. Even for the more ambulatory, street crime now curtailed such free movement.

Yankie Winters was assigned to stand by me and help me, the novice, with keeping the place in the siddur during the davening. He had just recently been bar mitzvah. In spite of Porter and those Marrano anti-learning-classes in the cellar at Beth Asher I could still read somewhat, but following the *chazzan* and keeping the place in the siddur was difficult. Translation was beyond me.

Like gathering together in a shelter of a hospital in a war zone during an air raid, they hobbled in, bent and broken old men and women, the women ducking in behind the *mechitzah*. Beaten bodies, wheel chairs and hobblers some holding intravenous drips. There had been a war. They had seen combat against the enemy—death—and they had been taken hostage. Invariably death won the war, but usually it was a war of attrition with deceptive lulls. The buck–toothed Dr. Harvey Lifschitz, family and Old Age Home dentist, favored filling cavities even for the terminally ill, greatly discounting his fees, often forfeiting payment from the more imminently dying.

Isaac Barowsky had begun writing his biography in his 90's. Some days he was clear, others not. He wanted to record it all asking, badgering, begging attendants and people in charge to organize a tape recorder for him. No one thought there was any value in that biography and getting the tape recorder was delayed. The matter was brought to

Rabbi Winters and he endorsed bringing the tape recorder. As the weeks went on and Isaac Barowsky sat and dictated it became increasingly clear that he wasn't clear. As he never asked for any replay, the attendants began setting up the tape recorder without tapes, turning the tapeless machine on for him to continue dictating. Though Rav Winters encouraged recording with tapes, sadly he accepted that even without them a certain *chessed* (act of kindness) quota was fulfilled.

One old man wandered behind the *mechitzah* and was promptly chased out by an old lady brandishing her cane and screaming, "Go where you belong, this is the place for the ladies!" I remembered wondered, watching an old woman on the subway applying her makeup and lipstick — for whom, for what? Yet whatever happens to those bodies, the core soul remains female. After a lifetime within those respective bodies such souls carried all the accrued codes and memories of those female bodies. Men-souls and women-souls. Behind the *mechitzah* that old-man-of-a-woman, was yet a woman-soul, and she defended her turf. Overheated as the room was, most people still wore sweaters. Always with his bow tie, often with spats, "Prince Albert," as the nurses called him, was invariably amongst the first ten men for the *minyan*.

About thirty men and ten women, some open-mouthed, glaze-eyed, fogged out, but most were familiar with the davening libretto, comfortably following the chazzan. Winters was the *chazzan*. Removing his black Shabbos fedora, he put on a *tallis* and began to lead the *Kabbalas Shabbos* (prayer of receiving Shabbat) to receive the Queen, Shabbos. He sang melodiously, and now he didn't stutter. So there you had it. Donning his cape of a *tallis*, exeunt Clark Kent, enter Superman. We could make a great duo, Winters and me. He only stammered when he spoke to men; when he spoke to G-d he did fine. Me? I did fine speaking to men. I only stammered when speaking to G-d.

Yankie Winters notwithstanding, I got lost a number of times in the prayers. After *davening*, Winters senior did his rounds, visiting the bedridden and making sure all had wine or grape juice and challah and helping them with the *Kiddush* recitation. Again we hit the streets for the walk back. Black, and some Puerto Rican kids running the streets. Gutted couches, disabled chairs and broken tables along the curbside, broken glass everywhere, sidewalks and gutters. Once more, some older black men wishing us Gut Shabbos.

Shabbos with the Winters meant no driving a car, no telephones, no switching lights on or off; Shabbos as an isolated island in a sea of time. A spiritual Swiss Family Robinson. The world was somewhere distantly beyond, all the external static now filtered out. We were marooned on a desert island in time and we had meantime chosen to stay, to cherish the preciousness of stretching to fix on the moment and each other.

Basically according to Torah tradition there were thirty-nine categories of creative or constructive endeavor, in which man was engaged during his workaday week. One was wont to say I drove, I wrote, I built, whereas a more accurate delineation would be—I chose to drive, and the Creator of us and it all, that Supreme Master of the Universe allowed, enabled, for the electric impulse in my brain to successfully move through the intricate network of nerves and cells touching and reaching to designated interim and ultimate targets, each in its very turn transmitting encoded messages to muscles and tendons duly empowered to instruct and implement function to achieve the intended act. How many steps along that seemingly instantaneous but truly complex and inter-dependent route are actually beyond our control? War-refugees at the Hebrew Home for the Aged to wit. To be candid and authentic one should say, "I chose to write and G-d guided the impulses of that decision to effect that happening." Weekdays a lower threshold of sanctity tolerates the vaguenesses and inaccuracies of our nature and speech. Come Shabbos and the diction and syntax of performance are refined, crystalized. By refraining from those Torah-termed creative and constructive activities one is elevated to a state of integrity—closer to the root reality of our existence—each Shabbos an editing, a re-writing of the sloppy weekday first draft of the narrative of my past week and coming attractions for the coming week; cutting, sharpening for a more pungent clearer version of me, to offer posterity, connecting to eternity. One that will stand the test, the scrutiny of time. Then if all those encumbrances—those dos and don'ts, and controls, seemed so excessively restrictive, then didn't Bill the Bard and Jimmy Joyce and Billy Yeats, Her-man, Ludwig and Amadeus all subject their muses to delicately calibrated configurations, imposing rules, regulations to contain, to obtain to, to direct and define the cumulative volcanic chaos of those creative passions and erupting muses? Rather than putting a lid on percolating energies, instead, these Torah Jews claimed only through such channeling was the integrity of liberation realized. If it is I that does, then I am limited to the mea-surable resources of that I. But, if it is the Divine Creator that does and I just chose to do who then knows where the cap really is. Result: A mystical sense of sublime liberation that permeates the Shabbos scene; a Source-linked I is a Source-Empowered I…. And yet for that one needed twenty-twenty I-sight. Whereas we of the roaming pronouns tended to a me-ness that had us my-opic.

They lost no time, Torah Jews, in translating the ethereal and subtle language of metaphysics into the lingua franca of action, the idiom of behavior, *halachah*. Ideas, norms, customs, all cooked directly into the gefilte fish and *cholent*, baked into the *challah* and if the workaday week was *melachah*-time (*halachically* creative endeavor, prohibited activity on Shabbat) promoting the illusory sense of self-propelled achievement, then Shabbos that dripping tic-toc of the imagined clock actually halted stopping all that seepage and leakage of mundane Mondays, all that random dribbling away, then so deftly Shabbos-patched with a snatch of eternity. As even sovereign territory has extra territorial embassies so this terrain in the County of Time reserves a seventh of its dominion for that space and place of transcendence – Shabbos; stubbornly regularly resurfacing that spiritual Brigadoon. The countdown was over, we were here now, at a place called Shabbos. Wardrobes, menus, tangibly sewing together threading body to soul.

Gefilte fish was introduced to avoid picking out the bones from the fish on Shabbos (separating bad from good, which was one of the prohibited activities). Food had to be brought to an halachically prepared, edible state before Shabbos, and then could be kept warm over a covered fire that was lit before Shabbos. Around the time of the formulation of the *Mishnah*, since the Sadducees rejected the Oral Law, they refrained from eating any food that was kept warm on Shabbos despite its having been cooked before Shabbos and having been placed on the covered (to avoid possible adjustment on Shabbos) fire that was lit before Shabbos. Hence, eating food that had previously been cooked and was kept warm in the halachic tradition was tantamount to a pledge of allegiance to the Oral Law. One who did not partake of such warm food on Shabbos was suspect of being a Sadducee. Hence the heimish-gourmet version of the cholent dish—the traditional rabbinic inspired stew-of-a-potion usually a potpourri of beans, potatoes, barley, meat, with various additions and deletions according to community, family chef. Pre-cooked, that simmering brew then sits on the covered low flame from the inception of Shabbos on Friday evening til the lunch meal Shabbos morning and is served steaming hot.

Two challahs to signify the double portion of mannah that fell Friday for those Jews in the desert so that they would not have to collect their daily allotments on Shabbos.

During the Winters' Shabbos meal courses were interspersed with songs from the traditional repertoire, the entire family joining in, with bit solos from the younger boys. Once again, Winters sang without stammering and then turned to quiz the children, from the youngest attending kindergarten to the eldest in high school on the Torah portion of the week. Children leaping and vying bursting to answer, perform. Winters' mother beamed with each answer. Rebbetzin Winters, his wife, also beamed, but Grandma Winters beamed like a fluorescent, audibly, the Rebbetzin, incandescently, quietly. Older children and adults riveted by the mini-monologues under the Kleig lights of the budding Lilliputian performers. If I had not felt sufficiently inadequate earlier, at the davening...now witnessing that whiz-kid quiz-kid session as they leaped and vied with each other to declaim, delightfully indicting, but indicting. Almost enough to make me lose my appetite. I wondered if they do this every Friday night, or might it not have been staged this Friday night to humble the haughty. But of course it was a part of the Shabbos tish-ritual. Of course. And of the courses: They came one upon the other and as premeditatedly *halachic* as they were, gefilte fish, chicken soup simmering on the blech, yet the resultant dishes were delicious. I could have gone for some dry wine but all they had was sweet wine. That single sip after Winters' Kiddush was more than enough of the syrupy stuff. But after the gefilte fish we had a few stiff l'chaims on some Cutty Sark. Daunting, as all those dos and don'ts were, the dos were less burdensome. Caloric expenditure of energy did not determine Shabbos don'ts; rather, by what the Torah defined as constructive and creative endeavor. In a room the table may be lifted and carried. Transference of a spoon from a public domain to a private domain or the converse was prohibited. The dos, such as Kiddush, praying, eating, singing, were easier than the don'ts, those categories of prohibited activity. One sage had explained it—based on the verse "*Ani yesheinah v'libi eir*—I am asleep but my heart is awake" — people are often asleep from the negative *mitzvahs* yet awake for the positive *mitzvahs*. The positive *mitzvah* is an extension of one's ego i.e. I am doing, whereas the negative *mitzvah* was constriction, I am not doing. Ego satisfaction that was present while expediting the positive mitzvah was absent for the negative *mitzvah*, passivity was inhibition, a constriction of self-expression, and thus harder to fulfill.

A few times during that first Shabbos with the Winters the very thought that I must hold out until Saturday night, that I could not—or should not—hop into my car and drive off, the very notion of that Divinely imposed immobility per se was oppressive. If they were on an extended idyllic—pastoral, metaphysical—picnic, Swiss Family Robinson–dik blocking out the noise and noisesomeness, the racket and the pollution of the world, yet I was marooned. Until the *Havdalah* service I was a castaway on that island, their island called Shabbos. Havdalah I learned would only be recited when three medium sized stars became visible.

Moishe the eight year old began prodding Rabbi Winters to tell me the "three star story." Winters called for a referendum, and it passed unanimously as the juvenile electorate rippled and swayed with conspiratorially smothered giggles. Rebbetzin Winters had a very distinguished and religious uncle, Mr. Wexler, a wealthy manufacturer and art collector who traveled the world. Usually he returned home for Shabbos. One such trip to Paris he had to remain for Shabbos. It turned out to be a beautiful day and after the morning davening and meal he went for a walk. Joining the viewers he stopped to look at a street exhibition of paintings spread along the sidewalk bordering a nearby park. One particular group of five pictures caught Mr. Wexler's eye. Strolling up and down the street at the edge of the park he studied the pictures. Shortly, the artist who had been lurking in the background appeared and informed Wexler in a mixture of French and English that each painting in the group sold for $500. Mr. Wexler explained in French that it was

Shabbos and as an Orthodox Jew he conducted no business transactions on Shabbos. The Parisian painter, studied Wexler thoughtfully, then answered in English: "Aha! $475 each."

"My good man, you seem not to have gotten the point, my religious laws don't allow me to buy or sell on the Shabbos," in French.

"$450," countered the artist.

"No you are still not getting the message. Look here, I am in Hotel La Maison Blanc on Rue de Rosier in the Pletzel and after dark when Shabbos is over if you haven't sold them we could talk."

"$425."

"After dark."

"Dark?"

"Obscurite sambre noire."

Late that Shabbos afternoon there was a knock at Wexler's door at the hotel and there stood the artist with five paintings.

"You are a little early, it's not quite night yet."

"Okay take all five for $400 each."

"Just be patient, Shabbos is almost over. Sit down please, as soon as its over we'll talk."

"Take four for $350 each."

"You still don't get it, the Shabbos just isn't over yet, soon, soon."

Jumping from his chair swinging open the door to the verandah the artist ran out and pointing to the sky screamed, "It's dark, it's dark! For sure it's dark. G-d knows it's dark! For seventeen years I live and paint and sell my paintings here in Paris and before that in Florence and before that in London and I have seen all kinds of methods and all kinds of bargaining tricks, but this is new. Okay. Take two $325 each."

Mr. Wexler joining the agitated artist on the verandah, "It's dark, now I just have to sight three stars."

"Three stars?" screamed the artist. "Okay, okay, fine $300 each, take two."

"Hang on just a few minutes more and we'll see the stars," Mr. Wexler pointing to the sky, and motioning to be patient.

"There, there is a star, and another one, and another one. Three stars. $265 each, take two."

"They have to be middle sized stars," explained Wexler.

"Middle sized?"

The artist now hysterical, throwing his hat to the floor, pulling at his hair.

"Okay, okay $250 just take one, $250."

Tzippy and Moshie were doubled up with laughter. Four-year-old Tully, initially upset, once again he hadn't caught why everyone was laughing, but quickly caught the bug and joined in. Rebbetzin Winters said no matter how many times the story was told the children laughed, maybe even more as time went on, anticipating each step. And it was true; Uncle Sigmund Wexler wasn't given to embellishing.

After the meal, Winters studied some *Pirkei Avos* (Ethics of the Fathers) with me, "Bbbe cautious in your dddealing with those in power, they only encourage you for their own advantage." And then later "dddon't say that when I have time I will learn, maybe you won't find the time." That was two years ago, and Winters then offered to learn with me on Saturdays if I was within walking distance, or on Sundays after the schoolyard softball games. Saturdays wouldn't work as I was still driving from Lawrence to those games but Sundays in the spring might work I explained. In the summer, right after the game I drove back with the guys to Lawrence. We headed for the beach, and I also headed home. As we were only in March, we agreed to learning on Sundays until the weather got warmer. He did throw out a standing Shabbos invitation to stay with them as well. I wasn't quite sure that I was ready for that. We got in a few sessions, some *Pirkei Avos* and some *Bava Metzia* (tractate). There was something intriguing about Talmud. It was tightly knit stuff. A kind of legal mathematical style, but concrete and somehow poetically gripping, abstract while thoroughly human. In fact reminiscent of Yaetes, "Rooted in the foul rag and bone shop of the human heart." The rhythmic range of focus global yet dramatically particular. Came June, we increased *Gemara*. I liked the way Winters went at it. That concern for phrasing; worrying the wording, the syntax into place, until it all fit. At times he coaxed, fondled, tickled the stiff staid squarish words until that text began to quiver, grimace, laugh, sing and dance. Summer came, and with it my resuming of Sundays returning with the guys to the beach and then home to Lawrence. Winters then came up with the suggestion of learning Thursday evenings and I began hitching and then, with my license, driving out Thursday evenings late to study *Gemara* with Winters. A few more times through the summer I did spend Shabbos with them as well. And once or twice I even stayed over Saturday night until Sunday morning games.

But that first Shabbos, when *Havdalah* came, it wasn't any too soon. I welcomed that separation ceremony ending the Shabbos that divided between Shabbos sanctity and the secular. Particularly appropriate the *Havdalah* that first Shabbos two years ago, as I was headed out to Babylon to meet Pat. What more apropos way of ending the Shabbos with Winters and beginning the evening with Pat than to make *Havdalah*, to separate the sanctified from the secular. I did think that it was pretty clever of these Jews to keep Shabbos for only twenty-five hours. There was something charming about the retiring from it all, that—"the world is too much with us"—syndrome whereas had it lasted any longer that first Shabbos I was seriously considering hitting the fire escape and making a getaway.

As time went on, a few more Shabbosim, and over the months I began to miss the Shabbos and the kids. Moishe traipsing in with one shoe on and one shoe missing stretching his open palmed hands out expressively claiming it had disappeared. Little Estie spinning like a top endlessly. She never got dizzy. The other kids tried to imitate her but could not. They fell along the way, while she continued on and on. A few times the baby of the house landed in my lap. Little Yossi was just at that stage of fixing his eyes on you, cooing, talking baby talk. Lying on his back in the playpen like those cartoon characters, legs moving rapidly as if they were running, but going nowhere. His arms waving joyously, enthusiastically as he coo-talked while legging that stationary-marathon.

Is any of our running, Dad's marathon as well, any more than running east on the belt moving west as if we were getting somewhere? Not sure why that fellow referred to his symphony as the "Unfinished Symphony"—which symphony is finished?

A brimming, bubbling, beaming bundle, Yossi. Amazing, that little creature. Those fingers so perfectly formed, the eyes, he was communicating, he wanted to connect. A person. He did connect. That entire chorus, that circling circus of kids had to do with Shabbos, with creation, with the Creator, and with owning up, testifying to it all. Magnetic. And those very restrictions, no phone, no car etc., seemed to work to bring them all together, that family. To an island, their island called Shabbos. Their designated space of tranquility surrounded on all sides by a tumultuous and stormy sea. Each Shabbos they were Swiss Family Robinson all over again. Guests were invited to alight on their isle...Me? Parachuting interloper. Tourist, viewing and charmed but only a visitor.

One of those Shabbosim late August, the kids were explaining to me what the importance of the Hebrew month of Elul was. "*Ani L'Dodi Vedodi Li*"— the first letters of the words formulate Elul, "I am to my beloved and my beloved is to me." That's a dedicated time of special proximity to the Divinity. The last games of the season. Pre-Rosh Hashanah. Pre-World Series. I noticed Winters' mother staring at me and trying to get my attention.

"So you loinink de *Mishnah* and *Gemara*, so dere it says an *am haaretz*, a person what he is ignorant, can't be a *chassid*, a real righteously person. So tink you, yourself, really you should right away go to *yeshivah*. Odervise vot kind of girl vill you gettink anyway? And vot you gonna be able to tell your own kinde, nutink if you don't learn sometink yourself. So I tink you should go to *yeshivah* right away."

"Right away?" choking a little on my cholent.

"Mom you shouldn't put him on the spot like that." The younger Rebbetzin.

"Dis is a free country, and I am not puttink him any place, I am tellink him where ahm tinkink he should put himself. Ahm tellink him vot is for him right to do. Vot's de matter, you don't tink he should go?"

"Of course I think it would be good for him, *yeshivah* is a wonderful experience but 'right away' might be a little hard for him." Younger Rebbetzin.

"Vat he's got such big business to give over? He trows a few tinks in a suitcase and fartik (finish)! So today is Shabbos if he can't go right away tomorrow, so he should go Monday."

"Look this is a ddemocracy so lets vvvvote," Winters turning towards the children and the Rebbetzin and his mother and resuming. "All in ffffavor of Stephen Yisroel Bloom going to *yeshivah* raise their hands."

The younger children leaped from their chairs yelling and laughing and jumping over me. "Yes! Yes! We want Steve to go to *yeshivah*! But he will still have to come to us for a Shabbos sometimes" added Moishe.

Get thee to a *yeshivah*! Wittenberg for Semites. More like Gulliver overrun by Lilliputians, half bemused, half intimidated. It turned out Winters had a specific *yeshivah* in mind. Yeshivas Kovna in Ellenville in the Catskills which was run by Rabbi Gordon, a colleague and friend of Reb Shimshon's. Winters himself had studied for a while under Rav Gordon when the *yeshivah* was in Brooklyn. The *yeshivah* began in Brownsville with the help of Reb Shimshon, immediately after the war. In 1952 Rav Gordon took the students up to the Catskills ostensibly for the summer, but at the end of that summer he announced he was keeping the *yeshivah* in Ellenville. Returning to Brooklyn only to pack up shop most of the fifty students at the *yeshivah* made the move with Rabbi Gordon. According to Winters, Rabbi Gordon was a world-renowned scholar of the analytical Lithuanian sort. A *talmid chacham* (talmudic scholar) of great depth and penetration, Rabbi Gordon had come to America with his family in the early thirties and had taught and served as a Rabbi in a few small congregations until he finally began the *yeshivah* in Brooklyn. Although he had learned some English along the way his classes were taught in Yiddish. He understood questions addressed to him in English but answered in Yiddish. On a one-to-one, Rabbi Gordon was willing to speak English. I was intrigued by the prospect of breaking the Talmudic code, of learning how to make an independent preparation of the esoteric page of the Gemara. Its highly condensed rhythmic reasoning, its cadence of question and answer, and enigmatic style, the careful cautious coddling reading of text, ever surprising, its tingling logic as it went about resolving apparent contradictions. Rabbi Gordon had been a contemporary of Henry Austryn Wolfson, and although they went their separate paths, Wolfson on to Harvard, and Rabbi Gordon to Brownsville and then Ellenville, they maintained a correspondence. Later, I was to hear in the *yeshivah* that the *mashgiach* (kashrut or student supervisor), Rav Lehman, was critical of Rav Gordon's relationship with Wolfson. If light years apart in Weltanschauung there were many shared sensitivities and experiences, including a continuing awe for the Talmud, though Rav Gordon held its authority to be binding and Wolfson brilliant but less than binding. Winters had a copy of Wolfson's 'Cresca's Critique of Aristotle' autographed and dedicated to Rabbi Gordon which Winters had borrowed. Each time Winters went to return it Gordon said there was no real hurry.

In the Talmudic method of text study, the starting point is the principle that any text that is deemed worthy of serious study must be assumed to have been written with such care and precision that every term, expression, generalization or exception is significant, not so much for what it states as for what it implies. The contents of ideas as well as the diction and phraseology in which they are clothed are to enter into the reasoning. This method is characteristic of the Tannaitic interpretation of the Bible from the earliest times; the belief in the divine origin of the Bible was sufficient justification for attaching importance to its external forms of expression. The same method was followed later by the Amoraim in their interpretation of the Mishnah and by their successors in the interpretation of the Talmud, and it continued to be applied to the later forms of rabbinic literature. Serious students themselves, accustomed to a rigid form of logical reasoning and to the usage of precise forms of expression, the Talmudic trained scholars attributed the same quality of precision and exactness to any authorative work, be it of divine origin or the product of the human mind. Their attitude toward the written word of any kind is like that of the jurist toward the external phrasing of statutes and laws, and perhaps also, in some respect, like that of the latest kind of historical and literary criticism which applies the method of psycho-analysis to the study of texts. This attitude toward texts had its necessary concomitant in what may again be called the Talmudic hypothetico-deductive method of text interpretation. Confronted with statement on any subject, the Talmud student will proceed to raise a series of questions before he satisfies himself of having understood its full meaning. If the statement is not clear enough, he will ask, "What does the author intend to say here? If it is too obvious he will again ask, "It is too plain, why then expressly say it" If it is a statement of fact or of a concrete instance, he will then ask, "What underlying principle does it involve?" If it is broad generalization, he will want to know exactly how much it is to include; and if it is an exception to the general rule, he will want to know how much it is to exclude. He will furthermore want to know all the circumstances under which a certain statement is true, and what qualifications are permissible. Statements apparently contradictory to each other will be reconciled by the discovery of some subtle distinction, and statements apparently irrelevant to each other will be subtly analyzed into their ultimate elements and shown to contain some common underlying principle. The harmonization of apparent contradictions and the inter-linking of apparent irrelevancies are two characteristic features of the Talmudic method of text study. And similarly every other phenomenon about the text becomes a matter of investigation. Why does the author use one word rather than another? What need was there for the mentioning of a specific instance as an illustration? Do certain authorities differ or not? If they do, why do they differ? All these are legitimate questions for the Talmudic student of texts. And any attempt to answer these questions calls for ingenuity and skill, the power of analysis and association, and the ability to set up hypotheses – and all these must be bolstered up by a wealth of accurate information and the use of good judgment. No limitation is set upon any subject; problems run into one another; they become intricate and interwoven, one throwing light upon the other. And there is a logic underlying this method of reasoning. It is the very same kind of logic which underlies any sort of scientific research, and by which one is enabled to form hypotheses, to test them and to formulate general laws. The Talmudic student approaches the study of texts in the same manner as the scientist approaches the study of nature. Just as the scientist proceeds on the assumption that there is a uniformity and continuity in nature so the Talmudic student proceeds on the assumption that there is a uniformity and continuity in human reasoning. Now this method of text interpretation is sometimes derogatorily referred to as Talmudic quibbling or pilpul. In truth, it is nothing but the application of the scientific method to the study of the texts.

- Crescas' Critique of Aristotle – Harry A. Wolfson

      Discussing the possibility of my going to Ellenville for the study of Talmud, Marty said that he once met a girl in Rockaway that hailed from the Bronx but he never followed up to visit her. There was nothing in the world worth going north of 42nd Street for, at any time. Anything beyond 42nd Street that wasn't available below 42nd Street was meaningless. I should ask the *yeshivah* to send me a correspondence course. Bam said it didn't make sense to miss so many games at the schoolyard, besides which his parents told him that they had checked out all that religious stuff and it was superstition. I asked him how he could be sure, he said he had faith. Besides which those pious tzaddikim in the Holocaust hadn't come off any better than anyone else. Tony said it was a splendid idea to know one's tradition from inside especially such a serious tradition of learning. If he were me he would do it.

Mom said it was a wonderful thing to learn about our religion— didn't so many people testify to the wisdom of the rabbis. Besides which, maybe I would decide to become a rabbi. It was fine with her. Dad said all those observances and studies took someone out of the mainstream and real success was in mastering how to move through the rapids of the mainstream; I would be going in reverse and carrying extra baggage to boot. As for being a rabbi, it wasn't a job for a Jewish boy. It wasn't what he had worked for and planned for. I tried to explain that I had no plan to become a rabbi. I was interested in "learning how to learn." The Talmud was the central opus of traditional Jewish literature. According to Winters it unlocked the great mysteries of life and our survival as Jews. The little I had learned was intriguing and studying the studiers they came across as impressive. I was interested in getting a handle on the methodology and technique and exploring some of those mysteries.

While I wasn't from the ranks of the *daveners*, I had my stand–in wailing walls: Those conjuring and crying places where I could peel the various layers of the onion of self, tearing apart the tiers, loosening tears as they brimmed and surfaced. So more than once upon a time, embarking seaward like Melville using his meager allowance for heading to the sea instead of buying a new coat, I too was sea bound, adding to and catching the spray of all those salty collected tears of countless bygone criers. Autumn and winter as well, I walked those deserted beaches especially at night, the ocean's pulsing incessance, the pumping pulmonary of the universe. Systolic and diastolic waves of crescendoing echoes, the tides without, mimicking the rhythmic tides within. Later at the *yeshivah* I was to hear Rav Gordon, quote from the mystical tradition that described the heaving and swelling of the waves as the pining reach of earthly waters to re-unite with the heavenly waters of the firmament from which they'd been sundered at Creation.

Or how many times of a late night in the Brownsville years wrestling with that doppelganger *dybbuk* who regularly grabbed me, held me in check, when loosening his grip a bit, I ascended the steps of our apartment house to the roof, praying for full release, and have him, that shadowy intruder rejoin the Wicked Witch of the West or any such nonesuch nefarious philistine furies yahoos and munchkins. And while the city streets lacked the soothing incessance of the sea, those streets yet had a resonating quirky syncopated pulse all their own. At times riveting in its kaleidoscopic shifting of intricacies, the turning traffic-charged swishing changes of neighborhoods. All those houses, apartment houses, four-family houses, tenebrous tenements all thick with people in contained motion. Countless vehicles, numbered each, by digit and state, mostly New York, — cars trucks, buses, cabs, mostly parked at that hour, but still late night traffic intermittently sluicing, zigzagging through the slotted black tarred streets. Coming and going to and from destinations where the other had been and exited. Betwixt and between all that brick and mortar weighted with life, reluctantly reassuring in its teeming and regenerating abundance, its colossal complexity, always that stirring sameness and separateness, the touching persistence and resistance of about to—never to—endless happenings of those myriad lives, loves, stories, games and dramas. Daytime, the hydra headed tenements and apartment houses–popping out from those windows, one by one, women's heads, men's heads, children's heads. In and out. At that hour the black and quiet blanketing of the mostly closed windows. Brooklyn's grand Punch and Judy show of the apartment houses was still. How many dreams, schemes, and disappointments. All those individual stories, ongoing critical, not so critical masses. All that one by oneness. Togetherness. Alongsideness. One by oneness.

Quickly I learned, and knew just where our turf ended. Where a white boy could or could not walk; North of Eastern Parkway going up Howard Avenue into Bed-Stuy or going east and north into Brownsville was off bounds. Where a Jewboy could not walk, Rockaway Fulton or Redhook or Canarsie. Those sons of Garibaldi and Parnell were no philosemites. Though I was blond and blue-eyed, the consummate Marrano, and Tony— if not hereditarily afflicted with being Semitic then physiognomically, symptomatically—he, Marty and Bam were more vulnerable. As patriotic Marrano I would not walk there if they could not. Uncles Uncas and Leatherstocking had taught me to put my ear to the sidewalk. You had to know the sounds and scents of that brick and concrete bush. Where the dangers lurked, where the beasts of prey gathered and ran. Finnegan and his seven brothers held that the family that preys together stays together. Jungle creatures had their law. Sometimes I fancied myself a Mowgli, and I would learn animal language, befriend them. Only then to think better of it. On the applied level that was Dad's thesis. What grabbed me more was the why—why was it like that? For them, I would always be different. Sometimes for me too. Was it just because that's the way it was for them? At the *yeshivah* they had their case for the why. Perhaps it was time to learn my language. Who were the founding Fathers? My founding Fathers? Webster, Franklin, Jefferson, Madison or Abraham, Isaac and Jacob:

a) Some of the above. b) All of the above. c) None of the above.

Which language was my language? Do you remember? Yes, I remember. Remember then, dearie, your soul is much older than mine. That lovely spring day, when Pat McQaude and I out walking in the open market place, down on Delancey Street weaving in and out of the festive carnival atmosphere of street stalls, shops, and pushcarts and one hawker had asked seven bucks for the colored beads and she had whispered to me "Let's Jew him down." Hey there! Look, Mom, I'm a verb! In the Oxford dictionary as well. Does it follow then, that if burglars shouldn't burglarize, that men should not womanize? Poetry and games are rooted in first–lived–days and first–sounded words the utter magical discovery of thingness, of becoming, those early wondrous sounds and words suffused with music. That melody haunts and lingers throughout one's life. Touching, and being touched by the heroics, the epical unfolding of one's larger than life, life. Partaking as it does then of foreverness and then with time, years, collapsing into fleetingness.

Mr. Barzun was on the ball when he noted if you want to understand America you must understand baseball. And if I was not a favorite son neither of the Wasp majority nor of that substantial if secondarily dominant, minority of Vatican loyalists, perhaps I was nevertheless an equal devotee — heir to Abner Doubleday. Didn't Benny, Bam, Jackie Rosen and I hit, run, and field with the best of them? Or was I merely an adopted son, no rightful heir to the nuances and subtleties of drag bunting, hook sliding, double plays, hitting behind the runner? Was that not my idiom as well? What odds would Nick the Greek give, or Moish the bookmaker at the poolroom on Saratoga and Livonia? Was it odd of G-d to choose the Jews? Not so odd, as they chose G-d; and thus to be at odds with all. The Idiom and the Oddity.

As had become his habit, on my visits this past year, Dad took Teddy out to the back yard to play catch. Teddy's neatly cropped green-grassed little league stadium in Hewlett had equidistant foul lines, with a perfectly centered center field. Whereas the PS 189 schoolyard, the court and foul lines, were quirky, unpredictable, full of obstacles. Teddy played hardball on soft grass courts. We played softball on concrete courts. Alvin Granatstein's mother critiqued, the nomenclature, when Alvin — hit in the head by a line drive off third base, unconscious — was taken to Beth El hospital with a concussion. "So just explain me so how come they call it a softball? Some softball." And if Robinson, Snider and Reese played on grass, then that was part of the Elysian fields and Zeus was on third and Apollo was pitching and H.M. Stephens was serving nectar, ambrosia in celestial chalices as preamble to the Messianic game of games. Perhaps our shorter mound, and bases, the bouncing on the concrete made up for some of the difference. Untold breaks, wounds and scars from running, sliding and colliding on that concrete. Hadn't Benny torn up his leg sliding on that concrete, changing the course of his history. As for G-d, He played hardball on concrete.

So what would it have been like if Musial, Marion and Slaughter and the rest of the Cardinals did not bring to mind the St. Louis the Struma and the Exodus? Or Finnegan and Blair, on Legion Street, hitting for distance two sewers, while bringing up "Jewish vermin" from that St. Louis hailing poet's poison pen. So let's us verbs verbalize To Jew or not to Jew, that is the question. Whether 'tis nobler...what is the *gematria* (numerical value) of noble? Of odd? And if it's "not so odd because they chose G-d"— maybe that's it! They volunteered. "They", not me. I never enlisted for that stiff-necked commando corps of the spirit that though dispersed throughout the lands of their exile, had infiltrated behind those enemy lines to scan and search that terrain for lost nuggets of truth. Those who despised us called us the conscience of the world. Yet, Winters claimed that, recognized or not, with or without awareness, that soul coded message of Sinai is inborn, a part of a Jew's systemic essence, of his/her innate inherent being. Tradition had it that the soul was taught Torah before it came to the world, and made to forget it the last moment to allow for challenge. Why then learn it in the first place? Because re-learning would always be recall, a déjà vu of the soul! So even if I hadn't volunteered for that expeditionary force, yet each dip of the bucket into that well of words of my unconscious was to draw and drink from those secret reminiscences, draughts of deep dark long-stored thoughts and phrases. Though I often tipped the pail and spilled those well-drawn waters, such was that invitation to quench my thirst to articulate my very me-ness as individual yet through the traditional tongue of our People. But if such was the language of self-actualization, only through verbalizing that Jewishness, my Jewishness, could I, would I actually still be me. So Pat was right, only by verbalizing the Jewish me could I be – to Jew or not to Jew. Not unlike the love-hate relationship of the *maskil* (proponent of enlightenment) who claimed that the halachasists had tied G-d up in phylacteries and fringes, I felt constrained. Given those givens, their givens, on their court, they claimed to have circumcised Sisyphus and circumscribed Odysseus even as he came careening around third base dashing so longingly for home plate. Was I though in a giving mood, mode? Was I not one of the T-shirt breed? Accustomed to running unencumbered with the wind! Not tied down by *tzitzis*. In a storm one rolls up the sails. And so I had to sort out their givens, my givens, givings and misgivings.

❑ ❑

When I visited Uncle Sid in Mt. Sinai Hospital he gave me another set of keys and asked me to organize closing up his atelier over the Mermaid's Tale. Looking at him was sad. Our own Dorian Gray finally done in. Short of breath, he had to rest from speaking every few minutes. Even from within the oxygen tent, it was still hard for him to breathe and talk. He whispered instructions, how to distribute the contents of his hideaway. Cousin Gregory was out in California and Roberta, was out of contact, last heard of studying ballet in Paris. Benny was off on one of his trips. A few years back, Sid had given me a set of keys to the atelier in exchange for attending to arrange a cleaning woman and handyman when necessary. When I commented on his magnanimity, Marty said, as usual, Sid got the better of the deal. Business was going down at the Mermaid's Tale. Sharing the atelier had been an incentive to come and bring some customers along. Most of the furnishings were to go to Sid's sister in Huntington, Long Island. A number of items were to go to Sid's office at the factory in Greenpoint, and when properly laundered to come home.

Tony was to arrange a moving truck with his uncle Augie, but there was a foul-up in their scheduling and the only vehicle available that day was Augie's Merry-Go-Round truck. The caged-in mobile mini whip which, from spring through fall toured Bensonhurst, Crown Heights, East Flatbush and Brownsville, belting out its canned hurdy-gurdy arrival as kids from around the block with nickels in their hands for their rides quickly gathered and lined up curbside. Marty, Bam, Tony, his cousins Don and Johnny and us, we carried down the couch, easy chairs, tables, lamps and kitchen furniture. When the place was about half empty, a certain sadness descended upon me. While I had used the place now and then, and that was always with a feeling of a kind of disloyalty to Dad—a kind of de facto acceptance of the atelier—yet had not Dad himself had his brand of spiritual peccadilloes in relation to his father? If Dad had kept some, or most man-man virtues, even if not as *mitzvah*, then most man-G-d rituals had been dropped. Here they were Sid's props, the miscellaneous appurtenances of an impertinent life. An extended celebration of applied chutzpah. A mutant Semitic hybris, indigenous to the goldene medinah. How much longer had it taken to gather all these furnishings than to dispose of them? All those hours of hosting and boasting—evaporated, presto! Winters quoted the Chofetz Chaim saying that everyone thought there was a club called *Chevrah Shtarber*—Society of Mortals—and every one of us felt that he himself had never taken out membership, never applied or filled out those forms, so surely he was never enrolled. Like maybe I am immortal. Everyone else joined that club but not me. Especially when looking at that three-by-five foot color photo of a grinning Sid with his players at the Mermaid's Tale's girls' softball team out in Alley Pond Park, more somatic than semitic. I, like Sid, had never chalked in for that "*Chevrah Shtarber*" team. Satyric and satiric that swaggering daguerreotype jarringly illusorily out of sync. Leo-the-Lip-Metternich might have agreed, "Baseball was in fact war by other means." If not sanctity, then at least a touch of muscular dignity adhered to the authentic reaching, stretching, contesting, jousting confrontations. Foxholes and dugouts were for men. Women weren't for fighting on either field. And here and there a Marrano surfaced from that underground dugout.

Driving through the streets with our load of Sid's furnishings, Tony put on the hurdy-gurdy recorder with some of the children's songs. "Oh dear what can the matter be." At the traffic lights a few times kids ran after us waving nickels. Monday we moved the stuff, Sid died on Thursday. Burgalizing, womanizing? Subject and predicate. But why predicate? Or maybe like the lady in Show Boat said, "Fish gotta swim birds gotta fly." So too we verbs had to verbalize. And maybe just like I didn't have to go through any bureau-cratic rigmarole or hazing process to join the fraternity of the *Chevrah Shtarber*, though skipping that procedure I already had and have full privileges of complete member-ship. Pre-awarded, free of charge, ipso facto, right of birth, right to join that Abrahamic commando corps as well. Without even having chalked in, I had been assigned an apriori priority.

❑ ❑

Like bookends; two funerals bordering either side of my first stay at the *yeshivah*, Sid and Miriam. Sid's funeral was scheduled to go out of the I.J. Morris Funeral Parlor on Church Avenue near Rockaway Parkway. Francine, picking up her black veil, dabbing at her eyes with her handkerchief, looked really broken. Gregory had come in the day before when things had turned really grim. Family, friends, men and women milled around Francine and Gregory. No one talked about Roberta. It seemed that no one really knew her whereabouts. Mom sat with Francine and held her as she sobbed. I kept picturing, sensing, feeling Sid's smiling wheeling and dealing presence. Even after seeing him at the hospital that continuing irrepressibility recommended he would bounce back. Iron man of *chutzpah* it was hard to reconcile with the inert Sid lying in the coffin. But even Lou Gherig fell.

"The regular rabbi, Rabbi Korn, is on vacation so Rabbi Goodman the assistant rabbi will officiate," came the explanation from Sid's cousin Laura. Second-string ser-vices for second-string biographies. Tangibly antiseptic the arrogance at funeral parlors, perfuming their personnel with a kind of formaldehyde-fixed complacency. Like for you plebeians death is a mystery, for us we have mastered it, tamed it, turned it into a science, a business. Just before the eulogy, I came across pinch-hit Rabbi Goodman in the men's room combing his hair, and straightening his tie and jacket. He studied himself in the mirror, and some notes from his pocket, produced a small bottle from his pocket, took two swigs, gargled energetically and emptied his mouth into the sink. He re-studied himself in the mirror, looked again at his notes and exited to the chapel. Goodman droned on about Sid's loyalty to his family and friends. Twice he called him Seymour. At the conclusion, Goodman stood and waited silently like he was expecting a rebuttal from the crowd. But only some loud crying, mostly from Francine, perhaps crying at the very discrepancy between Goodman's description and the reality she knew. I knew I would miss Sid. There was a grace to that energy and presence, that ongoing chutzpah/performance, stage front, before the klieg lights of life. If signifying nothing it had sound and fury.

Snaking through the city traffic, the funeral procession with head lights on. Red lights were for the merely living, death had its privileges. We drove out to the Montefiore cemetery in Long Island. Cemeteries, with their neatly laid out streets and signs, like toy towns. Missing only a little train. Perhaps it will yet come round the bend, shortly. Little white street signs with black lettering. Mount Sinai Street, Jerusalem Street, Jericho Place. Neatly planned, arranged patterns of interspersing roads servicing those yet vertical, crisscrossing the grey stone and white marble monuments of the indigenous horizontal. Patches of green at the edges, a tranquil eye pleasing setting. An architectural plan for dealing with death. All rather pastoral and orderly, under control—pleasantly freed of the stuffy, haughty officiousness of the funeral parlor people.

It was windy and the forty to fifty people, most with their collars up, gathering around the gaping hole. The tugging gravity of it all bunching, huddling, and I wondered—do we mourn more for the deceased, or more for our now increased sense of imminence of our own mortality? Standing, closely as people do at funerals, like we are all in it together against the enemy, death. Upright monuments for former players, like levers in the tabletop soccer game; today's players still upright with our lever monuments down, soon we will be down and our lever monuments will come up. No new strategy emerged from the huddle for righting already fallen players. Buck-toothed Harvey Lifschitz, Sid's vocal agnostic second cousin, and our family dentist, pulled me over to the side. He had meant to call me, he would have to cancel next week's appointment as he was going in for a hernia operation. Finding a tall monument, he leaned me back, and asked me to open my mouth, pulling out a pen flashlight he checked my teeth. You see it's like this Dr. Harvey—I have got this enormous cavity in my soul and every time I bite into life I get this throbbing truth-ache! Within a minute we were back in the somber huddle. Watching Dad choke back his sobs, a cry welled up in me. If this were a play or a serial movie, we could have a sequel. Like it only looked like it was all over. But. But—He as Producer of Producers had dictated an end that actually ended. Still, a few times I pictured Sid jumping up from the coffin and smiling and saying, "Didn't really think this was it did you?" The wind blew harder, pinning, wrapping people's coats against them. Like the wind was trying to fell them, us, the last of the standing in this field of the fallen. So hugging to the gravitas of this game.

Yisgadal veyiskadash, Gregory struggling with the jagged words of the Kaddish. Stumbling and bumbling the words from the transliterated text in the little crumpled booklet that had been handed to him. Slick and glistening the well-molded battleship grey metallic-looking coffin swaying in its double cinch as the hoist lifted that steely casket moving it into place over the gaping grave. And instead I saw Sid's glisteninig grey Caddy on that hoist like at a garage, or on a high pedestal at a car show, Sid as driver, propped up at the wheel all fitted out for his last drive, front and back blinkers flashing, radio blaring "Home, Home on the Range." Slowly rotating up there on high, the brilliant simonized sheen; hanging over the grave the glistening grey turning to a lovely grey-blue against the Long Island sky, the silvery gleam of the chrome, the brilliant white of the white-walled tires against their black, the thickly upholstered, richly appointed coupe de ville so majestically, glimmering, spinning then lowering down, down into the gaping pit. All those power turns on those road-hugging thick grooved tires, how warily perning on a gyre. Down, down into the grave. The metallic clang of the first shovelfuls of earth hitting roof and hood. Had they found Sid's last will and testament, that's the way he would have wanted it. *Yisgadal ve Yiskadash sh'mei rabbo.*

BOOK TWO
The Oddity

"How odd of G-d to choose the Jews."

William Norman Ewer 1924

"Not so odd, they chose G-d."

(possibly Leon Roth 1954)

Once upon a time The Paradise Lodge in Ellenville, spread over ten acres, was a summer haven for hundreds of hot and harried Jewish middle and upper middle-class city dwellers. Laboriously, they climbed the Wurtsboro Hills in overstuffed, overheating cars, desperately seeking respite for themselves and their children from the torrid summer pavements of the city. Servicing the carriage trade were the Concord, Grossingers, Nevele and a few others. The hoi polloi visited the tens of ungraded hotels and bungalow colonies that mushroomed each season, many of them disappearing from year to year. New ones appeared with the coming of each new season, old ones with new hats.

Paradise Lodge, high up on a hill at the top of a winding gravel driveway, sprawling ramshackle buildings with turrets and towers appearing haphazardly, as if a down-on-his-luck feudal lord had started to slap together a low budget summer palace, and gotten stuck along the way. Then subsequent in-receivership owners had completed various stages ad libbing and innovating along the way. By turns, aristocratic, pompous, heimishe, jovial, seedy, and spooky. Like the design had been made by a team made up of Frank Lloyd Wright, Charles Adams, Norman Rockwell, Molly Gertrude Berg and the editorial board of Mad magazine. When said seedy duke had gone bankrupt, and the cut rate castle had bounced around between some mortgage companies and banks, along came Sammy and his partner Dr. Seidel and their mostly Yiddish speaking consortium of Catskill people, maitre d's, cooks, waiters, musicians, comedians, impersonators, magicians. Many had come from the old country and banded together, pooled their resources, scrounged from moonlighting, borrowing, foraging, all to plunge in to the financial swim and make good the great dream of the Goldene Medina. Sammy knew the borscht belt scene well from his hotel hopping performances. Long after his first makeshift guerilla textile operation and partnership with Uncle Sid later in the Greenpoint factory, Sammy continued to dabble, with and without Sid, in property in the city and the mountains. A well thought of GP in the Catskills circuit, Seidel seemed also to have a veterinarian's skill for picking up symptoms of that ongoing epidemic of hoof and mouth disease that regularly afflicted the Catskill hotel flock. As if a vigilante band of outraged angels annually exacted retribution for all those summer holiday excesses of eating and cavorting, all that dancing in abandon, all that Bacchian imbibing. In seraphic anger then they inflicted that Catskill plague, ever afflicting those hill-dwelling hotel flocks. By mid-winter a dwindling population, felled by that recurrent foot and mouth plague.

By summer season old and new brash upstarts scrambling to begin. Despite parched liquidities and dried up overdrafts, despite the endemic economic epidemics of these mountain breeds, each year with its new bankruptcies, still there would be new buyers. Sammy and Seidel and their group picked up properties each winter and sold some of them off each summer. The Paradise Lodge had been bought by the group and then

Sammy and Seidel had bought out their partners. Rav Gordon, the *Rosh Yeshivah* of the Beis Chaim Yeshivah was once a Slabodka classmate of Seidel. Seidel had then become somewhat of a free-thinker. And Rav Gordon had decided to move the Yeshivah Beis Chaim from the Brownsville section of Brooklyn up to the mountains, Reb Shimshon approached Sammy who in turn spoke to Dr. Seidel and they were receptive to giving the premises free of charge to the *yeshivah*, for two years. And so in early September of 1951, shortly before Bobby Thompson's home run, on a late Sunday afternoon, while one long line of cars uniformly creeping like colored metallic ants, winding down from the hills towards the city, like towards some crumbs at the bottom, jamming up at the George Washington Bridge, across that lane, going up towards the mountains, in an all but free from traffic lane, a beat up wheezing bus with forty or so American born *yeshivah bachurim* heading to Ellenville to convert a casino into a beis medrash. There to listen to Yiddish lectures in Talmud from a Slabodka trained Talmudic scholar. By now the use of the facilities – initially assigned for two years had stretched to five. By the time I arrived, there were one hundred and fifty students at the *yeshivah*. It was 9:30 pm on a Thursday night when I jumped off my hitched ride on the main road, and made my way up the gravel driveway towards the main building. Voices from the beis medrash indicated the place was alive with activity. Opening the back door, I saw guys sitting at tables strewn with books. Big books, little books, old books with taped spines and new ones with colorful covers and gold lettering. Shelves mostly filled, but dozens and dozens of books, black, red, brown, green strewn over the tables and *shtenders* (lecterns). Some guys were dressed in suits and jackets, others in shirtsleeves, mostly white. Looking around that once-was-casino, filled with budding scholars, studying, concentrating, discussing, hollering, arguing, I wondered how the blazes could one think amidst all that din. What the devil was I doing here? High up on a promontory, this outpost like that Greek Isle of Mount Athos, exclusively for males. So here I was transported, exiled to this distant retreat of bespectacled ectomorphs. An occasional loose endomorph, decidedly less mesomorphs. Of a moment rising from their seats, donning their hats and jackets for the ten o'clock Maariv prayers. I wondered whether or not I could hold out for that month that I had dedicated for reconnaissance. Me, of the T-shirt credo, a devout practicing mesomorph. I remembered Winters' prep-pep-talk about the oral law as the key, the legend, to read the map of Judaism. Standing at that back door during *Maariv*, it was hard to get into the prayer. Like they swam naturally as I still splashed clumsily about. Haltingly self-consciously, I read some of the prayer. After the twenty minute *Maariv* service I was approached by one of the natives. He gladhanded me and said *"Shalom Aleichem."*

"Take me to your leader" I replied.

"Huhm... 'Leider', Yossi Leider he went home for Shabbos, he wasn't..."

"No, your leader, your Chief Rabbi, the dean."

"Oh, the *Rosh Yeshivah* – Rav Gordon. He's not here now. He will be here tomorrow morning for *davening*. He came in from the city and *davened Maariv* there. You don't know me. My name's Pinny Goodkin - guys call me Goody. What's your name? You need a bed? Or if you want I could walk you over to the *Rosh Yeshivah*'s home a little later or we could wait until tomorrow morning. Rav Gordon is home now. He learns until late at night. What about something to eat? I'll set it up. Would you like a salami sandwich? Or chicken? Or maybe *milchik* (dairy) altogether? Then I could go get the key to the canteen from Kalman Dorfman. Where are you from? Where do you learn. What..."

Goody's questions came in clusters and he did not stop for answers.

"I'll bet you are real tired. Maybe you just want to get to sleep? Or maybe some chocolate chip cookies I got from home yesterday? With milk or coffee? Who sent you here? Which *shiur* do you think you'll go into?"

"Steve Bloom, yes. Tomorrow! Yes. Fine. *Milchik*. Brooklyn. Didn't. Ad hoc. Rabbi Winters. Yes. Not yet. Yes, thank you. Coffee. Winters. Don't know."

The chocolate chip cookies were good. The coffee, lousy. Goody found Kalman the keeper of the keys and I was shown to a dormitory room. There were three beds. The room was plain almost bare except for some bookshelves and a wood closet. Neither of the other two occupants was around. They were either in the *beis medrash* learning or out. I left my stuff in the room and went out wandering a bit in the hall. I found a creaking staircase that wound its way up to a solitary attic–like room in one of the turrets. A bare, blindingly high watt incandescent bulb over–lit the room, which contained one table and two chairs. Ernest's—"A Clean Well Lit Place." was too lit. What does one need more? I had my copy of Yeats' Collected Poems with me and began thumbing through those lines. "I leave both faith and pride to young upstanding men, climbing the mountainside, ...now shall I make my soul compelling it to study in a learned school till the wreck of my body." I dozed and read and dozed and read until about 3 a.m. Finding my way back to the/my room, one of the occupants was there sleeping with the light out. The other two beds were empty. I went to sleep with my clothes on. In what seemed like minutes I was awakened to the *yeshivah* version of the town crier, the booming base voice of Chesky Schwartz marching down the low ceilinged corridor and screaming, "*Shtey uff! Shtey uff! Avoidos HaBoreh!*" "Wake up, wake up to serve the Creator!" That meant it was time to daven *Shacharis*, the morning prayer. It was actually only 7:00 a.m. and prayers began at 7:30, yet I felt like it was the middle of the night.

Though I had been outfitted with a pair of *tefillin* (by Rabbi Winters) and had donned them a few times, I was still a novice at that winding and unwinding. The *beis medrash* seemed to be about two thirds full when I got down there at 7:25. Now again almost all wore hats and jackets. Like as if after closing hours dozens of those suits from the high hanging racks in Louis Klugman's warehouse factory had come alive once more climbed down and sprouted bodies, some to learn and all to daven, those bodies disappearing, hiding out between *davening* times until the gong whence these yeshivishe part-Cinderella part genies hastened back to their racks and stacks disappearing bodies only to start again after closing time tomorrow. I would have to keep an ear peeled for that gong. Meeting with Rav Gordon was intriguing and disappointing. His English was sparse, my Yiddish worse. But the brilliantly clear blue eyes riveted me and there was warmth and humor at the corners of his eyes and lips. He read the letter Winters had given me and said, "You're learning about *yiush* from a ting what you losing without it having a *siman* and you learn about Abaye and Rava and if it's called still *yiush* ven you don't know you losing it — but if you know then you yes be *meyaesh* cos you got no *siman* and what dats called?"

"*Yiush shelo midaas.*" Potential despair of finding as if I would know I would surely despair of retrieving it.

"*Zeir gut* (very good), Yisroel. So one *talmid chacham* is saying that when someone is seeing so much books and is so much to learn so maybe you giving up hope you *meyaesh* from learning all dos books, so he's saying such a kind of *yiush* is coming from *Shelo Midaas*, only because he is not knowing that when you're learning is then coming the knowing, the understanding, first a little bit and then a little bit more. Like they are saying in the Gemara about Rabbi Akiva who he's being an *am ha'aretz* (ignorant person) until he is forty and then he is seeing water what is dripping on a rock and he is saying if the water what is so soft is making a hole in the rock what is so hard so by me the heart is soft and the Torah she is like fire so is then for sure she's going inside dat heart. So you, Yisroel, you only twenty years old, that's right so you can still be a big *talmid chacham*."

So I had a nineteen-and-a-half-year jump on Rabbi Akiva. But meanwhile, tutors had to be arranged for me. Since the *yeshivah* presumed that any student attending could make his own basic preparation of a folio page of the terse text of the *Gemara*—a *laines* or *laining* as they called it—then the classes, *shiurim*, were geared to closer readings of text focusing on subtleties, inferences weighing, challenging the defensibility of alternative interpretations. Using medieval and later commentaries for analyzing diction and syntax considering, measuring implications and their extensions. To begin, the *rebbi* would cite the seeming difficulties and throw it open for discussion proceeding to poke holes, shoot down some or all of the interpretations suggested by students, after which he would present his interpretation. Students would then have a go at the *rebbi's* rendition. Concepts and structure had to be consistent throughout the Talmud, semantically, logically, conceptually. Differences that arose in application of principles required resolutions. Preparation and usually review for the shiur were done with a fellow student, a *chavrusa*, (from the root form '*chaver*' meaning friend) a buddy system for safety sake when swimming in the sea of the Talmud. The vast and deep sea of the Talmud while thematically chartered by axioms, postulates and overarching concepts yet unmarked by punctuation. Each go at the text one must re-do the rhythm, emphasis, message. And like Rav Gordon was quoted as saying, "Life is unpunctuated. That is our job to supply the punctuation." The higher the *shiur* the more sophisticated the preparation that was expected. While I had a taste of some *Gemara* with those hours with Winters, now the half-hinting esoteric granite blocks of unpunctuated words towered above me and all around me. Before, I had passed quickly overhead as a tourist on a sightseeing flight, the landscape below looked at turns interesting, varied and attractive. If yet remote. Now I was stumbling on that hilly unpaved ground caught in a maze of boulders and mountains without a map. I was in need of a guide. A stranger, alone, lost, surrounded by natives. These Sherpa *yeshivah bachurim* had grown up on this rocky terrain. Generations of them had climbed the unpunctuated, tricky, unmarked trails. They knew the secret paths and spots. A few ad hoc tutor guides were organized to help prime me for the lowest shiur. Bachurim in Rabbi Gordon junior's shiur were fresh out of high school and on the average two and a half years younger than me. Even then, I needed priming to help keep up with the text. When I got past the words, the condensed rhythmic style of the Gemara had a fascination. Every implication had to be accounted for. No exhibition games. Everything went on record. A kind of tight, pulsating logical poetry. But the words were like cubes of ice, those Aramaic words, and they would not melt on my tongue.

Minchah was at 3 p.m. and *Maariv* at 10 p.m. One could fulfill one's obligation to *daven* by praying alone, but *davening* with a *minyan* was preferable; carried along by the energy of the *minyan*, the individual's prayers had added intensity, import, value. Rav Gordon, the *Rosh Yeshivah* was a product of the Slabodka Yeshivah in Europe. The *mashgiach* was from the Mir Yeshivah. They differed on certain areas of emphasis and approach. Rav Gordon allowed for a tacit dispensation for *bachurim* who learned late at night not to appear for *Shacharis*. Once the floodgates were open though, some late non–learners swept through as well. This amnesty policy was much to the chagrin of the *mashgiach* Rav Lehman. Performance, punctuality, excellence, in personal traits and general conduct and in service of G-d—all that was under the general purview of the *mashgiach*, the dean of men, Rav Lehman—though a scholar in his own right his renown was for his *tzidkus*, his saintliness and *avoda* (worship).

Rav Gordon was a recognized scholar of depth, an old-timer from the dwindling list of the long ball–four hundred hitters of that earlier pre-holocaust epoch that had great scholars in little *yeshivahs* or small pulpits in towns sprinkled around Lithuania, Latvia, Poland. The mavens agreed Rav Gordon was an MVP candidate, an unheralded winner, destined to be enshrined in that Cooperstown of *talmidei chachamin* in the sky. The Mash, as some people referred to the mashgiach, Rav Lehman, was a flawless infielder stopping hot grounders and carefully making the right plays with sober judgment and dedicated consistency, a competent 275 hitter. Breaking no records, yet by dint of an utter and overall perseverance for so many years and contests establishing a special reputation and name, his niche in the Torah world. Back in Brownsville about 8 or 9 years ago some *bachurim* in a moment of irreverence, had dubbed the sixty-five-year-old Rav Lehman, "The Shadow." Some identified the designation with Rav Lehman's recurring use of the term "like a passing shadow" from the *piyut* (liturgical verse) which referred to our physical existence as fleeting and insubstantial. Others noted the quiet softshoed–gumshoed private-eye appearances and disappearances he made onto and away from the scene of his surveillance. Still others pointed to his thinness, so thin he doesn't "cast a shadow" in fact, like a shadow, he cast no shadow. Still others pointed to his ethereal habits. As *baal avodah* (intense spiritual devotee) and ethicist par excellence, he was dedicated to an ever continuing fluoroscoping of soul and examining every seeming achievement for its potentially self-serving motivation. Even in learning. Whereas Rav Gordon applauded such achievements, the positive far outweighing any possible ego flaws, as such applause was necessary to churn the engines of creativity still he welcomed the Mash's critical persona and critique as it expanded, invigorated the debate and did prod for self-awareness.

The Mash's thinness, his meager diet and his black-garbed figure, all came together in 'The Shadow' and all agreed, that "The Shadow knows the evil that lurked in the hearts of men." While the stockier Rav Gordon also wore a black Prince Albert, yet even at seventy-five, he was full of verve and his blue eyes darted, laughed and sparkled as he sprang more than walked in conversation as well. The mashgiach walked slowly laboriously as if burdened down by humankind's personal and collective vulnerabilities, which had done us in so often in the past, and would likely do so in the future as well.

Aesthetic creative, engagement in Talmudic study lit up the *Rosh Yeshivah*'s eyes and there was a contagion to that intellectual-cum-theological exhilaration. While perforce he valued and shared the soul longings of the mashgiach's striving for personal and spiritual excellence, but the Rosh was somewhere on the continuum between hopeful and confident that through immersion in learning, "the rest" would one day fall into place. And he was cautiously skeptical of that "rest" that seemed to fall into place prior to in-depth scholarship, its quality and its longevity. However objective ideals and goals should be, yet our only avenue of access is through the subjective, trickily, walking, balancing across those high strung tight-ropes that connect me to they to It thrilling at all the scenic wonders en route. Along that climb there would always be basic *halachah*, shared and binding all, and the shifting sliding dimensions of add-on levels as one grew. Yesterday's option could become today's obligation. Such was the particularity on the commons of the contest for growth for a Torah Jew. It seemed to work for them and they seemed to work for it. Meanwhile I was still unemployed. Perhaps chronically unemploy-able.

Laibel Bronstein was one of the *elterer bachurim* (senior students), he was a budding 300 hitter in learning. A close disciple of the *Rosh Yeshivah*, Laibel was unhappy with the *mashgiach's* style and the heaviness of his lectures on *mussar* (ethics.) Frequently, after cataloging a list of difficulties of how personalities in the Torah (according to Torah description) on such high levels, could yet have erred so greatly, the *mashgiach* would resolve it with a sweeping — "*dos is der mentsch*", such is a man. Though the Talmud cautioned us to read any such shortcomings through the lens of traditional Talmudic interpretation yet on some level some shortcoming was at hand. Laibel was happier with the zing and blitz of the *Rosh Yeshivah's* resolutions of textual and conceptual problematics, and he enjoyed telling the story of one *yeshivah* where the stress was on *mussar*. The disciples there worked on themselves to continuously recognize and internalize that each and every one of them is a nothing; only G-d is Something, constantly rewilling all that is into existence, us included. "*Ich bin a gornisht*" (I am a nothing), was credo, mantra, anthem to be regularly repeated. One day a new disciple appeared and within a day he was mimicking the credo, "*Ich bin a gornisht.*" One veteran long time disciple responded, "*Kook ver maint az ehr is shein ah gornisht*," (Look who thinks he's already a nobody!)

The *Rosh Yeshivah* was of the *gadlos ha'adam* school; those who saw the greatness and reveled in the splendor and power of man's imagination and creativity. Each and every *bochur* inherently had that potential. If *mussar* and *gadlos ha'adom* each had a certain truth to them, yet the emphasis significantly shaped different personalities. Within the objective halachic perimeters, there were subjective choices. The same *mitzvahs* applied to all Jews in all ages yet different problems required different areas of stress. Life was not static, events and situations were constantly changing. The difference between the halachic Jew and the non-*halachic* Jew was not whether or not there would be change, it was how that change and what change could and should take place. *Halachasists*, proceeded from the assumption that the Torah contained the necessary resources to deal with each new exigency, from within that infrastructure the internal formulae prescribing a range of options, proscribing others. One does not have to step outside the halachic grid to respond, to innovate – but authority and range were crucial prerequisites. Only through rabbinic tradition could the range of possible valid applications be accessed. All possible halachic responses were potentially there in fact, built into that Sinaitic text waiting, ready to be deciphered to emerge at the right moment through the right application of that preciously protected core code. The continuing halachic discussion was a revolution from within, not from without; creativity— chiddush, the new innovative insight, came through delicate cerebral readings of complex postulates, excruciatingly careful juggling and balancing with newborn variables with the other hand. The non-halachasist does not grant that mystical axiom that all the resources lie within the normative tradition. As much as he might value the insights and sensitivities literarily, sentimentally, perforce he steps outside the grid to seek relief. That was/is/will be all the difference in the world. As contentious as the debates might be within the beis medrash of the Jewish people, yet they took place within that transcendentally time extended beis medrash. *Chidush* was rooted and enfranchised through this very Talmudic core. That 'democracy of the dead' was in fact applied; every Jew that lived voted and his ballots still counted. The Mussar movement, even according to its critics was a response from within. Chassidism even according to its critics was again a response from within. *Shinui* was a break from past, dabbling nostalgically, sporadically, selectively. *Haskalah* (enlightenment), came from without. Winters liked the analogy of the pitcher taking the sign throwing the ball towards the plate and as the ball reaches the batter's box, the batter throws down his bat, catches the ball and begins running across the infield, the outfield, in a broken field run. Interesting maneuver, wrong game. He has options, that batter: to bunt, go for the long ball, place his hit, hit behind the runner, wait the pitcher out. But one of the options is not to throw down the bat, catch the ball and run across the field in a broken field run. Wrong game.

Leibel Bronstein translated some of the *Rosh Yeshivah*'s Friday night Chumash classes for me. Pinny Goodkin, who found me as a foundling *am ha'aretz* on the *yeshivah*'s doorstep, took responsibility for translating the *mashgiach's shmooze* (inspirational and instructional talk by *mashgiach*) for me.

One of my roommates was Pinnie Meltzer. Pinnie's folks ran a men's hat shop, first in Brownsville and then in Crown Heights. Blacks, *yeshivah bachurim*, and old men wore hats. Pinnie was the family agent–outlet in the Catskills. With his return from the city now, the room was piled with boxes of felt hats, mostly black fedoras with some grey, brown and dark blues as well. At this season he still had straw hats as well. He also carried a small inventory of socks and ties. My father did not own a hat. Grandpa Bloom had one. When I studied with Winters I donned a *yarmulke*, but then like in the old days at the Talmud Torah classes in the basement at Stalin's *Shul*, as child Marrano I whipped it off as I hit the street. Here, for learning time, which was most of the day *bachurim* went about in *yarmulkes* and shirtsleeves. For davening, most donned hats and jackets. While according to some views halachically it was sufficient to *daven* just with a *yarmulke*, and in shirtsleeves, in the world of the *yeshivah* it was accepted that the *davening* should be treated with more formality, another dimension of dignity. When one had an opportunity to speak to the King—the King of Kings—preparing oneself was in order, helping focus one's mind and heart. Hat and jacket were de rigueur. It was quoted that, learning is when G-d speaks to us, *davening* is when we speak to G-d.

Pinnie was "In *Shidduchim*." That meant he was dating. *Yeshivah bachurim* did not date socially, casually. When they were ready to play for keeps they began dating. Anyone who knew a guy or girl was a potential *shadchan*. Parents usually acted as screening agents to help sort out the different possibilities, sometimes to do interviewing. Most guys also took counsel with either the *Rosh Yeshivah* or the *mashgiach*. With all the screening, interviewing, counseling, bachurim and girls took their own decisions. Some guys and girls decided quickly. Others went out a lot, meeting many times and many candidates, before deciding. Being "In *Shidduchim*" meant driving into the city, usually Thursday night, and returning to the *yeshivah* some time Sunday. Out of town *bachurim* had no shortage of hospitality for their stays in the city. Upon his return Pinnie usually replenished his haberdashery stock. Clean shaven, a dapper dresser, Pinnie followed that school of thought that natty grooming contributed to a positive self-image and confidence. The *Mash* and his devotees critiqued this position as posturing, and over–indulgence cloaked as instructional. Defenders of "style" explained the necessity to pay a minimal tariff when trafficking through cultural borders. Limited and external prices to protect, sometimes even enhance inner realities.

Laibel Bronstein quoted another *mashgiach* who said. "In de Mir, if someone took a shave in the middle of the week they called him a –'*pootzer*." (poseur). For the very pious one arbiter of piety was a close–cut haircut. Sporting a "*chup*" (wave) was narcisstic. Though there were pictures of the *Rosh Yeshivah* as a young man with a "*chup*." Pinnie had a "*chup*." Goodkin had no "*chup*" Laibel had no "*chup*" but he was reported to have explained that he deplored going to the barber and it was just more efficient to get a very short haircut. He insisted that in Platonic terms—in that world of essences—he in fact had an essential "*chup*" and while, as such, it was not visible, he knew that the *mashgiach*, The Shadow, knew of that essential though invisible "*chup*" that Laibel's soul sported.

Pinnie sang a lot of Hebrew songs, melodies, *niggunim*, without words. Only a few of those songs and niggunim had I heard at Winters table. More than half of the guys left the *yeshivah* a few evenings a week for college courses at Wurtsborough College half an hour away at Middletown. For the most part they treated college like it was a trade school. *Parnassah* required some preparation. For intellectual stimulation, and instruction for life, the *yeshivah* was the place. Pinnie was studying accounting. Though I had been told that we had another roommate—Mottel Werner, I had begun to doubt whether or not it was true. Mottel was never there. Not when I went to sleep at 1:00 or 2:00a.m. or when I awoke in the morning with the robust call of the *"vekker"* (waker) at 7:00 a.m. Mottel had been pointed out to me as he stood in the front of the *beis medrash* swaying over his *shtender*. But for days at a time I didn't see him in the room. His head, the protruding forehead, though not really abnormally large in relation to his body, dominated that thin body. Not a body with a head, but rather a head with a body. Sharp features with large grey eyes under thick glasses he would be tuned out at the beginning of a conversation, like you hadn't quite caught his station, then gradually as words wafted up and back he would bring you into focus and his short haircut highlighted that head as mind. No frills. His big black *yarmulke* sat crown–like on that scalp, signaling a kind of coronation of mind over matter.

In the moving scale of *din* (core halachic obligations) and beyond *din*, (individualized reaching for extra spiritual excellence) stretching that common baseline to leapfrog to higher levels could at times risk distortions. Misapplying emphases was like leaving the cap of the Coke off overnight and the fizz went out. Those bubbling energies, resources had been better husbanded for propelling today's growth within *din*. Laibel Bronstein was impatient with the presumptuously pious. *Halachah* is *halachah*, increased *frumkeit*, self imposed, must come from inside out, suspect when it comes from the outside in. Mottel Werner passed muster even according to Laibel. There were others that didn't.

My first days in the *beis medrash* were like months. While I didn't catch it happening surely the clock on the wall had not just stopped, but regularly jumped backwards as well. Like fasting on Yom Kippur and constantly checking the clock that sneaked backwards between viewings. Standing there now at the door of that once-was-casino-now-*beis medrash* studying the studiers, observing the observant, watching these *bachurim* cogitate, contemplate, gesticulate, articulate, arbitrate, tracing conceptual and thematic markings that they'd been trained to pick up, to track the scent and sense of landmarks and footprints of earlier scholars that had traveled these paths, climbed these valleys up these hills and peaks. Deerslayer and Uncas. Natives these *bachurim* , they knew the terrain. Sherpa-*yeshivaleit*, (yeshiva folk) all steeped and nurtured in the law and morés of moving, climbing, negotiating, surviving, on these breathtaking craggy Talmudic ascents and inclines. They thrived in this heady altitude, on these tricky twisting icy slopes, fed and sustained on the rugged mountain fare. Thorny questions, and lofty concepts framed in jagged Aramaic phrases, fit comfortably into their mouths. They chewed and digested those words. They. Not me. I was an outsider. A pampered urban dude. These heights brought the blood to my head. Not a Torah head, with body as disciple, instructed and informed by that head, but rather a Greek kind of head with body as instructor-conductor. Look quickly there's a centaur in center, deploying soul in the service of body celebrating and rhapsodizing physical-cum-aesthetic existence as end all, be all. Play ball! It's game time! Always!

I didn't receive or ever learn the libretto for this *yeshivah* performance. Perhaps even if I had the correct libretto, might it be that these Talmudically cerebral shibboleths just weren't for the lisping likes of Yankee me. I would always be the American New World "*greener*" tongue tied at this Yiddish-American pageant, stranger on the scene. And if one day perhaps Gladys Gooding would yet belt out "Hatikvah" or "Shalom Aleichem" from that right field score board and Cal Abrams would make his second coming, and instead of taking their hats off, the players while standing at attention would don their caps like in *shul* or *yeshivah*. Till then? I was aware that these kosher Sherpas claimed that the soul of every Jew prior to birth was taught all these clever homilies and arcanely coded word games and braided dialectics, and at the moment of birth was made to forget it all. That allowed for challenge and accomplishment. But then why learn it to begin with? Always then the difference between learning for the first time or recall. A déjà vu of the Jewish soul. What my Sherpa *chavrusa* was saying then was that one had to climb Sinai not just because it was there, but because I was there. Maybe yes. Maybe no. But even so. Since then I had been to a lot of other places. To Babylon, Persia, Greece, Rome, Bialystok, and Brooklyn. Treblinka and Auschwitz as well. Meanwhile, here on Long Island I'd once again resumed commuting up and back to Babylon. There are no Pat answers. So listen here guys, en-route between Asia and Europe, between Europe and the US of A I learned some new games and other tricks. And it seems I forgot some old ones.

My *chavrusa* hadn't shown, and sitting there staring at the *Gemara* trying to decipher the next few lines of elliptic allusive text, the guys all around me, inside that *beis medrash*, inside that text, discussing it from within, arguing it from within, their intensity, their straining delight, the cacophony of that crescendoing din welded into a jeer and routed me from the beis medrash. If I got down to the road quickly and was lucky, I could get a hitch into town, where I could still catch another hitch or the last bus back to Port Authority. If I was lucky. Like I felt the pinging, stinging, flipping of mental metal coins raining in my head. Pelting down. Heads I go, tails I stay. Maybe centauraly, more accurately tails I go, heads I stay and that internal cerebral downpour grew to a rocking storm. And then I saw him, tall and lanky coming up the winding road with his suitcase on his right shoulder adjusting his slipping hat with his left hand even while holding a folded umbrella.

"Where you headed stranger?" I asked.

"I wish I knew."

"Looking for the *yeshivah*?" Me.

"Yes and no. Sort of like if you know what I mean, but I guess you don't," checking his watch as he spoke. "See, usually about this time Sunday night, 'yes,' before and after a lot of 'nos.' But then again back home its three hours earlier so I am not sure. And then again I am usually not sure." The tall lanky one.

"Home? From?"

"Well Buffalo by way of Los Angeles," rolling his eyes.

"That's the long route to the Catskills." Me.

"Now you tell me."

"Besides which nobody comes from Buffalo."

And together: "Look who thinks he's a nobody."

"Where did you hear that? Not in LA or Buffalo."

"Kansas! Believe it or not, Kansas. See, I was hitching and these *yeshivah bachurim* were headed back east from a wedding out west and all of a sudden..."

"The road is under construction and you get rerouted"— As I confirmed his confirmation.

"Right that's it! How d'you know? And there's this yellow brick road right there in the middle of that desert that intersects with US 1 and somehow runs through Sinai as well. Also through Pinsk and Minsk."

"To Delancey Street and Maxwell Street and fields of flowing amber."

"That's it, you got it. You've been on that road too, huh? My G-d what are the odds of making it to the finish? You know what I mean like I don't mean nothing by it but it was really kind of odd of G-d! There you go. I do. I mean, I did. So here I was hitching and cruising the USA in a spiffy new Chevrolet, checking the horizon, the side and back mirrors, for little old Lucille in her merry Oldsmobile, and suddenly there is this alternate route with signs and crews waving flags and flares. 'Road under Destruction use Alternate Route' and there is an old Hornet stuffed like that circus car with *yeshivah bachurim* spilling out the windows and rumble seat, coming cross-country from a *chasunah* out in LA and they say 'come on in, its crowded anyway...'"

"And what pray tell do you intend to ask of our residing Rosh–Wizard of Odds?"
Me.

"Well, a *bissele* (little) courage and a *shtickle* (piece of) brain" and here straightening up to his full length and height grabbing at his chest summoning every available particle of meaning and fervor, surging mightily through his body up to his eyes and bouncing out through his tremoring lips, "A *gutta hartz* (a good heart) ...and you think like the wonderful Wizard of Odds might he also maybe be a *shtickle shaddchan* on the side, like maybe he could arrange a date with Dorothy?" Folding down to his former posture.

"Ah, I can see it all now, set back then a few years since Judy sang 'Over the Rainbow' it happened in a good guy America when Ted Williams was off to war, Mickey Owens dropped the third strike. As far as the eye could see amidst oceans of waving amber fields of wheat, inside the white picket fence, up on the unroofed section of that cozy wrap around white porch, the loveliest doggone sukkah in the whole darned state of Kansas, topped with fresh cut stalks of wheat, set inside with candles so serenely lit and the aroma of home grown, home ground fresh baked braided challahs, family singing Shalom Aleichem to the tune of America the Beautiful, sitting at that splendidly set festive table, Dorothy in her Shabbos finery, fussing a bunch of spiffy cherubic kids to the elegantly set white clothed table and suddenly there's a harsh rap at the sukkah door, and three white hooded figures standing in the doorway and one white hooded little boy and the boy walks up to your seven-year-old Yankie and pokes him in the chest, 'Why did you kill Jesus Christ?' and Yankie runs to you crying saying 'Daddy I didn't do it. I don't even know who he is, Daddy I didn't do it. I don't even know who he is.' And they read you a proclamation from the State Department all stamped and embossed and official–like and it says that if those Semites of European origin were to want to get into the US of A today, they would not be allowed in as per American restrictive immigration quota policy, so that anyone that actually accidentally got in earlier, since they wouldn't get in today, obviously it was a mistake, therefore all such closet aliens should immediately report to the New York or Galveston docks where fleets of ships have been made available, sponsored by combined State Department effort and the largesse of the Ford Company, who in turn amassed additional magnanimous private contributions from the Kennedys and others, so that all such originally east european semitic (lower case as per mr. t. s. eliot) alien types will then board the ships and under the flagship St. Louis the deportees will return to the lands of their origin. The State Department apologizes for any inconvenience incurred, no surcharge will be levied on the deportees for their mistaken sojourn in the land of the free and the home of the brave... And after having handed over the writ, they are joined by ten others, and they quickly dismantle the white picket fence, slap together a makeshift crucifix on the lawn and ignite it." Me.

"What about Aunty Emma Lazarus and the 'teeming refuse' from your shores?" Him.

"She must go as well they say." Together.

"She's already gone." Him.

"Then there is no problem they pronounce." Me

"Yeah, and that very night all choked up with sobs we hoist the *sukkah* onto an uncovered wagon, bundle up all our worldly belongings, toss them aboard and map out our course, our route, calculating how to re-hook up with the Yellow Brick Road." Him, sobbingly.

"Yeah. And men, women and children are ordered to pin on yellow brick badges (some with smiling pictures of FDR reaffirming our faith and hope to actually re-hook up with that Yellow Brick Road) ...by the way, you come anonymously or with a name?" Me.

"One of each."

"The name?"

"Isadore Stanley Seymour Isaacson, and you?"

"Stephen Bloom, a lot of the guys here call me by my Hebrew name, 'Yisroel,'" stretching out my hand.

"In that case Isadore Stanley Seymour Isaacson – alias Yitzchak."

"Isadore Stanley Seymour Isaacson, 'Izzy' – is he or isn't he Yitzchak?" I asked as he checked his watch to determine.

"Can you imagine that? I got one first cousin named Gordon Bloom and a second cousin named Stephen Morton." Izzy.

"A second first cousin or a first second cousin?" Me.

Placed together in Rav Gordon's son's *shiur* for 17-18 year olds which was the lowest *shiur*, Izzy and I were the oldest in the *shiur* and became *chavrusas*. Dovid Oberstein from the *Rosh Yeshivah's shiur*, who hailed from Williamsburg, tutored us for an hour before the *shiur*. During that time slot others in the *shiur* made their peer level preparation of the text. Given their Jewish day school and high school backgrounds, their vocabulary level and basic familiarity with the highly condensed, syncopated rhythm of the dialectic of the Gemara, that training gave them a good shot at a reasonably defensible reading. The hours that Izzy and I went at it together sans tutor were tough; we stammered, stumbled, and tripped along the way. Like some esoteric poetry whose subject matter was the entire, raw amorphous mass of life, in all its glory and measure, in all its detailed mundaneness. The grand, the gritty, the grizzly and the grim. Taking it on in all its daunting specificity, the entirety, the *halachah* offered contours for shaping, forming, melding and molding the substance of all the maddening chaos into definition. Given that premise that man-man prescriptions even talmudically derived had their origin in the very same Source of Sources as the man-G-d rituals and commands, it followed then, that strumming the web at one end vibrated at the other, all strands connecting us with each other and to the Divine. As the fellow said, "If there is no G-d then everything is permitted." And only if He Is, then everything counts, all the nitty gritty, all the rabble, babble and rubble of, 'where all the ladders start in the foul rag and bone shop of the heart,' and, maybe that 'ladder' was Jacob's ladder, no timeouts, that clock continuously running.

Torts and damages though on one level defined, assigned and refined by designated criteria, tractates, all their own, yet they and that had to do with tzitzis with citrons and Shabbos on the Grand level, threading through syntax and diction, the cosmos. Only thus could the market place, the four-poster and the sanctuary all be invested with a shared sanctity, all creations of the Creator there for the reconnecting to the Source. Not just the elevated liturgy of Yom Kippur and the sublimity of the Temple, the high priest's service therein – thereat, but rather all moments of all days were integrally related in that cosmically inclusive quotidian linkage.

A Bauhaus school of applied theology: 'G-d is in the details.' The *midrash* (non halachic Tanaic commentary) had it that as an architect works from his plan, so the Torah was designed first and then later the world from that plan. No square-peg-round-hole-syndrome here. We, our environments, are designed to express that Law; the ever twisting and turning monkey-wrenching of freewill, crucial to that Law. The written-oral axis was to give man a platform for creativity to join in reapplying the living law on an ongoing basis to an ever changing world. A Reb Yaakov was quoted as saying, " At Sinai G-d might have frozen the permutations and possibilities of change in the world, then a document presented at a certain point in a certain place could be applicable for all times." Instead though, He formulated and gave a law – an ectoplasmic law that infinitely regenerates in tandem with this changing world, yet according to His plan which He shared with us. Applying hermeneutic criteria for juggling how, who, and where. One Rav Soloveitchik told of a traveler in a mountainous area, coming to a great ravine that was traversed by a small and elegant looking bridge. He was told that the bridge had been put together by a poet who had never studied engineering. The poet had taken it on as a hobby, collected the materials over a period of years and put up the bridge. Rav Soloveitchik said that he would pay as a tourist to come and view the bridge. However, he would be loath to cross that bridge in a vehicle with his family. How could he be sure that the poet took into consideration all of the concerns, of the elements, and stresses that engineers are trained and equipped to deal with? Halachasists are engineers of law, bridging between generations, trained from Sinai on, generation to generation certified engineers of *halachah* instructed and interned studied in the axioms and postulates as applied to life issues, those core elements of internal and external stress. Halachasists proceeding from the premise that the resources, the rules for extrapolating and applying those resources come from within the system hence they work from within from that all embracing halachic grid. Creativity meant most efficient and imaginative derivation, explication and application of those *Masoretic* principles... Tingeing the contingent with perpetuity capturing it all and coloring the chaos, the randomness, the ephemeral with a transcendent sense of continuity. Only thus does our matter, being really matter. "Oh dear what can the matter be."

Sometimes sitting across from Izzy for those *lainings*, (independent preparation of Talmudic text) was like cooking dehydrated soup. Wedges of raw words, dried, sliced and diced, bring your mind to a boil, now squeeze and cook those truncated terms and bit-phrases in their own juices, in your juices, then salt and spice with commentaries to bring out the flavors. Finally—mouthing, chewing, sucking, those succulent grainy Aramaic bitefulls.

Wordsworth and Coleridge were *chavrusas*. William set out to capture the magical that resides, yet hides in the natural. All the wonders we regularly ignore. Like that passage in the Talmud that cites the contradiction: One verse saying that the earth is the L-rd's, and the other saying that the earth has been given to man.

Resolution: Prior to reciting the blessing it is G-d's but after reciting the blessing, once identifying the Source of the experience, we are entitled to partake. Pleasure fuels the energy of consciousness. As means to end it means. We did not have to be fashioned in such a manner—such that our taste buds respond to the delicious juices of the peach. Everything might have tasted like castor oil. For nutrition to also provide pleasure is invite to plug into the Source of it all. We, the peach, the relationship.

If one hasn't seen the ocean in thirty days, one recites a blessing. If one has seen it within thirty days no blessing is recited. Thirty days is the cycle that allows for renewal. *Chodesh*, the Hebrew name for month, also means renewal. Perhaps that is why women are exempted from *mitzvahs* that are time linked. She has her inner clock, less in danger of being disconnected from the rhythm of life. While he is at risk to become abstracted, unmoored. Time-linked *mitzvahs* reconnect him to the rhythm of existence.

Wordsworth–like, then, the blessing gives us the heightened consciousness to experience and re-experience an act with an ever-awakening sense of freshness, focus.

On the other hand Izzy was Colerigean. For him, the fantastical was normative. Ghosts and angels, spooky and magical happenings, imaginings of the extraordinary, abounded and surrounded his consciousness. His studies at medical school had merely confirmed his fixing his tent in that twilight zone where consciousness and unconsciousness, where death and life co-mingled. Thematically Colerigean less Samuel Taylor's aloofness which the poet needed for coolly crafting the couplets and stanzas that so gallantly sought to contain and structure the frenzy and the gloom, whipping the fantastical into elegant diction and phrasing "best possible words in best possible order." Izzy actually lived the frenzy, the chaos, and the gloom. Hounded as we both were the entire route by the ever present yelping and barking of those so dogged "So Whats."

Was or wasn't this the best possible order for all those tumbling words of the lexicon of our lives? Like when the lights were dimmed the words of the dictionary sneaked off the pages to dance and sing, cavort up and down around the walls and ceilings, the floors of our habitats. Wasn't writing about catching, capturing the ever melting import before it flees. Sounds like falling snowflakes touching down on the frozen slides of pages. Like dear dead Dylan rushing to a table upstairs, his arms full of words hoping they would not "drop before I made it to the table."

Rav Gordon quoted the Medrash that Avraham had a brother-like status in some regards to the creation and the Creator, a loyaly and commitment born of core connection. And that same word "*Ach*" (brother) "*LeAchot*" (to sew) to stitch together the disparate parts of the cloth of the world to mend the rips and tears. Sew be it. Sew what!

"If it does not seem a moment's thought,

Our stitching and unstitching has been naught."

Adam's Curse – Yeats.

Marty often referred back to his expulsion from those afternoon would be Talmud Torah classes in the basement at Beth Asher. That fateful day, as usual, Porter had given his writing assignment, and fallen asleep at his desk. Marty stood up in the back of the room on his chipped, scrawl scarred blue and red doodle idling tattoo embossed desk, tottering and sounded the *shul* shofar, announcing he'd heard that Maimonides said that the shofar was intended to "awaken the sleeping from their slumber." After sounding the shofar, like the fellow in Arsenic and Old Lace, Marty screamed, "Charge!" The wobbly desk tumbled as Marty leaped to the floor and led the class out the door and up the rickety steps to the air and street. Recorded in the annals of Beth Asher as "The ascension and escape of the child Marranos."

When principal Peter Lorre had hissingly ejected Marty from the classes at the Talmud Torah the next day, Marty referred to that as his "unwilling suspension of disbelief." But, then again what's the difference he added, "dis-belief or dat-belief?" Ours was to contemplate and comment on the business of the day. After all is said and left undone Marty said, critiquing the Sunday morning games was really what it was all about. Performance was merely means to the end: Commentary. Games, politics, wars and loves all fell under that rubric. Shades of Adam D'Lisle. Meanwhile, back at the *yeshivah*-ranch, when Izzy and I got stuck on some particularly difficult text, most of the time we would try to piece and puzzle together the words and syntax with a dictionary. That failing, we asked someone to explain the text to us. Running through those super packed, unpunctuated lines, was a non-stop marathon. It just kept going, and going. Surely moments of charging exhilaration in the stretching of one's mind, but more of the exhaustion of frustration that came with running that endless track and not finding the finish line. When lost in that never ending maze, we'd droop and sag into conversation. About growing up in Chicago, moving to Buffalo, and going to school in Los Angeles. About guys and girls. About shortstops and mystics. About his great aunt Sara who told him it's okay if he wants to be a doctor but just that he should remember not to be a doctor like his socialist Uncle Max, the doctor who practiced in a black neighborhood in Chicago's South Side—"Some doctor that Max. All he does is cure people!" I told Izzy about Marty, Tony and Bam, about the hearse, about Sroly, about Mom and Dad, and Teddy. About Pat, and the others. Like sometimes happens with kindred souls you can go back and reminisce like you had actually been through it together. Generating, gerrymandering instantaneous nostalgia.

That posse of *yeshivah bachurim* that had picked Izzy up in Kansas had taken him to Chicago. He spent Shabbos with them and then a few weeks in a *yeshivah* there. After continuing back to Buffalo he returned to *yeshivah* in Chicago. Though he hailed from Chicago he never knew there was a Yeshiva there. They gave him the address of the *yeshivah* in Ellenville when he was heading back east.

"So then there I was sitting on the banks of the Niagara River looking out to Grand Island. And while part of the time I was minding the river and part of the time I was minding me, trying to figure out which was the me that was doing the minding and which was the mind; but then this image of Noah, not from the ark, at least not that ark, but Ararat yes, in that, that's what he, Noah, this more recent Noah, wanted to rename Grand Island as haven for the Jews. And he threw in some Indians as well, in as much as he was convinced they were the lost ten tribes—which I plumb forgot that we had twelve tribes to begin with so as we can go ahead and lose ten of them and still be left with something, and I get into thinking about this girl I met at a basketball game in LA and she came from Brownsville, Texas not Brooklyn, and upon being queried what's a nice Jewish girl doing coming from Texas, she explained that her grandfather had come from Russia through the Galveston Plan and wound up roaming the Texas grasslands and punching cows for a parnassah, until he finished veterinary school on the side. And meanwhile back at the ranch he'd gone vegetarian, 'cause he didn't have a local shochet. And he became this bovine-*maven* (expert) and she had this picture of this Yiddish speaking, Russian born, vegetarian-veterinarian astride his horse, wearing his ten gallon homburg—the grandfather not the horse—him all leathery yet properly Semitic and bespectacled—I never saw a cowboy with spectacles before—him toting a book and his satchel, clad in a white doctor's tunic—his cattle-*kittel* (white garment worn at specific liturgical recitations) over his de rigueur plaid flannel shirt, and deep inside my own skull, the heavy fog causing low visibility going both ways, and I say to myself since no one else was around, at least no visible tangible conversational type, I figured I ought to say it right then and there like I wasn't sure when I was leaving too, and then there would really be no one to talk to, so I ups and says –or more like asks—so like whose side are we really on? The cowboys or the Indians? Such and sundry ponderings on the ponderosa and the rabbi's sermon on Shabbos about the disappearing Jewish community like the Buffalos disappearing and like who are they? We? I? Such and sundry misty mystical ruminations, aurora borealisdik predicaments imbroglios and conundrums lighting and darkening the horizons and haze of introspection by turns gladdening and glooming—Joe Btfsplk-dik, hum and the drum, the Mundane, the Tuesdane, the Wednesdane, of my reveries which as it has been noted in my case were pretty fantastical to begin with. Lo and behold I get home and there's this flyer for a lecture course at the Buffalo Jewish Center generally attended by *bubbies* and *zaidies* and meanwhile me and this cantor's daughter show up for 'The History of the Jews and the Ten Lost Tribes' and I say 'Oh my goodness someone was listening' and so the Israelites they are finally there in Israel and after some tough goings on after a while they seem to be doing pretty hunky-dory, actually copacetic, and I get to relax and lean back and doze off a little bit, and then boom, slam, bang, I wake up there's a new doctor Savana, Penguin—Nebuchadnezzar zapping it to us and we are chucked out into the Diaspora which this Viennese thin maestro of a free thinker instructor pronounced die-a-spora—causing me to picture endless chains of spores appearing and re-appearing. And he each time he exhaled 'hex-isle' like the spooky Hex Island that undoubtedly must be the source of all this mischief, and I conjure up Pinocchio stopping at the Island of Pleasure and doing all kinds of misdoings and a few middle aged affluent classmates during the course of said course at their golf course having sized up my send-this-boy-to-camp-look sponsor me for half a scholarship and the cantor's daughter also to go to the Federation Community Camp Tel Aviv Tepee in the Catskills subtitled Albert and Pearl Roth Summer Retreat for Adolescents. Albert Roth having been a Buffalo Jew who went to New York and made it on Seventh Avenue as a tie tycoon, he liked to say 'tie-coon,' who donated and dedicated said premises on certain conditions: like that it be a classy operation and all the help, waiters, busboys and counselors, and maintenance people, cooks and life guards had to wear at all times on the camp grounds an Albert Roth neck tie. Bails and boxes of ties filled the warehouse and I went as boat boy to cover the second half of my keep, and she as a nursery assistant, and after duly checking their fleet of half submerged row boats, the moss overgrown with algae, from the stagnated receding pond, buzzing with multitudinous miscellaneous flies, gnats, fireflies, wasps, hornets, darning needles, like airborne articulating punctuation, dots, dashes, periods, commas, hyphens, diving, gliding, buzzing, hovering, flashing, zipping, and then sometimes in formation, straightening and dive bombing. And one of those chefs is this wizened old cook who had a habit and a penchant for pickling all perishables, anything that wasn't moving, so this ancient marinator with an Albert Roth around his neck, he grabs the lapels of my tee shirt, pouring forth his heart and soul tearfully declaring that he must confess that it is he that's at fault that the Tel Aviv Tepee Albert and Pearl Roth Adolescent Retreat fleet isn't seaworthy. Three years ago at the beginning of the second week in December he and Bonzai Bill, the then Japanese short-order cook had come up from the city to check the pipes at the camp as it was freezing cold and he and B.B. proceeded to have a go at some bottles of rye and gin, fire water and kickapoo juice, that were just hanging around with nothing to do. And things warmed up. And very shortly Bonzai Bill the short order cook and the wizened old ancient marinator, are in a slug out, and Bonzai Bill finds this shot gun and promptly begins blasting away and chasing the ancient marinator around the camp and the ancient marinator heads for the lake which Albert Roth had particularly dedicated in his wife Pearl's honor and Bonzai Bill, sho-gun with a shotgun in hot pursuit sprays the dock with buckshot punctuating one after another of the idle fleet. Since that fateful day at Pearl's Harbor, the Tel Aviv Tepee Albert Roth Adolescent Retreat Fleet has never been..."

"December 7th ?"

"December 7th: And me I'm impressed, inducted, conducted, depressed into kitchen duty as there is no fleet, like I hang my already tattered soul on a hook in the pantry and wade into that culinary cave sinking knee deep, stomping and sloshing, slurping, glops and blobs, dollops and globs, minced mush, and sautéed muck, steaming monster cauldrons, stirred by cackling witches, brewing tartar's noses and lips of Jews and I am mired in the sinking slop, while everyone out there in the sunlight is boy-girling away from here 'til doomsday which seems anyway to loom overhead eminently imminent. Then one day there's this basketball game against Camp Cobras and a warm up game with Rubenstein's Rip Van Winkle Bungalow Colony Cove Hideaway as they had this real nice basketball court with proper stands for spectators right out at the edge of the lake where both games would take place, and they schlepped (pulled) me out of the cave to see sunlight for the first time in weeks and it became immediately apparent to me that Plato's prisoners in the cave were kitchen help and when exhumed from that world of shadows the blinding light of day had one blinking away like Don Winslow flash-blinking a message out to good guys in distress at sea, and like he picked up my message or had one of his own up there in the stands, with a mirror flashing to me, jumping and screaming and flashing to the court, there he was, the Ancient Marinator with his Albert Roth around his neck, waving wildly, towels, aprons, and the mirror, signaling me that Bonzai Bill was at center for the Corregidor Cobras and this summer time summari running up and down the court barefoot elbowing, body blocking and chopping our guys bruising and grinning down the would-be referees into submission, one little nine-year-old kid with tortoise shell glasses, hands my team mate Ziggy Sigfreund a box of thumb tacks and whispers to him, "like in the Laurel and Hardy picture," and Ziggy proceeds to unobtrusively sprinkle the court with tacks and soon Bonzai Bill is screaming and jumping with one foot in his mouth and he hobbles off into the horizon where the rising sun has started to drop, and meanwhile I trip and come up like a voodoo pin cushion and the kid says, 'I guess the plan wasn't foolproof' and grins. And I'm not sure whether to take it personally and I hobble over to the canteen to get some band aids and mercurochrome and there is a girl named Faith Ginsberg in a long sleeved high necked blouse all intent and wrought up busy mending the wings of some injured low flying sparrow, and after flapping my arms and chirping "G-d Bless America," "Hava Nagillah," "Alexander's Ragtime Band," and "Over the Wild Blue Yonder," and closing with "Over the Rainbow" she finally took note. And as one thing did not lead to another so when she said she had to catch a row boat at the waterfront to cut back across the lake that divided the Rip van Winkle Cove from Gottlieb's Garden of Eden Grove where she, Faith Ginsberg stayed, and from where she'd come to view the game and found the wounded bird, and I self impressed myself into naughty-cal-galley service all wound up to row, row, row the boat not so gently down the stream and losing no time I proceeded to fumble around with the oars like they were greased and hot and they keep springing out of the oar locks and she ducks twice as I almost clobber her and all the while I am eye-balling this cozy sheltered alcove off this little sandbox of an island in the middle of the lake and suddenly she whips out this Hebrew text and starts reading out aloud about perfecting the soul and that being the ultimate purpose of human existence. And such and sundry metaphysical contemplations and recitations and the oars go heavy on me like there is a thickness in the air and I can't cut through the ether and things are spook*ifying* up by the minute like this chilly dusk closing in and despite the soupy cool I start to shvitz (sweat) and she trembles and closes her eyes ever so slightly and I am really fearing maybe I did really clobber her poor Faith with the oars..."

"Ah yes, the Fear and Trembling, the Ether-Oaring."

"Yeh that's it."

"And then we're finally rowing, cruising and going no place fast and I suddenly realize that we're parked on what must be a sandbar or just maybe Jonah-like on the dome of the Loch Ness Monster... And suddenly Faith stands up in the row boat and right there with the text in hand turns to me and says 'Get thee to a *yeshivah*' and jumps out of the boat and onto the water and proceeds to walk over the water as I go 'oops wrong text.'"

"The veritable leap of Faith." Me.

❏ ❏

Time was told in the *yeshivah* by tractates. "Shimmy came in *Kedushin*, Tully in *Bava Metzia*, both left in *Bava Kamma*." Days revolved around learning *sedarim* (dedicated learning times) and prayers. Weeks around Shabbos, months around the Holidays. Learning was a means to an end, but also an end in itself. Data and know-how were prerequisite for performing the *mitzvahs*. But quality and quantity of the *mitzvahs* merged through depth in level of learning. Always a stratification of performances—the informed act penetrated and vibrated more deeply and lastingly in the individual soul, in the cosmos. Echoes were absorbed by the person from the environment and by the environment from the individual. Learning was spiritually, not just intellectually edifying. Verses, words, and letters that connected the Jew to his essence, and the Essence of it all. So could this learning require and receive such devotional scrutiny. This was G-d's plan for the universe, and we were invited, privileged, required to study it. The very studying was then an act of personal, national, universal sanctification. The *Rosh Yeshivah*, Rav Gordon was of the Lithuanian analytical *iyun* (scrutiny) school. Some Talmudists held that covering ground and having range and scope was of greater urgency. While Rav Gordon personally had that scope and range, yet his teaching methodology emphasized the in-depth on the spot penetration of syntax, diction, and the rationale behind the nuances and concepts, beckoning, urging, however implicitly, that the very aesthetic of that exploration was spiritually elevating.

For hours, days, weeks, Izzy and I vacillated between frustration at our ineptness, and exhilarating delight when we got the pshat (straightforward understanding) . We hung high in vertical-vertigo-like limbo catching aerial views of the talmud-scape of a map on the page below, lost and looking for landmarks. Overwhelming, that commitment of time and concentration. Most guys seemed to handle it with a good-naturedly cadet officer kind of discipline. For some, secular books, even other than those for parnassah-preparation, music, from classical to jazz, sports, hobbies could fit, squeezed in as adjuncts, for Torah lives. Here too there was a split. One group for whom the secular was holiday, R&R, temporary respite from the ongoing battle to regroup and gain more ground for sanctity. Then there were those for whom the secular was ever eminently eligible and redeemable gradually to become sanctified. Olam shanah nefesh, place, time, people, an ideal configuration was mitzvah, less than that could be neutral or slip-slide to transgression. A third group held that the secular, anything other than Torah study, unless for a quantifiable practical reason was a waste of time. Some rabbis encouraged athletics for health reasons. Those that did, were usually wary of competitive sports. Science had its place as key to appreciating G-d's handiworks. Some held that classical commentaries long ago understood the text to mean that the Creator incrementally implemented His micromanaging the process of Creation. Other than man. This soul endowed creature signals a new chapter. Literature was suspect as its design and appeal were unabashedly heart-grabbing, hitting mind and gut simultaneously. That required being more vigilant. Such critique was invariably aesthetic rather than content concerned, focusing on manner not message. Like Mr. Goldwyn responded when chastised about the superficiality of his films, "If I want to send a message I'll use Western Union."

Tzaddikim-masmidim (righteous, diligent and devoted) like Laibel and Mottel had internalized the quest, the pursuit of knowing Torah as an all-encompassing passion. All else had been excluded by Mottel. Laibel was still ever-amused at submitting frozen slides of slices of life under the microscope of Talmud. Not merely for comic relief, but life was a tractate that needed *iyun*-analysis as well and required consistency with all other tractates. The world had its Cobbs, Ruths, DiMaggios, and Williams. But one could not plan an entire nation of three fifty hitters and sluggers. Winters and then Laibel had begun to show us chapter and verse re the complex steps, the syncopated rhythms of learning and doing, study and action, each player ideally finding his position.

Learning could work even for the apostate. Esthetically. True, few would be prepared to pay that price of discipline, of hours and energy required to achieve the skills and techniques even if the esthetic dividends were there to be reaped for believers and non-believers. Dr. Seidel, H.A.Wolfson, make room for Stephen Bloom. Possibly.

More than just bringing to the table another angle of perception, the *chavrusa* system also mitigated the loneliness and humiliation of not understanding. After you slip down one of those hazy craggy slopes of confusion, having someone dangle a rope to pull you back to relative safety was reassuring and tumbling together was still better than tumbling alone. Sudden flashes of comprehension, the thrilling blitz of insight came from either side of the table. Of course, more thrilling if I caught and pointed to the flash of lightening first. *Davening* was a more troubling, stunning anomaly—all together—yet all alone. Tying into a *minyan* allowed for plugging in to the energy of that *minyan*, that mystically enfranchised quorum to recite, receive, reveal sanctity. Activating that relationship with one's Maker was after all, in the final analysis an analysis of the Final; Laibel quoted the Baal ShemTov (founder of Chasidism 1698-1760) as saying just as we expect to see the drowning man waving his head and arms desperately for help and survival, so should we not be surprised to find he who is truly confronting his Creator, during that moment of actually connected prayer, that *davener* waving his arms and head as well. Could it be then that drowning was comparable to *Yiush shelo mida'as* sinking while unaware of that sinking, could there yet be a rope of hope or float for remedial swimmers. Anyone see the lifeguard?

Though an occasional heretic was caught by the thrills of the intellectual enterprise, it would probably not be accurate to say that non-believer and believer would have equal aesthetic dividends. Pungent, poignant, as insights might be, yet when they take on the dimensions of the Ultimate Plan of us all, and it all, then by definition there is another relationship to the glow and aura of those insights. Words read on the page echoed and reverberated back through the corridors of history and shot forward to that invisible future. "The seeing of the sounds."

But *davening* alone or perhaps even more so with a quorum, of earnest devotees, when one, you, I, all three of us, weren't sure of what we were sure of, that was a different fettle of kitsh. When I skipped the *minyan* I stumbled through an adumbrated version of the regular prayer, usually within the halachically allotted perimeters of minimal recitation and maximal time boundary allotted for the morning prayers. When I made the *minyan*, watching the guys around me, so seemingly connected, and communicating, my line frequently just didn't go through. Either I got a busy signal or no connection. Frequently on Torah reading days, like a young Kafka sitting in *shul* with his father, I hid in some corner hoping no one would call me for an *Aliyah* (calling to recite blessing at Torah reading.) Laibel and Winters both claimed that when you understood the text, the references, the symbols and allusions of the liturgy, then intellect and soul meet and soar hand in wing. That text organized by the men of the Great Assembly was a minimum and additional private prayers could, should, be inserted. Nevertheless I hadn't quite sorted out what it was I wanted to ask for. Perhaps I should ask to know what to ask. Until then, like the thirsty fellow who stopped his wagon on the road to ask how far ahead was the inn, "*der kretchma*" and upon being told of the great distance till reaching that inn, he replied "*Vas tut man biz zu de kretchma?*" (what does one do until the inn?) Izzy said you had to try it on for size to see if it fit, and even if it pinched for a while if it was fitted properly eventually the pinching was likely to go away. "If it was fitted properly." Meanwhile it pinched.

August that year just about coincided with the Hebrew month of Elul, the last month of the Jewish calendar. Elul was a period of intense preparation and soul searching, leading as it did to the High Holy Days - Rosh Hashanah and Yom Kippur. Beginning with the first of Elul the shofar was sounded daily at the conclusion of the morning prayers. Talmudists held that to one degree or another, people were somnambulists, sleepwalking their way through life. Full spiritual consciousness was at least unconsciously avoided and usually consciously. Consciousness meant confronting responsibilities. Shrill and piercing as it was that sounding of the shofar, it was intended to awaken us from slumber. Having slept through various "*vekkers*" rounds, I did in fact awaken a number of times to the sounds of those primordial blasts coming from the *beis medrash* at the end of the davening. The *mashgiach* who normally delivered once a week talks during the third Shabbos meal, *shalosh seudos*, Elul time he now spoke twice a week. Like contenders closing in on a pennant playoff, the electricity in the air built up as we neared Rosh Hashanah and Yom Kippur which would be World Series Time. The *mashgiach* was fond of quoting Napoleon's remark that only when he was awake was he Napoleon the Emperor, when he slept he was just another peasant. Sleepwalking through life was tantamount to dozing under the quilt of the unconscious.

Yeshivah tradition had many *bachurim* learning through the night Thursday nights—the *mishmar* (learning vigil). Friday was only half a day of learning to allow for getting ready for Shabbos, which preparations could, unlike the week's usual afternoon learning, be carried out while yet somewhat tired and sleepy. Shabbos would offer more resting time. Some fellows turned out Fridays for basketball or baseball games in the park nearby.

At 2 a.m. Thursday night Pinny Goodkin, Izzy, and Duvy Levenberg asked me to join them as they were driving out to pick up some goodies at the kosher bakery in the little mountain town of Ellenville. That bakery also baked for a number of small rooming houses and little hotels in the area. Roads were deserted at that late hour, the town was asleep. Pulling up in the back of the bakeshop we caught and were caught by the aromatic scents luring us to a scene of heated action. Pinny, Duvy and Goody led the way through the back door from the parking lot into the boiler room of a ship atmosphere of the baking area. Sweating, aproned, flour-coated, the baking crew scurrying about dropping trays, bending, lifting, seemed to take no notice of us. Eventually one tall stoker sidled over, acknowledged Pinny and Duvy and took our order. A selection of chocolate-covered layer cakes and some pareve whipped cream things were chosen. More than enough was purchased for the guys back in the *beis medrash*. After getting back to the *yeshivah* and eating too much of the cake, Pinny said that each week at this time he swore off the gooky stuff, vowing not to come back next week. By next week though he would be back. It did work like that. Duvy said the message was more potent than The Shadow's *mussar schmooze* (lecture urging spiritual self-inventory). Goody questioned whether we really got the message and if we did, would we have gotten it without The Shadow's *shmooze*? What is the measure of getting it? Doesn't coming back indicate that we didn't get it? Or, can one get it and still come back for more?

Friday afternoons at the basketball games guys played without keeping score. And when they kept score, they didn't have too much of an inclination or an urgency to win. Izzy and I played hard to win. At 6'2" he was three and a half inches taller than me and we shoved and elbowed more than a bit for position under the boards. One gentle-souled *bachur* named Shia Englehard from Indianapolis, shocked at the pushing and elbowing, expressed his dismay, and I countered with "What do you think this is, a game?" Izzy out jumped me under the boards for rebounds, though I pulled a few and he outshot me on the inside. On the outside I did a little better. More often we played opposite each other. On the average he won two games to one of mine. One time Mottel showed up and popped a series of line drive setshots. Housed as it was in the basement of a former bank building the low ceilinged gymnasium at the Brownsville Yeshivah where he had studied had defined for eternity unarched setshots for its *bachurim*. It was said you could always pick out those *bachurim* from that *yeshivah* years later even after they left and played in open-air courts they still shot their setshots on line drives. Sometimes we were able to get enough guys together for a softball game. But they played, short of gloves and fielders and without calling balls and strikes. Other times with twelve or thirteen guys on a team. "Aw it's a *chessed*. What difference does it make? Let them play." Again, winning was not a factor, clearly this was reformed softball, and I was strictly observant, with a low tolerance level for such disregard of halachic softball. My obligations to my softball heritage could not be fulfilled with playing with this mendacious *minyan*. I resented their casual, cavalier approach to the *mitzvah*, the *Shulchan Aruch* of the game.

Like at the Winters' household, at the *yeshivah* the pre-Shabbos preparations crescendoed into a frenzy as zero hour came closer. Cleaning rooms, grounds, polishing shoes, shaving, showering and putting on one's finest. One's special Shabbos suit and hat. Peculiar, all that sartorial manner and style at the *yeshivah* on this continent of continence.

But they were dressing for the Shabbos Queen, who was about to arrive. And she did arrive, amidst graceful regal song, festive dress and tastefully spread and set dining room tables. Even here in the *yeshivah*-austere dining room noticeably upgraded for the occasion—the Shabbos filled the space. There was learning on Shabbos, but a more relaxed kind of learning. Throughout the meals songs and rather spontaneous discussions of the weekly Torah reading portion. Usually beginning with a question, conceptual or textual about the parshah, followed by some classical or individually innovative interpretation to resolve the problem.

At Shabbos davening they sang some of the passages of the liturgy. And depending on who the *chazzan* was, it ranged from acceptable to very nice. Shabbos meals at the *yeshivah* were more festive and elaborate. They were interspersed with songs, a few of which I had heard at Winters' Shabbos table. Izzy and I began finding ourselves looking forward to Shabbos, a day of actual-factual-satisfactual resting. If it wasn't quite yet as the Talmud described, "A sample of the world to come," still, it was an interlude of tranquility. Multiple and complex as were the laws governing the Shabbos, they forged into a kind of intricately filigreed shield, protecting one's space and peace on that island called Shabbos, a la Swiss Family Robinson. Occasionally the Rosh or The Shadow joined the bachurim for a Shabbos meal. Rav Gordon did not sing much but he enjoyed and encouraged lively melodies. The Shadow had his short list of dirges that he sang / lamented.

Saturday nights were the loneliest nights in the week. Even if Marty hadn't mailed me that packet of pinups: "Just to remind you of what you're missing." I did not need his reminders. On the screen of my memory, at night especially flashes of past attractions, reruns. Girls. Plain girls become attractive, attractive girls became pretty, and pretty girls beautiful. Re-released through MGM—My–Good–Monkishness—as often in retrospect there had been a certain re-writing, revisionist history. But the Talmud claims that G-d had a formula: "I created the Id and the antidote to the Id: learning Torah." *Tavlin*–antidote, also means spice–guaranteeing, spicing, the taking of pleasure. More than just occupying the imagination was meant by this strategy. Under the laser beam of Talmudic dialectic, at that point touching the core of the psyche, where body and soul link, that was the point of purification. Selectivity could then be applied, in, when, where, and how to take pleasure. When halachic criteria determine the context of the partaking then the experience was not just a recess from productivity, but rather a celebrating of the bonding of body and soul, Creator and creature. And that halachic selectivity was bulwark against boredom, ennui, that otherwise pulling whirlpool of shifting thresholds. They had their plan. For many of them it had worked. I was heir to a line for whom it hadn't worked. Yet pulling far back enough in my lineage perhaps I was hybrid. Enough to urge the lingering suspicion that it could not be casually, cavalierly written off. But like the fellow said, "*Biz tzu de kretchma*," what does one drink?

Given that man is essentially a psychological rather than logical entity—there would then be a need for guiding him to focus. Prayer is that moment of focus—re-establishing the proper ratio between creature and Creator. In principle Yom Kippur, the Day of Atonement, should have preceded Rosh Hashanah, the Day of Judgment. Yet the converse is true. One possible understanding the inversion is that Rosh Hashanah, the day when we, as it were, coronate G-d as King of Kings, that being identical with His ultimate judgment, and His being Sole Judge. For Him to need my endorsement would be a contradiction in terms. Yet it required my exit from routine to come to terms with that ratio, that actual proportion of Creator to creature. If every day was World Series time, World Series time would not be World Series time. Confronting the implications of that Coronation can bring one to an awareness that prepares the petitioner to speak to G-d, entitling one to enter into that Cosmic Dialogue. Calculating, establishing that ratio of Creator to creature earns one the privilege of prayer. And that moment of prayer a potentially existential catapult to elevate those praying: Who is that /our Interlocutor? Until then the dialogue lacks integrity. Rosh Hashanah as the day of my coronating the Divinity, i.e. my coming to terms with His supremacy, must then precede Yom Kippur. Like concentric circles, following, flowing one from another, the first of Elul, Rosh Hashanah, Yom Kippur. The week between Rosh Hashanah and Yom Kippur added another section of the prayer – Selichos. It began with a Saturday night, long, long, recitation, continuing on a daily basis with a shorter version. That Saturday night the atmosphere tingled with urgency and anxiety–coming that much closer to the finish line.

Watching the guys sway, sing, cry and reach, I thought of that description of the drowning man. Three divisions seemed to emerge from the hundred and fifty or so *bachurim* in the *yeshivah*: 1) The largest group, cadet-like responsible, fulfilling their obligations according to the code. Not too over-wrought, but serious. Pinny was in that group: 2) A smaller group mostly The Shadow's guys in overdrive, gunning their consciousnesses and consciences to the floor of their hearts, as bodies waved and vibrated like so many *lulavim* (palm branches) 3) A group of less than fifteen or so, like Laibel, Duvy and probably Mottel. Each in his own personal way had internalized that injunction of *Ivdu es Hashem b'simcha*—serve G-d with joy—and it not only affected them, but it affected those in their environment, immediate and extended. Like they could not suppress a certain inner joy at the compliment at the Divine invitation to engage in Cosmic Dialogue. However intimidating, yet thrilling as well. Cadets of group one – plugged into a two-pronged source of inspiration and guidance, emanating equally from the *Rosh Yeshivah* and the *maschgiach* who stood respectively in the *mizrach* (east) of the *beis medrash*, one on either side of the *aron kodesh*. The second group taking their lead from the *mashgiach*, more piously anxious, plugged into the high voltage Elul-tension that the Shadow emitted. Group three – Laibel, Duvy, my guys, while taking more note than usual of the *mashgiach's* presence, still took their lead from the *Rosh Yeshivah*. He, who as a young man had caught flakes of snow on frozen slides and scrutinized them, ever marveling at their shapes and symmetry, so even today he caught Elul flakes to do the same. "My guys," even while I wondered whether their words were my words. Maybe I had no script to recite, I was merely a walk-on. Soon to walk off. Still if any were "my guys," they were. Izzy felt guilty at not being in step with the second pious-anxious group, I had no such misgivings. Selichos that first night lasted one-and-a-half hours. A long one-and-a-half hours. A very long one-and-a-half hours. Coming attractions of Rosh Hashanah and Yom Kippur. The onset of the liturgical angst that would be the High Holy Days. That was eleven months ago and some of it was still with me today. That *Selichos* night, I was a spectator. A weary spectator. Stoic that he was, Izzy related to his weariness as endurance test. Spiritual excellence lies at the other end of the gauntlet-rainbow. One who could make it through the weariness— or better still— just because of that weariness attained to the desired spirituality. He refused to come with me right after the *Selichos* that first Saturday night when I announced that I was going to hitch into the city and head straight to the schoolyard to catch the Sunday morning games. I explained that I needed a short holiday escape from *davening, Selichos* and the *shmoozim*. Three weeks had gone by since I last joined the guys at ye olde schoolyard. There wouldn't be that many more games this season. In the past I had never missed more than a week at a time, and that was rare. Up in my dormitory room, I packed a change of clothes, my glove, thought about my tefillin, yes – no, took them and headed for the road. While I wasn't really sorted out yet where I stood ultimately in relation to Sinai and tefillin, now at least, I was on the *yeshivah* roster, and as team member a certain amount of loyalty had begun to prevail. Even if, at the end of the day it might turn out to only be a chalk in choose up game, meanwhile I was chalked in. At 2 a.m. on that mountain road which led through Ellenville to Monticello, the darkness was all-enveloping. Night in the country was uncontested, tangible, all was darkness. No city lights did battle with that all pervasive darkness. In turn that made morning and daylight more precious in the country. Meantime, the white and light of the stars up on high burned more brightly in the deep velvety black of the country sky. Less than ten minutes after I hit the road Izzy came running down the gravel driveway carrying a bag, short of breath and stood alongside me. "Going somewhere fellah?"

"Kinda," as he bent down to roll up his pajama pants that hung out from below his suit pants and pointed to Orion in the sky and said, "Did you ever notice that he's not so much an archer as really more accurately and actually a short stop leaping high up over the runner sliding into second base, his arm cocked towards first, about to complete the celestial double play?" Izzy.

"Tinkers to Evers to Chance." Me

"Not sure what became of Tinkers and Evers but Frank Chance became a manager." Izzy.

A dated big Oldsmobile pulled up and Izzy recognized Cantor Shapiro from Buffalo.

"What took so long, we've been waiting here for seven minutes already?" Izzy stretching his arms out in bewilderment.

"What luck...New York?" Me.

"Or Providence?" Izzy pointing skyward.

"Naw, Providence is the other way, we're heading to New York City." Cantor Shapiro.

"Yeh, yeh. We want New York – 'New York, New York, the Bronx is up and the Battery is down.' " Me singing.

"From Tinkers to Evers to Chance, " Izzy continuing, "My Uncle Louis had this autographed picture of them doing a double play."

"You know, I had a *shul* member, Waldman, that was interned at Fort Ontario with the thousand Jews they had there during the war—big heroes the Americans, saving then locking up 1,000 Jews after they finally let them in. And then when they let them out Waldman picked Providence to live, based on advice from someone who claimed to have a third cousin that liked it. His wife always complained that her luck to have such a shlemeil for a husband that goes and picks the smallest state in the union. Eventually they came to live in Buffalo and joined our congregation." The Cantor.

That night Cantor Shapiro had led the Selichos services at the Cypress Hotel in Kiamesha Lake. Now, he was on his way to Brooklyn to spend the day with his mother before turning around and heading back to Buffalo. Rosh Hashanah and Yom Kippur he would be back at his post at the Ohel Sholom Synagogue in Buffalo where Izzy had been an occasional congregant. The Cantor's radio was broken but he happily offered to regale us with his renditions of Rosh Hashanah liturgy, since he did want to stay awake and rehearsals "never hurt the best of them you know! Even Rizzuto and Coleman go out for pre-game infield practice!" Shapiro.

"Double play?" Izzy

Now together, "You can tinker around forever but frankly it's all managed by chance, or, or!"

Or...again together "Providence!"

Shapiro began singing *U'Nesane Tokef.* (give Divine validation) "Some holiday from davening." I whispered to Izzy.

"Like Louis Pasteur once said, "Chance favors the prepared mind." Me.

"Did he really once say that?" Izzy.

"Could be, chances are more than once!" Me.

"Methinks if G-d told Abraham, his progeny would be like the stars, up there, that Milky Way, like then, maybe the Torah was supposed to be that ultimate pasteurizing process." Izzy

"Yeah, maybe that's where Borenstein got his celestial grazing herd, his holy Holsteins from. 'If cows could talk they would serve pasteurized milk in heaven.' Where-as like the Rosh explained, we are compared to the sand, the dust and the stars. On the one hand the sand is like the breakers against the waves, and those waves are the on-slaught of the nations. And also the sand no matter how much gets carted away from the beachfront, the beach remains. So the people of Israel no matter how much persecution, defection and assimilation the people remain. The dust? The more you tread upon it, the tougher it gets. So it came to be that we developed our inner resiliency to anti-Semitism. Despise it? Yes! Outlast it? Yes! Sand and dust are from the collective perspective whereas that Milky Way, all those stars says King David, 'He counts the stars and gives each one its name.' Of all the inventory in G-d's bag of tricks, why fix on that counting? You and I look at the stars and say so what difference can their number and names be, and who could count them to begin with, so like what would be already, if there are a hundred less or fifty more? Like so who cares? But aha, that's it, the giving of the name is the designation of its function, yet that Divine assignment of purpose has it that there really is a finite number, and if any one is missing in Creation, Creation is then lacking."

"Gottchya! Pasteurized yeh. Homogenized no," and we moo-ed together.

Cruising down Route 17 Cantor Shapiro sang (portions of High Holy Day liturgy) *U'Nesane Tokef* (giving validity) and *V'Chein Tein Pachdecha* (bestow fear of You). "I guess He does have a sense of humor up There," Izzy pointing to the sky.

I asked the cantor how he managed singing at the synagogue without driving. He answered that surrounded by the congregation, and standing up at the podium, was like driving. He continued with strains and sections of the *chazan's* rendition of *V'Chol Ma'aminim* (and all believe).

"How come you came along?" Me to Izzy.

"Well, I figured like this, half a day I would be worrying about what you're doing and when you're coming back. The other half a day I would be angry at myself for being worried.

So I might as well spend the whole day with you anyhow. Besides which, you're taking my *chavrusa* with you."

On the Palisades Parkway, a few miles north of the George Washington Bridge we got a flat tire. Cantor Shapiro pulled over to the side and jumped out. Holding a flashlight and rummaging through his trunk he announced that the jack was broken. "I wonder if there is a song for this situation?" Izzy turning to me.

We took turns with the flashlight trying to flag down a car. There wasn't much traffic at that hour and the few cars that were on the Palisades zoomed by without stopping. One car slowed down, looked us over, *yarmulkes* and *tzitzis*, and hollered, "Get a horse, Jew," and the guy alongside as they were screeching off, "Why don't you hop a train to Auschwitz!" and they sped off into the night. After about twenty minutes waiting on the road, which seemed much longer, two black guys pulled over and offered to assist. When Izzy and I fumbled around with the crossbar they laughed and said they would do it faster, Cantor Shapiro offered the bigger guy $5 but he refused to take it. After they put the spare tire on, the little guy came back and took the $5.

Now the sun was coming up and the still thick green foliage of the Palisades was unveiled. Spring and summer were green, plush, adolescent. Autumn would soon be varied, matured golds, oranges, reds and maroons, amber hued and rust-colored leaves, majestic, courtly, elegant. Over the George Washington bridge and across the Harlem River Drive down the FDR. Cantor Shapiro wanted to save the Brooklyn Battery Tunnel toll. Down the FDR until Houston Street, we pulled off, headed to Canal and over to the Manhattan Bridge. Flatbush Avenue and Brooklyn were quieter. This city was near asleep. Just around the Grand Army Plaza across from the Brooklyn Museum, Cantor Shapiro dropped us off. He would be heading on to Borough Park and we could catch the New Lots subway to Brownsville.

How many times had I gone through those high ceilinged corridors and display halls of the museum? First on school trips. Then on dates. With Pat. She liked the burnished glistening knights in armor. I told her the story of the four heroic soldiers lining up to become knighted by the Queen. Each of the first three bowed down ceremoniously on his knees, prostrating himself as the Queen dubbed each, one by one with a jeweled sword and pronounced his knighthood. When the fourth, who was a Jew, came forward prohibited by Jewish law from prostrating himself before a human being, he merely bowed from the waist. Turning to her advisor, the Queen asked, "Wherefore is this *knight* different from all the knights of the year?" Pat didn't laugh, she had never been to a Seder. She said that must have been a glorious period to have been alive with chivalry and all. Pat had studied some of the Chanson Digest celebrating the heroes of the crusades. I told her that we Jews hadn't come through too well during that period. Firstly, I would still opt for modern plumbing rather than go back then. Secondly her heroes had been some pretty nasty fellows. Good old Godfrey of Bouillon frequently extolled for his piety and simplicity, the hero of many of those Chanson Digest, upon capturing Jerusalem in 1098 filled the synagogues with Jews and burnt them all. Pat said she didn't believe it. We were one day to chase over to the Grand Army Plaza, library and find sources. Later she refused to accept those sources.

That was over two years ago. Tonight, down the steps to the tiled tunnels of the subway station, Eastern Parkway just a few subway stops till the elevated station at Sutter Avenue. Tunneling underground until that ascent out of the caverns of the earth, out into the air, the light, the world. As the subway train climbed its way out of the ground, up the tracks of the El line, always a palpable sense of relief and surging optimism as we churned up the trestle of those elevated tracks. Lincoln Terrace Park to our right and Brownsville to our left. Rutland Road to our right and Sutter Avenue to our left. The marquee of the Sutter Avenue Theater. Till morning all the bustle and tumult of the weekday-market-day shopping on Sutter Avenue would be stilled. Awakening, erupting, exploding again with each new onset of the sun.

Following the first exodus, for a time that was the Maginot Line. Streams of passengers exiting the trains formed two lines. Blacks exited to Sutter Avenue and whites to Rutland Road. Before the Maginot Line crumbled, how often had I stood at the foot of those long high steps on the East Flatbush side, with those lines of white believers, now mostly black climbing up to the pagoda topped temple tucked so neatly there on high. Climbing lines of believers, penances in hand ascending the long high stairs to the lotus leaf turnstiles, presided over by a solitary mendicant, quietly sequestered in his booth of ritual meditation. Pilgrims depositing their coin offerings, continuing up to the next level to await the roaring metallic dragon that would engorge them, and descend with them into the bowels of the earth in search of rumored and legendary treasures. For years, Dad lined up to go and come with the believers. Thoreau must have had the subway in mind, "The mass of men lead lives of quiet desperation."

Miles of El tracks snaking along that range between monotonous, mountainous canyons of apartment houses. From different spots and distances the harsh sounds of the El somewhat varied. At times more muffled, at times more strident. The clacking metal wheels screeching at track bends, grinding over those steel tracks, like a thousand rickety metal-wheeled rickshaws racing. From closer, the trembling glacial crash and shaking of the entire terrain, like everything was splitting asunder and the earth was about to swallow us all. Maybe, like Korach and his cohorts, we too had rebelled against Moses.

High up on those grime coated girders, those tracks making their grinding, careening way south and then east where East 98 and Kings Highway met. Roaring trains, gloom-casting tracks over the streets below. Locals, shopkeepers, pedestrians, residents forever in perpetual dusk of that all-pervasive gloom cloud. A community of Joe Btfsplks. People living and working under the El learned to scream loudly when those harsh tremors and cymbalistic thunder blasts filled the gullies of their streets. Some chose to swallow a bit and wait for the rushing deafening waves of noise to peak and pass overhead. Further north and west white armies were regrouping. Conquering black and Puerto Rican battalions were pressing from the east, south, and northeast in their continuing putsch. Retreat was either westward or far beyond the east borders of East New York to Queens and Long Island.

Where East Flatbush and Brownsville met—our triangular isthmus—an anomalous, free-trade zone geographically Brownsville, territorially a short stretch of lovingly kept, kempt two family houses bordered on one side by a few well tended elevator apartment houses and by a few walk up tenements that still had white and black tenants who had resided there for years, voiced and showed their caring about their neighborhood. A few blocks of cropped hedges and cared-for homes made one almost forget this was Brownsville. Dad said it was inevitable that our neutral status would fall. Mom said it was a convenient place to live and we were close to the Hebrew Home for the Aged where Grandpa Bloom was. Itzik Lipman still owned a number of the buildings on the block and he continued to exude unqualified optimism for the neighborhood's future. Mom was impressed. Dad said if Itzik's buildings were in Manhattan then his prognosis for Brownsville would be more credible. I still had easy access to the schoolyard where we had lived, ten blocks over, where I had begun my career. Stalin's *Shul* was across the street from the schoolyard.

We moved from the schoolyard block to the Linden – Saratoga Isthmus in 1947, the year that Jackie Robinson came up to the Dodgers. Itzik's Isthmus – as we called it, according to most wouldn't last. Four years later we moved to Lawrence. Around the time of that moving, a group of black homeowners from along the edge of the triangle came to petition to Reb Shimshon and others not to sell. It had been their intention to live in an integrated neighborhood, when they moved here. They too were escaping the war-torn black ghettoes of Bed-Stuy, East New York and East Brownsville. But that wasn't the common mood of the rest of that black migration. That invasion wanted the whites gone. Reb Shimshon was of a mind to hold out. Vladimovsky and Kaufman, after losing their bid for purchasing the Ambassador Theater on Livonia Avenue (which was just on the wrong side of the tracks), now wanted the *shul* for their Yiddish theater revival troupe. If anyway the building was falling into disuse, at least it should serve some purpose for the Jewish community. Reb Shimshon had a *halachic* opposition to the Yiddish theater. Besides the specific breaches of modesty in their performances, they were the epitome of cynicism, and anti-religiosity, *haskalah*. Other *baalei batim* told Vladimovsky and Kaufman that their plan could not work anyway. Just as there were no longer congregants to attend Beth Asher there would no longer be Jews for the Yiddish theater. Their rebuttal: A theater could be traveled to by car, people from outlying areas within short commutes could come to a theater. An Orthodox synagogue had to be walking distance for Shabbos. Beth Asher backed in and under the elevated tracks between Saratoga and Rockaway Avenue stations. Sometimes as the trains roared overhead the floor, the furnishings, trembled, scoring high on the Richter scale, as if the earth was in fact about to rip open. Perhaps it really would be prudent to finally decide whether we were with Moses or Korach.

It was said that Benny once hit a home run from Brooklyn to the Bronx: A towering high blast over the left center fence that entered the open window of a passing, speeding train heading from Brownsville towards Manhattan and the Bronx. Train stops notwithstanding, merely breath catching, final destination defined landing.

This Sunday as usual, the first official game in the schoolyard was scheduled for 9:00 a.m. but starting time was usually closer to 9:20. We had a few hours. I led Izzy across to the park and we hopped the fence and lay down in that caged in patch of grass. *Davening* was scheduled for 8:00 a.m 'til 8:40 at Stalin *Shul*. We would chalk in first, before we went across to *daven*. We slept for a while and were awakened by bugles and drums of a parade marching down Saratoga Avenue towards Linden Boulevard. Izzy turned his ear to the ground. "I left my stethoscope at home, but methinks I hear the enemy approaching!" It was an American Legion veterans of foreign wars parade, "Like the fella said 'I seen the enemy and he is us.' One day there might be a parade of veterans of local wars," I explained.

We chalked in on the first base line and headed across the infield, outfield, out the left field gate across the street, towards Stalin's *Shul*. Andrew and Sroly were pulling up in front of Beth Asher discharging dwarfs for the Sunday morning *minyan*. Along the street a few disemboweled couches and chairs, some guys with brooms would be sweeping the glass off the infield. Standing at home plate guys took turns fungoing balls out to the outfield. Weekdays and Shabbos Stalin *shul* had for years become a de facto relic, only Sunday mornings it came to life. Like Madame Tussaud's exhibits climbing from off their pedestals and from behind their glass enclosures to come down to daven; or Brigadoon–like hibernating in mist from Sunday to Sunday, but here these actors were not preserved in their youthful state. In just the three weeks that I had been away at the *yeshivah* Reb Shimshon had grown taller, gaunter, older than I remembered him. More Lincolnesque, but also more grey-white semitically Lincolnesque. Again, the penetrating look, that piercing gaze. *Halachic* protocol required delaying other than perfunctory greetings until after the morning prayer. Izzy had more practice with putting on *tefillin* for some years prior to coming to the *yeshivah*, but I had improved a bit these last weeks. Wrapping black straps and black boxes, tying mind, heart and action together. Head phylacteries four compartments four parchments; conceptually to consider perspectives, angles, views. Arm phylactery one compartment, one parchment, symbolizing action as a singularity, contained, defined by time and space.

In the *yeshivah* the guys *davened* slowly, here Reb Shimshon's dwarfs were on fast forward. Notwithstanding our joining this guerilla octogenarian *minyan* yet the musty, dusty atmosphere of the corridors and that weekday sanctuary were heavy with emptiness and aging. Back in the *yeshivah beis medrash* up in Ellenville, invariably by midday the tables were strewn with *seforim*. Big ones, dark ones, light ones, thick and thin ones. On a rotation basis each evening *bachurim* returned *seforim* to their shelves. Invigorating, that *yeshivishe* chaos. A kind of rhythmic clutter-to-order-ferment and around again, like an inseparable by-product of the creative process. At Beth Asher seforim thick with dust in their yellowing, browning, cracking disuse, saddeningly inert. Quickly the octogenarian dwarfs manned their regular positions. Every Sunday was Old Timers Day at Beth Asher. But not just a ceremonial game, but rather a game-game to be recorded by The Official Scorer, old timers *davening* counted. Inescapable the stabbing poignancy the absence of a farm system. No rookies coming up. A dwindling roster.

"For a long time you didn't being here." Grumpy, looking at me and continuing.

"When is not coming for a few weeks someone here, is probable for sure he's not coming no more. But you a young fellah so dat's being ah difference. You heard maybe dat Katz the president, he died? Believe me for such a funeral really true was not worth for him de trouble to bothering to die. His daughter didn't want for de rabbi to speak Yiddish and nobody is coming. Just one week later Levine is dying and was a *za* (such) nice crowd, it was coming a lot from his family and real old timers still around from Flatbush and Queens and Canarsie for him—a lot from people dey coming and the Rav speaking for everyone to cry."

Along the walls, white marbled tablets with inscribed epitaphs dedicated by and for former congregants and families. Tiny bulbs, unlit, on the large bronze *yahrzeit* (anniversary of departure of kin) memorial plaque with the slim black plaques noting dates of demise of the memorialized. Reb Shimshon vigilantly recorded and acknowledged each *yahrzeit*, lighting the corresponding bulbs on their dates. One large plaque engraved with American and Jewish flags, "For our boys who perished in the armed services. Joey Feldman, Eddie Kessler, Hymie Berkowitz, Stanley Katz, Jerome Blustein, Teddy Lapidus, Seymour Novack." Teddy Lapidus I knew. When I was just ten-years-old, too young to play in the Saturday and Sunday morning games I used to come to watch those major contests of the week and Teddy was a regular shortstop. According to most, Benny was the best pitcher and power hitter in the history of the schoolyard. Jackie Rosen of blessed memory had a better batting average but he did not hit the long ball as often. Teddy Lapidus was a good fielder and runner, as good as Jackie, but had a weaker stick.

At the conclusion of the prayer as per Elul custom the *shofar* was sounded. Oft times psalms were recited for a sick member, friend or relative. After the *davening* it was Rav Shimshon's custom to learn a *halachah* with the *minyan*. Still wrapped with his *tallis* and *tefillin* Reb Shimshon began to explain a *halachah* to the dwarfs, reading the text of the *Shulchan Aruch* and translating it into Yiddish, and Izzy and I managed to piece together into English "A *Beis Knesset* (synagogue) that was destroyed, the premises retain a certain residual sanctity."

Still wrapped in his *tallis* and *tefillin* Reb Shimshon greeted me warmly. "How is going the learning? How is the *Rosh Yeshivah*?" I introduced Izzy, and he seemed to melt as Reb Shimshon peered through him, through me then abstractly in to space. Excusing himself, Reb Shimshon was hurrying out to the hospital. Miriam was sick. The *Tehillim* had been for her. Reb Shimshon rushed off, the familiar limping gait.

Rewinding all the old reels of those old frames of the schoolyard, the neighborhood, Stalin's *Shul*, to re-view them, now together with Izzy. Not so much as a dying man flashing his disappearing life across the screen of his memory, but more as wanting Izzy my newfound *chavrusa* to see, not just hear, the sounds, the colors of my bygone days. To retroactively, anachronistically, click him, into those days of yore. As participant. After all, only through some hitch in execution by a rookie angel with two left wings, had Izzy been mistakenly placed in Buffalo and LA. Surely he was meant to be in Brownsville and East Flatbush. That must have been what the initial Divine plan had intended. Now, walking together through Beth Asher basement Talmud Torah, down the bleakly lit narrow corridor, by the airless cubicles that served as classrooms, in days of yore. Like I could feel the ghosts of all those bright-eyed, bubbling-but-bored, boys and girls, rarely even inadvertently moved or touched by those classes. Budding Marranos reluctantly donning our *yarmulkes*, heading down those sagging steps to the basement. By turns angry, intimidated and now and then bemused by that cavalcade of sad-faced failed clowns strutting through our lives, the circus side-show of masquerading scholars—freak instructors, fat ladies, dwarfs, thin men, fat men, bah, baw, behing, yawningly, to exasperation, to distraction. Wonder of wonders, Porter who could smoke a complete cigarette down to ash while yet leaving it hanging from his lips, without handling the butt, without inhaling or ever exhaling, even while swallowing down a hot cup of tea poured from the whistling kettle to the cup and gulped down in seconds, without ever removing the long, glowing, increasing bending ash.

Impatiently waiting for the bell, to rush out and up those creaking-sagging steps, Marrano-like, to whip off our *yarmulkes* once more to rejoin America the beautiful in all its boundless, vibrating, joyous, goyish, romp and dance.

Upstairs in the vaulted muraled main sanctuary, even then used only on Shabbos and holidays, at its center three steps up the *bimah* (synagogue table for Torah reading) as per tradition higher than the pews—from that spot the ritual reading of the Torah scrolls took place, Shabbos, Monday and Thursday. That's where Benny never showed for his bar mitzvah *aliyah*, and seven years later – seven years ago – I appeared for my bar mitzvah. Haltingly, hauntingly memorable, not then and surely not today my place. Dad wanted to have my *aliyah* in a Conservative Synagogue out in Lawrence, since we were planning to move there. Mom objected to the Lawrence Synagogue, Grandpa Bloom would not be comfortable there. He was still living in Brownsville in his own apartment at the time. Although we had moved further from the synagogue to our extra territorial isthmus we were within walking distance. Grandpa Bloom lived only a ten-minute walk from the *shul*.

On this very site the War of the Roses had and was still raging through the years. President Katz, the Rose brothers and nephews, Rosenman and Rosenstein together with Klein, Kaufman, Goldlist and Vladimovsky with them led the rebellion against Reb Shimshon. In the trenches with Reb Shimshon Rosenkranz, Rosenman, Stein, Zaks, Grandpa Bloom and the dwarfs. Though losing the battle of the ark in the east, (it was completed during Reb Shimshon's absence in World War II). Reb Shimshon did lead his house of "red roses" to four victories: 1) The *mishaberach* for the Russians in World War II, before his departure; 2) The *mechitzah* separating the men and women after his return from the war; 3) Using the Gdanske *sefer* Torah with the blood stains on the borders; 4) Shooting down the men's club and sauna program combined with Liberal Synagogue.

Losses had been sustained on both sides. The present battle over the sale of the property was still raging. Cease-fires, re-groupings, attrition of manpower and armaments had impeded the pace of the conflict on both sides. But those were only temporary truces, no actual peace treaty. Stalling as a tactic had been employed by Reb Shimshon's forces when they held time was in their favor. That had worked well in the men's club sauna confrontation. The more the neighborhood changed the less plausible any such idea of investment had become. The present dispute over the property, and Vladimovsky's scheme to turn it into a Yiddish theater revival group seemed equally improbable, untenable with the present demography. But Vladimovsky continued to take no notice claiming neighborhoods experience cycles and even if the re-Judaizing of Brownsville and East Flatbush would never really take place, utilizing the building for a theater group did not require a neighborhood–based clientele. Yeats had his Lady Gregory, so Vladimovsky had his Mrs. Greenberg. She had an agenda to keep Jewish tenants for her tenement. Vis-à-vis the black and Puerto Rican church groups that were vying for the Beth Asher premises delaying made things worse. There were pressures and threats from the two battling groups as they fought for control of the neighborhood and Reb Shimshon's resistance persisted regarding selling the synagogue to the cynically secular yiddishists or the anti-semitic church group. Part Lone Ranger, part Don Quixote, Reb Shimshon rode on to the scene. At times more one than the other, other times a *shaatnez*-like mixture. More recently the voyage of the SS Pequod-cum-Beth-Asher had Reb Shimshon as Captain Ahab and I had chalked in for this whale of a journey...searching my horizons for a exilically improvised wailing wall.

One Saturday night two years ago I came straight from a date to the schoolyard. Arriving after 3 a.m., I noticed the lights in the *shul*. Instead of lying down on the grass in the park across Saratoga Avenue or on the concrete of the schoolyard in a corner against a wire fence which I had done a number of times, this time I went across to the *shul*. The main sanctuary was locked. I went around to the vestibule door leading to the corridor that led there and to the steps to the basement weekday *beis medrash* and Talmud Torah classes. It was open. Following the lone dim light, all but defeated by the darkness, down the steps to the basement across the dank corridor and up the steps leading to the lobby of the main sanctuary. Doors were open and lights were on. Holding the back door just a little ajar, I could see in. Standing alone three steps up on that raised square railed bimah under those high vaulted ceilings, like in a boxing ring, like John Garfield's punchy tormented black trainer after learning of the champ's throwing the bout, shadow-boxing his way around the ring to an empty arena all alone jabbing and pounding away at the ghosts of old opponents. So Reb Shimshon circled the railing of the *bimah* punching out his lines, delivering his *drashah* to the ghosts in those empty pews. Speaking first in a low, slow manner, he stopped, thought, grimaced, feigned a move or two and belted out some heartfelt soul-felt point at his invisible audience. Quoting Hebrew, Aramaic phrases his Yiddish now quicker, louder, more emphatic, lifting his arms as he spoke to the vacant benches. His words echoing through the empty chambers up the walls to the women's section, those syllables seemed to bounce back down and around the sanctuary reverberating, vibrating in their electric impact. After about twenty minutes I closed the door and left. It was chilling, riveting. I walked away, and came back again ten minutes later and he was going strongly. I stayed for about another fifteen minutes. When I left he was still at it.

Winters later claimed that given the supremely allusive compressed style of the Talmud, it was not unusual for a scholar even when by himself to himself, to articulate his points, his ideas, to develop and clarify his insights. Now having been eight months in the *yeshivah* I had been witness to that. But that time was different, Reb Shimshon was in fact addressing the congregation that wasn't there, engaging those ghosts whom he actually saw. I'd shared these stories with Izzy. And now he could see for himself Stalin's *Shul*, the bussed in octogenarian glee club *minyan* of dwarfs. He could actually identify Grumpy, Sleepy, Zaks, Rosenman and a few of the others. Reb Shimshon had headed out immediately after davening to see Miriam at the hospital, but the dwarfs insisted that we make a *l'chaim* for some *yahrtzeit* with schnapps. Canadian Club, crackers and herring had been arranged on the back table at the close of the *davening*.

❏ ❏

The hearse was parked alongside the left field fence. Bam and Marty were already there. The pitchers, Zip and Red Moish, had just started picking their teams. Each about ten years my senior, I had watched them play long before I was chosen into games. Most of the players were five to seven years older than me. Zip with exaggerated irritation, "Who's this Isadore Stanley Seymour Isaacson guy?" Izzy had chalked in with his full name. He stumbled forward, saluted and stood at attention. Zip studied him up and down and pronounced, "Too long a strike zone!" Izzy buckled his knees, crouched and bent over. Red Moish sizing him up, "Me, I like guys with long arms that can pull even outside pitches in this yard, that's real important."

Izzy straightened up proudly to his full height measuring and stroking the air with an imaginary bat the full length of his arms away from his body. "You look like a first baseman kid, you got the stretch," Red Moish.

Izzy now reached for a star and responded, "Ah shucks, they all say that."

Tarzan Weiss was chosen by Moish reluctantly. Moish was angry at him for having missed a throw from Coffee Cooperstein the previous week. All agreed that it was Coffee's poor throw but Red Moish said that Tarzan should have picked it up anyway. While he could not ignore Tarzan's hitting, Red Moish wanted to remove Tarzan to the outfield, and put Izzy on first base. When it came time to take the field Tarzan Weiss just went straight to first base, planting himself there. Red Moish ordered Izzy to stay at first base. Izzy, Stan Laurel-ed it, waving his arms and mumbling helplessly, hopelessly. Tarzan Weiss picked up Izzy carried him out to right field and deposited him. Right field in the PS 189 schoolyard was an alley between the intrusive concrete handball court and the caged in unused over-weeded school garden. No one else in the schoolyard would have stood up to Red Moish, only Tarzan Weiss could get away with that.

During warm-up, a few throws were tossed out to the outfield and Izzy did some of his Jerry Lewis knock-kneed twerpy sad clowning, climaxing with sudden and miraculous snatches of the flyballs. Not many guys laughed. Even if we only put up two dollars a head, to cover cost of balls, bats with the remaining proceeds going to the winners (and now a portion paying for protecting our cars from smashed windows, missing hubcaps, antennae, and tires), still, playing was a serious business. Marty enjoyed Izzy, Bam was indifferent.

It felt good to be back in the schoolyard in an orthodox game with definitive "*halachic*" rulings. Though even here at the schoolyard, much of the oral tradition was given to dispute, i.e. balks, running with the pitch, high chops, pick offs, yet - balls and strikes counted; there was a defined number of players, balls and strikes, and innings.

Izzy was in right and I was in center but the handball court blocked our view of each other. Picasso had his green period and his blue period. Most often I preferred center, occasionally shortstop, center was pastoral, shortstop urban. Sometimes in the outfield waiting and wading through so much inaction picturing a Yucca Forest outcropping in the Mojave Desert, bare branches stretched out and up – Joshua trees they called them – reaching heavenward like in prayer – or perhaps petrified outfielders groping, hoping for the flyball. Prayers and players.

Late Saturday mornings were, by common consent, for the local fifteen-and-six-teen-year-olds. Eight years ago on such a Saturday morning, from deeper in East Browns-ville a roaming horde led by Finnegan of the Snake Pit Dukes with five of his brothers and thirty goons descended en masse to the schoolyard. Mostly Irish, some Italian, pegged pants bargain basement bunch of barbarians with slicked back hair, gently arched waved peaks rising in pompadours but slightly, carefully, tousled and cascading onto their fore-heads, they blocked off the exits and surrounded the less than ten younger guys that were there. I was twelve at the time and that pretty much exempted me from direct conflict. Finnegan and his dukes, while they had no interest in a fair fight, nevertheless wanted sufficient appearance that could be construed as such when later reported and reviewed, that there had been substantial resistance. We, little "punks" had observer status. About half-hour before game time. While ten of our guys were taking batting practice, others hanging around at the edge of the court, Finnegan's seventeen-and eighteen-year-olds descended. Then Finnegan himself walked up to home plate and began with a declaration of annexation of the court. The schoolyard was public property and he and his gang were now taking over. Four or five of his guys holding steel pipes and big-buckled studded belts clobbered Ira Gershman and Irving Berliner who stood their ground and refused to walk off the court. They were knocked down and kicked around. Some of the desperadoes had their captives empty their pockets on to the court. I felt my stomach churning, if only I had a gun, and if I don't, can't G-d send a thunderbolt? Tarzan Weiss and Red Moish would be here only tomorrow. If only they could show now.

MM Roth also stood firm. As usual he seemed oblivious to the goings on. Short, pudgy, prematurely balding with gaps in his teeth MM had always been in the schoolyard. Year after year he'd been left-back at school and in the schoolyard as well. He was older than all the guys that came down Sunday mornings. Court jester, mascot, MM's partially toothless grin belied his memory bank of hundreds of schoolyard games. A quasi–official status had been awarded to MM's versions of statistics and plays. As "PS 189 idiot-savant" he never played and never missed a game. But most uncanny was his sound simulation capability. A la Marty Glickman —"Today's Baseball" — MM did brilliant replays of past games. His cracking bats and thumping catches were astonishingly real. Like a recording machine, he had the sounds down pat, and he could recall and replay specific innings and games as far back as fifteen years ago. MM could also open bottles of Pepsi and Coke with his remaining teeth, often he projectile-spit the tops high into the air catching them again in his mouth. Irwin Schwartz, left crippled in one leg after a bout of polio, usually umped. Unofficially he became official scorer, till something was hotly contested. Irwin sometimes challenged sequences in MM's golden oldies. MM's recollections were undoc-umented. After a game, Irwin would go home to his archives and come back with written documentation. Those records included batting averages, RBIs, home runs, extra base hits, fielding averages, ERAs. MM was always grinning. Irwin never smiled. Finnegan and ten of his goons surrounded MM where he continued to stand as if the onslaught had not occurred. Short, balding, paunchy, gap-toothed MM face to face with the tall, blond muscular tattooed Irishman. Hawk nose tilted upwards to meet pug nose. Brown eyes to blue eyes. Though it was said that he had been dishonorably discharged from the U.S. Navy, Finnegan wore his eagles and flag tattoo over his biceps proudly. Surveying the deployment of his thirty odd thugs, the blocked off gates, he gloated. Like dropping down too quickly in an elevator, my heart and stomach leaped up to the back of my throat and into my mouth.

At that very moment of truth, MM erupted a volcanic burp, a colossal greps that shook the Richter scale. And then another. And another. Thundering and reverberating through the canyons, the high escarpments, and palisades of the tall buildings that bordered the schoolyard. Through the alleys, around the school building and through the open yard. Successive massive eruptions exploding mightily rattling glass and causing the terrain to tremble. Finnegan stood astonished. Paralyzed. And immediately with hardly a breath in between, MM erupting in that crazy surging hyena laugh that leaped up from somewhere from within his depths volumes louder than the shrill canned cackling of that hag-like cuckoo that presided over the haunted house on the midway near the Mermaid's Tale in Coney Island. No one was sure of MM's parentage. Someone said that old man Roth had been a union organizer that had been done in. Others claimed that MM's parents had been patients at Kings County Asylum. But MM Roth was a neighborhood fixture. His laugh that day pealed through the yard. And then to the streets. One kid selling iced soda and beer from an open bucket in a stroller carriage handed MM a bottle of beer which he proceeded to pop open with those few remaining teeth, eject the cap high into the air and catch it in his mouth. He then spit it out up high through the air scoring a basket on the court behind the pitcher's mound. Finnegan laughed. First lightly. Tentatively. Then fully, heartily. Placing his arm around MM's shoulder they laughed and laughed. Together. Others began laughing. Gershman and Berliner were freed. Finnegan declared a pact, a protective alliance. He collected his gang, ordering them to return what they had taken and they departed. Such was the saga of, "The Greps of Roth." To be included in the Guinness Book of Records, the world's most stupendous burp; dubbed by Marty, "The greps that daunted a thousand micks." In the aftermath of Finnegan's retreat, MM attained a newfound celebrity status; in Finnegan's wake MM was a hero.

MM's glory was re-established some six or seven years later after Benny took over management of the Mermaid's Tale and a few local hoods appeared and demanded protection money. MM was sitting with us at a corner table and Moishe the singing waiter from Bucharest clued us in what was happening at Benny's table. Without warning MM opened verbal fire filling the air with simulated blasting gun shots, smashing glass and crumbling plaster. Everyone hit the floor. Except us. MM stopped to sip his beer and re-loaded, the culprits ran for the door. We heard tell that they eventually returned but with a newfound respect. Most guys in the schoolyard agreed that MM was best at war. He should get a Nobel War Prize. His canon shots and exploding bombs, screeching roaring planes strafing enemy positions were frighteningly real.

Another schoolyard legend was Sroly's broken field run. "Salugee" was popular amongst the younger kids. Usually a ball, a cap, a pack of cards that was used in the games of "Packs" was grabbed from some kid, and tossed by the grabbers up and back eluding the rushing reaching efforts of the owner to retrieve his property.

A few months after the war ended in 1945 a fifteen-year-old Sroly with red, orange *payos* (sidelocks), short-cropped hair—a Chassidic anachronism—turned up without any family in the neighborhood. Small clusters of such Jews that looked like that lived in Williamsburg and on the East Side. Through some friends of friends, Sroly was apprenticed part time to Mendel the butcher who was a closet *chassid*, and had his shop on Sutter Avenue not far from where we lived. We bought our meat there. Within days of his arrival Sroly, who spoke no English, was strolling near the schoolyard and some kids grabbed his *yarmulke* and screamed "salugee." Five kids formed a circle and someone taped the *yarmulke* to a "clincher" (adhesive tape was often around to bandage and recover torn clinchers) and they began tossing it up and back between them. Sroly at first stunned and immobilized, began to chase his *yarmulke* as it flew up and back on the clincher. He moved surprisingly quickly, deftly, with jerking bursts of speed, but also with a special grace. A few more kids joined in the "salugee" circle and about eight guys were now in the circle and that made it harder. One boy hesitated momentarily long enough for Sroly to rush him and spear the *yarmulke–ed* clincher just as it began to ascend.

The following week Sroly hanging on the fence and watching a two-hand touch football game (or more accurately it should have been called two–hand shove) and when a kid named Bernie twisted his leg and had to be replaced, Sroly was inducted with sign language and gestures as replacement. No one spoke Yiddish, and Sroly knew no English. In the very first play, a partially blocked pass was fumbled and then again deflected by another would be interceptor. The football landed in Sroly's hands. Guys rushed him. Sroly screamed "salugee" and headed across the concrete court. Initially assisted by a few well-placed blocks he deftly dodged, pursuing opponents as he dashed across the schoolyard. Then, instead of stopping at the fence he exited the gate and kept going. Some guys laughed and others screamed as they ran out after him. An ad hoc posse formed and streamed out of the schoolyard and into the street after Sroly. Down the middle of Rockaway Avenue, on-coming drivers honked, some stopped and exited their cars to gawk, Sroly, orange-red *peyos* flying behind him, streaked and weaved his way gracefully towards Linden Boulevard. Moving from the road to the sidewalk and back again eluding his chasers he continued to run. Kids along the route joined the posse but Sroly stayed way out in front. Guys said that Jackie Rosen came close a few times but never quite caught Sroly. At Saratoga and Livonia Sroly turned and headed towards the El. Most reports had it that he bounded the steps, stopping only momentarily at the platform to throw the football back down and jumped onto the New Lots train that was heading towards Sutter Avenue. Winters said that Sroly had jumped the turnstile and after failing to get the fellow in the booth to accept the owed fare, he later dropped it off at the booth. Schoolyard lore.

Today Marty had on his Marrano baseball cap. Sometimes he just hung around first base line commenting on plays and calls. Of late he often split the umping with Irwin. Bam and Tony attributed Marty's lack of motivation to play to his spikes debacle two years back. He had turned up for a few games wearing spikes and guys had argued that it was impossible to play with spikes on concrete. Marty had been obstinate and demanded documentation that it was prohibited. Then one Sunday, with Tarzan Weiss present the argument exploded and he picked Marty up by his ankles, hung him upside down, took off the spikes, replaced Marty on the ground and said that if he ever comes back with the spikes again it will be the last time he comes to the schoolyard. Every once in a while Bam would bring it up and ask, "So how come, Marty, you gave in about the spikes?"

"It was unreasonable to deny the cogency of Tarzan's logic." Marty.

The first three hitters against Zip all hit automatic outs into the right field garden. In all my years, first as a spectator, then as a player, I have never seen that happen. Zip said that he had been developing his screwball. Marty said Zip was a screwball. Biggy said the new right fielder put a hex on them. Upon hearing that, Izzy, out in right field, swelling with pride, exhaled onto his nails, polished them, knowingly against his chest and smiled triumphantly.

Although Jackie Robinson was and would remain my favorite player, yet for a short time Cal Abrams captured a special place in my heart and imagination. A real live Jewish boy on the Dodgers, and add to that his bursting onto the scene with a blazing hitting streak. Through those initial weeks hitting over three seventy. True, Goody Rosen had been around, but only as a utility player—and he was on his way out, as I was coming in. Goody never made any great mark. Clearly, Cal Abrams was destined to be the Messiah, despite his awkward penchant of hitting to left field although he was a lefty. Eventually fielders pulled a right-handed pull hitter shift on him. But those first weeks he continued to get hits. When challenged why this left handed Jew hit to left field I explained the peculiarity since we Jews read from right to left—in fact baseball/softball was essentially Semitic in its roots running as we read, counter-clockwise, like Jewish history—going against the clock, against the stream. Maybe that's what Dad had in mind with his racing theory of race. At least unconsciously. Football, basketball, soccer and hockey were governed by space and clocks. Baseball went beyond time and space. Baseball courts were not standardized, outfields each had their own quirky dimensions. Extra-inning games could go on forever and the home run over the outfield wall or fence whether into the flowing anonymous crowds or out of the park went somewhere very far into the great beyond, touching, rubbing with the forever, brushing with eternity. Infields, including the mound, were fixed irrevocable, halachically ninety feet, sixty feet. Whereas like in *galus*, each outfield *kehilla* had its special dynamics of communal space yet within the traditional court. Economics, culture, politics, indigenous to that locale shaping customs for that outfield/community. So there were: Ashkenazim, Lithuanian, Chassidim, Yekkies (each with its various subdivisions) and Sephardim (each with its multitude of breakdowns), Yemenites, the variegated dress, music and styles were outfield-like, serving as shock absorbers protecting the non-negotiable infield. *Halachic* communities differed from each other in custom while sharing core root halachic norms. Non-halachic communities stepped off the court outside the grid, changing infield measurements. New game; different game.

Ebbets Fields, home runs into Bedford Avenue, landing in the street, the cars, the houses, an extended court, as were Brass Rail, Van Heusen, Tydol, signs all part of the playing field. The market place was in play, long drives ricocheting off those multi-colored tattooed patches that lined the outfields were happening on court at this time and place. So in Judaism the market place, the home, every facet of existence was under the *halachic* purview, sanctifiable through Torah. Football and basketball were soundless. Hockey whacks slid not soared. Softball, baseball, the carbine crack of the bat resonated throughout the stadium, shooting that inscribed seamed orb of tightly packed parchment skyward, with its imprinted messages heavenbound, gently arcing, peaking then tipping earthward with the Cosmic answer – safe or out. Even the padded thump of the speared line drive was audible. Dribbling, bumping across the basketball court was tangential, incidental to the decisive moment. Here the hit, the catch, was the event.

The schoolyard was crowded in by broad three story, four, five story tenements – older narrower buildings or light colored bricks, topped by dirty cornices. Taller buildings, especially the ones with elevators were called apartment houses. Those soiled discolored cornices atop the tenements sat like silly silk top hats on peddlers. Surrounded on two sides by apartment houses and the third side by tenements, the open space of the schoolyard was closed on the fourth side by the gothic fortress like edifice of PS 189.

July and August, escaping airless claustrophobic apartments, neighborhood people brought out chairs to sit in front of the tenements, apartment houses. Especially in the evenings. In the day time mostly women, at night men and women. Kids on bikes weaved in and around the men and women who recited their regular lines by heart without scripts regarding landlords, neighbors, children, shopping, movies, politics. Sylvia Sidney's Street Scene. A bit less crowded than the East Side, but more crowded than Flatbush. Bensonhurst, Canarsie. In all the years we lived there, I never saw Mom sitting with them. She was always busy. Either inside our apartment or outside. Coming and going she would exchange cordial words, more than pleasantries. She liked people. She liked to be liked by people. But she had no time. Dad was selective about whom he liked. Four nights a week Dad, after returning from the accounting office in Manhattan, attended law school classes. He regularly returned angry at Professor Thomas's posturing and histrionics and at his classmate, the president of Beth Asher's son Melvin Katz and his imitative posturing and affectation. But Dad also followed Thomas' instructions and painstakingly prepared and delivered solo perorations to the living room mirror.

With Dad still not speaking with me, since I had moved out of our Lawrence home, it would have been awkward taking Izzy out to Lawrence to meet the family. As it happened, Teddy was away in camp in the Adirondacks and Dad and Mom were away for the weekend, so I did not have to grapple with the problem. Instead, after the game we would stay in Brooklyn and stop by Winters' place to refuel. Izzy got one hit. And he hit another long ball out to center field. I got two hits, and though we lost, we had acquitted ourselves reasonably well. Red Moish told me as we were leaving that I could bring Izzy back again.

Rebbetzin Winters was out with some of the children visiting her mother in Crown Heights. Ten-year-old Tzippy and the Rabbi were organizing lunch for the kids that had remained behind. I counted about five children including the infant in Winters' arms. Winters' smile was accompanied by his focused look, which as he spoke turned even pleasantries into real talk. His stuttering made his words more measured inviting responses in kind. Each time the baby, Yossi, cried, Winters cooed, gurgled or clucked towards him rhythmically setting off his phrases. Like Victor Borge's verbal punctuation. Studying Yossi, that striving bursting sense of self, those fingers, limbs, eyes, I once again landed on the side of teleology over randomness. And if there were quirks, bleeps, kashas (as they said in the Yeshiva) Intelligent design still worked better than any alternative. Tracking that race as Mr. Darwin astride his streaking eohippus contemplated the eye, that blind leap from not seeing to seeing he and his mount kept coming up Charley-horsed.

When we got to talking about the *yeshivah* it did not take too much time for Winters to get into the *"sugya"* (subject discussion) of the *Gemara* that we were learning. Stammering his way through Tosafos' (medieval commentary) interpretation of the question and the answer, and the questions on *Tosafos* from the *Ketzos* (latter day commentary), as Yossi continued to punctuate the remarks with gurgles, coos and clucks. At first Yossi seemed entertained, but as we went on he became less impressed. Now he was crying loudly. Standing up now Winters threw Yossi up in the air, in split seconds there was a bubbling laugh. Then without any advance notice it switched into a cry. All the while Winters continued his staccato stuttering analysis of *Tosafos* and the *Ketzos*. Each time Winters tossed Yossi up, Izzy's plastic countenance puckered into amazement covering his ears with his long arms as if in fear of a missed reception. When four-year-old Tully burst onto the scene hotly pursued by six-year-old Chaim, Winters deposited Yossi in Izzy's arms. Frozen with fright Izzy delivered a quick medley of Rock a Bye Baby, Oh Dear What Can the Matter Be, Lambs Eat Oats and Does Eat Oats and Little Lambs Eat Ivy. Yossi thought it over carefully and just as Winters succeeded in imposing a kind of truce in the shoot out between Tully and Chaim, Yossi exploded into tears once more. Palming the crying bundle like a basketball, Izzy returned him to Winters. Both Tully and Chaim cocked their thumbs and aimed their index fingers at Izzy. "Why d'you make my brother cry?" challenged Chaim. Tully shook his head in agreement. Banging shots aimed from those little extended fingers, Izzy grabbed his chest and stomach, doubled up and fell to the floor. As he rolled over the second time Chaim said, "We got him." At that moment the Rebbetzin and the rest of the brood appeared. Rushing to her Chaim and Tully bubbling, tumblingly show-and-telling how they had come to Yossi's defense and done in Izzy. Sitting up on the floor Izzy Stan Laurel-ed his way up, sobbing, grimacing, haplessly, word-choked, in his defenseless defense. Weeks passed and a few times I dreamed of Nicholas' Cantonist *chappers* (Tzarist employed kidnappers) coming after Tully and Chaim grabbing them pressing them into batches of screaming youngsters, six, seven, eight and eleven year old recruits, kidnapped to serve their twenty five years in the Tsar's army.

Six months had passed since Reb Shimshon's infamous *Mincha* at the Mermaid's Tale, on the Rebbetzin's *yahrtzeit*. They had said *Tehillim* that day for Miriam who was critically ill. Maybe those prayers had something to do with her hanging on for the next six months. Like some heroine from a Russian novel, it was said that Miriam's eyes and speeches had burned more intensely the last months. Until finally one day she collapsed during a feverishly fervent presentation at the Workman's Circle Center on

East Broadway in Manhattan.

The call from Reb Shimshon came while Izzy and I were tangling with Rav Winters in the sugya of 'avad inish' – (A man taking the law into his own hands). Reb Shimshon was calling from Beth Israel Hospital in Manhattan. Miriam had just died, and her husband Solly Zemeroff had arranged for the last rites to take place at a non-sectarian funeral parlor, the Workers Brotherhood Funeral Parlor on Essex Street. Two of the main union and party people were going out of town Monday morning and grave-diggers did not work on Sundays so it was arranged that burial would take place early Monday morning at 8 a.m. but the eulogies and the viewing of the departed would take place all day Sunday. And that way no one would have to miss work, "employers were heartless and they would dock their workers otherwise."

Reb Shimshon had a different scenario in mind. Miriam was to have a tradition-al Jewish funeral at a Jewish cemetery with the *Kaddish* being recited. He called Rabbi Winters to commandeer me and the hearse into action. My credentials for the position began in heredity and climaxed in position. Wasn't I Itcha Bloom's grandson? Hadn't Reb Itcha stood in the trenches with Reb Shimshon through the ongoing War of the Roses, and I drove a hearse. Now, Reb Shimshon could speak to me shorthand as well. A mitzvah was an absolute objective obligation. Once established, that one was dealing with a mitzvah, it followed then there was a responsibility to help get it done. One might differ regarding priorities, that's why learning-learning was so crucial to the system. Only the cool well-reasoned *pilpul* (Talmudic dialectic) could sort out the variables and as-sign each point its proper place and weight arriving at an operative conclusion. Most of the business of daily life was neither definitively *mitzvah* nor transgression, rather an amorphous mass that could be shaped, molded into one or the other. Burial of a deceased who had no one else to deal with that burial was in fact a definitive *mitzvah*.

"Its [2] ah big *mitzvah* for to brink deh *niftar* to be buryink, ah special ah *mess mitzvah mit* such ah niftar vere dere is no one for to doink de buryink ven dere is not dere somevone somebody else vott can do de *mitzvah*. It's den an extra big *chessed*. A special *chessed* is vot ve callink a *chessed shel emes*—a truly *chessed*. Dat's meanink ven de vone vot is doink him dat *chessed* is not doink him dat *chessed* for vantink dey should do him vone day back a *chessed*. Cos ven you doink for a *mess mitzvah* den is a *chessed shel emes*, ah truly vone. And even ahm de tatter ahm beink an old man and is notink you gonne need me for vot ahm can do for you. So is really de true ah *chessed shel emes*. You hearink me Yisroel?" Reb Shimshon turning to me.

<hr>

For the benefit of those who do not speak Yinglish, please see the translation in the Appendix, page 205.

After tracking down Marty, Bam and the hearse, and consulting with Pastor Thomas and Tony and his Uncle Augie, Rabbi Winters and Reb Shimshon, we worked out our plan. Uncle Augie had access to special order caskets; what they called in the trade "The London Coach Casket"—equipped with a hidden bottom berth—a "Bay Ridge Special" for situations that required modest anonymous unobtrusive burials. In this case, we would use it to pick up Miriam from Beth Israel Hospital, and have some unidentified unclaimed cadaver, preferably also a Caucasian woman around forty years old, in the bottom berth. Pastor Thomas had "the lay of the land" at the Kings County Morgue, and he felt he could fulfill our order. Tonight after the eulogy, and the viewing of the deceased at the Workman's Brotherhood Funeral Parlor, someone would have to be on hand after closing to later remove Miriam to the parking lot where our hearse would be waiting. The remaining anonymous cadaver in the bottom berth would then be elevated to the upper level. That casket would be guarded till the next morning by an attendant who Pastor Thomas had found ready to cooperate. Pastor Thomas and Uncle Augie had, in their own ways for various reasons, gone similar routes before. We had some trouble arranging to get the pick-up orders from the Workman's Brotherhood Funeral Parlor driver, but that was finally worked out. Rabbi Winters said it was a pleasure working with socialists, they understood the value of a dollar. At 2 a.m. Sunday morning, Bam and Sroly were dispatched and headed out to Bay Ridge to meet Augie where they would be taken to collect the London Coach Casket. Marty, Izzy and I had the hearse and we were to meet them after we had made our pick up at the Kings County Morgue. Pastor Thomas was at the morgue arranging for our passenger. Winters was with Reb Shimshon at Beth Israel Hospital where they had prepared for us to replace the Brotherhood Funeral driver and make the pick up of Miriam at the hospital morgue. Pastor Thomas and a hospital guard came wheeling out a full body bag on a high stretcher. After exchanging a few words with Thomas the guard disappeared and we lifted the body bag into the hearse.

"Now lookee here boys, I done gone out an got us a considerable discount, instead of a hundred and twenty-five bucks this here poor unfortunate, G-d rest his soul, is only gonna cost us sixty-five dollars, but I must advise one and all concerned hereto that we gotta make double sure tomorrow they don't start no peeking around in the morning about the box before the burial. Being as time was going to beat us to the finish line here and we had to beat that there genuinely deadly deadline, and there was no expired white woman handy on the premises to be had, I settled for the best one hundred and ten pound corpse that was available. Now that just happened to be a colored man, and under the circumstances— and boys I think we is all really agreed that we is under the circumstances—that was a lot better for sure than a two hundred pound white man, under the circumstances!"

THE IDIOM AND THE ODDITY | 147

"Are you for real? A black man, you gotta be kidding?" Bam with surprise.

"Now fellas, that there tone sounds like downright prejudice. For all we know he could have come from real decent folks that poor devil—let's call him Lester—even if it was a knife wound that finally did him in. I sure did not expect to find that kind of an attitude from you fellas."

"Come on Thomas, you know what we mean." Bam again.

"Ah remember, my friends, ain't no one ever played the "Star Spangled Banner" with just using the white keys or just using the black ones. Got to use both the white and the black keys to play that there national anthem. Right gentlemen? And we got us a real considerable discount thrown in to boot. Only sixty-five bucks."

I called from the street telephone near the Kings County emergency exit. Sroly and Bam were already at Augie's Used Car Lot with the London Coach Casket in Sroly's van. Surrounded by an outer row of simonized glistening cars for sale Sroly's camouflaged beat up dented van seemed suited for transporting coffins behind the lines. Later, removing the coffin from Sroly's car onto the ground, we opened the bottom berth with its hidden hinge and placed our passenger to rest. Lifting the coffin we now placed it in the hearse and set out to pick up Miriam at Beth Israel.

Up the sleeping streets of Brooklyn, thinking about what that other Thomas said, "Only the dead know Brooklyn." Bypassing the Manhattan Bridge we headed for the Brooklyn Bridge. That would get us to the FDR Drive north and up to 21st Street where we could cut over to Beth Israel on East 17th. No question about it. FDR had drive. He made it to the top. Churchill said FDR was a mediocre intellect in a first-rate personality. A charming hustler. How many Jews had sat by their radios enthralled and reassured by those cunningly cozy and caring fireside chats while their brothers, cousins, mothers and fathers were systematically being murdered in Europe? FDR and Winnie did know, but those listeners did not know that they knew and that they could have, should have, stalled, postponed, bought, bartered for saving hundreds of thousands. But the gates of England, Palestine and America were hermetically sealed. And the railroad tracks leading to the gas chambers were not bombed, though the Czech underground had supplied the information and the maps... Miriam would be placed in the upper berth of the double-decker casket later to be removed and the lower passenger upped to the top berth for the Workman's Circle burial Monday morning. Sunday, Miriam would stay in place till the viewing was over and Sunday night be removed to the parking lot where we could join Reb Shimshon for her traditional burial at a Jewish cemetery. It had been arranged with the driver that we would make the pick up of Miriam from Beth Israel Hospital. If the right guard was on duty he'd help, otherwise we would carry the extra heavy double-berth coffin. From the hospital we would deliver her to the Workman's Circle Funeral Parlor. Solly said there was no point being at the Funeral Parlor at 7 a.m. Monday morning. Funeral ceremonies were bourgeois indulgences, institutionalized and superstitious and capitalistic exploitation. He would take his leave Sunday evening and had no intention of appearing Monday morning. Solly and Miriam's fellow travelers agreed.

At the hospital the nurse providing the release for Miriam's body looked up, studied us, and said "You guys don't look like drivers." Izzy all touched and bashful looked at her and said. "Aw, you're just saying that!" Reb Shimshon refusing help carried Miriam out in the bodybag. Like she was alive and sleeping he hugged his precious bundle, tears rolled down from his eyes as he spoke to her the entire time. "Soon now *mein kind* ahm takink you for alvays to home *mein kind*. Ahm no-more leavink you again *mein kind*. Just a few hours den I'm comink quick and takink you dis time for good mein kind." I could hear Izzy choking back his cries. Just when I thought I had myself in check somewhere from deep within a heaving sob leaped up and out of me. Miriam was placed in the upper berth of the London Coach Casket and we drove to the Workman's Brotherhood Funeral Parlor. The right guard was on duty and helped us carry in the casket. He looked up, winked and said, "She must have been a big lady, G-d rest her soul."

"My kind of socialist." Izzy.

After delivering Miriam to the funeral parlor, Reb Shimshon headed over to a *shul* a block away on Houston Street to *daven Shacharis* and spend the day saying *Tehillim* for Miriam. We followed him to *daven Shacharis*. We had until 8:30 pm to return to the funeral parlor when the last viewers would be leaving. At that time Leonard, the evening watchman, was scheduled to allow us to stay behind when the others had left. Sometime in the middle of the night we could up Lester and exit with Miriam to the hearse that would be waiting in the parking lot to be taken for a proper *halachic* burial. Lester, then having been upped, would be duly buried in the morning as Miriam. Someone would have to attend to the coffin not being opened before the burial. According to Pastor Thomas, that had cost thirty five dollars to make sure that Lester would go that last mile as Miriam without the coffin being viewed.

As the last viewers were exiting, we hung around the john for a while. Leonard came and told us that we could exit and sit down and relax in the waiting room. We fell asleep on the sofas until about 3 a.m. when Leonard awoke us in a bit of a frenzy. Leonard's wife had been rushed to the hospital with an appendicitis attack and he had to leave. Regulations required that he called the alternate watchman, Johnny Blake, to come down. Blake would be there within fifteen minutes. We could rest assured that by four thirty, quarter to five Blake would have gone to sleep on the sofa in the waiting room, that was his habit. Until then, Leonard suggested that we select caskets and lie down until we could sneak out with Miriam. Leaving the lids just a bit ajar would provide enough air. "To tell you the honest truth, I myself occasionally grab a catnap in one of those coffins." Leading us to the display room he pointed out a few coffins that were more or less comfortable. He reassured us that he knew Blake's pattern, and for sure Blake would soon be asleep. Until then we could rest for an hour or so. Climbing into the casket like an open baby-grand piano, Izzy turned to me.

"While I am pretty copasetic with, 'for instance dying' but I may turn out green about the McCoy." Izzy.

"I guess I am more yellow than green." Me responding.

Together, "A tisket, a tasket a green and yellow casket."

"Let's say for instance that you were G-d." Me turning to Izzy.

"Oh my G-d! Okay, just for instance," here sticking his head out of the casket again looking up apologetically toward the ceiling and beyond, then like a turtle pulling his head back in. "But I tell you it's hard to 'for instance' that you're G-d when your legs are cramped. You know what I mean?" Izzy with concern.

"And up there in the celestial court…" Me.

"I am not so sure Stevie, like Omnipresent and so maybe, but omnipotent and omniscient? I just don't know."

"Just for instance." Me.

"OK for instance."

"So in come these low flying seraphs from the Divine Justice Department; some say they were originally *Litvak*- Sheriffs (Serrifs) now promoted, and they supply all the chapter and verse for the docket of prosecution. All those scramblings and scribblings, those poet-tasting peccadilloes." Me.

"Got ya, like things just keep going from bed to verse and back and again and besides which who is that weary looking angel with the clipped wings sitting on the railings?"

"Why dat's da-fence attorney. He just can't climb down and go one way or the other." Me.

"He's got to earn his wings, let him say something." Izzy.

"He's caught, can't decide which defense. Labile inanity or temporary insanity?" Me.

"Nothing permanent." Izzy.

"No nothing permanent. Though that does seem pretty permanent that lack of permanence, at least for the time being. You know what I mean? But then again down on Sutter and Ralph Alfredo's Beauty Parlor did permanent waves! All those lines of helmeted women like visiting Martians on view. At least temporarily till the next wave." Me.

"I read somewhere about Jews in Berlin that hid out during the war, like, in this pull out drawer under a bed where they spent most of their time playing harmonicas, and they called themselves symphonic submarines. And there was this guy Hershler who wrote his dissertation at the University of Freiberg on the Demonic in Religion. .... Also I once saw these toothless triplets on Ted Mack's Amateur Hour that did the harmonic in precision." Me.

"They didn't even win. Some one-armed juggler from Peoria flipping a dozen flaming daggers up on a high wire riding a unicycle suspended over eleven fire breathing dragons, four panthers, three jaguars with six vultures, a remodeled Archaeopteryx with an overhauled Messerschmitt motor coming from one side and seventeen hara–kiri grinning Japs on the other side—he won." Izzy.

"Yeah the usual stuff…So this German actress who was hiding them out: Hershler from the University of Freiberg, and his actor friend, so one day she comes back to the apartment and opens the door and finds these two devout atheists between blasts of the harmonica singing out at the top of their lungs 'Shema Yisrael.'" Me.

" Ever since I broke my leg sliding into third base against the Devils my legs have cramped, especially my left leg, especially whenever I lie down in a coffin." Izzy.

"Were you safe or out?" Me.

"Well it sort of got complicated." Izzy.

"For a change." Me.

"The umpire had hayfever, sneezed and closed his eyes!" Izzy.

"*Aleph, Beis, Gimmel, Daled, Hei,*" Porter had an allergy to '*Gimmels*' more than '*Heis*', he used to cough and gasp when he *gimmeled*, he had *gimmel*-fever." Me.

"So we flipped this coin." Izzy.

"Seymour Sternfeld from Ralph Avenue had this two headed quarter, he got it from some Puerto Rican kid on Pitkin Avenue and they called it Sternfeld's Latin Quarter." Me.

"Harvey Alvin Mersky from Lawrence Avenue had the most beautiful set of baseball cards and coins. He had this double-tailed dime, vintage 1929 which year everyone came up tails first, in fact Chicago was inundated with those double-tailed dimes. Harvey Alvin Mersky's father went into this tailspin and landed with the entire family back east at his grandmother's home in the Bronx peddling ice cream. Harvey prematurely inherited his father's collection, his Dad having become this depressed Good Humor Man. Harvey used to keep his baseball cards in the freezer of the Good Humor truck next to the creamsicles, 'so they would last.' Eventually he had the soggiest set of cards on the block… So maybe Keats was wrong after all and things of beauty do pass into nothingness." Izzy.

"I heard say that Sadya said that only the Creator can pull off the big trick. Just as only He can make something from nothing then only He can make nothing from something." Me.

"But I will tell you Stevie, for instance, Divine or no, I have to climb out and find a john. Me and Pharaoh pretending to be a divinity and Moshe catching him going to relieve himself by the river Nile." Izzy.

"Yeh, imagine that, the whole Cecile B. DeMille production of plagues and that old codger of a Pharaoh he persists and resists. Like Pharaoh was the first Nile–ist." Me.

"So there was this time when I was an intern and I used to take my beauty naps in July and August in the Cook County Hospital morgue as that was the coolest quietest place to rest and that's when I learned to play dead, and one day when the supervisor came by ranting and raving about sloppy procedures and comes by my table jabbing me a few times in the kidneys and says,… 'look at this cadaver, I am sure it's been out of the refrigerator for hours. Just look at that color…' And me, though I wasn't prone to argue, like the fellah says, still I thought boy am I glad my Mom ain't here, 'cos she would take it real personal after pouring down my gullet all that chicken soup and gefilte fish and kishke." Izzy.

"You think that when the time comes you will be better at being dead than someone that had no practice?" Me.

"Ah shucks, it ain't that hard, it kind of comes with the territory. But now I begin to wonder about 'for instance' dying and dying–dying." Izzy.

"One time Winters showed me this heavy Hebraic tome by a seventeenth century mystic where he described the soul-body relationship as a shoe that slips on and covers only the very tip and extremity of the soul that actually, though not visibly, stretches beyond into other spheres." Me.

"What did he say about sneakers?" Izzy.

"Well last year Yom Kippur night I was walking the Brownsville Streets with Winters and his honorable number one son to *shul* in the Old Age Home, and there we were all in our Shabbos finery, suits and hats all decked out and each of us wearing sneakers instead of shoes due to the Yom Kippur prohibition regarding wearing shoes. One of the black guys hanging out on the corner of Bristol and Clarke turns to his buddy as we go by and says, 'Man there must be a track meet at the *shul* tonight.'" Me.

"So a coffin is like galoshes I guess." Izzy.

"Whereas when Socrates considered the possibilities regarding death he said it's either the big undisturbed sleep which all agree is restful and pleasant, or getting to meet up finally with that all-star team of heroes, of leaders and philosophers and getting finally to *schmooze* it out with them…

But, I wonder…like who says that final sleep is anything at all like the sleep from which we do awake all refreshed and invigorated— cause here we never let go completely, and refreshment is experienced only post-sleep. Whereas diving into the big void, plunging into that eternal abyss of nullity that ain't just some cat nap nor beauty nap, inasmuch as one is stuck there for eternity." Me.

"Boy that's a long time." Izzy.

"Like being on the Long Island Expressway—foreverness!" Me.

"And even if you go his other route, so who says there aren't genuinely grimmer and bleaker routes that he did not consider? Like I heard the BQE ain't no picnic either!" Izzy.

"Wasn't it Rabelais who said at the very end that he is setting out, 'in search of the great perhaps'?" Me.

"Maybe." Izzy.

Neither the padding in the coffin nor the pillows were comfortable. A sickening, dizzying, perfume scent suffused the bedding. The berth was narrow and the sides much higher than I had pictured from the outside. I kept thinking I saw the lid beginning to slip closed. As good as he was at being dead Izzy—that apprenticeship had been served at an open table morgue—here Izzy was uncomfortable. His legs were really cramped. Maybe Izzy and I like Tom Sawyer and Huck Finn, maybe we would get to hear our own eulogies.

"What if we both fall asleep?" Izzy.

"I guess the shovel thud hitting the lid would wake us up." Me.

"Be lovely now to hear Berel screaming 'Shtey uff! Shtey uff avoidas HabBoireh!' (Wake up, Wake up to serve the Creator) "Did you ever get round to doing your will Stevie?" Izzy.

"Two years ago after a New Year's Eve bash, I thought that was it and I quickly scribbled out my last will and testament. I left my Rawlings mitt to my kid brother Teddy, my books to Marty, my interest in the hearse to Marty and Bam... now I guess I've got my *tefillin* to worry about. You know I really wouldn't want them to switch hearses on me, it just wouldn't be the same cruising that last mile in a strange vehicle... And that picture we took of Jackie Robinson by the roll-up door in the right field corner of Sullivan and Bedford where the players exited and kids and guys waiting to get autographs, no one could be identified until the door came all the way up except Jackie. Only the pigeon-toed shoes came into view and we knew it was him! That picture is also for Teddy. I guess my *tefillin* and *Gemara Bava Metzia* to you Izzy." Me choking up.

"Better take a second choice too! I should have had my stethoscope bronzed for my Mom, my hypodermic needle to Laibel and my autographed picture of Phil Cavaretta to my seven-year-old nephew Philip. My tefillin I borrowed from a guy in Buffalo." Here choking on his words, "and my *tzitzis* to you Stevie,...Did the ticking of your watch get louder? Or is that my heartbeat?" Izzy.

We did doze off a bit and I woke suddenly looking up at the lid.

"Oh my G-d I fell asleep. Steve are you there? Steve are you there." Izzy.

"I guess there really will be a resurrection of the dead." Me.

Quietly we exited our coffins and I told Izzy to wait as I checked the waiting room sofa to see if Blake was really asleep. He was. It was 4:15 a.m. The metal door exiting to the parking lot was at the other side of the large casket display room. The London Coach Casket had been placed in the refrigeration room and we had to get Miriam out and Lester up to the top. Leonard the number one watchman had said he would be back to make sure that the casket was sealed properly before morning. Now he was gone.

When we got to the refrigeration room we opened the casket and found Lester already on top with a note inside saying that Leonard had removed Miriam to a stretcher in the side room and Lester's coffin would be properly sealed.

"Boy this place is cold. I guess either we've been resurrected or we did not go to that other place. Cause boy this sure is cold." Izzy.

"Maybe that's really what that place is, really like so cold you can never get warm, and all the promotion about heat so that no one will bring along sweaters, coats and gloves and the cold will really get them." Me.

After checking to see that it was Miriam, we picked her up, placed her on a stretcher and carried her out of the side refrigeration room through the display room around the caskets.

"Be careful don't trip or make any noise." Me.

Opening the metal door to the parking lot, it creaked as we exited. Reb Shimshon was waiting, rushed towards us and took Miriam from the stretcher into his arms and placed her gently into a simple pine coffin that was waiting in the back of the hearse. Bam was driving.

"I think I heard some noises as we were closing the door." Me.

"That was just my heart coming back down from my mouth." Izzy.

"No I think there was a movement inside the room there." Me.

"Maybe Lester stood up for the 'Star Spangled Banner.'" Izzy.

Jumping into the hearse we sped off for New Montefiore Cemetery. I took the wheel. A grave plot had been secured there, but there would be no gravediggers on hand. Rav Winters was scheduled to meet us there with Marty and four dwarfs to make our *minyan* so Reb Shimshon could recite *Kaddish*. Dark as the streets were from time to time as we were driving I thought I saw somebody in the back mirror following us. Izzy said all body snatchers think someone is following them. I headed down Second Avenue towards the Brooklyn Bridge. Manhattan was not sleeping but not fully awake. Crossing the Brooklyn Bridge into Brooklyn any number of cars were behind us but it was hard to tell if there was somebody really following us.

On to the BQE out to the Long Island Expressway and then to the Southern State, less cars and I was doing seventy-five miles an hour passing the occasional lonely car in the right lane. Reb Shimshon continued to recite *Tehillim* all along the route. Izzy whispered in my ear, "Does *Tehillim* help for driving too?" as we swerved sharply around a bend.

Reb Shimshon directed me as we got off the Parkway to the cemetery. The stonework, the iron fences and gate of the new Montefiore cemetery were fortress-like. Like the old gag about people dying to get in. Here the mechitzah was for real. Passport and visa should be required to enter this new jurisdictional realm. Maybe that Greek was right, dying, not being dead seemed to be the real nasty part. Struggling to hold on. The pain, the agony. No groaning or contorting over here after crossing the border into the Sovereign State of the Dead. Not willing to let go, therein lies the pain; whereas here in the Sovereign State of the Dead in this land of the horizontal, all of the harried hurried rushing, squealing and mumbling was halted. A dominion of passivity and pacificity. All languages translated into the global tongue-of-quiet. Listening carefully one could hear the quiet, in this internationally recognized speech free zone. Any time, all the time, this universal chorus and its time honored timelessly silent anthem. Esperanto wasn't the real international language. Quiet was. Spooky quiet. Faces and words offer clues to what the speaker is thinking and feeling. Chaplin versus Jolson. Oft times Chaplin encouraged being taken for Jewish. The odd man out little tramp on screen and off the screen the archetypical silent outsider, socialist. Al Jolson, Jazz Singer that first talkie, a verbalizing Jew-boy, a *chazzan* singing. Deceptions, disavowals, dissemblings, dysanagnosia notwithstanding. Tone, gesture, grimace, indicated at least inklings of intent. But what the blazes are these disembodied mute souls up to? Though we could sense their presence, yet no hint of what's on their invisible expressionless yet so present minds. Aren't we and they fighting for turf? We of the sound and fury signify alien-nation intruders on their Commonwealth of Quietude. Border skirmishes erupt regularly as we, the yet ambulatory, try to encroach upon the borders of their terrain. With their population growth, and our population growth, and limited land supply, clashes were inevitable. Grasping for dominion while each and every officer and soldier of ours is suspect at any given moment of turn-coating to join the enemy. Dear dead Dylan and sundry other dying romantics had it that since the cycle redoes itself, the green fuse forces its way forth from the dust and rust of the earth and so life ultimately triumphs. But the Chofetz Chaim said we—all of us—were passport holders. Citizens of that Sovereign State of Ultimate Reticence. Like it or not, no one of us could renounce that citizenship. Resurfacing as brunch for some munching bovines, providing provender for the continuing cosmic cycle was no solace for my sense of me.

Once again, the neatly laid out tranquil streets of the little Cemetery Town, of Mortality County. Our Town. Marty was waiting with Winters, Sroly, Sleepy, Grumpy, Happy and Dopey to make our *minyan*. After numerous phone calls and notes left, Marty was unable to locate Benny. Ten of us alongside the open grave that'd been dug by Reb Shimshon, Winters and the dwarfs before we arrived. Removing the plain pine coffin from the hearse, we carried Miriam to her grave. Hand-held hoist and cinch were fixed into place to lower the coffin into the gaping gap. Grumpy held a flashlight as Rav Winters guided the hoist, and the casket dropped slowly into the grave. Reb Shimshon began to shovel the piled dirt from the edge of the grave onto the coffin. It was a *mitzvah* to bury the dead. Each one of the *minyan* took a turn shoveling.

"Dis[3] vas a *minhag*—a custom, by special *kehillos* in *der heim* in Europe dat ven someone dyink dey takink de table from de dinink room dat on dat table dey feedink dere guests and vas doink *mitzvas* from *hachnosos orchim* - givink hospital. From dis table dey takink him apart de table and makink de box for to bury de man or de voman vat dey dyink, so dat de *mitzvos* vat dey doink from *hachnosos orchim* should goink along mit dem to de grave… And in Dvinsk in *Pay-Vov* ven Reb Meir Simcha was dyink dey takink de piece from *de shtender* dat he usink to stand all de time and learn by him, and put *de shtender* by him in de grave… So I'm rememberink in *der heim* my Mirele's little *sharfer*, such a small brown closet mit tree drawers, vone big vone vot Mirele and her sisters and de broders is keepink tings dere. Mirele she had dere a doll vot she lovink him and playink mit him on top from *de sharfer*. Dat doll de *zaida*, my Sorele's father, givink Mirele dat time vot he brought from *Varsha* and von day Sorele, my Rebbetzin, is busy cleanink and de doll is not der and she is askink Mirele and Mirele she starts cryink mit dos big black eyes shinink mit tears and Mirele she is sayink dat de Dubinsky girl vot she is only nine and Mirele is eleven and de fadder from de Dubinsky girl is dyink and she don't have no fadder and no *zeida*, and no doll, *nebech*, so Mirele is givink de doll but please ve shouldn't tellink zeida vot he brought dat doll all de vay from Varsha… *Oi mein kind, mein sheine* Mirele… I should have him here dat *sharferle* dat closet from da doll from da scarves and gloves vich you took from drawers and givink away to differens *kinde* from dat *sharferle* ve should make him de box for my Mirele for to bury her from dat *sharfele*… *Ribono Shel Olam* vhen ve not havink de *Beis Mikdash* den ve are not havink de *mizbei'ach* but den you givink us *Ribono Shel Olam* a test and is comink *tzoros* and is every Jew not only just a *Kohen*, a priest, but is everyone den making a *mizbei'ach* in his own house in the *heime* and bringink so many sacrifices - *korbanos, Ribono Shel Olam. Ribono Shel Olam* you know dat is standink here a *Tatta* from a *maidele* and a *mishpoche* vat is all *korbanos. Mein Gutt* You knowink the real true dat my Mirele was a *gutte neshamah* and she vos gettink *fafeirt*. Ven dey needink me, my Rebbetzin Sorele, de Mamme and my *sheine kinde*, Yossel, *olev hasholem*, Yankele, *olev*

---

3 For the benefit of those who do not speak Yinglish, please see the translation in the Appendix, page 205.

hasholem, Itzik, *olev hasholem*, Channi *aleha hasholem* and Perele, *aleha hasholem* over dere, dey going up on de *mizbei'ach* – dere den ahm beink here. And Benny and Mirele over here. Den ven dey needink me here and ahm over dere and is going out a fire over dere from de *Shamayim* and the fire is burninck everytink in de vay. So many *kinderlech* ve givink on the *mizbei'ach* in de *heim*. *Oy* Yossel! Itzik! Channi! Yankele! Perele! Mirele! *Ribono Shel Olam!* So many *kinderlach* and *gutte, reiner neshomes*! Ahm rememberink, I am not forgettink de story from the *yid* in Spain, fahr five hundret years, runnink tzu Portugal, and den runnink from dere to Morocco gettink away on de udder side from de *yam* and dere his wife and children is gettink sick and dyink. And he is cryink to You: *Ribono Shel Olam!* Dey are takink from me everytink vat ahm, havink mein job, mein *kovod*, mein money, mein house and ahm havink to run away in de night like a tief only cause ahm ah *yid* and de 'Catolicen' becomink *meshugah* mit hate and ahm comink to Morroco *mit mein veib un kinde* and ahm tinkink ve have nottink but we are livink and den here dey all gettink sick and dyink *de mishpoche* – de whole family.' And he is sayink to *Ribono Shel Olam* 'You takink from me everytink, first *mein shtelle*, den *mein house, mein kovod*, everytink and now *mein veib* and *kinde*, for vot I don't knowink but is left only one ting by me and dat You don't take him away from me — dat's beink mine, dat's stayink by me *Ribono Shel Olam*. De *bitochon* — de fait dat all vat You doink, dat was for ah good even ahm not seeink de good *mit mein mentscheleche* eyes but dat's *mein* property belongink to me, dat *bitochon*, dat stays by me *Ribbono Shel Olam!* Ahm knowink dat iz comink back *neshomos* to fixink tinks vot dey breaking ven dey here de first time, so mit mein eyes I am never seeink de whole from de picture. Ahm not beink der to beginnink dis velt and I am not beink der to de finish. And ahm not forgivink de Germans, de Cossacks, de Babylons, de Spanish, de Polish, de Lituavanians, de Russians vat dey murderink us. Ahm knowink dat dey have *bechira*—choosink and ahm knowin dat you lookink on my Mirele's *neshamah* also like a *korban* from de *milchoma* and please *Ribonah Shel Olam* look on dis coffin like ahm makink him from dat *sharfele* and all the *goodskeit* from dat little *maidele* back in *de heim* mit de big black eyes is goink *mit* right now *mit* my Mirele. But you should forgivink me *Ribono Shel Olam* cos still ahm a *Tatta* and de heart is tzebrochen, broken like the *ershta luchos* and just like dey havink a special place in the *oren* for de first broken *luchos* also for broken hearts is needed ah special place by you *Ribono Shel Olam*, a special *oren*. *Oy* Mirele, *mein* Mirele please be moichel – forgivink your Tatta so much *vot de emes* ahm lovink you, ahm vasn't dere ven you needink me, *de Ribono Shel Olam* He knows dat ahm tryink *maidele*. He knows dat I am lovink you *mit* Yossel, *mit* Yankele, *mit de Mamme, mit* Itzik, *mit* Channi, *mit* Perele and Benny he should be *gezunt* and I am knowink, like Bruriah de wife from Reb Meir is sayink to him ven dere sons is dyink and he is not knowink yet, only she is knowink and she is askink him vot is *de halachah* ven is givink someone a borrow, a loan and den is vantink back the *pikadon*—de ting, de loan. And is sayink Reb Meir vat's de question for sure he has to givink him back cos it's only a borrow and den Bruriah is showink de two sons dat de *Ribono Shel Olam* givink dem for a borrow and now he is taking dem back. Is like ahm buryink here Yossel *mit* Yankele *mit* Itzik, *mit* Channi, *mit* Perele togeder *mit* Mirele. Is not for de *Rebbetzin* and me the *zechus* to valk *de kinde* to *de chupah* and for to seeink *eineklach* mit big black eyes. *Mein teirah* Mirele." Sobbingly.

"*Yisgadal veyiskadash shmei rabba.*" (Glorified and sanctified be His name) Brittle, granite, mosaic incantation, jagged words cutting quickly, sharply through the dark and quiet piercing to the quick of my bone. Our rag–tag *minyan* of dwarfs, Marranos, fiddlers, infielders and infidels, answering "*Yehei shmei rabba.*" In that perennially losing and demeaning bout with death, Jews manage to salvage a modicum core of ironic dignity with that incantation - recitation. Each soul a reflector of the Light of G-dliness in this world adding to the greater glory of the Creator. With the demise of a given soul and that reflector now absent, theoretically to result in a possible diminution of that Glory. And since He has no needs this was then necessary for us; to self-actualize, flex our spiritual muscles. Taking up on behalf of G-d, facing down our mortality, a fleeting moment of audacious privilege, reaching, touching Sublimity. Petitioning, praying for the replenishment of that light of G-dliness here in this world, our world.

After the *Kaddish*, Reb Shimshon, bending over to place a stone on the grave— "*Schloff mein kind, schloff* "—sleep, my child, sleep. Reb Shimshon repeating, twice and then a third time, "*Schloff mein kind, schloff.*" Then turning back again once more "Tell de Mamme, tell Sorele, not too long I comink also to be mit you and *de kinde* (children). It's such a long time I'm not seeink everybody. Tell de Mamme, tell de kinde soon I comink. And dis time ahm stayink."

❑   ❑

I was not anxious to get back to the *yeshivah*. Rosh Hashanah at the *yeshivah* did not beckon. If Izzy wasn't with me I might not have gone back. Then. Eventually? Maybe. Maybe probably. But not then. Once upon a time Rosh Hashanah at Beth Asher and then later at the Old Age Home had been serious enough to have some authenticity, tentative authenticity. If you go for authenticity. Temple Israel out in Lawrence was a social event, congregants there for the fashion show, walk-ons and spectators, not participants in the services. The theatrics of the cantor and the choir were less than Off-Broadway.

When Dylan Thomas paraphrasing that shepherd dedicated his poems in 'the love of man and praise of G-d' because he'd be a "damn fool if he didn't." What did that mean? He mean? It mean? How does meaning come to mean?

At the *yeshivah* it would be the tingling intensity of World Series and final examination time all wrapped up in one. *Elul, Selichos, Teshuvah* crackling electrically in the
air. Crescendoing from *Rosh Chodesh Elul, Selichos,* to the Big Game. Now we were there.
Preliminary exams and playoffs had been attended to. For better or for worse. Enough
to qualify. Faces, expressions, were now more sober. True, that Laibel and Pinnie and the
Rosh Yeshivah would still smile frequently. Not comic relief but rather the joy at being
enjoined, privileged to be invited to mark the anniversary of creation together with The
Creator. By now even the cadets had been mustered into shape. Time had run out. The
stakes were big. Biggest.

At Beth Asher or at the Old Age Home things weren't that intense to begin with,
old-timer games that I could straddle as participant–spectator, stepping in and out of
the action. There was them, and me. In the *yeshivah* it wouldn't be like that. With each
peer-powered vibrant *Shema* and *Amen,* each and every sounded and silent verse and
phrase, they all were declaring, inviting, urging, nay even demanding my engagement,
my participation. Beyond the stark tangible energy of their magnetic sincerity was the
sum total of all those hours in the trenches together, fending off despair, inertia, apathy,
the axis power enemies of learning and performance, the hydra–headed *galus.* Gathering
the courage to make an offense out of the defense. Together. We had sailed the seas of the
Talmud as a crew. Our crew. Like units here and there volunteering for special duty on the
flagship aircraft carrier of our fleet. From there, sorties flown to strafe enemy positions
soften the beachheads of attrition and assimilation. Now it was time to hit those beaches.
Down into the barges and head for the shores. Not to join these guys, these *bachurim,* was
copping out. They counted each voice, each additional soul, each added presence in that
war against national and religious annihilation. Notwithstanding our offense, they, me,
we were still surrounded. For so many centuries we had held on. Once again, ours was
to hold on till the fresh troops of the next generation would be called up. And so it was.
Intimidating, inspiring, confusing, boring, frustrating, beckoning, electrifying, exhaust-
ing. By turns and then all at once. Beginning in sequence, then concurrently we were
altogether and all alone. An orchestration of simultaneous solos.

New Year's Eve at Times Square was not Rosh Hashanah. That seething Bacchian Day of the Locust, crowding, milling, frantically celebrating, sought and fostered
mindlessness. At the *yeshivah* each choral rendition of each piyut scraped off another
layer of unconscious covering of consciousness closer and closer to that core of me-ness,
of self. Once exposed, now that self was heard and felt with an incipient stunning and
trembling starkness. Times Square with all its forced jocularity was a melting into a press-

ing and anxious oblivion. Beth Asher Rosh Hashanah had its poignancy the last octa-septuagenarian glee club on the reservation. Not a summoning to form and perform as at the *yeshivah*.

Generally speaking man's I–sight was poor. Hopelessly poor. Consciously and unconsciously our perceptions and responses were governed by a reigning me–ness. How does or might this or that or the other effect or pertain to me. We were all my-opic. Rosh Hashanah was an exercise in confronting that Otherness; The Utter Otherness. Like it or not, will it or not, there is that Supreme Objective Consciousness that ultimately likes it, us, our performance or not, and has willed it, us, into being with our field of options. At once diminishing, and elevating. As Prime Mover He was also Prime Discussant. The One Interlocutor one could not ignore. One could not walk away from that discussion. There was nowhere to go. Demeaning, yet elevating. My Maker, The Maker, our exchange was cosmic. Reverberating through space and time, permeated with Supreme Dignity and though there was a script and libretto for my lines, that recitation became my empha-sis and provoked, anticipated ad libbing and applauding. Alone. Together. That davening that liturgical rendering ever encircled by those swaying bodies, corralled by that cho-rale, ensconced within those mystical, mellow, muscular, masculine voices thundering the *Shema* for extended moments tears and joy mingling, at those very moments. Singing the subtle phrases, the import-laden nuances of diction and syntax, the learning powered davening of this *bachur*-corp-squadron, man made, that thunder. Yet alternating, for me, with who needs, requires this? That response not recorded in any *siddur* or *machzor*. *Yeshivah-bachur*hood, their arcane surging Hebraic, Aramaic, marching choir. So rabbin-ically clever, so allusive, suggestive, connective, symbolic, below and above the lyric and music. Perhaps instead, for me to wander off alone to some rolling green veldt near a lake, or better yet at the seashore, by myself. To be myself, alone with myself, touch the inces-sance, the infinity of the source of it all as me, only me. And so what if those excursions invariably luxuriate into one version or another of celebration of that me–ness. As seen through my I–sight. Me, watching me, watching myself watching. Lake and sea were then merely rippling reflections of me. If so, all I could see in seeing that sea would be some sweet, salty, murky images of me.

Perhaps then, one, I, did require these squads of choric incursions into the im-mediacy of my aural oral range, these quorums of liturgic troops, sounding their anthems, pleading, parading, through the twisting roads and paths of exile, and when stumbling they helped draw me up onto the road, the route, to that root joint commonality of our plight and the countless shared and unshared grand and petty nobilities and humiliations of our peoplehood and mortality. To go it alone was to play deaf to the dinning, crashing drums and cymbals of our marching history. Those private ventures invariably floundered and squandered, then reached for the common shares of public stock. This Yeshiva world steadfastly persisted in claiming we'd been awarded preferred shares.

If *Elul* had been the playoffs, and Rosh Hashanah the World Series, then Yom Kippur was the ninth inning of the last game of a tied series and we were coming from behind. Being judged presumed that one had free will. Responsibility. What had been achieved Rosh Hashanah through the festive meals, complementing the shofar and prayer, was on Yom Kippur attained through fasting and prayer. Nor had those meals been a gala splash. Rather a considered conscious eating, a decisive breaking of bread to give thoughtful tribute and gratitude to being part of that honor guard endowed with free will a commissioned commando vanguard. From within those ranks, an expeditionary force sallying out, clearing terrain and establishing footholds for the armies of Man. A specially trained unit skilled in the martial arts for the hand to spirit combat in the wars of body and soul. Simultaneously loyalist and revolutionary. Now the cadets were really into it. Mottel was in another sphere. Laibel was moved. Izzy was struggling like me with being there and not being there, and struggling with the struggling.

One Rebbe had put it, on *Tishah B'Av* who can eat? On Yom Kippur who needs to eat? No mindless abandon to this halachic ecstasy. Rather a kind of cerebral rejoicing and trembling at this standing on the tips of the toes of one's soul to reach far beyond one's normal reach. But the toes of our souls weren't meant for standing that way day in day out, only once a year we could do that. At most. The opening and closing opera / ballet of the Jewish soul.

With only one short break, the long, long davening started at 6:30 a.m. and around noon some of it had become tedious. I was weary. Some songs and rhythms pleasant, but there was a lot of private reading, recitation and vocalization by the chazzan and the congregation. Like being lost in a desert drifting through endless dunes of words. Time stopped. The clock stagnated. Again I thought, if I turned quickly enough I would catch those hands moving backwards. Just when I thought of bolting from the *beis medrash* and declaring my own intermission, just then a melody caught me and the lilt kept me in check. As sung by the guys that proud yearning vigor, a kind of ongoing anthem of allegiance, for the moment lining up just right with the vibrating metal of the tuning fork of my mettle. For the moment. A gull of the flock, I stretched my wings, arcing, soaring skywards together. For that moment.

Winters had said that we didn't get major league cantors at Beth Asher. Those mustached, beardless, pompous, poseurs, so transparently I–ing and eye-ing themselves all fitted out in their canonicals. Posing. Self-indulgingly lyrical leaps so off-putting. Some were bad, others were worse. Even those with range and pleasing voices were performers not *daveners*. Genuine moments at Beth Asher had been when the congregation somewhat joined in the singing and overcame the *chazzan*.

At the *yeshivah* the *rebbei'im* and a few married students led the prayers. Everything was in-house. No mercenaries. The *Rosh Yeshivah's* son-in-law, Rabbi Davis had a lovely tenor voice. Not strong, but moving. Leading the mussaf prayer, The Shadow had a kind of saying–singing, a kind of shadowy whispering incantation, while deeply–felt style. Since the Prophets had hung up their mikes, man's talking to G-d was monological, His answers came in pantomime. Or as a ventriloquist, like throwing his voice through one dummy or another. At Beth Asher, High Holidays for most of the congregants there had been frequent self-legislated intermissions often graduating to long interludes spent outside the synagogue. At the *yeshivah* I longed for such an interlude. At Beth Asher even while the prayers continued in the sanctuary, at times there were more congregants in the corridors and lobbies than inside the synagogue. Steps, streets, around the synagogue filled with once–a–yearers. At Temple Shalom in Lawrence, prayers served as interlude from the promenading, the strolling and strutting over the grounds, lobbies and parking lots as primary business. At the *yeshivah*, no breaks. This was it. Each play was now being recorded by that most Official of Official scorekeepers, tallied in the Cosmic scoreboard in the sky. Close calls weren't sorted out by flipping coins. Routinely, during the year our bodies were to be used. Pleasure itself, could be harnessed in the service of the Creator and the very pleasure was redeemable and a necessary resource. Time, place and people, the right configuration comprised a spiritually successful event. Yom Kippur we were challenged to be angelic. As if without bodies. As if. Like you needed that condensed existentially ethereal prayerthon once a year in order to reach the yearlong goal of successfully directing the body and its proclivities. Breaking the Bronco! Minding the matter. Because it mattered to Him, it mattered, my matter. Never mind! Oh dear what can the matter be? But while there was no promenading here at the *yeshivah*, a part of me was still rescanning, reviewing old scenes on the screen of my memory, there, back, then, now. Beth Asher. Temple Shalom. The *yeshivah*.

They'd coined a new flip for this court—a body-flip, pinky square for real this time, now it really counts. Meanwhile where was I, it, we, all of us? Heads or tails? It wouldn't quite do to forget that back then at Beth Asher and at Temple Shalom, if the davening had not pulled me in, yet the interludes had also grown tiresome. Also the human traffic. Tailgating, tailrating. Surveying the landscape. Suddenly then, there at the *yeshivah*, bachurim singing, surging, with a militantly lilting but lovely soaring arcing melody, maybe to be, maybe not to be. Heads or Tails? Hymn or her? Or would a battalion-choir of anti-semitic Cossacks be as riveting...? "Searching for the great perhaps."

The *shofar* at the climax and the spontaneous burst of dancing after the shrill peculiarly pleasant signaling at the end of Yom Kippur did work. Neither Beth Asher nor Temple Shalom had ended that way. That singing circle, their voices, the cumulative pent up nuclear energy transformed into electric particles of joy. Like the cascading of Niagara of Yom Kippur, energy immediately harnessed for home use for the workaday week, for the coming season. That singing circle, voices reaching, joining in joy—forging a cumulative pent up burst of nuclear energy transformed by Yom Kippur into voltage delicately designed for collective and individual use. For the workaday week. For the coming seasons, the routine of the year.

❏ ❏

Sukkos time most guys headed home. With only a few days between Yom Kippur and *Sukkos* it was a busy time organizing lulav and esrog and getting the *sukkah* up. Pinny and Laibel asked me to come along with them to the East Side Canal Street where street vendors were lined up at their improvised long board tables assembled on wooden horses surrounded by boxes of *lulavim* and *esrogim* to hawk. Awkwardly, at that open-air traditional bazaar, I followed Pinny and Laibel as they made their way through the stands and merchandise knowingly. Dozens of people milled and browsed inspecting the wares. People checked for the halachic requirements, first the minimal halachic pre-requisites for fulfilling the *mitzvahs*, then the added dimension to look for an aesthetic excellence that amplified the core halachah and its fulfillment. In order of priority, first the base line then the beautifying. "*Hondling*" (bargaining) — Pat would have said "Jewing" for the price was acceptable, expected. That was Sunday. On Monday I spent a few hours helping Rabbi Winters put up his *sukkah*. Pinny and Laibel and a few other guys invited me to stay with them the first two days of *Sukkos* which were holidays, Shabbos-like, *Yom Tov*. Carrying, cooking and cooking related activities were allowed on Yom Tov, but otherwise like on Shabbos there was refraining from other kinds of halachically defined constructive activity. Following the Yom Tov days there were the intermediate days of *Chol Hamo'ed*, which would be followed by another *Yom Tov*. Each of those slices had two days. A hero sandwich. *Simchas Torah*, the climax of the *Sukkos Holiday*, when the year's cycle reading of the Torah was culminated, would be a festive occasion of dancing and singing with the *sifrei Torah*. Most guys returned back to the *yeshivah* for *Simchas Torah* (festive Holiday of conclusion of Torah reading at end of *Succot*).

This would be my first time actually eating in a *sukkah*. I had stopped in once or twice after *davening* with Grandpa Bloom to make *Kiddush* in the Beth Asher synagogue with Reb Shimshon, but I never sat down to a full meal there. During *Sukkos*, Reb Shimshon would sit alone in that makeshift branch covered booth which he and Andy

Panda put up each year in the little courtyard of the *shul*. He ate and sang alone through most of the Yom Tov. Mr. Gordon, pale, balding, post office worker from Bristol Street was the only congregant who actually built his own *sukkah* yearly on his third floor fire escape. Other Beth Asher congregants often came in for *Kiddush* and left. About half an hour walk away was Rav Winters' *sukkah*. He was, and wasn't, a congregant; for the most part he attended his own *minyan* at the Old Age Home. Harvest time was chosen as the time to commemorate those temporary huts that sheltered the Jews during their sojourn in the desert. Ecclesiastes is read on the Shabbos of *Chol Hamo'ed Sukkos* as well. When bringing in the bounty from the field that was the time to be reminded that the material world is transitory. Now you have it, tomorrow you don't. Today you are, tomorrow you aren't. Those two most important facts of life. 1) It is. 2) Then it won't be. The *Rosh Yeshivah* quoted a commentary who said, "For most people their money has them, they don't have their money." Particularly, at that moment when the bounty of the crop might lead to headiness one is required to exit one's regular domicile and dwell for seven days in a temporary dwelling. How then is *Sukkos* yet so ironically a festive and joyous occasion? Undoing the illusion of material permanence is liberating, exciting, essentially joyous for one's soul, stepping rhythmically to the heartbeat of reality.

The story was told of the saintly Chofetz Chaim some forty odd years ago receiving a very prestigious visitor into his humble surroundings in Radin. When asked by this wealthy industrialist how it could be that he, the renowned Rabbi of Russia, Lithuania, Europe and the world—he, the Chofetz Chaim, author of such great halachic works—how could it be that he lived in such meager surroundings; where was the furniture appropriate for his stature and position? The Chofetz Chaim responded by asking the guest where was his furniture? The guest responded, "I am traveling, I am just passing through." To which the Chofetz Chaim answered, "Me too. I am just passing through."

That's what the *sukkah* is all about. Contrary to Mr. Goldwyn, these Jews thought and behaved like everything eating, sleeping, singing, dancing, everything had a message. Not just Western Union.

If eating and sleeping in that lean–to shack of a *sukkah* demonstrated and dramatized the ephemerality of the material, then most American Jews seemed to hold otherwise. Dwellings and possessions were deemed permanent. Surely that's why Providential Guidance had ordained that in this velvet–lined version of *galus*, the message of impermanence was sent in another manner. Through the ongoing shifting of neighborhoods, just as they were settling in, the Jews, they would have to move. Arriving from the shtetl to the East Side, from the East Side to Brownsville, from Brownsville to East Flatbush, from East Flatbush to Long Island, from Long Island to Scarsdale. Where next?

Still, the wandering Jew. If so, there was a case to be made for traveling lightly. It's easier, so much easier, to get up and go; to move quickly along that route, through these high-ways and byways of even this goldene galus. But instead, evidence indicated that more and more baggage was being accumulated at each stop along the way. Reb Shimshon was at home in the *sukkah*. He traveled lightly. So were most of the guys in the *yeshivah*. For them it fit, that added sense of joy, sitting in the *sukkah*, just because of jettisoning accumulated excess cargo. Of a moment, this moment, the liberating opportunity, to really run, climb, baggage–less. Unburdened. A tactile exhilaration in hitting and hear-ing that gong of truth. Like that Hit Parade revolving stage, that ongoing theatre perfor-mance, our tragic–comic existence we come to treat the props and backdrops, however temporary, yet as if they, we, were here to stay. Method–acting like Brando becoming the part. One day, rather soon, other actors will use these props and appurtenances in turn to be followed by other players who will in turn...

I should tell Dad about this. It would suit his credo of "The Race." Running without carrying any excess burdens, to rip and roar across those lanes and tracks of history. And then, piling more into the bulging bundles on our backs has us running so much slower. But Dad and I are still not speaking. Truth has it that since Lawrence, Dad has been more intent upon stuffing his backpack with more of the collectibles, the bric-a-brac, the casted, molded, crafted trophies of the Winners' Circle. But as Rav Gordon and Rav Winters often say, "a silent *chavrusa* (study partner) is no *chavrusa*." Dad was silent.

One time a few years ago I arrived straight from a Saturday night date or party to the schoolyard at 4 or 5 a.m. I curled up against the sag and bend of the wire fence along the first base line and dozed until chalk in time. I had my spot along the fence where the concave sag fit. It was early October, *Sukkos*–time and I was just about to doze off when it began to rain. I chased across the street to Beth Asher, but all the doors were locked. I climbed the fence of the little courtyard and made my way into the *sukkah*. In warm climates Jews sleep in the *sukkah*. In America it's rare. Though rain would come through the branches, it was better than sleeping out in the open schoolyard. One of the guys at the *yeshivah* had shown me the thought of the Vilna Gaon, that there are only two *mitzvahs* that encompass our entire bodies: the mitzvah of inhabiting Israel, the Land; and the mitzvah of *sukkah*. All other mitzvahs we perform with only a part of the body. These two mitzvahs we enter into the mitzvah, completely engulfed within the *mitzvah*. That's why ideally one should eat, learn, rest, even sleep in the *sukkah*. Inclement climate brought an exemption. More than an exemption, it was counterproductive when defin-itively uncomfortable to remain in the *sukkah*. Thus was there a question of whether or not by sleeping in the drizzle in the *sukkah*, whether I had fulfilled any *mitzvah*. When it rains one is exempt, but perhaps that exemption only applies for someone who has a house to enter into, to escape from the rain. For me the *sukkah* was the best option of shelter from the rain!

Aren't all man-made structures however tall, complex, and imposing really only sukkahs of one sort or another. Temporary. The Empire State building was a tallish concrete sukkah. The Chrysler Building, the Chanin Building sukkahs all. Will these buildings be standing as they are today some centuries hence? More intricate and less intricate, more beautiful and less beautiful. Frank Lloyd Wright,–Bauhaus–*Sukkas*.

'*Ah sukkalah ah kleina*,' with melody.

Ah Sukkaleh ah kleina

fuhn breitilich gemeine

hub ich mir a Sukkaleh gemacht

bdekt dem dach mit a bissele sach

zits ich mir in Sukkas by di nacht

A vint, a kalte

vus blus duch di shpalter

leshen zich di lichtelech zeyer fil

es iz mir a chiddush

vi ich mach mir kiddush

uhn di lichtelech zey brennan gantz shtil

Beym ershten gericht,

mit a blassen gezicht

trugt mir meyn tuchterel areyn

zi shtelt es avek

uhn zogt mit grois shrek

Tattele di sukka falt balt eyn

Zein nisht keyn nahr

und hub nisht kein tzar

zol dir di sukka nit tohn bank

es iz shoin guhr

tzvei toizand yuhr

uhn di sukkaleh zi shteyt nuch gantz fein

A sukkaleh, quite small,

Wooden planks for each wall;

Lovingly I stood them upright.

I laid thatch as a ceiling

And now, filled with deep feeling,

I sit in my *sukkaleh* at night.

A chill wind attacks,

Blowing through the cracks;

The candles, they flicker and yearn.

It's so strange a thing

That as the *Kiddush* I sing,

The flames, calmed, now quietly burn.

In comes my daughter,

Bearing hot food and water;

Worry on her face like a pall.

She just stands there shaking

And, her voice nearly breaking,

She says

"*Tattenyu*, the *sukkah's* going to fall!"

Dear daughter, don't be foolish;

It hasn't fallen yet.

The *sukkah's* fine; banish your fright.

There have been many such fears,

For nigh two thousand years;

Yet the *sukkelah* still standing upright.

Whose *Sukkah* will outlast?

Now, it was still summer. Izzy had come in for Operation Jeremiah—our Tishah B'Av Beth Asher mission. Arriving Erev Shabbos he stayed with me in my inverted basement garret and we ate Shabbos meals with the Winters, *shalosh seudos* at the Old Age Home and a late *melave malkah* at the Winters. We drove out to Coney Island after the *melave malkah* and met Bam and Marty at the Mermaid's Tale to have some beers. Décor, furnishings, had grown seedier with the passing years. Staff and clientele had also changed; I didn't recognize any of the waiters. Neither Sid nor Benny were around. We went over the strategy for tomorrow night at Beth Asher. Izzy headed to his cousin in Woodmere.

It was 3 a.m. by the time I got back to my place and dozed off in my clothes. At 8 a.m. I jumped up and ran to the Sunday morning *minyan* at Beth Asher. This would be the last Sunday *Shacharis* in the history of Beth Asher. Tonight, the last *Maariv*, but this was the last *Shacharis*. Dwarfs were pulling up in front of the *shul* and convening. Sroly in his van, Andy in his pick-up truck, were dropping off some of our guerilla *minyan*. Across the street, in the schoolyard, the softball recruits were limbering up and chalking in. For a time the bussing policy worked for Beth Asher and PS 189.

Two softball games in the blistering August sun. It was The Nine Days and to-night would be *Tishah B'Av*. Bam and Marty would drop me at my parents and head off for the beach. Had it not been The Nine Days, *erev Tishah B'Av* I would have joined them. Real *yeshivah bachurim* did not go mixed swimming at all, even not during The Nine Days. I had bought in on some of the mitzvahs. What Rav Winters called the supermarket syndrome. Shopping around with my cart I'd picked some *mitzvahs* off the shelves. *Shabbos, kashrus, tefillin*. Though, those as well were on trial purchases. Yet? Or? Maybe like a new pair of shoes I was wearing them around a bit until they stopped pinching. And like with that new pair of shoes I also reserved the right to switch back to the old ones when the new ones pinched too much. Or bury them somewhere in my closet perhaps eventually to find some shoeless recipient to receive them. 'All or nothing' was a compelling principle, logically on mark, yet I was decidedly undecided, a kind of young hound circling, encircling, searching for the spot where I would eventually lie down, meanwhile continuing my roundabouts, sniffing, but not yet quite ready to collapse.

During The Nine Days I elected not to join them at the beach. Somewhere in the labyrinthine recesses of my inner soul, a piece of that collective memory of the *churban* and holocausts still resounded. An echo, a groan, a cry, was faintly audible in the chambers of the inner ears of that Jewish soul of mine. Faint, but audible. Laibel had once said that perhaps I was a *gilgul* (reincarnation) of some Jew who had lived through that *churban* (destruction) and had been sent back again to tidy up the mess left on the desk of that earlier life. Thinking about tonight, again palpitations, and the sudden plunge of the gut, again, like falling quickly in an elevator. Round and round that maze of a thorny mulberry bush unable to escape that Joe Btfsplk-dik *dybbuk*, who seemed to have settled his gloom cloud over me. Maybe in earlier *gilgulim* I had been on other Pequod-like failed missions, starcrossed voyages, recorded if not recollected in me and my various *galus* meanderings.

□   □

Dad was in the backyard catching with Teddy. Mom was also there preparing food on the barbecue, that last family vestige of the kosher rite, our suburban altar erected out of filial allegiance, today only occasionally activated for pious progeny. She would then wrap left-over victuals in tin foil and bags for me to take back to Brooklyn.

So call me Israel. And when the slicks of grime in the gutters of the cityscape become too slippery, when the quotidian daily redundancies grew thick and smothering, and the velvet-lined angst, the softened grind of being and not being, of winning and losing, of being a winner-loser, of Jewing and not Jewing, of verbalizing and not verbalizing; whether 'tis nobler to act or to sit pat or perhaps Patless. I could still re-enter that Sadie Hawkins Day race couldn't I? Could I not atavistically return to my pre-Sinaitic at least partially pagan status? Of late when such doubts and glooms grabbed me, then chasing through the streets, the alleys, walkways and courtyards of Brooklyn and Manhattan, and rather than Melville–like knocking people's hats off, I might go and recruit me a *minyan* for Minchah and start slapping hats on people instead. Or like that poet I could find my way to the Rockaway coast, drift with the ebb, do the dead man's float out into the sucking grating tide into the roil and boil of those seething sibilants of my existence. Seas and ships, schoolyards, subways, *shuls* and synagogues, Jewesses and *shiksahs*. And here I was in this fenced in compound chalking on to a voyage on the Pequod-cum-Beth-Asher. Waves of collective reveries reverentially washing over my consciousness. Now the Santa Maria, with the Nina and the Pinta right alongside. My fellow Marranos impressed from such schoolyard–like fenced in compounds back there, then all chalked in to discover a new world — the old one having become impossibly grim.

Our Maritime Marrano-Mafia: Zaccuto touching up his astronomical charts. And when Isabella considered diverting her pledge of the crown jewels to finance the war against the Moors to Columbus' expedition it turned out not to be necessary. Santangel and the confiscated properties of exiled Jews sponsored that trip. As Professor Herbert B. Adams said, "Not jewels but Jews were the real financial basis of the first expedition of Columbus." It happened 465 years ago, it's happening today. De Torres translating from Spanish to Yiddish for Reb Shimshon. Columbus readying his log with the customary big "Beis-Hei" (Boruch Hashem, at the outset of writing traditional blessing G-d for that ability) in bold black ink in the right hand corner inscribing 5252, the date of the Jewish calendar. *Erev Tishah B'Av* and Chaim Chaskel Columbus, Genovese Marrano, also known as Christopher, noted the traditional date of the destruction of the Temple as 68AD and postponed the voyage from *Tishah B'Av* to a day later. Then. Now, we were in the pews of that seaman's sanctuary down at the docks. Those pews pickled in the briny sweat, sighs and tears of sundry saddened and lost seamen. Widows, missing buddies, fathers, sons and daughters. Walls lined with marble cenotaphs memorializing long gone, short gone, kith and kin who had sailed the seas of galus. Inscribed and dedicated by the bereaved. The storms of this longest exile. Reb Shimshon high up in the bow-like pul- pit preaching, gesticulating to his motley weather-beaten congregants. Waiters from the Mermaid's Tale, Uncle Sid resurrected with other long deceased former congregants. Mr. Katz, as usual, nodding off through the sermon. Rosenstein, Rosenberg attentive, approv- ing. The remaining dwarfs, chins shelf high at their built-in, fold-out prayer book holders. Seas are contradictory, unpredictable. Soft and harsh. "C"s are soft and harsh. Coney Is- land and cenotaph. Sheeny and kike could also have been spelled with Cs. Soft and harsh. We seamen and C–men. Whelan, Tony and Andrew were there too. Whelan's all but shaven glistening black head under the light of the swinging ceiling wheel like lantern. Reb Shimshon spoke about Yonah fleeing his responsibility and signing up instead for the voyage to Tarshish. The storm. The sailors' lottery. The whale. The miracle. Coelacanths. "C"s soft and hard, that once thought to be anachronistic outdated extinct specie. Then lo and behold sighted off the coast of the Cape! There they are! Alive and swimming! Like schools of Coelacanths we Jews! Expected to, thought to disappear become extinct. Research and theories notwithstanding, predictions and declarations of imminent extinction and strategically concentrated schemes, planned pogroms; with it all, in face of it all, schools of Jews regularly sighted swimming off global coasts. Jewish schools. *Yeshivahs*. Salmon and herring–like swimming upstream against the current to breed and thus had those fish become staples of the Jewish diet.

Reb Shimshon shrouded in his cape-like caftan stretched and waved his arms. A captain in a caftan remonstrating against desertion, preaching and reaching out for recruitment. To enlist gallant souls, to accompany him on his voyage. To chase around the seven seas and pursue that rare elusive White Coelacanth, to lower his praying de- votional *minyan* of wailing sailors in that adjunct smaller boat to harpoon and rope in that long-thought-gone yet surviving extra-ordinary school of fish. Check scales and fins for *kashrus*, clean and bone, grind the meat down and cook into delectable gefilte fish patties, for Shabbos and Yom Tov. Reb Shimshon now tugging at his white beard pondering the point he was expounding. Maybe that's the secret of *galus* survival, quietly, clandestinely feeding on White Coelacanths, and noshing on salmon and herring. Reb Shimshon bending towards his listeners, with that piercing penetrating stare, target after target around the hall, one by one, locking eyes with his listeners, those fidgeting squirm- ing listeners. Like at a shooting gallery, one by one–ing them down. Now straightening up to his full six–foot plus height.

Tarshish–bound, that ship, caught unexpectedly in a raging sea, sailors pray and petition (the Talmud says sailors tend to be believers) and after casting a ballot to determine the likely cause of the raging storm, they turned to the mysterious Yonah. When questioned he admits he is fleeing from his G-d and his G-d's command to go to Ninveh and rebuke the people. Yonah assumes responsibility for the storm as direct expression of G-d's wrath. He recommends they remove him from the ship predicting the storm will relent when they drop him off. They attempt to near the shore to deboard him, but are unsuccessful and finally, asking forgiveness, reluctantly they cast him from the storm-torn ship into the raging sea. And even as the sea quieted the sailors were filled with remorse.

Reb Shimshon pauses momentarily, the floor is moving. The ceiling lamps swaying slowly, quickly, wildly, the scratch and clang of metal on metal, of colliding, slipping furniture. The entire hulk and bulk of Beth Asher moving out of its moorings, breaking loose and out to the harbor, out to sea, rolling, sailing to the great deep expanse. On deck now, Reb Shimshon up on the bow studying the waters. Waves lapping against the hull of the tall imposing square-rigged HMS Beth Asher. Goody high up in the crow's nest with a telescope affixed to his eye, scanning and rotating, searching the seas for signs of that rogue White Coelacanth, that maverick of mavericks. We American Marranos, especially suited for that expedition, like Columbus' recruits. To spy and search them out, those inexplicably existent denizens of the ocean with their vestigial lungs, we with our vestigial Jewishness. A friendly ship sighted by Goody and they boat-bellow their greeting. Meshugana Morris bellows back resounding basso buffo horn-like tones. After days of empty calm Goody from up high in the crow's nest screaming 'ship ahoy on the north east horizon.' Reb Shimshon at the tip of the fiddle bow with Reb Winters both peering forward. Perched up high on the jib boom gathering cord, Mottel battening down flapping ropes of the mizzenmast, Laibel climbing down from tightening a spanker running over to join Reb Shimshon and Rav Winters.

"They are flying the Jolly Roger!" as that square-rigged man of war, that hulking galleon came into view at the edge of the horizon. "All hands on deck, they are flying the Jolly Roger!" From somewhere "Prepare for battle, prepare for battle!" Only one musty, antique paltry cannon on the HMS Beth Asher. And one dusty, rusty round of dated ammunition. "One should not rely on miracles, let's be practical let's *daven*." Mottel organizing a *minyan* and a *chazzan* to say *Tehillim*. Now coming into closer view the Jolly Roger with additional flags furling and unfurling in the wind, emblemed, emblazoned with the ancient and medieval devices of Egypt, Babylonia, France, England, Persia, Spain, Germany. A motley crew of pirates. Also a swastika and hammer and sickle. A proper man of war the S.S. Amalek unveiling double tiers of cannons the length of the ship, like the toothy grinding grin of a monster about to pounce. Variegated warriors, corsairs, armed with swords, knives and guns anxiously hanging from ropes and masts straining to leap.

Reb Shimshon recites the *Shema*, Rabbi Winters lights the fuse of the lone archaic cannon. Izzy and *Meshugana* Morris on deck as the S.S. Amalek pulls within shooting and shouting range. Our single cannon fires and their cannons fire. Their round of shells fall in the sea, in a circle all around HMS Beth Asher. Our feeble single shot fells a pole and knocks over a lantern. *Meshugana* Morris lets leap from his barrel chest a voluminous volley of consecutive verbal explosions. Stunned buccaneers on the S.S. Amalek fall to the deck ducking the impact of MM's fulminating fusillade of exposed explosions. Verbal bombs and vocalized volleys of shells. Meanwhile the felled lantern has lit the sails and the masts are tottering as the fire rages across the deck of the S.S. Amalek. Pirates fall to the deck. Flaming, falling sails and poles hitting the deck. Planks and walls of the vessel catching fire, smoke and walls of flames everywhere. Burning, cracking, crackling masts, poles, ropes and sails. Frantic screaming and frenetic racing and failed attempts to quell the leaping fires engulfing the deck. MM pounding the air relentlessly with thundering barrages of roaring reverberating fusillade. An extended thickening hiss and the S.S. Amalek tips forward, sinks, and disappears into a closing sea.

Once again Reb Shimshon up at the bow peering out to the north east, his beard whipped back across his right shoulder in the sea wind. Goody up again in the crow's nest stern side, Whelan squatting on a capstan whitening his black face with shaving foam, and smooth-shaving his beard with a harpoon. Izzy checking first the pulse and then the eyes of a sick sailor. At the westerly side Pinnie, Bam, Marty, Laibel, MM on deck munching matzah and gefilte fish sandwiches as the gallant windjammer HMS Beth Asher speeds its way due east now seeking out the elusive White Coelacanth. Behind us in the west the sun, like G-d's own golden yo-yo, a burning sinking orange orb dipping, dropping seaward. Pinny running the decks to make sure everyone had *davened Minchah*. A kind of fluid joy in trembling the utter endlessness of the sea...

Mellow *shofar* blasts like honking, then more shrill soundings waking me from my sleep, my dream. Heeding Dad's injunction not to pull the hearse up in front of the house, Bam and Marty were waiting at the corner. I had slept for about an hour and they were waiting. Mom had the sandwiches packed and ready. There would be some tuna, salmon and gefilte fish, but also cold cuts. I would keep the Mendel purchased cold cuts until the afternoon of the day after *Tishah B'Av* when halachically one could eat meat again. Bam and Marty would go at it now.

Mom handed me the packages. For her this was still my extended, however prolonged, picnic in Brownsville. One day, soon hopefully, that picnic would end and things would again be just as they had been. Deep in her heart she knew that's the way it would turn out. Dad thought otherwise. And meantime he could not forgive the mean-time.

Still, in the backyard catching with Teddy, he would ignore my departure as he had my arrival. Sometimes Teddy would break to come out and say hello/goodbye, sometimes not. He was good at picking up on the intensity of Dad's mood, he was on to the 'whether-vein.' Sometimes he even sneaked a half smile, more eyes than mouth. After my stalling a little then some more, it appeared that Teddy wasn't coming out. Mom gave me that "there–are–things–that–are–felt–and–can't–be–said" look. And while she seemed on the verge of crying, she switched quickly to a smile. As I crossed Central Avenue near the corner where the hearse was parked I turned back once and Teddy wasn't there. Nor Mom.

Marty and Bam had picked up Izzy before they had come to get me. Usually, upon being picked up, Bam and Marty would report on the days collecting and cataloguing beach fauna. Today would be different though. If it wasn't pre–*Tishah B'Av* for Bam and Marty the way it was for Izzy and me, yet tonight's proposed caper also had them rather heavy. I jumped into the hearse. A pervasive sense of purpose was palpably thick in the air. Still tucked and lurking in some dark corner of my mind, that observer that studied me being me, noting the increasingly anxious sense of a risky mission. We drove off like it was a B29 and our flight and goal were crucial for the cause, laced with peril. I preferred to drive, and Marty and Bam went to the rear of the hearse, Izzy sat next to me.

As usual, most drivers on the road offered that special deference to the hearse. Driving on Seagirt Boulevard and then under the Rockaway Freeway elevated train, on our left spreading towards the beach the summer clapboard bungalow sea-front community of Rockaway; summer squatters. Along about Arverne began blocks filled with patches of converted now all–year–round shanty–town dwellings for migrant semi and wholly destitute blacks and Puerto-Ricans. Then once again the beach people coming from a day in the sun. Some towing kids. All lugging the requisite equipment for relaxation, chairs, tubes, pails and shovels, blankets and large bath towels. Wet sandy miscellaneous paraphernalia of a day of fun and sun at the beach. Floppy hats, straw hats and caps. People half dressed, just baked bodies, red, brown and black and white. Whites looking to be darker, blacks looking to be lighter. Female cakewalking and promenading were not merely introductory, means, and preparatory, rather goal and feting of her femininity. Whereas that ubiquitous smart masculine strut calculated flex and stride as necessary and exultant, yet ever preliminary to be measured by results. *Tachlis.*

Belle Harbor, solid brick and stone, moderately elegant to utterly elegant, all-year-round-homes. And summer homes. Along the sandy marshy shoulders of Beach Channel Drive camping families settled in, settling in. Some came to fish in the bay strip between Cross Bay Boulevard and Marine Park Bridge. More blacks than whites. Sometimes we drove over the Cross Bay Bridge passing through Howard Beach. Boat people and their invariably white-to-gray neat well-kept clapboard and aluminum sided homes. Houses on water stilts. Fronting, as if floating on the bay. Goysville. Any Jewish boy rolling the dice on the board of the game of galus and landing here would have to take ten steps back. On to the Belt Parkway. We'd risk the ticket, in our once–was commercial vehicle. Belt Parkway, the concrete cummerbund that encircled the Brooklyn bulge with a bit of overlap clasping in Queens. Gulls gracefully ascending, arcing, dipping and then climbing again equally picturesque over the bay or the garbage dumps of East New York and Canarsie. On the concrete belt speeding cars like projectiles from pinball machines surging and zipping forward in and out of their lanes. Every twenty or thirty cars a zig-zagging Indianapolis speedway driver searching for his lost track.

Through the rear view mirror I watched Marty and Bam awaiting zero hour. Marty adjusting and re-adjusting his Marrano cap. Soon we would be over enemy territory and it would be jump time.

"What are you thinking about?" Marty to Izzy.

"Come on Izzy you gotta be up–beat!" Bam interjecting.

"Well, I am two thirds there — I am beat...! Okay, so like I guess I oughta think about making it out. I got it. I am picturing a whole 'nother picture. There's this grey shingle house with wide wrap around porch, out in Dayton. And there are weeping willows and there's this piano teacher on the corner of Elm and Maple and the girl that came by every Tuesday at 5 for a lesson. So like if we make it out, I'd really kind of like to take them out for supper the two of them to the kosher deli and..." Again Izzy choking up.

"Come on Izzy, you'll do it, it's easy as kosher apple pie." Marty.

"Well, it's not so simple" with a cry in his voice, "I wish it were but I'll tell yet it's just not like you think."

"Okay, let us hear why it isn't so simple, tell us why..." Marty.

"Well if you guys really want to know," here losing his fight to check the cry, "it's like this — only 'cos you really want to know right?"

"Right" in unison this time Marty and Bam.

"Well firstly, I never took any piano lessons, I never had a piano teacher."

"Now how much do you think it costs to get a piano teacher?" Me.

"But there was no teacher, and there was no girl." Izzy sobbing.

"The yellow pages are full of piano teachers." Marty.

"And the girl," Izzy sobbing more heavily.

"We'll get us a *shadchan*!" Me.

"But guys, I'm sure there is no kosher deli in Dayton!" Izzy.

"We'll import some salami and rolls." Me and Bam.

"Are you ready?" Izzy.

"Ready." Izzy, Bam and Me.

"I've never been to Dayton in my life!" Izzy.

"Big deal, so how much can a Greyhound bus direct to Dayton cost?" Marty

"I feel better already. Don't forget the pickles and mustard." Izzy.

Turning off the Belt Parkway at the Pennsylvania exit, that black strip of pavement traced and lined rather than altered the primeval contours and topography of those untamed heaths. Closer to the bay, sandy marshy terrain. Further away from the water high grown weeds interspersing the grime, oil, fumes and debris of garages, junkyards and heavy-duty factories. The soiled soil of the East New York Canarsie swampland-workland. Eviscerated carcasses of abandoned cars. Windowless, tireless, seatless. Chewed to the bone. Burnt and vacant like blanching cattle skulls in the desert. Dipping and bouncing with the rolling turf, the sags and swells of Pennsylvania Avenue, the bats and balls in the back of the hearse rolled and banged noisily. By the junk yards, mounds and mounds, of once mobile, stacked, dumped and heaped car shells. Like tossed by a whirling cyclone, some piled more neatly, most chaotically. Masses of motionless hulks. There had been a car-holocaust. Next the smelting furnaces.

Some gas station personnel were noticeably squeamish when we pulled up with the hearse. But doing the 2 a.m. shift at the Pennsylvania Sunoco station at the end of the East New York wasteland, his predecessors and this attendant had undoubtedly, while filling them up, had their own fill over the years of a variety of innovative land fill programs and projects. Murder Incorporated had favored the area, though it was prudent not to discuss what had been seen in those wee hours of the morning. Squarely, cartoon-like, absurdly festive, yellow and blue Sunoco pumps amidst the grease, litter and dirt, but the overall squalor of the station could not be overcome by the celebratory bright colored robots. Somewhere, I had seen the thesis propounded that after a time, dogs and their masters came to resemble each other. High-boned with his tail between his legs the huge

German shepherd blended in with the general greasy décor of that surly gas station and its attendant. The loping gait of the dog mimicked that of his two-legged companion. Whereas that jowly uniformed biped with his hang-dog look had acquired a low guttural growl, now lowly directed at us.

Hearses should not have to stop at gas stations and line up with all those other plebian cars. Just as hearses were awarded traffic privileges, so ought they to have a comparable deference for their other mundane needs. Hoisted up for a grease and oil change or some repair was the worst indignity. Mechanics poking and puttering about the under-innards of that hearse, draining, spraying gas and oil, and smells and greasy surfaces was a mockery of the dignity of the hearse and its calling.

At the east end of the heath across Pennsylvania Avenue, the batting range. Now dark and deserted. Thursday night at eleven it had been jumping with people and noise. Robot pitchers like from an out of space team. Quarters, duly inserted in those mechanized *pushkas* (charity coin box), and the automated Martian hurlers raising their erector set arms firing their pellets. Usually with some accuracy. Usually. Bam always came with his own bat. There was that unforgettable time when he began connecting solidly on the first few throws sending, soaring shots beyond the lights into the night. Suddenly from Bam's cage, "Hey! These pitches are hitting the ground before the plate, what kind of crazy range is this!? Do something will ya! Quick do something! It's wasting pitches. It costs money!"

"S'what you goin' so crazy for? Dat's like de real thing, de real McCoy. Some pitchers lose their control like dis here is the real thing. You should oughta appreciate it," the short flap–eared mousy looking guy with the nervous darting eyes, and the wide wide mouth—we called him Mickey Mouth—rolling the change in the pocket of his grey apron-front as he defensively came towards Bam's cage. "Like de real McCoy."

By now Marty and others were yelling as well. "Moron, if we wanted the real McCoy we could have stayed in the schoolyard and not fed quarters to your monsters." Marty.

Mickey Mouth pulled the juice and went out to the pitching battery. About five minutes of tinkering and he switched the juice back on. Running low to the ground like trying to avoid being picked off by enemy snipers he returned to the spectator side of the cages. Of a moment from all ten cages, terrified screams, as the pitches now went directly at the batters, swiftly bombarding them. Pitch after pitch directly at the hitters, while a few of the cage doors jammed and batters could not escape. Ducking the firing of those Martian hurlers Mickey Mouth crouched, crawled out to the firing battery and pulled the juice again. About twenty men and a few women gathered around Mickey Mouth and demanded their money back.

"What are you knocking me out? Dems the breaks, like the real McCoy." Mickey Mouth. One tall hitter said he got hit in his pitching arm and he's going to sue. With Mickey Mouth's sneer one muscular guy promptly lifted Mickey Mouth upside down and holding him from his legs shook out his apron-front of coins. Shades of Tarzan Weiss. Quickly the crowd collected the coins from the ground and dispersed. That was a year ago. Tonight everything was enveloped in a foreboding darkness. Wistfully glancing at the batting range as we pulled off the Sunoco station, Marty said it might be more efficient if we had mechanical women like mechanical pitchers. A lot less bother, waste of energy and confusion. Izzy said in fact there were mechanical women but they had a different name for them.

Rav Winters had told me the story of the maskilim who had come to Rav Chaim Oizer with a petition. Reb Chaim Oizer the *Dayan* of Vilna who used to write two intricately reasoned responsa simultaneously, one with his right hand and one with his left hand—so were there eye witnesses who testified. These medical students, maskilim who had bolted from the religious community, were put upon by the Polish authorities and the registrar at the medical school, to pressure the Jewish community to supply more cadavers for research. Ostensibly there had been a relaxation of university attendance quotas for Jews—but still there were problems. The most recent critique offered by the registrar, claimed that since Jews did not submit their bodies for autopsies, Jewish medical students were learning their medicine on gentile cadavers. (There were unique *halachic* exceptions when a one-to-one relationship between a cause of death and a possible remedy for a similarly sick person might be identified. Possible yet, to be quantified by *Halachic* authority.) This was unfair. Unless the Jewish community would begin donating cadavers for research there could be no continuation of the study by the Jewish medical students. The young *maskilim*'s proposal was then, that given the poverty and conditions in Poland at the time there were a number of Jewish prostitutes— these women had an extraordinarily high mortality rates. Yet, their bodies as well were not allowed to be submitted for autopsy by the Jewish community. Could Reb Chaim Oizer not re–evaluate that decision and allow these women's bodies to be donated to the medical schools for such research? Reb Chaim Oizer stared down at his open Gemara then looked up at them and said, "I know what you think of these women. You think you know what I think of them. But neither of us have any indication what G-d thinks of them! They are Jewish girls who, however they have gone astray, they are Jewish."

Back into the hearse, quitting the Sunoco station, closing in on East New York, the encroaching crowding in of civilization. Leaving behind the primeval heath, the marshes, the bay, the swamps, the dipping gulls. Now instead stretching, extending walls of brick and window began. Building packed streets. Square and angular, tall and squat, thick and thicker, taller and lower houses. Regularly rectangular blocks, oddly interspersed with irregularly truncated lots and structures, tenements strung with metallic fire escapes like petrified distended concertinas. All that brick and concrete, jigsawed and interlocking lined with never ending lines of parked cars.

Night brought some respite from the din of all that growling, colliding frenetic density. Brooklyn, the sprawling magnitude. Not the slim elegant obelisks of the Manhattan skyline, but instead these thick shorter herds, buildings, tenements and houses like inert mastodons frozen in huddled immobility. Like once they had roamed these planes, these fields, valleys and dunes in an earlier epoch, then checked by some prehistoric cataclysm that had frozen and fixed them brick like, square and stiff, atrophied; once power strong herds running, yet these streets of brick–rock canyons and concrete mazes still vibrated with periodic echoes, rumblings of those accumulated collected once upon a time hoof beats. And one could still feel the tremors. Like so many urban Leather-Stocking and Deerslayer city dwellers we'd learned while young to hear and feel those scents and sounds. Somewhere deep in the well of the urban unconscious it was feared that one day the thrall would end and the stampeding rampage would once again resume, the myriad pounding hoof beats would once more thunder through the bluffs and hollows over the urban range the plains of the cityscape over the Brooklyn prairies and plateaus. Subliminaly far off yet intermittently imminent first as whisper, then thicker and louder that however antiquated ancient roar re-echoing now and again howlingly pounding its way into the syncopated clashing, clacking, bleating din of the El trains. Growling, groaning, clogging traffic, foreboding crescendo of those rushing oncoming myriad hoof beats. Doomsday. An incipient trepidation, the gnawing knowing repressed anxiety of city people, ever just below the surface. Maybe that's what the fellow meant when he said, "Only the dead know Brooklyn."

Under the little mason work bridge that shouldered the occasional desultory freight train at the edge of Canarsie—usually just a few cars but sometimes seemingly endless random linking of box cars with scores of haphazardly different markings. What did Reb Shimshon, Sammy and Gabriel think when they saw box car trains? Just beyond Itzik's Isthmus the Brownsville East New York Canarsie triangle of factories: faceless stone-slab, nameless brick and concrete steel plants, sundry sorted sordid factories and workshops. Discarded relic metal debris, piled, strewn broken twisted once–were tools no longer functional, deserted rusted machines lining the half paved, once paved, nonpaved, wild grown, muddy, oil slick streets and driveways.

In the hearse we had four passengers. *Meshugana* Morris, Reb Shimshon, Winters and three dwarfs would be brought by Sroly to complete our *minyan*.

A few Beth Asher artifacts would have to be cleared out. One *sefer* Torah, its silver crown and pointer.

Overhead, from a block away the piercing screech of the El train bending along Livonia Avenue towards deeper East New York. At the spot where Uncle Sid had decked Abie Rellis' goon. Driving along Sutter Avenue shops, steel grates locking in mannequins, jailed in display windows — perhaps to keep them from escaping? A few gutted storefronts and buildings. Everywhere broken glass on the streets, gutters and sidewalks. Again gouged out couches and broken chairs along the curbsides. At night Beth Asher really did appear ship–like at the pier of the canal, that inky murky edge of fluid road, Beth Asher docked at its triangular roadway wharf of a sidewalk. The HMS Beth Asher manned by ghosts who flitted over the decks through the hold, the staterooms and cabins below. Tonight, we would be shipping out. Crew returning to their point of origin. Tonight's Maariv would be the last prayer at Beth Asher.

The marooned HMS Beth Asher, this fortress of ghosts….. Unlocking the big padlock that bolted the tall front metal door, then pulling open that creaking straining door, resisting on its rusted hinges. The war was over. I went in alone with a flashlight and some candles and matches for backup. For a few weeks already the electricity had been off. Though I had run through this empty building a number of times with Andy Panda of late, now it was more palpably empty. A hovering tangible emptiness, the ceiling was higher, corridors had become wider and longer, the darkness and emptiness merged to overwhelm the flashlight. The very ether of the atmosphere had been emptied and blown away by unseen demonic forces. An invisible herd of silent dragons inhaling and sucking me into the black and blackening vacuum, pulling me into a threatening, all–enveloping pit of emptiness.

For the last seven years the Sunday morning *minyan* was the only *minyan* at Beth Asher and was held in the small *beis medrash* in the basement. But tonight's last Maariv, last prayer at Beth Asher, was to be held in the main sanctuary upstairs. So had Reb Shimshon requested. Marty and Bam weren't from the *daveners* but tonight they would be part of our *minyan*. We left ten *siddurim* and ten copies of the *kinnos* (prayers of lamentations), with Lamentations in them as well. Those *kinnos*, printed in flimsy pamphlets, in many congregations were not kept from year to year, a kind of expression of optimism that 'til next *Tishah B'Av* the Temple would be rebuilt. In those congregations where the *kinnos* were not retained they were consigned to *sheimos* (fragments of holy script), those depositories of torn and unusable pages from holy texts reserved to be buried. At Beth Asher the kinnos were kept from year to year, in retrospect perhaps the entire structure had been one great *sheimos* bin.

Long before I actually stumbled upon Reb Shimshon speaking to the empty pews in to the sanctuary I had heard that he gave such spooky *drashas* to the visiting ghosts of former congregants.

Now again, high up on those steps standing in the candlelit squared–off railed–in *bimah* platform, tall, hoary, white bearded, black caftaned, himself apparitional and apocalyptic in the flickering candle light. Winters had commissioned me to make those last rounds through rooms, halls, sanctuary, basement, offices—like that pre-Pesach last search for *chametz*. Checking the premises alternately with flashlight and candle for left-over articles. If I did not have a feather, I did find a half filled bottle of Three Feathers. Probably one of those bottles from which Mr. Zaks regularly filled emptied Canadian Club bottles. Shutting the flashlight I sat down way in the back, in the last row as I had done other times when coming across one of Reb Shimshon's soliloquy *drashas*. Caught in the cross drafts of that tall vaulted hall the single orange *yahrtzeit* candle near him on the *bimah* danced feverishly. It seemed that Reb Shimshon could not make me out sitting in that last row in the east part of the dark sanctuary near the back door.

Walking around the platform he peered into the darkness, the empty pews seat by seat like the seats were occupied. Now, with his left hand on the corner rail-post his face and eyes catching the reflection of the quivering orange flame.

"So [4] I'm seeink you comink back for the last *Kaddish* by Beth Asher, Kaufman, Katz, de Rose boys, Rosenkrantz... like vas yesterday ahm rememberink ven she vas dyink your veib in Bet El Hospital and you son Marvin de psychologist is away in de college in Boston and you askink him for to comink to see his Mamme before is too late and he's tellink you dat he's beink busy workink on a hexperiment mit rats for monits and is time now for dem to do a special ting and anyway is not no difference since de Mamme vill probable not knowink whose dere and whose not dere so its not no difference and you comink cryink to me Katz and you sayink 'dis is a *mentsch*?! Is by him more important de rats den his own Mamme.' So now is comink de time Katz and ahm askink you for to re-membink twenty-five years ago ven I'm askink you should send de boy to ah *yeshivah* and first you are laughink and den you mad on me and den you gettink mad again on me ven ahm askink again and den is comink de funeral and he's not sayink de Kaddish for his Mamme cos he said is for him not meanink anytink. An you sittink by me and cryink how terrible is to have a son vot he not sayink no Kaddish for his Mamme and ahm tellink you ahm not havink a patent for turnink back de clock, and I know you tinkink so he not goink to say Kaddish for you neider. Oy Katz, gleib mir dats der iz difference kinds from korbanos, iz sacrifices vot is korban tzibbur vat every Jew is havink to bringink ven he is likink or no, and deres korbanos yochid, a privata korban, but der is also vot de mentsch is makink a privata chiyuv, and its der vot he's bringink cos he's vantink himself decidink vot he is not supposed to bringink also. De Rebbetzin and me un de kinde in dat gehin-nom dere ahm also bringink korbanos. You hear me Ketzele? Five korbanos, mit de Eu-rope'ishe yidden vot dey vent up on de mizbei'ach and is dere sacrifices but is not by us to decidink over dere. Den He is havink rachmonos de Ribono Shel Olam and is givink us a goldene galus, a goldene medinah in America but ve goink and den makink here from dis goldene medinah our own privata korbans vat He's not askink and He's not van-tink and we not havink to do dem... You knowink my Miriam and Benny and ahm not being here ven dey needink me. And de Rebbetzin is all alone but you Katz, you here, you havink de parnassah is going by you de gesheft and before ahm goink to dat hell over der ahm beggink you den for to teachink him Marvin in a *yeshivah* and no, and den vhen you so sick also by de end in Unity Hospital and Goldberg's nephew de doctor sayink is only days you askink me I should say de *Kaddish* for you and you not even askink for Marvin to come because you knowink he's not comink. '*Sof davar hakol nishma.*'(At the climax all is clear) It says in de Midrash by de funeral dat's tellink us ven dey sayink de *Kaddish* and de *hesped* how is vas de man's life. By dat end iz tellink us all from de beginning; and de middle, de whole story ve knowink from dat end... And you, Rappaport, ven you callink me in de middle from de night and your vife is screamink ven your daughter Rosie com-ink home from Syracuse with a *sheigitz*, and Rosenberg, when your Arlene is comink home pregnant from de mountains—tell me Rappaport and Rosenberg, you askink me before they're goink to Syracuse and to de mountains? No, you laughink on de old man mit de beard vot talks Yiddish and den dat same minut vot ahm runnink down dat hell and fire over dere dats burnink over dere mit dat *sefer* Torah from de Gdansker Jew vot he's givink me, de zelber minut you here in Beth Asher while I am runnink in de night like a tief over der, in de middle from de night mit de *sefer* Torah—and dat same minut you tearink down de *mechitzah* in Beth Asher. You here in de *goldene medina*h and ahm der in *gehinnom* and you decidink dats de most important ting for to use you hands un you hearts un you heads, for tearink down de *mechitzah*... Oy de Roses, oy Katz, oy Weiss, you so sure you knowink better, such big *chachamim*, you sayink ve not needink dem de *mechitzah* and by you, Berkowitz, it's going so good de junk business and den de building business—so good dat you movink away from Brownsville to Long Island den ahm com-ink to you in Great Neck in dat big house and ahm askink you for a loan one time for de *yeshivah* in Ellenville vat dere's a leak in de roof by dem, and von time for Horowitz cos he's losink his job, you are makink *mit* de nose. And for four months you *dreyink* me, next veek, tomorrow, next veek and ahm callink and final ahm stoppink even to askink you. And now by you, *de gesheft* is *in der erd*, and is like dat story from de Chofetz Chaim vhen is comink to him a yid vot says to him ahm not forgivink you Chofetz Chaim vat you doink to me. And the Chofetz Chaim is not knowink vat he's doink him and he's tellink him de Jew dat vonce in 1915, 'you comink to me for de *yeshivah* in Radin and days you asking me for to givink a donation and ahm not givink de donation and den is comink de Bolsheviks in 1917 and takink from me everytink, de whole *fabrick* and *sechorah* and leavink me mit notink, so now ahm tellink you de true ven you comink dat time if you pressink me more so maybe iz possible I'm givink den, so at least today I am havink still de *mitzvah*, but now 'cos you not pressink me, ahm not havink not de money and not de *mitzvah*, ahm empty'... So even if you not comink and tellink me Berkowitz ahm knowink vat you tinkink in your heart today, you not havink de *mitzvah* and not havink de *fabrick*... Silberman and Kalman you givink den de *gelt* for Horowitz ven he's losink his job and de *yeshivah* also a little bit trough de years you givink sometink for *tzeddakah*. Ahm rememberink all the *tzores* vot you makink here in de *shul* but I ahm also not forgettink de *mitzvos* vot you doink also. From de beginnink ven ahm comink here alone to America and de Rebbetzin is stayink back in de shtetl and you vantink puttink the *aron kodesh* in de *maarav* and not in de *mizrach* and Bloom and Stein and Rosenman is *mit* me and Veiss and Katz and Berkowitz and de Roses is *mit* dem. And takink de architect and makink de plans vat dey vant before ahm goink de second time to dat *gehinnom* for to lookink for de Rebbetzin *mit de kinde*—ven ve still only in de basement downstairs, ahm movink him de *aron kodesh* togeder mit Bloom and Rosenman back to de *mizrach* but den vhen ahm not here you doink the vay you vant him and putting him in de *maarav*. Oy is always vos a *shul* mit de *farkerte aron kodesh* mit de *farkerte luchos*. And also de *mechitzah* and de mishebeirach for Stalin's Russia and de *sefer* Torah mit de blood from dat Gdansker *yid* and now again like ven you vantink to make him a *shul* mit ah *shvitz*, ah mens' club mit a tiny *minyan* mit a *mechitzah* and a big *minyan* mitout a *mechitzah* and now you vantink to sell him de whole buildink. Ven is den the trials der in Nuremberg after the *milchamah* is sayink von from dose Nazis *yimach shimum* dat ven dey askink dat Nazi how is possible dat dey doink all such terrible tings to men, vomen and childrens and murderink, shootink an' in de gas chambers and everytink all de *tzores* dey doink to such innocental peoples and iz sayink de Nazi by de court vot you expectink de Nazis all dey doink is better organizirt vot for two tousand years de church is teachink un spreadink and makink pogroms dat de Jews is not human beinks and iz by dem like ah *mitzvah* for to makink dem *tzores*, terrible *geferliche tzores*. Vat by dem dey makink dem for *tzaddikim* dem vat is makink more *tzores* for us and is callink dem "saints", people vos is makink de biggest *tzores* and killink and catchink and *shmadink* more *Yiddishe kinde*— and to dem I should sellink de *shul*? To dem dis *shul* mit all vats here, de problems here still is vas still a *shul* and dese valls is *eidim*, is hearink all dat *davenin* is stucked in de valls and is in de ceilink in de plaster in de wood in de brick, all dat *davenin* and also Schwartz and Katz and De Roses and Vladimirsky and de others vot dey vant it should be a yiddishe teatre for to take him de *zal* vere all de *davenin* Rosh Hashona and Yom Kippur and makink from dat a platz for makink jokes from Torah and de mitzvahs mit nivul peh and znus and all de maskilim all you doink is lookink on Yiddishkeit like mit a kook from de eyes from a *goy* and even vorser, and from everythink is joke and *shmutz* and from dat you callink Yiddish 'kulture' 'cos you talkink *Yiddish* not *goyish*? Listen vot I'm tellink you den pouring salt on a *shtickle chazzer* dats not makink him kosher by de *Ribono Shel Olam*. You knowink here all de time, all de beautiful *kinde* dat's comink to *daven* and learn de *aleph beis* how much ahm tryink for dem dey should goink to an *emesse yeshivah* but from all de years ahm not *matzliach*—only mit Sendelman's boy and Bernstein de plumbber's daughter. And even dough all does years I'm knowink how *shvach* is de Talmud Torah so maybe from de *sheine kinde* one day some from dem rememberink a little bit from dat *Shema*, and how I ahm tellink you Katz and Rosenman all den vat iz goink happenink ven de *sheine kinde* is growink up, *takke* dats vot *nebech* happenink. Ah *novi* ahm not, but ve know vot is de *galus* everyvere de *galus* is no good when de *goyim* is good to us ve forget and gettink *shikker* and den runnink to be like does *goyim* and is no good ven dey no good to us and making us *tzores azay* is no good and *azay* is no good. Is today *Tishah B'Av* vat is dere in *Eichah* de *Novi* writink *kara alai mo-ed* callink de time. Is true strange 'cause "mo'ed" meanink usual ah holiday and ahm also losink Miriam and Benny so many years away. Ven dey dere ahm here— ven dey here ahm dere. Only now I am talkink to You, *Ribono Shel Olam*, You knowink the true, how ven someone is *shikker* by him no more the *koach* for to doink what he has to doink; after so much years Europe and so much insultments, *tzores* ven dey don't givink us to breathe an ve chokink so den for de Jews ven dey comink to America ve don't take him de *chessed* like a *matona*—like a present, and in de stead ve gettink *farshikkeret*—drunk in de same air vot dey lettink de Jews to breathe ve forgettink, but ven is someone *shikker* is *pottur*—unresponsible, is den he not havink responsible for his hactions... All dose *Shabbosim*, so many *Shabbosim* de Rebbetzin, *mein* Sorele, alone mit de *kinde*, and me, ahm over dere alone and de whole time ahm *davenen* dat vill be ah ness for dem comink back but my Yankele, Yossel, Itzik, Channi and Perele is goink up on *de mizbei'ach mit millioner anderer kinde, un elter mentschen.* A Slabodke *yid* is tellink me dat by dem in de slave camp is a question *mit de tefillin* on Tisha B'Av ven you not supposed to puttink on de *tefillin* in de mornink but in de afternoon, but for dem dey not comink back til iz dark and ahm seeink de eyes of *mein kinde* on thousands, millioner udder *kinde* vot for dem de night and dark comink early in der lives and dey never goink to see de morning to put on de *tefillin*, iz not for me to take mine boys to *barmitzvah* and *tefillin*, and every night ahm seeink Yankele, Yossel, Channi, Itzik and Perele dere dey standink in de clothes vot dey are wearink and how dey are lookink on me dat last time dat ahm seeink dem den ahm leavink for de goink to America and seven-year old Perele in dat yellow Shabbos dress vot she vant to vere because ahm goink, Perele mit de big black eyes like Miriam is cryink and sayink ve not goink seeink you no more Pappa, no more, and ahm sayink no mine *sheine maidele* soon I am bringink you to America mit me soon de whole family. But Perele still sayink 'No papa no papa.' ... But *Ribono Shel Olam* mein Perele vas beink right not me, oy Sorele *meine taireh froi* ahm seeink in you eyes dat you knowink den in you heart dat Perele is right and ve all not comink togeder no more, de whole family, no more."

Standing on the bimah platform, that raised square at the center of the great empty hall again like a boxer in a ring, but now even more like that loyal black trainer of Garfield's, that punchy devoted ex-boxer turned trainer, writhing with disappointment, chasing imaginary adversaries around that deserted ring, in the empty vaulted *shul* arena. Stalking phantom opponents, swinging quickly, sharply, wildly at the air, ducking ghost punches that black man sweating profusely, reliving, refighting every old bout. Finally, collapsing to the floor of the ring. But Reb Shimshon did not fall. A few times he faltered, choking back the cry in his voice, and continued. Standing up now, firm and listening hearing something I could not hear. An 'amen' leaped not from his throat, but from somewhere deep in his heart. Only he heard it, that ethereal Kaddish. Chanted by the ghosts of those former congregants. That phantasmagoric quorum returning to Beth Asher each to recite his own Kaddish, that Kaddish that their children could not / would not say for them. Another heart rending 'amen' leaped out and "*Yehei shmei rabba.*"

[5] "So *Ribono Shel Olam*, ahm keepink here de *shul* all dos years ven no more *yidden* in the neighborhood so dese *neshamos* can comink back to sayink here dere own *Kaddish*, vat de kinde dat dey hardly never is bringink here to *daven* is not goink to sayink for dem. So dere is no more goink for to be here de *shul* from Beth Asher. You knowink *Ribono Shel Olam de tzores* vot ahm havink here all dese years and you knowink dat I'm *moichel* dem, de Roses, Katz, Vladimovsky, Berkowitz and all from dem in de *Olam Ha'emes* and dese *chevrah* vot still here still now makink me *tzores*. Ve havink too much trouble, too much *tzores, Ribono Shel Olam* and ve are *fartummelt un farshikkert*. Now is comink de time ven is no more goink to be de *shul* ahm knowink dat I am not givink him dis *shul* not for "*laitzim*" to make ah Yiddishe teatre, vhere dey are makink *choizek*—ah joke from de Torah and not for dose *goyim* what dey makink two tousand years pogroms making to preparink for Hitler, *yemachshemo*. So dere is no goink to be here no *shul* no more and de *minyan* for de *neshomos* from the *alter mispalelim*, dey are goink need a new

---

5 For the benefit of those who do not speak Yinglish, please see the translation in the Appendix, page 209.

place to say dere own *Kaddish* or maybe like is sayink in de *Shulchan Aruch*, is still holy dis place dis ground and even if is not here no more de *shul* dey comink back here to dis place vhere vas de *shul* so long still to sayink dere own *Kaddish*."

At first glance there seems to be little relationship between the state of mourning and the text of the Kaddish, the text praying for the greatness and sanctification of G-d's name. One Chassidic master explained that each soul initially sent to the world is a reflector of a certain bit of G-dliness in this world, a mirror reflecting that light of G-dliness on earth. With the departure of any given soul, there is that much diminution then of that portion of the revealed Presence that had been in our sphere of existence. Family, as closest observers and recipients of that specific spirituality are most alert to the loss, that reduction in spiritual energy in their environs. And so they are charged with petitioning the Creator to replenish that missing manifestation of G-d's presence. i.e. the recitation of the Kaddish. Yisgadal... To regrow that sanctity within our space *Yisgadal veyiskadash shmei rabba*.

That was two days ago on "*Zayin B'Av*," 7th of *Av*. Tony's cousins the Pindalfo Wrecking Boys wanted the walls and ceiling to implode towards the center. Studying the structural plans, they placed explosives around the two main support beams. That would do it. Throughout our history it had been that way, we implode first and only then the host goyim detonate and devastate us, explode us from without. After we have imploded. But that "want ad" that the Master Planner places in the Providential Times: "Wanted vicious tyrant, seasoned evil-doer, with c.v. substantiating merciless nefarious track record, to mete out retribution..." That ad is then voluntarily responded to by the Nebuchadnezzars, Pharaohs, Hamans, Torquemadas, Chmielneckis, Nicholases, Hitlers and Stalins of the world. Of their free will they earned their evil wins sadistically, satanically, indulging their hate. Such is their culpability. I told Tony that we took him and the Pindalfo boys because, "You Romans have been in the Temple destroying business from time immemorial!" And like that congregation in Gdansk, where the Jews got together just before the Nazis could take the *shul* and turn it into a stable or a brothel as they had done with synagogues elsewhere, those Jews themselves blew up the *shul* rather than see it so desecrated. Rabbi Winters explained that Reb Shimshon also differentiated between Gdansk and the Beth Asher situation, but all those notoriously nasty Yiddishist broadsides at *halachic* observance and the cumulatively inimical track record of the Church to Jews through history, culminating with Pastor Thomas' hate campaign in particular, had disqualified each of those two alternatives. That left the Gdansk plan.

Tishah B'Av night we gathered together then, for that last *Maariv* at Beth Asher. Not having electricity was fitting, as anyway the custom was to act as mourners, to sit upon the floor and read the text, chant the Lamentations and the *Maariv* by candlelight. Candles and matches had been prepared. Rabbi Winters led the prayers. Once again no stammering. He smoothly lilted through the *Maariv* in that ironically, paradox-ically-pleasant, controlled-sadness, of a mode and began the touching elegiac plaintive reading of Lamentations. "Even in the land of dispersion we become ministers to our masters"—teach the commentaries on that verse—like 1492 the Abarbanel with Ferdi-nand and Isabella, needed as he was for his economic genius, yet rejecting their offer to stay on even with a select *minyan* in Spain, explained the Abarbanel what will be with the other expelled Jews will be with me. It was then. It is now. After Maariv I went to make one last check in the downstairs weekday *beis medrash* with Izzy. The flashlight had died and Izzy walked close behind me carrying a flickering candle.

"Do you think ghosts believe in people?" Izzy.

"So how many people do you know that you can believe in?" Me.

Izzy wet his finger and began ceremoniously, chalking an invisible list on the blackboard of the air. Reviewing the list he shook his head, and began erasing, chalking, erasing, and re–chalking his unseen list in the air. Finally winding his thumb talmudi-cally in a few warm-up strokes, he lifted his arms and set his face to his, 'I–am–stumped' expression and pose.

"Maybe perhaps we could borrow that willing suspension of disbelief? But then again what's the difference dis–belief or dat–belief?" Me.

"You need collateral to borrow. Actually I got a few sixteen inch soft balls left over from my years in Chicago..." Izzy.

"No good in New York." Me.

"We could wash them in Brand X and watch them shrink!" Izzy.

"My Dad knew this guy in the textile business whose daughter had this complex and they took her to this shy shrink who wore purple ties..." Me.

"Yeah", and together now "One of those shrinking violets!" Izzy and Me.

"Ever since the time some patient clobbered him with an unabridged tome of Burton's Anatomy of Melancholy, he began noticeably shrinking from violence and land-ing as it did on his head that massive volume, it left him with a distinct depression!" Me.

Together, "That's heavy stuff."

Reb Shimshon's last *Kaddish* pierced through the dimly lit hall echoing, resounding through the darkness.

"*Yisgadal veyiskadash*" his voice choking, yet defiant, he stopped, continued. A few dwarfs scurried in and out of the room. For *Shemoneh Esrei* we turned east away from the platform of the architect's original ark. Then, following Reb Shimshon, the *minyan* lined up one by one to kiss the doors of the small improvised ark that had been set up on the east side of the sanctuary. Both had been emptied, and the larger ark that had been in the west had already been removed. Now we picked up and carried out the empty make-shift *aron kodesh* that was in the east.

Tony and the Pindalfo boys advised us that everything was in place. Reb Shim-shon climbed the steps to the *ezras nashim* to get one last look at the entire sanctuary from above. There, where the *Rebbetzin*, Rebbetzin Havisham appeared and waited each Shabbos in her black dress with the large white polka dots and rounded white collar. Waiting for Benny to show for his bar mitzvah, no–show Benny. Zaks had offered to take bets, who would show first, Benny for his *bar mitzvah* or the *Mashiach* to redeem the Jews. Zaks laughing and crying as we exited turning to me, asked, "I should lock the door?" It was hard looking directly at Reb Shimshon, that long–deep–depressing, cutting sadness etched into his face. Was this what the Talmud meant when they said that the building of youth is destruction and the destruction of elders is building? Or perhaps we had really jumped on the Pequod–cum–Beth Asher and were on our way to oblivion. Reb Shimshon, Winters, Zaks, Rosenberg and the dwarfs held with Reb Shimshon; Marty and Bam held the Pequod thesis. But they also held: So what? The Pindalfo boys were for hire. While in practice I had thrown my lot in with Reb Shimshon, Winters and Zaks, I con-tinued to have moments of doubting. And in suite, doubting my doubting. While there was no injunction to sound the shofar on *Tishah B'Av*, yet that sounding was allowed at urgent moments of turmoil and tragedy for a community or congregation in deep stress. Reb Shimshon pulled out a black *shofar* from somewhere within his caftan and began sounding the *tekiyah*, (long unbroken sound) *teruah*, (quick short sounds) *tekiyah*. We exited the building now and standing on the street and he again sounded. *Tekiyah, teruah, tekiyah*. A few mellow sounding notes and then rippingly wild bleats as of an impaired shrieking beast. Echoing, bounding through the blackness of the city streets. Now gath-ered together across the street at the entrance to the deserted schoolyard shrouded by mountains of brick and mortar, our rag–tag guerilla *minyan* turning towards Beth Asher. "*Yisgadal Veyiskadash*." My stomach leaped to my mouth. Three bronchially rasping loud dull thuds in quick succession and the building collapsed. Inwards, like a tent. Crumpled, crumbled. Except for the eastern wall mostly standing amid the rubble and debris of the torn beams and ripped plaster strewn over the lot. My eyes burned.

❑ ❑

The corridors, stairways and courtrooms themselves all had that antiseptic sterile hospital odor. Germ free, story free, emotionless. Carefully wiped clean of humanity after each session. Even after the first hearing and the bail posting it all seemed so dream like, story like, as if the film would end and the lights would flick on and I would be back in the real world, my world. Meanwhile, a bored bailiff read a *megillah* (long story) list of charges against Reb Shimshon and me for executing the explosion and Marty, Bam, Andy and the Pindalfo boys for being accessories. Malicious destruction by intent of a synagogue, disturbing the peace, unlawful use of explosives, endangering property and persons.

I had appeared in traffic court once for a speeding ticket. A few times as spectator in night court with Pat or Marty and Tony for entertainment. Now I was the entertainment.

Fitted out in his black gown with all the practiced expressionlessness, still a little too proud and carefully coiffed, Judge Lombardy, sitting, presiding from on high, every so often, shifting the papers before him. Maybe those canonicals, vestments came from the same store where Cantor Weiss shopped. Judge Lombardy also looks like he might gargle with raw eggs. Maybe that was sheet music in front of him that he was sorting out. He cleared his throat and I waited for the "Star Spangled Banner," "America the Beautiful." Or maybe if this was a day of judgment he would also do "*U'Nesane Tokef.*" (He shall enforce).

Those cardboard cutouts called the jury, that random sampling of our society, that blindfolded willy-nilly selection and elimination process that affirmed our national faith in the soundness, goodness of Everyman, now one by one officiously fidgeting into position to weigh and decide the fates of the lives before them. If they had not chalked in yet this happpenstance configuration was still a choose-up/pick-up-game jury.

VANDALS DESTROY SYNAGOGUE, had been the Daily News headline. And later, INSIDE JOB. SYNAGOGUE FIREBOMBED in the Daily Mirror. The New York Post—BROOKLYN SYNAGOGUE DESTROYED.

Lefkowitz had told us not to speak with reporters as they hovered and crawled about like ants over crumbs, making the most of the least. Judge Lombardy as well had decided for a temporary embargo on interviewing: Too many emotional and religious overtones that could exacerbate feelings and moods prejudicing sound judgment inside and outside the courtroom.

Eight men and four women lined the jury. Marty's father, Bam's parents, Rabbi

Winters and Andy's daughter sat up front studying, trying to aim some eye contact at those cardboard cutouts like at a shooting gallery. Mom and Bam's mother in their black hats and veils like they were attending a funeral. Oscar Wilde said of that Lady supporter she knew exactly which hat to wear to meet him upon his release from jail. It hurt, that 'my–son–the–terrorist–but–he's–mine–anyway' look, but especially Bam's parents dressed in their soberest and finest like that meant they respected the severity of the proceedings, the system, the court, the judge, and perhaps he and the jury would be touched by their obeisance.

Marty's father in his sixties, slim wizened once upholsterer, now cab driver, with his flat tweed cap in his lap, till today whenever he spoke it was like he still had a mouthful of nails and was careful not to move or open his lips too much.

"How can we ever go ahead and prosecute vandals and hooligans who go about destroying and defacing houses of prayer, public and communal property and then on the other hand allow this kind of flagrant violation of peace and order? A democratic and just society must be evenhanded and consistent in meting out his rewards and punishments. It is unconscionable and un-American to pardon, to assign any impunity to a particular group merely as a function of that group's religious beliefs: Today they destroy their congregational buildings, nor was it their personal property, albeit empty buildings but the public's buildings; tomorrow that same logic of license would destroy populated buildings destroying life and limb as well." Melvin Katz's prime disciple and prosecutor Morton Williams.

"Objection, your honor, the prosecutor's leap from the question before this court of property damage, to an imagined scenario of loss of human life is a light year's leap into fantasizing and has no relevance or bearing to the case at hand." Our lawyer Lefkowitz, was Rabbi Winters' brother-in-law.

"Objection sustained," Judge Lombardy.

"The incorporating charter of Beth Asher states, 'Inasmuch as the members and their duly elected board voted and determined that the premises and resources of this facility and organization are dedicated to establishing and maintaining an Orthodox *minyan*, as such all board members, Rabbi and Sexton, must be Sabbath observing Orthodox Jews and committed to furthering the ideals and goals of Torah observance." Lefkowitz reading from the paper in his hand.

"A charter is merely an expression of the will and the organization at a given time in a given context When past members are replaced by new ones that charter in fact must be amended to meet the present needs of the new members." Prosecutor.

"A charter is the equivalent of a constitution. Could an amendment to the US constitution determine to return to being a British Colony? Or a monarchy? Or return the land to the Indians? By definition a founding charter cannot be rescinded. Means and ways of fulfilling the charter are negotiable but not the essence, the core raison de etre of the organization; to act otherwise is breaking with its continuity, rejecting the founding organization in favor of a new reality which it constituted to be unconstitutional!" Lefkowitz.

"Charters are charters and constitutions are constitutions. Who is to say what is core and what is not core? Maybe, in fact surely, accommodating the social-cultural-spiritual needs of the present Jewish community is the core mission of that organization. Given the demography and socioeconomic realities that prevailed at that point those needs were best expressed through an Orthodox service. Today the community has other norms and needs, and I stress, norms of expressing those needs, feelings, loyalties and duties." Prosecutor.

"What if an entire community of KKK members emigrated to Brownsville East Flatbush and then as bona fide neighborhood residents they applied to become members at Beth Asher?" Lefkowitz.

"Beth Asher is a Jewish community resource. Members are morally and legally honor bound to respect..." Prosecutor.

"As determined by whom? How Jewish is Jewish? What if these KKK members like bagels and lox and gefilte fish and Yiddishe klezmer music?" Lefkowitz

"Where, pray tell, does it state in the charter that the synagogue may be destroyed? Under what authority could such a decision be taken and executed?" Prosecutor.

"The charter states that the premises may not be used for any purposes other than an *halachic minyan*!" Lefkowitz.

Judge Lombardy called Reb Shimshon to the stand.

"So ahm seeink in front from me ah jury vot iz twelve difference nice peoples from Brooklyn. But ahm also tinkink and seeink a few tousand years from mein people de souls from de twelve tribes in front from me now vot dey is also sittink here. An dey knowink all de *tzores* vot is livink tru our people in de history, in England, France, Spain, Poland, Hungary, Germany but also by de Araba... Den ve comink to a place America vot iz givink us to breatd and to live, like Jews if ve vontink."

"Your honor, I fail to see the relevance of this historic diversion." Prosecutor.

"Mr. Prosecutor, that is in fact the crux of the matter before us. The very obligation of Beth Asher management to realize its historic mandate to fulfill its raison d'etre with integrity." Lefkowitz.

"Objection overruled."

"Just [6] like iz vas by de Jewish people ven dey comink out from Hegypt and dey gettink de Torah and Moshe is not comink down from Sinai ven dey tinkink he said he comink and dey makink de *goldene* calf..."

"Your honor, is it not an infraction of our sacred principle of separation of church and state to have bible lessons in a US courtroom?" Prosecutor.

"Quite the contrary, your honor. Inasmuch as our federal and state governments have enfranchised individuals to join together in groups and form those institutions that best express their interests and beliefs, said institutions may in turn establish the necessary by-laws to achieve those ends, binding members and non-members to respect those norms, hence it is logically necessary to understand the premises and the consistency which flows thereon from actions taken to express those historic mandates and beliefs." Lefkowitz.

"My G-d, if that's not metaphysics I don't know what is! And metaphysics has no place in an American court of law!" Prosecutor.

"For the record, your honor, it is my esteemed colleague who introduced the L-rd to the discussion not me! Though I list myself as a believer... Surely it is the province of the court to monitor contractual undertakings. A charter and its bylaws are a three party covenant: the members between themselves, the members and the community and always standing as guarantor for fulfillment of such trusts, the government. To be honored, if you will pardon the expression, in good faith."

"Objection overruled." Judge Lombardy now smiling.

"In addition to which my colleague's question was actually from whence the license and/or obligation to implode the synagogue?" Lefkowitz.

"Explode!" Prosecutor.

"Implode!" Lefkowitz.

"Well well, so the honorable defense attorney's expertise extends beyond metaphysics to semantics as well." Prosecutor.

---

6 For the benefit of those who do not speak Yinglish, please see the translation in the Appendix, page 209.

"While that may or may not be so it is of the utmost relevance the implosion–explosion difference; an explosion thrusts debris outward for distances. An implosion properly prepared and managed after clearing lower walls and creating enough open space on the bottom levels collapses central support pillars one by one, beginning at the center and moving to the extremities. This method has the collapsing and the debris falling inward, downward. Absolutely no neighbors or passersby were exposed to risk!" Lefkowitz.

"Rabbi, do you do plagues and split seas as well?" Prosecutor.

"I think I see where my esteemed colleague is going and I would like to put him on notice that Pharoah and Korach have already been casted from local neighborhood talent." Lefkowitz.

"Gentlemen," Judge Lombardy smiling, tapping his table softly with his gavel, "I think we have strayed."

"That we have your honor, that we have." Lefkowitz.

Dad pulled out the old Beth Asher demolition permit he had and gave it to Lefkowitz. Three days later Judge Lombardy ended the proceedings with a *mussar* talk, exhorting us to be more cautious in the future.

❑   ❑

Of the two *sifrei Torah* left at Reb Shimshon's apartment, one was to be on loan to the Old Age Home as long as a *minyan* functioned there, the Gdanske Jew's *sefer Torah* with the blood on the borders was to go to the Kovna Yeshiva in Ellenville. Reb Shimshon asked me to drive him with the *sefer Torah* up to Ellenville one day. He had been invited to come and live there acting as a resource person for the *beis medrash*. Some *bochurim* understood Yiddish, more understood Reb Shimshon's Yiddish–English. He was considering trying it for a time. "Mein Sorele always sayink 'So much better to go to *chasunahs* (weddings) den *levayahs* (funerals)' no matter how tired she beink she always goink to a *chasunah*."...... We scheduled driving up for the *Elul* semester. That would give us a few weeks.

If the Abrahamic code and its inductively arrived–at–postulate was right and there was a design and a Designer, then in fact He had designs upon me. Why and how to build the edifice of one's existence. And these *yeshivishe* architects and draftsmen went with Mr. Van de Rohe's halacha, "G-d is in the details." Could it just be one exaggerated exceptionally enduring edifice complex? That night I spent flipping metaphysical quoins in my heart and head, go and stay, or go and come back. About 2 a.m. I walked over to the schoolyard, looked across at the rubble of the demolished building—the fall of the House of Asher. Of building and wrecking.

Like when I came on a Saturday night for an early Sunday morning game I found my spot where the sag of the fence fit my back sat down and dozed off.

So in G-d's game we were playing hardball on the concrete of the schoolyard. Their team lined up along the first base line most cloaked and caped in white sheets, a few yellow sheeted players in their dug-out and bullpen. From that haunted scoreboard the last notes of The Star Spangled Banner, The Yellow Robes of Access and Die Meistersinger. Meshugana Morris Roth standing along the third base line with our team did an impressive verbal drum roll. Our players draped in black sanbenitos with yellow trimming and a yellow badge below the knees, all wearing talleisim: myself, Bam, Marty, Rabbi Winters, Sroly, Laibel, Izzy, Mottel, Cal Abrams, Hank Greenberg. The opposing team argued it was hardball and you play with nine men, we argued it was the school yard and concrete and we were the home team and we played with ten. t.s.elliott metrically hissed, "They always imagine themselves to be the home team." We took the field with ten. After a scoreless top of the first they reluctantly took the field with ten.

Each draped in his white sheet, Mencken at first base, J. Edgar Hoover at second, Father Coughlin at short stop, third H. G. Wells, Nicholas 1st at short center, Thomas Edison in left, Theodore Dreiser center, Henry Ford in right. t.s. eliot was pitching spitballs with Ezra Pound catching. Umpiring behind the plate was Joseph P. Kennedy Snr. He examined the concrete scuffed and scruffy ball; the black lettering on the dampened white horsehide parchment could hardly be read.

Two out and I was up. Reb Shimshon was coaching at first base and Rav Gordon at third. As expected the first two pitches came right at me. Reb Shimshon signaled to watch now for the spitball–curve. Izzy, cavorting off third base, slow motion pantomiming a forward and backward race, tzitzis flying in the breeze; Sroly pirouetting, dancing off first base pulling his black hood over his head and slipping into his mock bullfight chassunah routine. All we needed was a single to win. Or maybe a double steal. That would be another argument, can one steal on a concrete court. Having ruled to play with ten men must we be consistent? Or, after all it was a "hard-ball" contest. If I waited for the fast ball I could go for the fence. Though all we needed was a single to win. It was getting dark. Time out. Kennedy ran to the mound, waved his arms and called the game on account of darkness. Izzy screamed, "You can't do that in the middle of an inning." "Says who?" hollered Mencken. I woke up.

In a few hours I would drive Reb Shimshon in the hearse with the Gdanske *sefer*

Torah, to Ellenville, that parchment with its blood stained margins... whereas those other smaller parchment passages folded script in squared–black–inkwell–like boxes, my tefillin—take them or not take them? Frozen cubes of that primordial liquid darkness, like attempting to contain, to explain, the ever surfacing night of Golus. Blackened boxes and straps of hide, covering quill-penned black lettered verse merging, messaging. While the text for both was the same, the hand container had only one compartment and parchment, the head container four. On the mind level we entertain, juggle multiple and even contradictory concepts; action is singular. That black hand box placed opposite the heart, urging, unifying mind, heart and action... Mystics held that initially the soul is reluctant to come down to this earthly sphere, perhaps the wrapping of those straps and boxes was like tying body and soul together keeping that anxious soul from escaping this body... Maybe like a crazed Thomas Mitchell on the docks frantic that his soul had fled.

At the *Yeshiva* I had seen the Responsa of Rav Ephraim Oshry, from the Kovno slave labor camp which he survived, retrieved after the war. One contraband pair of *tefillin* was passed around each morning before they were marched to their slave labor. *Tisha B'Av* custom had it not to don *tefillin* until the afternoon. Each day the prisoners were taken out at dawn not to return until after sunset. Should they then break the *Tisha B'Av* custom by putting on the *tefillin* even this *Tisha B'Av* morning, otherwise they would lose the *mitzvah*?... Sheep to the slaughter? Like it or not that was damned heroic, in step with a kind of dignity, loyalty, to their *halachic* criteria, reaching, touching the very heavens from the midst of Hades... yet, but, does that really tie into me to bind the Stephen to the Yisrael in Bloom?

Rav Gordon said such decisions should ideally be made when one is in a learning mode. Pursuing the "Great Perhaps?" Perhaps. Or maybe unrelentingly pursued by The Great. Pursuing, perusing. My *tefillin* with those special passages were in the cockpit of the hearse, in the glove compartment. Like that fellow down under who came up with a black box to record and monitor troubled flights, so perhaps I one day with these black boxes would help decipher my flight. Taking them meant keeping my options open. Rather odd that wrapping business. Passages of rite, right there in the hearse. Tying the passenger to generations of Jews that wrapped those *tefillin* from Sinai to Babylonia to the secret *bar mitzvahs* of frightened Marrano boys whispering *Shma* in their cellars in Malaga, to the Cantonist *bar mitzvah* boy that smiled like Teddy almost strangled when caught donning his contraband *tefillin* in Nicholas' Minsk... But is the *gematria* of outrage – truth? What are the odds? Of all this oddity? I could go down to the poolroom and find me a bookie and do Pascal's bet... Books and bookies... If I stay, have to arrange a driver to bring back the hearse. Coming down would be a lot easier. Ah! the gravity of it all. I do wonder how my Sherpa bochurim are doing up there in the mountains. Never did find

Norgay Tenzing. Climb those hills because they are there. They keep insisting I was there. Time to rehearse? Then now. All that climbing. I should tune up the hearse.

An end.

❏ ❏

Weighting for Echoes

"*Verter zol men vegn un nit tseyln.*" Words should be weighed, not counted."
                                                    – *Yiddish aphorism*

"Translation is at best an echo."   – *George Borrow*

"When I experience anything, I experience it as a thing and a word at the same time, both equally amazing."   – *Dylan Thomas*

And as paraphrased by James Sutherland: Writing the "Ballad of the Long Legged Bait" had been 'like carrying a huge armful of words to a table he thought was upstairs, and wondering if he could reach it in time, or if it would still be there.'

Isn't the transition from idea to expression an attempted act of translation?

שפריך שפראך - און די אויסנאם
Shprich-shprach un de oisnam The Idiom and the Oddity

Glossary

a gutta hartz	a good heart
aleph beis	alphabet
aliyah	calling to the Torah reading
am ha'aretz	ignorant person
aron kodesh	holy ark
avodah	worship
baal avodah	sincere worshipper
baalei batim	lay leadership
bachur/im	single student/s
Bava Metzia	tractate
bechira	choice
beit Knesset	synagogue
beis medrash	study hall
Beis Hamikdash	Holy Temple (in Jerusalem)
bidi'eved	post facto
bimah	synagogue table for Torah reading
bissele	a little
bitochon	faith
blech	covering over fire for keeping food warm (on Shabbos)
bubbies	grandmothers
chavrusah	study partner
chayas	beasts
chazzan	cantor
chazzanus	cantorial rendition
chessed	act of kindness
chevrah	a community or group
chiddush	the new innovative insight

chiyuv	obligation
cholent	traditional Shabbos dish
chol hamoed	intermediary days of Holiday
challahs	Shabbos loaves
chametz	prohibited wheat product on Pesach
charedi	dedicatedly religious Jew
chasid	follower of one of the disciples of the Baal Shem Tov
chasunah	wedding
chup	wave in the hair
churban	destruction
davening	praying
der erd	the earth
der heim	the home
din	law
drashah / drashos	sermon/s
dreying	manoeuvre
Eichah	Lamentations
eidim	witnesses
eineklach	grandchildren
elter bachurim	senior students
emmes	truth
erev	day before
ershta luchos	First Tablets (10 Commandments)
esrog	citron
ezras nashim	women's section
febrick	factory
fafeirt	misled
fargin	wholeheartedly grant
farkerte luchos	opposite tablets
farshikkert	drunk

farshtunkener	lousy
fartummelt	confused
frumkeit	religiosity
gabbai/m	lay sexton/s
gadlus ha'adam	greatness of man
galus / galusdik	exile
geferliche	terrible
gehinnom	Hades
gemara	Talmud tractate
gematria	numerical value
gesheft	business
gezeirah	edict
gilgul	reincarnation
gleib mir	believe me
goldene medinah	golden country
goodskeit	goodness
goyish	gentile
greeners	newly arrived immigrants
greps	burp
Gut Shabbos	Good Shabbos
hachnassas orchim	hospitality of guests
hashgachah	Providence /Kosher supervision
halachasists	Proponents of Talmudic law
haskalah	"enlightenment"
hechsher	to determine kosher
heim	home
heimish	home-like
hesped	eulogy
hondling	bargaining
iyun	scrutiny

Kabbalas Shabbos	to receive that Shabbat (festively)
kaddish /kaddeshim	specially sanctified prayer at times specifically for mourning
kapparos	atonement ritual
kashas	questions
kavod	honor
kehilla	community
ketzos	latter-day analytical commentary
kibitz	running commentary
kiddush	small morning repast for occasions
kinde	children
kinnos	prayers of lamentations
kittel	white garment worn at specific liturgical recitations
koach	power
korban / korbanos	sacrifice/s
kugel	traditional Shabbos dish
laining	reading of the Torah or independent preparation of Talmudic text
laitzim	cynics
landsleit/landsman	countrymen
Litvishe	Lithuanian
lulav	palm branch (Succos mitzvah)
maarav	west
maariv	evening prayers
machzor	High Holiday prayer book
maftir s	election from Prophets climaxing weekly Torah reading
maidele	girl
mamzer	bastard
maror	bitter herbs (served at Pesach Seder)
mashgiach	Kashrus or student supervisor

mashgiach's schmooze	inspirational and instructional talk of mashgiach
maskilim	proponents of "enlightenment"
masmidim	diligent and devoted
matana	gift
maven	expert
mechitzah	divider (in halachic synagogue between men and women)
mein sheine maidele	my beautiful girl
mein teirah froi	my precious wife
melachah	halachically constructive endeavour
melava malka	special meal denoting the departure of the Sabbath Queen
mess mitzvah	deceased one is obligated to bury
meya'esh	abandon hope
midrash	non halachic Tanaic commentary
milchik	dairy
milchomo	war
mincha	afternoon prayer
mine kind	my child
minyan	ten males to pray
misheberach	blessing
mishnah	first recording of Oral Commentary
mishpoche	family
mispalelim	prayers
mitzvahs	Torah ordained good deeds
mizbei'ach	altar
mizrach	east
moichel	forgive
muktzeh	items we refrain from using on Shabbat
mussar	ethics

nachas	spiritual satisfaction
neshamos	souls
ness	miracle
niftar	deceased
niggun	melody
nivul peh	profanity
novi	Prophet
Olam Ha'emes	World of Truth (to come)
pareve	neither meat or dairy
parnassah	livelihood
parshah	portion of the Torah
payos	sidelocks
pikadon	loan
pilpul	Talmudic dialectic
Pirkei Avos	Ethics of The Fathers
piyut	liturgical verse
platz	demise (usually metaphorical)
pshat	straightforward understanding
punkt	exact
pushka	receptacle for donations (usually coins)
putzer	dandy
rachmonos	mercy
Rebbi	teacher
Rebbe's tish	ritual gathering of Chasidim
Ribono Shel Olam	Master of the Universe
reiner neshomes	pure souls
rosh yeshivah	dean of Yeshiva
schloff	sleep
sechel	wisdom
sechorah	merchandise

sedarim	dedicated learning time or literature
sefer Torah	Torah scroll
seforim	sacred books
Selichos	prayers for forgiveness
Shaatnez	halachic prohibition of joining certain items animate
	& inanimate
Shabbosdike	Shabbos-like
Shabbosim	plural of Shabbos
Shadchan	matchmaker
shalom Aleichem	greeting - literally 'peace be with you'
shalosh seudos	the third Shabbos meal
shamayim	heavens
sharfer	bureau
sheigitz	gentile
sheimos	remnants of holy script
sheine kinde	beautiful children
shema	prayer declaring commitment and belief
shemoneh-esrei	Amidah recited three times daily
shidduch/im	match/es (usually for marriage)
shikker	drunk
shiksah	non-Jewish woman
shiur / shiruim	class/es
shivah	traditional week of mourning
shlemeil	fool
sh'lo midaas	from not knowing
shmadink	forcibly converting
shmattah	remnant of garment
shmear	smear
shmoozim	talks focused on ethical and spiritual improvement;
	interactive discussion

shmutz	dirt
shnorred	begged
shochet	ritual slaughterer
shofar	ram's horn
shteler	position
shtender	lectern
shtickle chazzer	a piece of pork
Shulchan Aruch	Code of Law
Shvach	weak
shvitz	sweat
siddur	prayer book - plural siddurim
Sifrei Torah	Torah scrolls
siman	identifying feature
sof davor hakol nishma	at the climax all is clear
stam	generally
sugya	subject discussion
tachlis	goal
takke	actually
talmid chacham	scholar
Tatta	father
tish	festive holiday table
Tisha B'Av	9th of Av
Tosafos	classical medieval commentary
tumult / tumulter	generator of action
tsaddikim	righteous
tzaddakah	philanthropy
tzidkus	righteousness and/or saintliness
tzitzis	four cornered garment with halachic fringes
tzores	misfortunes
veib	wife

veker	waker
yahrzeit	anniversary of departure of kin
yam	ocean
yenem	others
yeshivaleit	yeshiva graduates
yimach shimum	may their names be obliterated
yiush	abandoning hope
zaides	grandparents
zechus	merit
zeir gut	very good
zelber	the same
zhid	Jew
znus	adultery

Appendix

Yinglish* Translations

Modern research has it that appendix may not be vestigial. The following translations are provided for the benefit of those who don't speak Yinglish. For full understanding and reading pleasure, it is suggested that you return to the original Yinglish sections in the text after reading the translations. Hurt, it can't.

Sam Benito's brother

Page 26

FOOTNOTE 1 "So how come Weiss before I was gone for four years in that *Gehinnom* over there your wife came to me crying that you are never home. When you are not working you are busy playing cards and drinking with your cronies. So that's the only time you can find to give your wife is the *Ribbono Shel Olom*'s time, no other time? But you are mistaken, all time is the *Ribbono Shel Olam*'s time and you did not understand it then and you still don't understand it today."

Page 144

FOOTNOTE 2 "It is always a *mitzvah* to bury the departed, but when there is no one else to do it, it is another dimension of *mitzvah*, a unique kindness that is described as a true kindness. Frequently when we are gracious to another it is with anticipation of receiving a kindness in return. Where there is no such possibility of a return gesture, that is called an authentic kindness. In this case not just the departed, but I will not be positioned to return that kindness and so it is a genuinely authentic *mitzvah* of kindess, Yisroel."

Page 155

FOOTNOTE 3 "There was a custom in certain communities in Europe that when someone died, they dismantled the table to make the coffin for the deceased, so that the departed soul's merits should accompany him to his final judgment. In Dvinsk 1926 when Reb Meir Simcha was dying, he asked for a piece of the lectern by which he learned to be included in the burial.

And so I recall back home my little Mirele's bureau with three drawers and she and her sisters and brothers kept things there. Mirele prized a doll that her grandfather, my Sorele's

---

* Yinglish: A blend of English and Yiddish, esp. one spoken in the United States; a form of English containing many Yiddishisms or a form of Yiddish containing many Anglicisms (Oxford English Dictionary).

father, gave her after he came back from Warsaw. One day Sorele is cleaning and looking for the doll and cannot find it, when asked, Mirele cries and explains that her friend the Dubinsky is only 9 and Mirele is 11 and the Dubinsky girl's father died and she does not have a father or a grandfather or a doll so Mirele gave her the doll but please not to tell Grandpa. Oh my child my lovely Mirele, I should have that bureau here now and the scarves and gloves which you took from those drawers and gave away to your friends and I should take from that wood pieces for your burial as well.

Master of the World, when the Temple is there we have an altar to bring sacrifices, and then when the Temple is not there you test us with retribution and every Jew is like a Priest and must bring sacrifices on the altar. So many sacrifices, our Master. You know my G-d that I am a father of this girl and of a family that have all been sacrifices. You my G-d know that Mirele was a precious soul that became derailed. When they needed me, my Rebbetzin Sorele, their mother and those beautiful children Yossel, Yankel, Itzik, Chani, Perele of blessed memory all sacrificed on that altar over there then I was here, and Benny and Mirele were needing me here, I was there. So many children, pure souls on that altar.

I also remember the story of the Jew in Spain 500 years ago, escaping to Portugal, then from there to Morocco where his children and wife take sick and die; and he cries to You Master of the Universe, everything I had was taken from me, position, dignity, money, home and I had to run like a thief in the night from Spain to Portugal then Portugal to Morocco because those Catholics went mad with hate. And when his family died he looked to the Heavens that Jew in Morocco and said, "You took it all from me but there is one thing that is still left with me; that is my faith that for reasons that I don't see there was some plan to this all. That faith belongs to me and can never be taken away from me.

As we know that we are always coming in in the middle of the scene we weren't there at Creation and we don't stay long enough to see the conclusion. And I am not forgiving the Germans the Cossacks, the Babylonians, the Spanish, the Polish, the Lithuanians the Russians for their killing us, they had free will ... and so this precious soul of Mirele is also like a sacrifice of the war. Please G-d look at this simple coffin as if it was made from that bureau and all the kindness of that little girl back in Europe with the big black eyes is attending this burial. But please forgive me G-d I am still a father and my heart is broken like the first tablets which had a special place in the Holy Ark there is also a special place by you I know for broken hearts a special ark. Mirele please forgive your father that as much as I loved you I was not there when you needed me but G-d knows, my child, that I tried.

He knows that I loved you, Yosel, Yankel, your mother, Itzik, Chani, Perele and Benny, he should be healthy and like Bruria the wife of Reb Meir asks him when somebody borrows something from another and the owner asks for it to be returned what is the law and he replied of course it must be returned; and she then told him that their sons had been taken back by G-d. So right now at this funeral it is like I am burying Yosel, Yankel, Itzik, Chani, Perele together with Merele. We never had those burials. The Rebbetzin and I did not have the merit to walk our children to the chupah and see grandchildren with big black eyes like Mirele."

Page 179

FOOTNOTE 4 "So I see you have come back to Beth Asher Kaufman, Katz, Rose Brothers, Rosenkranz for your own *Kaddish* — which your children cannot or won't recite. It seems like it was yesterday when your wife was dying in the hospital and your son the psychologist, Marvin, in Boston refused to come down for a parting visit to his dying mother explaining he was at a crucial point in an experiment with some mice and did not want to leave and anyway his mother would probably not know the difference if he was there or not. And you cried to me Katz what kind of person is that? Those mice are more important than his mother. So now I ask you Katz to remember that 25 years ago I asked you to send Marvin to Yeshiva. At first you laughed at me and then you became angry and angrier when I asked again. And at his mother's funeral he did not say *Kaddish* as it had no "meaning" to him anyway. And you Katz sat with me crying how terrible it is to have a son that refuses to say *Kaddish* for his mother. And I told you that no one has a way to turn the clock back. And I know that you know that he won't say *Kaddish* for you either.

There are two kinds of sacrifices in the Torah, Katz, public and private. The public sacrifices required of the Jewish people are most often not up to us. The five sacrifices that were taken from me in Europe were not up to me. And then here in this golden country, comfortable Golus this land of mercy so many of us are bringing private sacrifices that G-d did not require. My Miriam and my Rebbetzin and Benny all alone here. But you Katz, your business was doing very well and then when you got sick we stood there in Unity Hospital and Goldberg's nephew the doctor said you only have a few days then you asked me to say the *Kaddish* for you because you know Marvin won't say it. At a funeral from the *Kaddish* and eulogies we understand what a man's life was.

And you Rapaport, you called me in the middle of the night when your daughter Rosie came home with a gentile and Rosenberg when your Arlene came home pregnant from the mountains. Did either of you discuss with me before they went to Syracuse and the mountains. Instead you laughed at the old man with the beard who talks Yiddish. While I was running over there in that flaming hell with the *sefer* Torah that the Gdanske Jew gave me. That very moment you were here in Beth Asher while I was running through the night like a thief holding that *sefer* Torah and that very moment you tore down the *Mechitzah* (divider) in Beth Asher. You are here in this golden country and I am over there in hell and you decide that is the most important thing to use your hands, heart and head for, to tear down the *Mechitzah*.

The Roses, Katz, Weiss you are convinced that you are such wise men you know that we don't need the *Mechitzah*. Berkowitz your junk business going so well that you were able to move from Brownsville to Long Island and when I came to your big home in Great Neck and I asked you for a loan to fix the leak in the roof in the Yeshiva in Ellenville and you were unhappy and for months toyed with me and now your business has collapsed and like the man who came to the Chofetz Chaim in 1917 and complained that the Chofetz Chaim had come to him in 1915 for a donation for the Yeshiva and he had refused, then in 1917 the Bolsheviks came and took away his business and he cried to the Chofetz Chaim that "Had you pressured me in 1915 I might have responded, now I don't have either not the business and not the merit of the *mitzvah*." And I know Berkowitz that that is what you are thinking now.

Silverman and Kalman you gave me money for Horowitz when he lost his job and the Yeshiva also a little bit through the years and some other charity. I remember all the problems you created in the shul but I also don't forget the *Mitzvahs* that you did. At the beginning when I came here alone and the Rebbetzin was back in the shtetl in Europe, your wanting to put the *Aron Kodesh* in the west not in the east. And Bloom and Stein and Rosenman were with me and Weiss and Katz and Berkowitz and the Roses with them. And taking the architect and making the plans before I went that second time into that hell to look for the Rebbetzin and the children, while we were still in the basement downstairs and Bloom and Rosenman helped me move the temporary Aron back to the east. And then when I was not here you redid it in the west. From day one this was a shul with opposite facing tablets. And the *Mechitzah* and the blessing for Stalin *shul* and the *sefer* Torah with the blood in the parchment from the Gdanske Jew. And then when you wanted to make it a shul with a sauna and a men's club, a tiny minyan with a *mechitzah* and a big *minyan* without a *mechitzah*, and now finally you want to sell the whole building, and to whom?

At the Nuremberg trials after the war when they asked one of those Nazi officers how was it possible to be so bestial to men women and children all that murdering, shooting and the gas chambers killing so many innocent people and the Nazi officer explained all the Germans did was improve technically upon a few thousand years of church-led and promoted hate and pogroms against Jews, as they are less than human. Like it was a great *mitzvah* to cause them pain and anguish. Even making saints out of people who did the most hateful things to the most Jews. I won't sell the *shul* to them. With all its shortcomings this shul, these walls absorbed so much sincere prayer and testify to many *mitzvahs* that were done here ... and Schwartz, Katz and the Rose and Vladermersky that wanted to make a Yiddish theatre in that very place where there were prayers for *Rosh Hashanah* and *Yom Kippur*, that theatre dedicated to making a mockery of Torah and *Mitzvahs*, profanity and moral looseness endorsed by the enlightenment; you look at Judaism from the eyes of a gentile and even worse and you call that culture. When you pour salt on pork it does not make it kosher. G-d knows how I encouraged numbers of these beautiful boys and girls in the *Talmud Torah* to go to a real Yeshiva. Only succeeding with Sendelman's boy and Bernstein the plumber's daughter.

And I know how weak the *Talmud Torah* was but I continued to pray that from the *Shma* that was said here maybe something good might come and for the most part as anticipated the worst came true. And though I am not a prophet I could see and told you Katz and Rosenman where it was all going. The exile is destructive either way, when the goyim are good to us we forget and get drunk and run to be accepted and try to disappear. And when they pursue us, surely that is no good. Today we are to read Lamentations, the prophet talks of this day of destruction as a holiday. My poor Miriam and Benny caught up there while I was here and here while I was there. And now I speak directly to You, my G-d. You know that when someone is drunk he cannot really perform and so after so many years of pain and punishment in Europe the coming to this wonderful place America they became drunk and forgot that it is a gift and a kindness to bring us here.

All those *Shabbosim* my Rebbetzin Sorele alone with the children and I am alone over there praying for a miracle, running and praying to find some clue about my Yankele, Yossel, Itzik, Chani and Perele but they were sacrificed on the altar with so many millions of other children and adults. And every night I picture leaving the family and the children standing there to say goodbye and the clothes they wore and how they looked at me that last time when I was going to America and seven-year-old Perele in her *Shabbos* dress with her big black eyes like Miriam was crying and saying that we are not going to see you any more Papa, and I said "No, soon I am going to bring you and the family to America." But my G-d, Perele was right and Sorele I saw in your eyes that you knew that she was right.

Page 183

FOOTNOTE 5 "So G-d, I kept the synagogue all these years even though there are no Jews in the neighborhood, so that those souls that had prayed here could come back to recite their own *Kaddish*, as their children that rarely were brought here, never came, would come back to recite it for them. So that is the end of the story of Beth Asher. You know G-d the aggravation that I had all those years and you know that I forgive them, the Roses, Katz, Vladimovsky, Berkowitz and all those that have gone on and even the ones creating such problems now. Our people have been too confused and too intoxicated. But I cannot give this shul building to the professional mockers of our tradition for a Yiddish theatre. Nor to those who for two thousand years have persecuted us and prepared the way for Hitler. So those souls that had to come back to recite their own Kaddish perhaps even if the building is no longer here, maybe this place where it once was retains a certain sanctity for them to return to say that *Kaddish*."

Page 190

FOOTNOTE 6 "Just like when Moses received the Tablets and found the Jews had created a Golden Calf, he smashed the Tablets, as they were no longer the appropriate recipients of those Tablets, so with this synagogue, when the responsibility to fulfill these ideals was forfeited so was the right and need for these buildings."

About the Author

An elderly Chassidic Jew on his way to the doctor was accompanied by a friend. After the consultation the friend asked the patient, "What did he say?" Waving his hands up in the air the patient said, "Ahh he gave it a name."

Sam Benito